# STAY WITH ME
## THE ANDERSONS, BOOK 1

## ALEXA POWERS

Published by: Alexa Powers

Copyright: © 2014 Alexa Powers

Cover Design by: Courtney Lopes, E-book Formatting Fairies

Copy Editing by: Janell Parque

ISBN: 978-0-9905667-1-7

# ACKNOWLEGEMENTS

There are so many people I need to thank for helping me get this book from my computer hard drive and into your hands.

First of all, to my beautiful children, who were my biggest cheerleaders and endured countless hours of listening to me go on and on about Emma and Noah, as if they're real people. Because, in my mind, they are. You are a constant inspiration and the reason I work so hard in everything I do. Mommy loves you.

To Lynn, Elaine, Lisa, Suzanne, Teresa, and Alex. All of you lovely ladies kept me motivated to continue, and for that, I can't thank you enough. Your words of encouragement helped more than you'll ever know, and I'm thankful for each and every one of you.

To the Formatting Fairies and Julie, in particular, for being patient and kind to a new author who felt a bit lost in the wilderness. And to Janell for her brilliant editing and to Courtney for my fantastic cover design. Thank you. Thank you. Thank you.

And last, but certainly not least, my readers, thank you for taking time out of your busy lives to read my book. I hope you love Emma and Noah's story as much as I enjoyed writing it.

# CHAPTER 1

As she pushed her luggage cart through Auckland International Airport to begin a year of studying abroad in New Zealand, Emma Anderson couldn't wait to see what adventures lay ahead for her. Ignoring the twinge in her lower back after the long flight from Charlotte, North Carolina, she welcomed the new day with open arms and a large cup of black tea from the coffee shop.

Warm December air greeted her and was in stark contrast to the chilly temperatures she'd left behind. Taking a deep breath, she was thankful for the balmy weather and sunshine of the Southern Hemisphere this time of year.

Emma slowed her footsteps for a moment, taking time to appreciate the sight of two people exchanging a hongi, their foreheads and noses pressed together in a traditional Maori greeting, and couldn't have stopped the silly grin from spreading across her face if she tried. She was finally in New Zealand, Aotearoa: Land of the Long White Cloud.

With almost two months to settle in before school would begin, she needed to master two things…driving on the wrong side of the road and the Great New Zealand Vowel Shift.

Having visited New Zealand since she was a toddler, she'd grown accustomed to the Kiwi accent, but it was always a bit of a shock when someone said a perfectly innocent word like 'deck' and it sounded as if they were saying 'dick'. As a young girl, when she first discovered the word referred to a certain part of the male anatomy, it usually resulted in a fit of giggles, which inevitably led to her mother scowling at her, while trying not to laugh herself.

Yes, if she could master those two things, she'd be well and truly on her way to being a good Kiwi.

Emma gathered her long sandy blonde hair into a loose bun and turned at the sound of her name being called as her cousin, Lily Bradshaw, and Lily's fiancé, Josh Thornton, enthusiastically greeted her.

Lily and Josh's wedding was in three short weeks, and Emma had arrived early so she could help fulfill her duties as Lily's maid of honor. Assisting Lily had proven difficult from so far away, but now that she'd arrived in Auckland, she'd finally feel useful.

Even though they grew up on separate continents, they'd always been as close as sisters, and the frequent visits throughout their lives had cemented the bond between them.

Lily's parents, Emma's Aunt Mary and Uncle Bob, met at New York University and moved to his native New Zealand after graduation, raising their family in the affluent suburbs of Auckland. Emma's mother missed her sister terribly, and it was undeniably hard to live so far away from each other, but she always said it made seeing her that much sweeter.

Since childhood, Lily and Emma had dreamed of Emma coming to stay in New Zealand, and now that the time was finally here, she couldn't be more excited. Emma had always loved New Zealand, so the decision was an easy one, even though most of her friends chose to study abroad in Europe.

Lily's dark hair was pulled back into a ponytail, exposing flawless olive skin, which was makeup free, except for a light smudge of lip-gloss. And her round emerald-green eyes were full of energy, despite the early hour.

Lily had a face that most models would envy and a body to match it, but the truly wonderful thing about her was that she was just as beautiful on the inside as the outside.

"Oh, my God! I'm so happy you're finally here!" Lily exclaimed excitedly, her green eyes brimming with moisture.

"I know! I've missed you so much. I still can't believe it. Everyone back home sends their love, and my mom said to give you an extra hug from her." Emma reached for Lily, wrapping her arms around her tightly...and winced. "It was a long flight and my back is killing me," she moaned, as she massaged the knot in her lower back.

"You must be knackered. Let's get home and then you can have a nap." Lily stepped back, but continued to hold onto Emma's arms, as if she might disappear if she let go. She took a long look at Emma and smiled. "I still can't believe you're going to be with me until November. We're going to have so much fun, and you're going to love our new place. I've got your room ready, and you can walk to school. We were lucky to get this unit when it came available. It's more space than we need, but now we have room for you, *and* we have a view of the harbor."

Instead of living in an apartment with people she didn't know, Emma was thrilled to be staying with Lily and Josh until it was time for her to move back home, to finish her studies at Appalachian State University in Boone, North Carolina.

"Wow, I can't wait to see it. Surprisingly, I'm not really that tired. My dad gave me a sleeping pill that I took after I got on the plane in Los Angeles, so I slept most of the flight. I just ache from head to toe from sitting for so long. Maybe we could go on a walk later and then a hot bath should take care of it." Emma smiled at Josh as he stood patiently to the side, watching her and Lily. "Hi, Josh."

"Hi, Emma, it's good to see you again. I'll get your bags in the car so we can get you home. But first, come here and let me have a hug," he demanded, as he gently nudged Lily out of the way and embraced Emma, his large frame towering over her.

Even though Josh no longer played rugby professionally, he certainly hadn't lost his rock-hard physique. With warm brown eyes and adorable dimples, Josh's good looks made him a favorite with the female fans...and a few of the male ones too, she suspected. But since the day he met Lily, he only had eyes for her.

"It's great to see you, too. Wow, I always forget how big you are," Emma laughed, as Josh enveloped her in his muscular arms. "Are you sure you don't mind having a roommate? I could've found an apartment, you know."

"No worries. It's not a bother at all." His cheeky grin was on full display, as he gave Emma a sincere smile. "You're always welcome. Now let's get out of here and get you sorted."

While Josh loaded Emma's luggage into the car, she lifted her guitar off the cart, carefully placing it in the back seat, then settled in for the drive home. As Lily prattled on, Emma watched as the landscape changed from the densely populated suburbs to the urban Central Business District of Auckland.

"I promised my parents that we'd come over for tea tomorrow night. Mum's about to burst, she's so excited you're here," Lily continued, as Josh maneuvered the car into the parking garage and pulled into his reserved parking space.

Making their way into the elevator that would take them to the 12th floor, and Emma's new home for the next eleven months, Emma settled her guitar in front of her legs and leaned against the railing, hoping to relieve the pressure on her back.

"I've missed you guys. A few weeks over school breaks is never enough," Emma sincerely stated, feeling nostalgic for her time spent in New Zealand. Summer vacations visiting Lily, her Aunt Mary and Uncle Bob, and Lily's older brother Robbie, who'd recently relocated to Australia for work, were always the highlight of her year. "How is everyone?"

"Well, my mum's driving me crazy with the wedding coming up so soon. She's always on me about something I've forgotten or some appointment she's made for us. I always thought the bride was supposed to drive everyone mad, but mum's ready for a nervous breakdown." Lily's troubled pout left Emma wondering what she'd gotten herself into.

"She's not that bad," Josh spoke up, defending his future mother-in-law. "She just wants your day to be perfect, and you're her only daughter, after all, so this will be her only chance to put on the show. Give her a break, Lil."

"I know, I know. I just wish sometimes that we could elope. When I think of everything that's still to be done, I think I might break out in hives." Turning her attention back to Emma, she flashed her a tense smile. "We have a fitting the day after tomorrow. I spoke to Ali, and she and Katie are getting theirs done next week before they come over," Lily released a weary sigh, and Emma could see the wedding preparations were taking their toll on her.

"I shouldn't need any modifications to mine. It'll probably just need a press to get the wrinkles out," Emma reassured her, not wanting to add any additional stress.

"Okay. Good. They should be able to take care of that at the dress shop. And, here we are," Lily announced, waving her arms at the opening elevator doors like a game show hostess revealing the contestant's prize winnings.

Josh came to a stop in front of the door to their home and unlocked it, then held it open while waiting for Lily and Emma to walk through, before following them inside with Emma's luggage.

Emma's eyes were immediately drawn to the wall of floor to ceiling windows, which revealed an unobstructed view of Auckland's waterfront. The large lounge was comfortably decorated with black leather couches and a wrought iron coffee table, along with coordinating end tables.

Mounted on the wall above the fireplace was a big screen TV that seemed to be a necessity for men these days. Flanking the fireplace on both sides were built-in bookcases filled with electronic equipment, movies, books, and framed pictures of family and friends of the couple.

Scattered throughout the bookshelves were photos of Josh playing rugby, before the knee injury that ended his career prematurely. He'd been one of the best rugby players in the world, and losing his career had been a devastating blow.

Spotting a photo of her and Lily taken that past summer, during Lily's visit to Emma's home in North Carolina, she couldn't help but smile. The image captured the moment they jumped into the pool while holding hands. Their long hair stood on end and they were both laughing, as they plunged into the refreshing water.

Emma startled as Lily commented over her shoulder. "We had so much fun that day, but my God, it was hotter than hell. I thought I was going to melt."

"You get used to it, I guess. It doesn't really bother me too much, but it helps to have a pool to cool off in. Living in Boone has definitely reduced my tolerance for the heat and humidity, though. It's much cooler in the mountains."

Emma's gaze drifted to the artwork decorating the walls. "Are these yours, Lily?"

Lily's eyes followed Emma's line of sight towards a photo of the Eifel Tower that had been enlarged and hung prominently in the dining area. "Yeah. I took that one on holiday in Paris last year. I've started putting them on canvas, as you can see, and a few boutiques are carrying them. Been selling quite well, actually. I've also had a few showings at a local gallery."

"Wow. That's amazing, Lil. How did I not know this? Why didn't you tell me?"

"Well, it just sort of happened by accident. One of our neighbors stopped by to welcome us to the building and I had a few sitting in the lounge waiting for Josh to hang them. He owns a gallery and asked to see some of my other photos, and one thing led to another. Photography has always been a hobby, and I love taking pictures, as you know, but it's weird to think that someone I don't know has one of my photos hanging in their home," Lily remarked, looking around the room at the artistic photographs adorning the walls.

"I guess, but it's also a huge compliment," Emma stated honestly. Lily's photographs possessed a uniquely beautiful quality and Emma was pleased to see that others appreciated them as much as she did.

"Thanks, Em. It's still so new and a bit overwhelming, with the wedding and everything," Lily exhaled with an exasperated sigh.

The lounge opened up to a modern kitchen and dining area, which shared the same remarkable view of the balcony and beyond. Sleek dark cabinetry complimented the décor, and the dining table and chairs were constructed from the same material as the kitchen cabinets.

Emma wondered if they ever used the kitchen, since Lily had always been such a disaster in the room she affectionately referred to as 'the microwave', and had to bite her lip to keep from snickering. She could remember many failed attempts over the years that usually ended with a pizza being ordered.

"I always forget how beautiful it is here," Emma beamed, as she watched a sailboat gliding easily through the crystal blue waters of Waitemata Harbour, its colorful sails billowing in the breeze. "I can't imagine waking up to this every day."

"Well, get used to it. This is your home for the rest of the year. It never gets old, though." Lily came to a stop next to Emma, taking in the view alongside her. "I still have to pinch myself sometimes."

"I can't see myself ever looking out at that and not being in awe. It's absolutely beautiful. And it's so much warmer here than back home right now. We've gotten so much snow in Boone this winter. It's pretty, but driving in it is such a hassle and I've been trying to get home as much as possible to see everybody," Emma inhaled a shaky breath, the sting of tears burning her eyes. "It just dawned on me that I'm really here. I think I might cry."

Lily pulled Emma down onto the couch and into an embrace so strong that it cracked her back. For such a skinny thing, Lily was surprisingly strong.

"It's okay to cry, Emma. I can't imagine leaving my family and friends and traveling halfway around the world to boot. But I want you to be happy here. Let's get you sorted, then you can take a nap, and we'll go out to lunch when you wake up," Lily comforted her as she held Emma.

"I *am* happy to be here. You know how long I've wanted to do this. I'm just going to miss everyone. And when I think how much Abby will grow while I'm gone, it makes my heart hurt." Emma's six-month-old niece had completely enchanted her, and just the thought of missing the next year of her life left Emma instantly homesick. "I think I'll lie down for a little while after I unpack…let everything sink in and let my back relax a little. Sitting in that plane seat for so long has done a number on it." Emma gingerly raised herself off the sofa and followed Lily into her new room.

"Here's your room. I hope you like it. I know it's not as big as yours back home, but it's better than a dorm room, I'd say."

A queen-sized bed, with a large espresso-stained headboard, dominated the room and was covered with decorative pillows and a cool gray comforter. The matching dresser and night tables left very little space for anything else, but were more than enough. The room was sophisticated and elegant, just like Lily.

"It's perfect. I spent my freshman year in a room smaller than this that I had to share with someone else. Trust me, this room is more than sufficient." Emma walked to the sliding doors leading to the balcony, then turned to face Lily. "I love you, Lily. Thanks for having me. I'm so happy to be here, I can't even tell you. And your house is beautiful."

"Thanks. You know how much I love you. And Josh loves you, too. We're chuffed you're staying with us," Lily paused, her hands excitedly clasping together. "Now…I've saved the best for last. The pièce de résistance."

Emma dutifully followed Lily to the opened door leading into the bathroom, on the opposite wall from the sliding glass doors.

Peeking her head around the doorframe, Emma's eyes scanned the large bathroom. The room was sleek and modern, with ceramic tiles on the floor and shower stall. But the main feature, that had Emma wanting to jump up and down, was the large soaking tub.

"I think my heart just did a happy dance," Emma giggled, already picturing herself taking a relaxing bath, surrounded by fragrant bubbles. "Oh, before I forget, do I have to share the bathroom with guests?"

"No. They'll use the half-bath by the laundry room. This bathroom's shared with the third bedroom, but we use that room as an office, so it's all yours."

Emma released a breath she didn't realize she was holding, relieved she wouldn't have to worry about storing her things away every day. "Oh, thank God! I was afraid one of Josh's friends would come in here and have to stare at all my stuff."

"No worries 'bout that. The only person who ever uses this bathroom is Josh's friend, Noah. He lives in Takapuna, on the beach, and when he's in the city he stays here sometimes, so he doesn't have to drive home after a night at the pub," Lily hastily continued, pointing to a door next to the vanity. "Here's the linen closet. It's stocked with towels and such, but there's some free shelf space for your things too."

"You are the hostess with the mostest," Emma laughed. "You sound like such a grown up. When did that happen?"

"Well, once Josh and I became homeowners, I decided it was time to embrace my domestic side. I even learned how to cook, too. Poor Josh," Lily grimaced, bashfully looking at her feet. "He had to suffer through some pretty awful meals in the beginning, but he was a good sport about it and I'm happy to say that I've improved a lot. I don't have a very diverse offering, I'm afraid, but every now and again I get adventurous and break out a cookbook to try something new. As long as I follow the recipe, it's usually edible."

"Well, I've been living on my own for a few years now, so I learned how to cook out of necessity. I had three options...spend money I didn't have on take out, go hungry, or learn how to feed myself. I'm actually a pretty good cook now. So, that's one way I can help out around here."

"I'd love that. And I'm so glad you're here, Emma. I'm going to see what Josh is up to while you get unpacked," Lily said, hugging Emma once more, then left the room.

Thankful for the alone time to gather her thoughts, Emma inhaled a deep breath as she unzipped her suitcases and started unpacking her things. Carefully placing the framed photographs of family and friends she'd brought with her on the dresser and night table, she took a moment to appreciate each one.

It'd been a long and exhausting day and it wasn't even lunchtime yet. Saying goodbye to her family had been a lot harder than she anticipated. She knew she wasn't leaving forever, but eleven months was an awfully long time, no matter how you looked at it.

Seeing her sister Alison cry, as she waved goodbye, Emma almost returned her ticket and stayed home. Out of her five siblings, she was closest with Ali and saying goodbye to her was the hardest of all.

# CHAPTER 2

Emma woke from her nap feeling refreshed and ready to take on her first day in New Zealand. The sun streamed in through the open curtains, warming her skin, and she was tempted to pinch herself to make sure she wasn't dreaming.

Looking at the clock on the night table, she calculated the time difference while reaching for her phone.

"Emma! It's so good to hear your voice. We miss you already!"

"I miss you too, Mom, but I've only been gone a day," she delicately reminded her.

"I know sweetheart, but I started missing you the minute you got on that plane." Her mother let out an unsteady breath and Emma could tell she was trying to hold herself together. "We were just sitting down for dinner, or maybe I should call it *tea*. Get you speaking like a good Kiwi, eh?" she chuckled before continuing. "How was your flight?"

"It wasn't too bad, I was able to sleep after I took the pill Daddy gave me. I won't keep you, though. I just wanted to let you know that I got here in one piece," Emma assured her, as she tried to ignore the stab of loneliness she felt at the sound of Abby's loud shriek ringing through the phone line.

"You know I always have time for you, Emma." The sadness in her mother's voice was palpable, and Emma ached for the comfort of her mother's arms. "You're never a bother. You know that."

Fighting the tears gathering along her lashes, Emma sighed in agreement, "I know." Needing to get off the phone before she became a blubbering mess, she hurriedly changed the subject. "I've already unpacked and we're going out for lunch, so I really do need to go, but I'll talk to you soon. Give Daddy a hug for me and tell everyone I miss them."

"Will do, sweetheart. Love you."

"I love you too, Mom. Enjoy your *tea*." Her mother's easy laughter relieved some of the tightness gripping her chest, and Emma quickly said her goodbyes before disconnecting the phone.

Clutching her pillow, staring blindly out the glass doors to the harbor beyond, Emma finally allowed the pent up tears to escape, letting them fall freely down her cheeks.

In her mind's eye she could see her family sitting around the kitchen table in their comfortable home, laughing and arguing with one another. All of her brothers and sisters were home, which unfortunately didn't happen very often. They were a close-knit family, but like most, they led busy lives that limited the time they spent together as a group.

Wiping the tears from her face, Emma freshened up in the bathroom before walking into the lounge to see if Lily and Josh were ready for lunch.

"Oh good, I'm glad you're awake. I'm starving," Lily said, as she glanced up from the magazine she was flipping through, before setting it on the coffee table. "There's a café down the block that you'll love. They have a chicken salad croissant that's to die for."

"I could go for that. I'm actually really hungry, too. Where's Josh?"

"Oh…um…He's getting dressed and should be ready in a few minutes," Lily replied, blushing shyly and avoiding eye contact with Emma, an obvious sign that they'd been getting busy while Emma was busy taking a nap.

Emma couldn't resist teasing her cousin as she squirmed on the couch. "Oh, really? That's funny because when I went to my room a few hours ago, he was fully clothed."

"What can I say? He's insatiable." Lily was trying her level-best not to laugh and Emma watched with delight as her normally unflappable cousin's blush deepened, spreading from her cheeks down her neck. "I'm too hungry to talk about anything. *Especially that.* Changing the subject now; did you get everything unpacked? I can help if you need me to."

"Thanks, but I've already finished. I didn't bring that much stuff with me. It was too expensive to ship all of my things, so I only brought what I could fit in my suitcases. We're going to have to do some serious shopping in the next few weeks."

"Yes! There's a cute boutique next to the café. We can pop in there after lunch and have a look around."

After a lunch consisting of two delicious chicken salad croissants for Emma and Lily, and enough food to feed four people for Josh, it was time to go shopping. Josh kissed Lily and gave Emma a peck on the cheek, then headed home as Emma and Lily entered the trendy boutique.

Emma immediately spotted a few tops she liked, and was thrilled to see the reasonable prices. "I was afraid I wouldn't be able to afford anything, but with these prices, I can actually get a few things."

"I love this dress. Here. Try it on," Lily demanded, handing Emma a yellow knit dress with thin spaghetti straps. "It'll look great on you. Have you been going to a tanning bed? How are you still so dark in the middle of winter?"

"No, it was so hot last summer, as I'm sure you can recall, and by the end of summer I was really tan. This is nothing compared to what I looked like a few months ago. It just hasn't faded all the way yet," Emma answered, as she made her way to the dressing room with her selections.

Leaving the store with bags in hand, Emma slid her arm across Lily's shoulder and squeezed her tightly. "I'm so happy I'm here. This has been a lot of fun. Two of my favorite things…you and shopping."

"Ditto!" Lily laughed. "Now we need to go out someplace where you can show off your banging body in that new dress. I know," Lily continued happily. "Let's go dancing tomorrow night. Do you think you'll be up for it?"

"Don't see why not. And I haven't been out dancing in *forever*. I have the perfect shoes to wear too." Emma wasn't so sure about the banging body part, but just the thought of dancing the night away gave her an extra spring in her step.

While growing up, being told how lucky she was to be tall and thin was of no comfort to her when all she felt was gangly and awkward. But eventually, she'd come to terms with her body after years of insecurity.

Countless hours spent doing laps in the pool had given her lean muscles, and an impressive set of guns, and maturity had given her feminine curves. Now, when someone commented on her appearance, she just thanked them, before politely changing the subject.

The following morning, Emma groaned as she made a mental note to remember to close the curtains before bed from now on. Bright sunlight flooded her room, making it impossible to fall back to sleep, and the effort it would take to close the curtains seemed pointless.

Checking her phone, she found a text message from her best friend, Chris. Trying to figure out what time it was in North Carolina was too much work for her drowsy brain, so she just slid her finger along the bottom of the phone to unlock it.

"Wanted to check in to see how it's going. It's been crazy here. Miss you!"

Of all her friends, she'd miss him the most. They'd been best friends since childhood, when he and his family moved in next door.

When the time came, they'd decided to go to Appalachian State together, and they now shared a two-bedroom home close to campus. The cozy cottage's location near King Street was perfect. They could walk home from the bars and restaurants after a night out with friends, and the AppalCART stopped right down the street, so they didn't have to walk or drive to school if the weather was bad.

The small home reeked of stale beer and cigarette smoke when they'd moved in, but it was sufficient, even though the closet space left a lot to be desired for any female resident. They'd made it their own with hand-me-down furniture and thrift store finds, the eclectic mixture somehow coming together to fit their personalities perfectly.

"Miss you too. Do tell :) Everything's great here," Emma texted back.

Surprised by how fast he responded, she jumped when her phone buzzed.

Relaxing against her pillows, she laughed as Chris described some of the more outrageous antics that had taken place at Emma's ex-boyfriend Tyler's house the previous night.

Most of her friends were home for the holidays from their various college towns, and getting together before they headed back to school or overseas. As usual, copious amounts of alcohol were consumed and Chris was hung-over and wanting attention. She loved him to death, but the man was such a baby whenever he didn't feel well and his flair for drama always made her eyes roll.

Walking into the kitchen, she found Lily and Josh in the middle of a sloppy kiss, as the water heated for their morning tea. "Do you guys ever come up for air? It's too early to be subjected to that," Emma quipped, shaking her head.

Josh let out a hearty laugh, but never took his eyes off of Lily. "It's never too early to kiss my girl." He gave Lily a sweet smile as he placed a chaste kiss on the tip of her nose.

"I'm sure. I just don't need to see the two of you sucking face first thing in the morning, that's all. At least not before I get some caffeine in my system," Emma teased. "How much longer till it's done?"

"Oh, Emma, it'll be ready in a minute. Here's a cup," Lily twisted, still enveloped in Josh's arms, and took a cup from the cabinet above the hot water dispenser. She placed a tea bag in it and slid the cup across the counter to Emma.

After adding water, along with milk and honey to her liking, Emma took a sip as she eyed Josh and Lily playfully cuddling, with a pang of jealousy. It wasn't that she wanted Josh, but she missed having what they shared. It had been six months since her break up with Tyler, and she was tired of being alone.

Watching them together reminded her of how it once was with Tyler. Until he decided that monogamy 'just wasn't working for him', leaving her heartbroken and wondering where it all went wrong.

Looking back now, the warning signs were as obvious as bright red flares exploding against the midnight sky. But, at the time, she felt confused and abandoned by the man she thought she'd spend the rest of her life with.

Seeing him in the bars around Boone after their breakup was hard enough, but witnessing his latest one night stand hanging all over him was absolutely cruel at times.

After too many pints of ice cream and more boxes of tissues than she could count, she'd finally accepted reality and reluctantly admitted that he wasn't the one for her. Tyler was a genuinely nice guy and had been a good boyfriend, but he clearly had a few wild oats in need of sowing before he settled down.

Lesson learned. She'd moved on.

Anyway, it was impossible to avoid Tyler at home or in Boone, since they grew up together and shared the same group of friends. But as time went on, it had gotten easier, until finally, it hardly bothered her at all. Hardly.

It still hurt sometimes, especially when she remembered how sweet he could be and the future they'd planned together. In the back of her mind, when she let her guard down, she thought maybe someday the planets would align, and they'd get back together.

Best not to think about it, though, their timing had never been right and probably never would be. The truth was that she missed the idea of marriage and children more than she missed the man. That had to mean something.

"Gotta go, babe," Josh announced, as he emerged from their bedroom. Slinging his gym bag over his shoulder, he rinsed his empty cup in the sink, then placed it in the dishwasher.

"Okay, see you later," Lily reached out, snagging him by the arm for a goodbye kiss that lingered a little too long, making Emma feel like she was intruding.

"Ugh, not again," Emma grunted good-naturedly.

Josh gave Emma a mischievous smirk. "You know…the more you protest, the more I'm gonna do it. Right?"

"Yeah, yeah. Whatever," Emma bit back a laugh. "Don't you have somewhere to go?"

"As a matter of fact, I do. Have to keep this body in tip-top shape, so my lovely bride here doesn't cut me loose." His hand tapped his midsection animatedly, while he gave Lily the dimpled smile that still had businesses clamoring for his endorsement. "Can't get too soft."

"Never. Going. To. Happen." Lily reached for him again, placing a hand behind his neck, and pulled him to her for another kiss. "You can't get rid of me that easily, Mr. Thornton."

"Good to know, Ms. Bradshaw. Now, I do need to go. Meeting some mates for a workout." He leaned down and deposited a quick kiss on her lips, before heading for the door.

Emma called out to him, "Bye, Josh."

"See ya later, Emma."

As the door clicked shut behind him, Lily turned her attention back to Emma.

"Now that we're alone, we need to go over some wedding stuff before we go to dinner tonight. My mum will be mad if I haven't brought you up to snuff." Lily's perfectly shaped brows drew together, and she looked like the weight of the world rested upon her shoulders.

Emma and Lily took their seats at the dining table to go over the wedding plans. While they ate breakfast, Lily opened a folder, spreading its contents over the table in front of them. Then the two of them proceeded to go over each item.

Dress, check. Flowers, check. Menu, check. Photographer, check.

The seating chart was the last obstacle. The task was as complicated and politically-charged as a White House dinner. Who sat with whom and the location of their table were of vital importance. No wonder it wasn't completed yet. Eyeing the floor plan with the tables mapped out and guest's names written in pencil, Emma noticed the paper wearing thin from the names being changed so many times.

Who knew that planning a wedding was so complicated? Emma's head was spinning as she tried to concentrate, and having no idea who most of the guests were wasn't helping. There were so many moving parts to keep track of and Lily was determined that everything would go off without a hitch, and Emma was determined to help ease her burden.

Even though Lily joked about slacking when it came to wedding preparations, it was clear she had everything under control. It was a well-oiled machine.

Emma wasn't sure how much help she'd been, but Lily seemed to relax once they'd finished. "What time are we going to your parents' for dinner?" she asked.

"Around five o'clock. That way we can get to the club before it gets too crowded."

"I'm still trying to adjust to the time difference. That's like midnight my time," Emma noted. "Good thing I'm up late most nights, so that's not much of a stretch for me."

"You'll adjust in no time. Speaking of that, it's going to be interesting to see how Abby handles the time difference. We may have a very cranky baby on our hands," Lily uttered the comment offhandedly, but worry lines were creasing her brow once again.

Despite Lily's valid concerns, Emma couldn't help but smile when she thought of Abby. Her sister Alison's daughter was the cutest baby on the planet. But her favorite thing about Abby was that she loved to cuddle, which was a good thing since her feet rarely touched the floor.

Abby's dark brown hair and eyes were in stark contrast to Ali's blonde hair and light blue eyes, and a striking reminder of Abby's father. Ali had also studied abroad in New Zealand, and met the charming Evan Thompson while working on his parent's horse farm. She'd fallen hard and fast for the handsome rugby player, but came home brokenhearted and pregnant.

"God, I miss that baby. Abby is the sweetest thing *ever*," Emma gushed. "We may have to find a babysitter for her, though. Ali keeps her on a pretty tight schedule and she's sleeping through the night now, so I don't think she'll be willing to mess with it."

"Well, being a single mum must be hard for her. I can't believe Evan didn't ask her to move back here with him. I really thought he would."

"I think she did too. She was devastated when she first came home. Then, when she found out she was pregnant," Emma's voice faded, remembering the long nights spent consoling her heartbroken sister, "well, let's just say, it wasn't what she planned for her life. But I think it's safe to say that, even though Abby wasn't expected, Ali wouldn't trade her for anything in the world. Neither would any of us. I also think that having a baby to focus on helped her get over Evan."

"Maybe one day he'll realize what he's missing and do the right thing," Lily sighed, as she carefully folded the seating chart and placed it back into the folder.

"Ali told me that when she's here for the wedding she's going to try to talk to him. See if he wants to see Abby while she's here," Emma added, hoping her sister wasn't disappointed again.

"Hopefully, he'll take her up on the offer. Maybe seeing her will be the push he needs. As far as I know, he's not seeing anyone."

"I don't see Ali going down that road again, but it would be nice if he'd come to visit Abby. I can't imagine only seeing your child a few times a year, but maybe mothers are different than fathers. Although, I think my father would have followed my mother to the ends of the earth and back again. With or without her having his children. Maybe it's just that Evan is missing the parenting gene or something."

"I guess. I still thought he would've at least *asked* her to come back, though. Even if they weren't together. So he could see Abby grow up. Be a part of her life. Evan's a good man and that's what's so confusing about all of this."

"He never asked her to move here as far as I know. She won't talk about it. I think she was holding out hope that they could still be a family. She knew he couldn't visit during the rugby season, but when he never came back when the season ended…well, she was crushed all over again."

Even though Ali refused to discuss Evan's absence in his daughter's life, Emma knew it cut her to the quick. Her sister put on a brave face for everyone, but Emma saw the quiet sorrow veiled beneath the cheerful façade.

Lily silently nodded her head in agreement.

"Only this time it wasn't just for herself, but for Abby too," she continued. "Ali was so upset, she thought about sending his child support money back, but my dad wouldn't allow it. He said, 'One way or another, Evan Thompson is going to take care of his daughter'," Emma stiffened her shoulders, mimicking her father.

"And so he should," Lily frowned. "Well, maybe they can work out a visitation schedule while she's here. It won't be easy living so far from each other, but that's what's best for Abby, eh? Is Ali seeing anyone?"

"She's had a few dates since Abby was born, but nothing serious. She's really just focused on being a mommy. She's moving into a rental home that my parents own, when the lease is up for the current tenants. Maybe once she's out of my parents' house she'll feel more comfortable dating."

"I can see that. Your mum is going to miss having such easy access to Abby, though."

"We avoid the topic like the plague. She cries if you bring it up. But the house is only a few miles from them, so I'm sure my mom will be over there all the time."

Emma knew Ali appreciated everyone's help with Abby, especially the way their mother doted on her only grandchild. But she also knew that her sister was desperate for some privacy, and was counting the days until she and Abby had a home of their own.

"I can only imagine. My mum's already asking when we're going to provide a grandchild for her. I have to keep reminding her that I'm not even married yet. Can't I enjoy my honeymoon before being barefoot and pregnant?" Lily complained half-heartedly.

"Aw…you're going to be such a good mommy, Lily. And the thought of you pregnant makes me a little weepy. A little baby bump. A little baby Josh growing inside you."

"There is nothing *little* about Josh," Lily winked mischievously. "They may have to cut the thing out of me. I don't think my lady parts can handle pushing out a Thornton baby."

"Ugh…*way* too much information, Lily." Emma shuddered dramatically at the visual.

# CHAPTER 3

Getting ready for dinner, Emma felt overdressed as she studied her reflection in the mirror. Her figure-hugging new dress was perfect for a night out on the town, but showed way too much skin for a casual dinner with family. The soft yellow color reminded her of the daffodils that grew in her mother's garden back home, but that was where the sweetness ended.

Storing a white cardigan in her purse for later, she glanced in the mirror one last time. After applying a thin coat of lip gloss, she headed into the lounge, where she found Lily and Josh waiting for her.

"You look lovely, Emma," Lily trilled upon seeing her. "I love those sandals with the dress, too. You're going to have all the boys queuing up to take notice of you."

Emma did her best 'Single Ladies' impression, her Sasha Fierce face firmly in place with her hand flipping back and forth dramatically, as she came to a stop in front of Lily.

"Dork," Lily giggled.

Ignoring Lily's fairly accurate observation, and Josh's loud snicker, Emma continued her impromptu performance. She loved being silly. Having spent endless hours with her sister Katie perfecting the epic dance moves in the Beyoncé video, she knew it by heart, but stopped herself before she broke out the full routine.

Sliding a strand of hair behind her ear, Emma laughed along with her cousin. "Seriously, though, I really don't care. I just feel like dancing tonight, but it is more fun when you have a partner."

"I don't think that will be an issue. My guess is you'll have more than a few, and if not, then I'll take pity on you. Josh doesn't like to dance anyway, only does it to keep me happy," Lily mentioned, as she wrapped her arm around Josh's waist, ushering them out the door.

As soon as they pulled into the driveway of Lily's childhood home, the front door swung open and her Aunt Mary rushed down the walkway towards Emma.

"Oh, my dear, it's so good to see you!" Her hands clutched her cheeks as she gave Emma the once-over. "You look wonderful, and I've made your favorite roast beef and Yorkshire pudding," Aunt Mary overflowed with joy, as she pulled Emma into a long embrace, then kissed both her cheeks.

"It's good to see you, too. I've missed you." Emma looked over her aunt's shoulder and spotted her uncle patiently waiting for his turn. "Hi, Uncle Bob."

"Hey, sweet pea. I'm glad you're here," he smiled, folding his arms around her.

"I'm glad I'm here, too." Emma wound her arm around his, as they walked into the house.

Uncle Bob raised his glass to toast Emma's visit once they gathered around the table for dinner. "Welcome to New Zealand, Emma. May your time here be well spent, and full of happiness. Cheers!"

"Cheers!" everyone replied in unison, then tucked happily into their meals.

"Has Lily brought you up to date on all the wedding plans?" Aunt Mary asked Emma, during a lull in the conversation.

Emma swallowed a bite of beef before she responded. "Yes, I think so. It looks like everything is right on schedule. I'm getting so excited and, now that I'm here, I'm happy to help."

"Your being here is such a blessing, Emma. There's still so much to be done and we need all the help we can get, I'm afraid." Aunt Mary flicked a concerned look in Lily's direction.

"Well, we spent a few hours this morning going over everything. I must say, you've done a wonderful job helping Lily, and I know how much she appreciates it." Emma tried her best to reassure her Aunt.

"She knows I would've been lost without her. I'm not that organized. And I didn't realize how much work it was going to be to put everything together," Lily paused, smiling at her mother devotedly. "Thank you, Mum. I don't say it enough, but I really do appreciate everything you've done for me. I hope you know that."

"Well, it's not every day that your only daughter gets married. And to such a wonderful young man, too," she said, regarding Josh affectionately. "I just want your day to be perfect."

"It will be. It's exactly what I dreamed of, and you've helped make that happen for me. So, thank you, and you too, Daddy."

"You're welcome, sweetheart," Aunt Mary lovingly patted Lily's hand, clearly relieved that everything was in order.

"Well, we couldn't be happier that you've found a man worthy of you," Uncle Bob grinned, tilting his glass towards Josh.

"Good as gold. I'm a lucky man," Josh lifted his glass, returning the gesture.

"Well...before we all start to cry, we need to get going. Do you mind if we don't stay to help clean up, Mum?" Lily asked hopefully, getting up from the table.

"No, it's fine. Your father will help me. Just take your plates into the kitchen and we'll finish up. Go have fun and we'll see you soon," Aunt Mary answered her, as she escorted them into the kitchen.

Parking the car at home, they walked the few blocks to the club on the waterfront in Auckland's CBD, Central Business District. Stepping inside, Lily took Emma by the hand and led her to a table, as Josh turned for the bar to order their drinks.

Looking around the small club, Emma drummed her fingers on the table to the beat of the music. The techno remix streaming through the sound system was catchy and had a good dance beat to it. She noticed that there were only a few people on the dance floor, but it was still early.

"Wait a few hours and you won't be able to move out there," Lily pointed out, as if reading her mind. "That's when we usually leave, though. I hope you don't mind. I can't stand it when it gets really loud, and everyone's all sweaty. The only sweaty man I want near me is the one who put this lovely ring on my finger." Lily held her hand out in front of her, admiring her gorgeous engagement ring, then slid her gaze to Josh as he arrived with their drinks.

"Whenever you're ready to go, just let me know," Emma responded, as Josh placed a bottle of beer in front of her, before sliding into the booth next to Lily. "Thanks, Josh. I'll get the next round."

"Drinks are our shout tonight. Your welcome to En Zed from us," he toasted, tipping his bottle in Emma's direction.

"Absolutely!" Lily agreed emphatically, cringing when she set her beer down a little harder than she meant to.

"I'm the one who should be buying. To pay you back for putting me up for the next year. A few rounds of drinks will hardly cover it," Emma protested.

Lily gave her a playful smirk, daring Emma to quarrel with her, but letting her know, in no uncertain terms, that doing so would be fruitless. "It's no use arguing, Emma."

Finding no quarter in Josh's stubborn expression either, Emma conceded defeat and smiled gratefully. "Thanks, guys."

Lily tilted her face towards Josh, as she rested her chin in the palm of her hand. "So, who's meeting us here?"

"Noah and Dustin. Not sure who else will be tagging along, though, or who will end up with us as the night progresses," Josh replied, lifting the bottle in front of him for a long drink.

"Well, I'm looking forward to meeting your friends. You want to dance, Lily?"

"Sure. Just let me finish my beer. Bottoms up," Lily quickly downed the rest of her drink, then turned towards Josh. "Can you watch our purses, baby? We won't be too long. Maybe order us another round."

The pulse from the loud music vibrated through Emma's veins, as they danced together. It felt good to release some energy and dancing always did the trick. Lily's graceful movements drew Emma further into the rhythm of the song as they laughed, while performing the latest dance obsession and some classic hip-hop moves.

One song turned into another, and another, until they were both out of breath and in need of refreshments.

Walking towards the table, Emma saw that two men had joined Josh, occupying the bench seat across from him, where she'd been sitting earlier. Two very large and attractive men, Emma couldn't help but notice. Lily slid over, making room for Emma next to her, and Josh placed two frosty beers in front of them.

"Emma, these fine young blokes are my mates, Noah and Dustin." Josh aimed his bottle at each of the handsome men. "Noah, Dustin, this is Lily's cousin Emma. She's from America and staying with us while she's at university this year."

"It's nice to meet you, Emma. Welcome to En Zed. I'm Noah Parker," Noah smiled, as he reached his hand across the table to her. His large hand dwarfed hers, and his grip was strong, but not overwhelming.

"Yes, nice to meet you, Emma. I'm Dustin Conrad," Dustin greeted Emma, taking her hand in his and giving it a gentle squeeze.

Dustin was cute, in a boy next door sort of way, but Noah...Noah was all that and so much more.

Are New Zealand men better looking than the men back home, or is it just their sexy accents? She asked herself. It must be a combination of both. There was no denying that Noah and Dustin were exceptionally good looking men, in a rugged sort of way. But when you added in their Kiwi accent, it just catapulted them into a different stratosphere.

Noah had the most beautiful pair of crystal blue eyes she'd ever seen, which appeared even brighter against his deeply tanned skin. And his wavy dark brown hair was just long enough to catch the collar of his dress shirt, and had her fingers itching to feel the softness of it.

Shocked by the shiver of awareness that raced down her spine, Emma felt goose bumps rise across her skin when Noah's full lips parted, adorably turning up at the corners, and Emma was sure that one flash of that sinfully sexy smile had women swooning at his feet.

"So, you're from America." Distracted by the touch of Noah's leg, as it brushed against hers under the table, and still trying to recover from the unexpected loss of most of her brain cells from the impact of his killer smile, Emma almost missed his comment.

The man should seriously come with a warning label pinned to his shirt.

"Yes, North Carolina," Emma managed to say, trying to disguise how flustered she was, while picking at the label of her beer nervously. She was in major trouble if one inadvertent bump of his knee against hers had her ready to crawl into his lap and purr like a kitten.

His shirt was nicely filled out by an impressive set of shoulders, and a pair of biceps which were currently stretching the confines of their sleeves to their breaking point. He must work out a lot, Emma concluded. Muscles like that were gained from years of training and hard work.

Emma kept finding her gaze landing on Noah's hands, though. She'd never really paid much attention to, or found a man's hands particularly fetching before, but she couldn't take her eyes off them. They were strong and masculine...and big. And sexy.

Yikes, normally two beers wasn't enough to get her buzzed, but her head was swimming already. The alcohol content in the local brew Josh had gotten her must have been higher than what she was used to, because she couldn't think straight.

"I love this song. You have to dance with me," Lily shoved Emma from the booth and dragged her away from the table, startling her from the dreamlike state she'd found herself in.

"What are you doing?" Emma yelled to her over the music. "You almost knocked me over."

"Stopping you from making a right fool of yourself. Thought I was going to have to wipe the drool off your bloody chin. Noah gets enough attention when he's out. He doesn't need you, of all people, behaving like that. Seriously, Emma, it was about to get embarrassing," Lily chastised her resolutely, while trying not to laugh.

"I wasn't that bad," Emma objected, with suddenly-eroding confidence. "Was I? I didn't think it was to the point of having to break out a bib. That wasn't fair, though, you should have warned me."

"Yeah, yeah, he's dead sexy. You'd have to be blind not to notice. Got that sorted. Now control yourself," Lily giggled, and gave Emma a spin as a new song started.

"Would you like to dance?" Emma turned to find a fair-haired man executing some serious dance moves, while waiting for an answer.

"Sure. Do you mind, Lil?"

"No. It's fine. I'm getting tired anyway. Need to sit for a while. Have fun, you two," she quipped, as she slipped away.


"So that's Emma, eh? Her pictures didn't do her justice. She's very pretty." Noah tried to sound unaffected but was failing miserably, as he eyed Emma on the dance floor. Pretty was an understatement. She was gorgeous.

As if her emerald green eyes and shiny blonde hair, which he was sure was naturally kissed by the sun and not from a bottle, weren't enough to get his motor running, her smile just about took his breath away. And the sexy yellow dress she was wearing, which was currently hugging her curves in all the right places, drew his eyes to a pair of long legs that he was sure would star in more than a few of his fantasies.

She was lean but muscular, athletic. And he'd always had a weakness for leggy blondes.

Everything about the way she looked appealed to him. Now, he just needed to see if she was more than just a pretty face. He'd heard Lily talk about her over the years, but surprisingly, had never met her until tonight.

"Yeah, she's a beauty. A total sweetheart. Lily's chuffed she's finally made it here," Josh replied thoughtfully, while watching Lily approach the table. "Hey, babe. Who's the bloke with Emma?"

"Don't know. He just asked her to dance and I was a bit knackered so..." her voice trailed off as she took the seat next to Josh.

"Just let me know when you're ready to go, and we'll head home." Josh reached out his hand to his weary-looking fiancée.

"Okay. I just need to rest for a few and then I'll be right," she assured Josh, as she nuzzled beside him, resting their joined hands on his thigh.

As the song came to an end, Noah slid from the booth, stalking towards Emma and the randy bugger who was eyeing her a little too fondly for his liking. Sizing up the competition was something Noah was used to, what he did for a living, and from the looks of things, this man wouldn't be a problem for much longer.

"Excuse me, mate, but I'd like to dance with the lady now," Noah glared intimidatingly down at the shorter man, then turned to Emma. "If it's alright with you, Emma?" he added sweetly.

"Um...okay." Emma watched as her dance partner took a step back, unintentionally making room for Noah to slide between them.

The annoyed look on the man's face, as he jerked his head towards Noah, was quickly replaced with one of surprise as recognition set in. "Good as gold, mate. Nice to meet you, Emma," he smiled, raising his hand to wave goodbye.

"Bye," Emma awkwardly returned the gesture, before focusing her attention on Noah as a popular hip-hop song began to play.

Noah stood back and watched in awe as Emma started moving to the music. Damn, she looked good as her body swayed seductively and her arms lifted above her head. The motion highlighted the swell of her round breasts, as well as exposing more of her long legs. And silky blonde hair fell softly over bare shoulders, as she turned her head from side to side.

Settling closer to her, he slid his arm around her waist and gently maneuvered her body against his as they moved together as one. She felt so good in his arms, and when she looked up at him through thick, dark lashes, he almost gave into the urge to kiss her.

Striking green eyes, sprinkled with tiny yellow flecks, had his heart doing a little flip in his chest when they met his. There was something about her that intrigued him; all he could think of was that he wanted to know everything about her.

"You're a great dancer. Do you go out a lot back home?" Noah asked curiously, trying to find out if she was a party girl seeking the spotlight.

Noah was looking for someone to settle down with, not trip the light fantastic. After indulging a bit too much, he was tired of club girls and groupies. He was ready for more.

Watching Josh fall in love with Lily had made him long for that too. Lily complemented Josh in a way that no other woman had before. They were truly happy together. Noah was impressed with Lily's devotion to his best friend as she stood by Josh, supporting him during his career-ending injury.

Josh wasn't always pleasant to be around back then, but Lily never piked out. She helped see him through his recovery, then never left his side when he received the heartbreaking news that he'd never play again.

Noah wanted a partner who'd stick with him through the good times and the bad times, someone to go the distance with. He was weary of the dating scene and wanted the security and comfort of a loving relationship. He wanted someone to come home to at night and eventually have a few kids with.

"Thanks, but no. I don't get to go out dancing that often. There aren't a lot of dance clubs in Boone, where I go to school. You're more apt to find a pool table than a dance floor in the bars there. At least the ones that I go to. But I do love to dance, so it's nice to get out once in a while and let off some steam." Noah couldn't help but smile as his hand splayed across her lower back.

Trying to focus on anything other than the way her lithe body was caressing him, or the movement of her soft lips as she spoke, was proving extremely difficult. But with a herculean effort, he forced his mind off the feel of her soft curves, and back to the conversation at hand.

"Where is Boone? I've never heard of it," he inquired sincerely.

"It's a small town in the mountains of North Carolina," Emma paused, and when the tip of her tongue peeked out to moisten her lip, Noah was sure he was about to thoroughly embarrass himself. "Um…have you always lived in Auckland?" she asked.

"No, I grew up in Hamilton. My father's a professor at the university there. I try to visit as much as I can, but Auckland's home to me now. I moved here for university and then got picked up by the team I play for, the Blues. That's how I met Josh. We were roomies when we traveled, so we spent a lot of time together."

"Ah, I probably should have guessed you played rugby, based on how big you are," Emma giggled adorably, pulling away slightly to admire his muscular physique. "I've never been to Hamilton; the only place I've been south of the Auckland area is Wellington."

"Wellington's a great place. Lots to do there," he held onto her as a new song began to play. It was slower and he was thankful she didn't move away.

Noah liked that she was tall, and the added height from the sexy sandals she was wearing aligned their bodies perfectly. As if waking from a long slumber, his body came to life as her softness pressed against him. And his fingers itched to slide over the round globe of her bum, to find their home there.

Warm breath tickled his ear as she leaned against him, to be heard over the music, and for a brief moment, her smooth cheek brushed against his. He had to physically restrain himself from tilting his head just slightly to the left, to capture her lips with his.

Afraid of scaring her off, he focused instead on the sound of her voice and the overwhelming realization that something had shifted inside of him. And the fact that that realization didn't send him sprinting for the nearest exit should have freaked him out, but it didn't, it comforted him.

Emma hesitated, not wanting to appear too eager, but then gave into the desire to hold Noah close as she wound her arms around his neck, twirling a lock of his hair around her finger. "I'm sure it is. I'd like to visit while I'm here. We went so many years ago that I don't really remember much, except going to the zoo. I cried when my parents let my older brothers feed the lion, but said I was too little," she glowered, the memory of sitting idly by while they got to do the one thing she'd been looking forward to still irritated her.

"Well, maybe you could come down for a match with Josh and Lily. I could show you the sights. Hopefully leave you with a better impression this time around. And if you still want to get up close and personal with a lion, I think that could be arranged." He gave her a promising smile that left her a bit breathless.

"Thanks, Noah, I'd love that."

Emma wondered how it was possible for his grip to be firm yet relaxed at the same time. The heat from his hand, holding her snugly against him, was making it hard to concentrate on anything other than his touch. His thighs brushed against hers as they moved to the music, in a slow rhythmic dance, and the rest of the crowd melted away, leaving only the two of them on the dance floor.

Little sparks of electricity followed the circles his fingers were tracing on her back, and she tried to remember the last time she'd been so aware of another's touch before...and couldn't.

At five-foot nine Emma wasn't a short woman, but Noah had to be at least six-foot three, if she had to guess, and surprisingly, she felt small next to him. She fit perfectly against his broad muscular chest, her head tucked into the crook of his neck as they swayed together.

When the song ended, Noah was uncomfortable with the size of the crowd that had grown thick around them. Ignoring the curious glances from the people surrounding them, he took her hand in his and led her back to the table.

Not missing the moment Lily spotted their linked fingers, based on the sly smile that spread across her face, he reluctantly let go of Emma's hand as she slipped into the space next to Lily. Taking the seat across from her, he let his knee rest against hers under the table, still wanting to feel the connection.

He watched as Emma slid a long lock of hair behind her ear, then took a sip from the bottle of beer that Lily placed in front of her. After she set the bottle down her tongue skimmed the length of her lips from corner to corner, leaving a sheen of moisture in its path, and Noah wasn't sure how much more he could take.

Trying to concentrate on the discussion taking place around him, he was jolted from his wandering thoughts of Emma's pretty mouth, and the naughty things he'd prefer she was doing with it, by the sound of her laughter. Noah closed his eyes to savor the sound of it. It was the infectious kind of laugh that left anyone who was lucky enough to hear it…happy.

Emma nudged his knee with hers, and damn if he didn't want to reach under the table and run his fingers up the length of her thigh. "I think they're trying to get your attention, Noah."

Following her line of vision, he twisted to see a pair of scantily-clad girls grinding against each other, eyeing him intently. The look on their faces, clearly an invitation to more than just a go on the dance floor.

Noah snickered and had to smile at the irritated look on Emma's face. "Seriously? That's not my style. I don't like to share. *Especially in the bedroom*," winking at Emma, while tapping beers with Josh, he didn't miss the way her pupils dilated at his statement. Interesting. Maybe he wasn't the only one who felt like they'd been struck by lightning.

# CHAPTER 4

"Do you mind if we go, Emma?" Lily asked hopefully. "It's getting too loud in here. My ears are starting to ring."

"Not at all," Emma sneered, glancing at the two women, who were now so close to their table, they were practically giving him a lap dance.

"You need a lift, Noah?" Dustin asked, as he stood to his feet.

"No. Left my car at Josh's place. I'll walk back with them." Saying goodbye to Dustin, he guided Emma through the crowd, glad to be out of there. He wasn't all that comfortable with large crowds, or predatory women, for that matter.

Exiting the club, he watched Emma pull a white sweater from her bag.

"Here, let me help you with that," he offered, as he took the sweater, holding it up behind her.

"Well, aren't you a gentleman? Thanks," Emma mused happily, glancing over her shoulder at him. Pulling her hair from its entrapment beneath the sweater, her long locks fell in shimmery waves down her back, and he wanted to comb his fingers through it. To feel its softness.

"My mum raised me right," he beamed with pride, thankful his parents had always emphasized the importance of good manners while he was growing up.

"My compliments to her then." Emma gave him a flirty smile, and the soft glow from the street light cast an angelic halo around the crown of her head.

Falling into step next to her, he was grateful for the peacefulness of the foot path, as they walked together in a companionable silence behind Josh and Lily. He'd needed a few minutes to gather his racing thoughts. Giving up, Noah shoved his hands in his pockets to resist touching her, when what he really wanted was to put his arm around her, to feel her warmth, to tuck her protectively under his shoulder. Or maybe just hold her hand.

"You know…you didn't have to leave just because we did," Emma said, breaking the silence, as she turned towards Noah.

"You trying to get rid of me already, eh?" he teased, and Emma instantly wanted to swallow her words, to take them back.

Cocking her head to the side, Emma looked at him curiously, hoping he wasn't offended by her comment. "I didn't mean it like that. I just…I don't know. Forget I said anything." Giggling nervously, Emma felt the heat of a blush tinting her cheeks, which she was sure was evident even on the darkened street.

"I'm just giving you a hard time," Noah joked, as if sensing her discomfort. "We usually don't stay too late anyway. Just go to relax and have a few, then head home. Oi, I sound terribly boring, don't I?"

"No. Not at all," Emma hurried to assure him. "I'm home or at a friend's place most nights. I lead a pretty quiet life in Boone. I like it that way, though." She'd never thought of her life in Boone as boring, she just enjoyed a peaceful, quiet life, with as little drama as possible.

"I reckon you might be right. Being boring isn't so bad after all," Noah agreed, giving her a gentle nudge with his shoulder.

"You're not boring, Noah. Boring people have nothing relevant or interesting to add to a conversation. They're just, blah, blah, blah."

When she lifted her hand and pinched her fingers and thumb together, in sync with her last remark, an irresistible smile spread across his lips, before accepting her compliment. "Thanks."

"I wouldn't say that preferring a quiet life makes someone boring either. I love that I can drive down the Blue Ridge Parkway in any direction, hike to a beautiful overlook and spend hours there just reading a book, playing my guitar, or watching the clouds float by…just enjoying the beauty of nature. Now, to some, they'd be bored out of their minds…restless. But for me…" she paused, reliving some of her favorite memories. "it's a little slice of heaven. It's all in how you choose to look at it, I guess. Does that make sense?" She glanced at him to gauge his reaction, looking for reassurance.

"Perfect," he answered honestly. "There's something about being alone with your thoughts that puts things in perspective. Living on my own, I have a lot of quiet time, by myself."

"Well, my brother and sister both live in Boone. And a bunch of friends that I've known my whole life live there too. So, I don't get a lot of alone time," she chuckled. "There's always someone around. I have a roommate too and he's usually home. But it's nice to get away once in a while."

Well, damn. He didn't see that coming. "He? You live with someone?" He didn't like the thought of her with another man…at all, and was a bit taken aback by the sudden twinge behind his breastbone.

"I live with my friend, Chris. But we're not *together, together*. Ew…no. I can't even think about that without feeling dirty. He's like a brother to me. Love him to death, but have no desire to see him naked in any way, shape, or form," Emma laughed, flashing Noah a dazzling smile that left him a bit shell shocked, and relieved that her roommate was securely in the friend zone.

Silently giving thanks that she was still available, he asked, "So…do you have a lot of blokes as friends?"

"Yeah, I do actually. I have female friends too, of course. But I'd have to admit that most of my friends are male. Less drama with men, I've found over the years. What about you? I'm sure you have a lot of friends of the female persuasion?"

Noah offered a reluctant laugh, then admitted, "Not really, most of my mates are guys I play footy with or used to play with, like Josh. I have female friends, but they're mostly the partners of my mates, like Lily. I spent almost all my free time growing up playing footy or training, so there wasn't a lot of time for anything else. Reckon I missed out on all the drama, yeah?" he agreed, then hurriedly continued, not wanting to sound like a total loser. "It's not that I didn't have girlfriends, but once the relationship was over, we didn't stay friends or anything, just went our separate ways."

"I'm friends with most of my exes," Emma replied openly. "Maybe not right away, but over time. It's not like we call each other to shoot the breeze or anything, but if we see each other at a party or out somewhere, we can hang out and it not be awkward. That would upset me. I've genuinely liked most of the guys I've dated and enjoyed their company."

"How many exes are there?" Noah probed, curiosity getting the best of him, but not wanting to press. "You don't have to answer that if you don't want to," he added quickly.

"I don't mind. There aren't that many. Thankfully," she hesitated, but continued, "I've had three serious relationships, but I've had boyfriends that never went much further than a few dates or going to a party together. I'm too picky, I think. At least that's what I've been told on a number of occasions," she finished with a resigned sigh.

"Nothing wrong with being selective, I'd say, eh?" Noah assured her.

"My mother always drilled the saying, 'Be careful who you associate with because that's who you will date, and who you date is who you will fall in love with, and who you fall in love with is who you will marry…So be careful who you associate with.' into our heads. I can't tell you how many times she said that to me," Emma smiled thoughtfully with a soft, almost imperceptible, shrug of her shoulder.

"Sounds like a very wise woman." A very wise woman indeed. He'd met more than his fair share of crazy women over the course of his rugby career. He was sure Emma's mother would definitely *not* approve of them…or his mum either, for that matter. That's why he rarely brought anyone home to meet his parents.

"She *is* a wise woman. My parents are still happily married after thirty-five years, so she must be doing something right." Emma's parents were still madly in love, and set the standard for a happy and healthy marriage, and the type of relationship that Emma hoped to have one day.

"Too right, I'd say. Any other nuggets of wisdom?"

"Well, let's see…Life's too short to waste it being unhappy. Always treat people the way you'd like to be treated. If at first you don't succeed, try, try again. And… don't forget to pack your undies." At Noah's loud outburst of laughter, Emma couldn't help but join in. "Don't laugh. It's not funny. I actually did that once."

"I guess that's good advice then, eh?" Noah chuckled, still amused by her cheeky comment, as they entered the lobby and turned towards the lift.

Emma's easy smile lit up her entire face. "Words to live by."

Catching up to Lily and Josh as the doors to the lift opened, Noah stood next to Emma as she leaned against the wall. Lily was watching them suspiciously, and he didn't blame her. He'd been falling all over himself to gain Emma's attention all night, and was practically making love to her on the dance floor. Lily knew him well enough to know that he was interested in her cousin. Very interested.

As soon as they walked through the front door, Lily caught Emma by the arm and dragged her into the kitchen, while calling out to Josh and Noah. "What can we get you to drink?"

"I'll have a beer, babe," Josh shouted out to her as he took a seat in the lounge.

"Me too, babe," Noah requested with a hearty laugh.

"Funny, Noah," Lily answered back sarcastically, then faced Emma and continued quietly. "So, what's going on with you and Noah? I thought I was going to have to throw a bucket of ice water on the two of you. He was just about shagging you on the dance floor and *you* didn't look like you were complaining." Lily poked an accusatory finger at Emma, then snorted while leaning into the refrigerator, grabbing four beers.

Shaking her head, Emma leaned her hip against the counter. "We were just dancing, Lil. That's how most people do it, if you haven't noticed. I'm not saying that I minded, though. All I can think when I look at him is…well…I have trouble thinking when I look at him, actually. He certainly wasn't slapped with the ugly stick," she laughed, as Lily cocked her head and glanced at her sideways. "What?"

"The ugly stick?" Lily snickered. "Yeah, well it looked like some kind of primitive mating ritual from where I was sitting," she pointed out gleefully, as she opened a drawer, shifting the contents around until she landed on the bottle opener.

"Ha. Ha. That was nothing compared to what those floozies would have done to him out there," Emma declared ruefully, wincing at the thought of the two women with Noah, then again at the sudden pang of jealousy that came over her.

"Yeah, well, he's not interested in that, I can tell you. Noah's been around for a fair few years in the public spotlight; he knows better than to get mixed up with the likes of them. Doesn't stop girls from trying one on, though." Lily exhaled a long breath in sympathy for her friend. "If they knew him at all, they'd know better. Girls like that just want to brag to their friends that they bagged an All Black. But that's not who he is. Do you know what I mean?"

"I think so. Obviously, I don't know him that well. But from the few hours I spent with him tonight, that's pretty clear. He seems like a nice guy," Emma answered honestly. From what she'd witnessed he appeared to be well-mannered and considerate…two very important qualities, she thought to herself.

"He is," Lily uttered simply, handing Emma two beers and starting for the lounge.

Emma handed Noah his beer, and settled onto her side of the couch. Glancing at Noah as he lifted his beer, he flashed an irresistible smile in her direction, before putting the bottle to his lips for a long swig.

Hypnotized, as his Adams Apple bobbed up and down when he swallowed, Emma wondered why she'd never noticed that on anyone before. Maybe it was just Noah, but it was one of the sexiest things she'd ever seen.

"Emma, how would you like to go to the beach after New Year's?" Josh asked, drawing her attention away from Noah. "We're going to a party in Devonport, but then were hoping to get away for a few days. A quick holiday before we get busy with the final push to the wedding."

"I'd love that, as long as you won't mind having a third wheel on your vacation." The beach sounded wonderful, but she was on a budget and wasn't sure she could afford the luxury of a vacation. "And as long as the hotel isn't too expensive. I still have a lot of stuff to buy for school and such. If so, I can always stay here. I don't mind."

"Wouldn't have asked if we didn't want your company, Emma. But Noah has a bach on Papamoa Beach on the Bay of Plenty, so it wouldn't cost you anything," Josh answered cheerfully.

"A what? What's a bach?" She didn't want to sound stupid, but she had no idea what they were talking about.

"I guess it's what you'd call a vacation home," Noah explained.

"Oh, so who'd be going with us?" Emma probed, her eyes locking on Lily nervously.

"Just the four of us. It's so nice there this time of year. You'll love it," Lily gushed, as if it was no big deal.

It felt like a big deal to Emma, though. If she was being completely honest, she liked the idea of spending more time with Noah, getting to know him better. But this felt like too much, too soon. Like a double date that was going to last for days.

What if he got on her nerves? What would she do then? She'd be stuck there. A few days of sun and surf might be worth it, though, even if he turned out to be a total douche.

But what if he thought she was like one of the girls from the club? Was he expecting an easy hook-up for the week?

Being a famous rugby player, Noah was probably used to women throwing themselves at him. Would he expect that from her too? She wasn't a virgin, but wasn't a one night stand kind of girl either. Had she given him the impression that she was? She hoped not, because she didn't do that. Ever.

"Um...would there be room for all of us?" Emma could feel her face heating up as she started to blush, and she was becoming increasingly annoyed with Lily for putting her in the situation in the first place.

"Yes, of course. We'd have our own rooms, but I think Josh and Lily might want to share," Noah chimed in, his sweet smile helping to put her at ease.

Giving herself a moment to think, she took a long pull from her drink, the cool liquid sliding down her throat, as she worked to quiet her churning emotions.

Over the years she'd taken plenty of vacations with her male friends, and occasionally she'd been the only girl. So, why was the thought of spending time at the beach with Noah so unnerving? She knew the reason and he was sitting within striking distance, looking sexier than any man had a right to.

With more confidence than she actually felt, she calmly responded, "Alright. I'd love to go. Actually, I love the beach. Now, what about the party? Will they mind if you bring me along since they don't know me?"

"Nah, they won't mind at all. No worries. And they live on Queens Parade so we'll have the perfect spot to watch the fireworks display," Josh replied, then irreverently added. "You might even find some lucky bugger to give you a kiss at midnight."

"Yeah, right," Emma snorted, then feeling embarrassed, started fidgeting on the couch. "What kind of girl do you think I am, Josh?"

"The kind that clearly needs to lighten up a bit, based on your reaction every time you catch me innocently kissing Lily."

Innocent my ass, she thought to herself.

Emma had been called a lot of things over the years, but uptight wasn't one of them. She was a go-with-the-flow kind of girl, so Josh's comment stung a little.

"For the record, I've only said something when you were ready to take her on the kitchen counter with me standing two feet away, *innocently* trying to enjoy my morning cup of tea," she clarified, aiming for a touch of snark, but instead landing on the whiney side of petulance.

"Well, I do some of my best work in the kitchen. Lots to work with. I've been missing that since you moved in," Josh winked, giving her a mischievous smirk, then slid Lily closer to him on the couch and kissed her soundly.

"Ugh...see what I have to put up with?" She looked to Noah for sympathy and found none, as he only laughed at Josh's response.

Emma scowled at Lily. "Please tell me you sterilize the counters."

"Of course, Emma. We have to eat off of them too, you know," Lily answered back, after pulling away from Josh.

"You sure you want to sit there, Emma?" Josh lifted his eyebrows suggestively, nodding towards her spot on the couch.

"Are you kidding me? Is nowhere safe around here?" Emma laughed, trying her best not to cringe.

"Hmm...let me think," Josh paused for dramatic effect, drumming his fingers across his chin, as he considered his retort, "Nope," he concluded decisively.

"Oh. My. God. I give up. Please tell me you at least put clean sheets on my bed," she joked halfheartedly, thinking she may need to do some laundry.

"Don't worry, Emma. I can see the wheels spinning in that pretty head of yours," Lily chuckled, trying to reassure her. "Your room has been properly cleaned."

"Thanks, Lil." Even though she knew Josh was only trying to get a rise out of her, she still didn't relish the thought of sleeping on dirty sheets.

"Well, speaking of my bed. I think I'm going to hit it." Emma hoisted herself off the couch, coming to her feet.

After giving Lily and Josh a hug, she turned to Noah, briefly contemplating whether or not she should give in to the urge to give him one too.

Making up her mind for her, Noah stood and took a step towards Emma. "Good night, Emma. It was great to finally meet you." He smiled as he folded his strong arms around her, then bent down and gave her a quick kiss on the cheek. At the tender gesture she unconsciously squeezed him tightly around the waist, shamelessly inhaling his musky scent.

His warmth enveloped her and she reluctantly released him after a long minute. "Good night, Noah. It was really nice meeting you, too. I had a lot of fun tonight." She leaned down, picked up her sandals, and headed to her room.

# CHAPTER 5

Waking in the morning, Emma groaned as she realized she'd once again forgotten to close the curtains. Making a mental note to call home, she left the warmth of her bed for some water in the kitchen.

As she stuck her head in the refrigerator in search of a bottle of water, she was startled by Noah's voice behind her. "Good morning, Emma." The smooth cadence of his voice set the hairs on the back of her neck on end, and sent a little shiver down her spine.

Quickly straightening, she turned towards him…and froze. Standing before her was what could only be described as perfection, but even that didn't do him justice. People wrote songs about a body like his, usually a cautionary tale ending in heartbreak, but as she paused to absorb the visual impact, she understood the temptation.

Leaning against the door frame, looking scrumptiously rumpled, wearing only a pair of black gym shorts, which sat dangerously low on his narrow hips, was the most gorgeous man she'd ever seen. Sweet mother of God, she thought to herself, clutching the bottle of water, needing something to hold onto.

It took every ounce of self-restraint she could muster not to reach out and touch him, just to make sure he was real and not a figment of her overactive imagination. She could feel her body temperature rising at an alarming rate, and was thankful for the still-opened refrigerator door providing cool air to soothe her heated skin.

Fully clothed Noah left her warm and fuzzy and wanting to cuddle. Shirtless Noah left her hot and bothered and wanting to copulate.

Swallowing past the lump that had formed in her throat, her eyes drifted to a pair of muscular arms, crossed over his bare chest, and an eight pack of chiseled abs, all contours and ridges, just begging to be explored.

A thin line of dark hair below his navel disappeared into his shorts, drawing her eyes lower, and when they landed on what appeared to be a rather impressive package, she forgot how to breathe.

Noah Parker had a duty to pass on his DNA for the good of mankind. And her ovaries were currently jostling for position, as they lined up to volunteer for service.

Finally dragging her eyes to meet his, she found him, much to her distress, watching her with a knowing grin.

*Busted.*

"Um…Good morning, Noah," she squeaked, her voice an octave higher than normal, betraying her level of utter humiliation.

Standing in the doorway, Noah had had a choice view of her bum as she bent over, humming a tune while rummaging through the fridge. Taking advantage of the fact that she was oblivious to his presence, he'd let his eyes wander over a pair of shapely legs that went on forever, and were the things dreams were made of. Wet dreams.

"I was just about to put some water on for tea," she visibly gulped, and a pretty pink tinted her cheeks. "I think I had a bit too much to drink last night. I need some caffeine to get my brain in gear."

She may've needed caffeine to get her mind in gear, but Noah's was locked and loaded, and as he took in the sight of her, ready for some fun.

"Should I flex for you, Emma? Give you the gun show?" Noah couldn't resist giving her a hard time, as he flexed his biceps, not embarrassed at all by her obvious appreciation of his physique.

As a professional sportsman his livelihood depended on taking care of his body. Any weakness would be exploited by his opponent and could cost him his position on the team, so he spent countless hours on physical conditioning, even in the off season.

He wasn't as ripped as some of the other fellas on the team, but the ladies seemed to like the results. And looking at the adorable blush coloring her cheeks, Emma liked what she was seeing...just fine.

"Um..." She paused, completely mortified and at a loss for words. "I...I wasn't expecting to see you. And then all this...I'm only human, after all," she stammered, waving her hand up and down, then grimaced, realizing she'd just said that out loud.

"I'm just teasing you, Emma." Noah lowered his arms to his side, and she breathed a sigh of relief. "Probably should've had some water before bed, I reckon. And I'd kill for a cuppa, if you don't mind."

Thankful for the change in topic, to safer territory, Emma tried to focus on the task at hand, before she made an even bigger fool of herself. "I don't mind at all. I didn't know you were spending the night here. Where'd you sleep?" she inquired, turning to make their tea.

"On the couch, I'm afraid. I used to have a comfy bed to sleep in when I stayed over, but it has a much prettier occupant now. I've been replaced," he frowned, reaching for two cups in the cabinet, and placing them on the counter next to her.

"Oh, I'm sorry. Lily mentioned you stayed over sometimes, but it never occurred to me last night," she admitted apologetically, knowing he couldn't have gotten much rest on the couch.

"No worries. The couch was surprisingly comfortable, considering I couldn't roll over without falling off," he fibbed. His back was killing him, but he didn't want to make her feel bad, so he'd never admit that to her.

Emma's lips curled into a pretty pout. "You're way too big to fit on that couch. If I'd known, I would've let you have the bed."

"Like I said, no worries. I slept like a baby." Curiosity getting the better of him, Noah switched gears. "So, tell me about your family. I know you have a brother and a sister that live in Boone. Do you have any other siblings?"

"There're six of us," she laughed, that enchanting laugh that left him wanting... well everything.

"That's a lot of seats around the dinner table," he observed good-naturedly.

"Yeah. You learned to eat pretty fast with three older brothers. They took a deep breath and the food was gone." Growing up, dinner was always an adventure. Most of the time it was loud and fun, but she could also remember plenty of teary exits from the table, after someone got their feelings hurt.

"I'm sure. Did you leave the table without enough to eat? Is that why you're so thin?" he asked, a concerned frown tainting his handsome face.

"Oh, I like food *way* too much to go without. Trust me," she chuckled, shaking her head. "But I've always been pretty active, with dance classes and then I started swimming, not to mention the endless hiking trails in Boone." She poured the steaming water into their cups. "How do you take it?"

"Just a little milk, please." He paused as she prepared their tea. "Thank you." Then smiled appreciatively as she slid his cup to him.

Noah watched, mesmerized, as she lifted the cup to her lips, and then blew on the hot liquid before taking a sip.

"Mmm. Just what the doctor ordered," she closed her eyes, releasing a sexy moan and he almost choked.

Not wanting to be obvious, he allowed his eyes to quickly skim the length of her. She wore a form-fitting tank top and a pair of scandalously short shorts that barely covered her perfectly rounded bum and left her impossibly long legs on full display.

"What does the 'A' stand for?" he asked, pointing to the bold yellow 'A' on the front of her black tank top, letting his eyes linger there for a long moment, enjoying the view.

Good Lord, she wasn't wearing a bra and her nipples were on high alert. Forcing his eyes back up to her face, he started to panic when he felt a stirring low in his belly, and willed his body into submission before he completely humiliated himself.

"Appalachian State. It's where I go to school. Home of the Mountaineers," she happily chirped, as she walked into the lounge. And as if attached to an invisible leash, he dutifully followed.

Taking a blanket off the back of the couch, she settled into the chair and propped her feet on the coffee table, crossing her legs at the ankles. Snatching the blanket from her hands would probably be ill advised, but that's exactly what he wanted to do when she proceeded to cover herself with the offending scrap of material.

Pity, Noah thought, as he made himself comfortable on the couch opposite her. Watching as she snuggled into the cushions, he didn't think he'd ever tire of looking at her, and found himself longing to hold her, to kiss her. Every mouth-watering inch of her.

Her clean face exposed flawless skin, surrounded by a thick mass of sun-kissed blonde hair that obviously hadn't been brushed yet, but still left him wanting to twirl it around his fingers. She was a natural beauty, with the prettiest green eyes he'd ever seen, and his only thought as he gazed at her was that he could happily wake up to that face every day, for the rest of his days.

Noah wasn't entirely surprised by his reaction to her; she was absolutely gorgeous and dead sexy too. But more importantly, the more time he spent with her, he realized that she was much more than just a pretty face.

Emma was smart and fun to be around, but she also possessed that elusive quality that you could never explain with mere words, it just was. Even so, he wasn't normally so smitten so quickly, and jumping to forever was going way too fast for him.

"So, what do you study at Appalachian State?" he asked, needing to keep his mind on the conversation at hand and away from thoughts of forever with a woman he'd only just met.

"I'm getting my bachelor's degree in management, with a concentration in entrepreneurship. I started out as a pharmacy major, but decided it wasn't for me after a few years, so it's taken me a bit longer to finish school. But most of my friends have changed their majors too, or gone on to get their master's degree, so most of us are still in Boone."

"That's quite the shift in majors. What brought that on?"

"Oh, I don't know really. Just realized that it wasn't for me. I wanted something I could do from home, if I needed to work once I had kids."

"Well, that makes sense. How old are you? If you don't mind me asking."

"I don't mind you asking, and I'm twenty four. I'll have one semester left when I get back home. Then I'm finally done with school," she paused, and a look of what he assumed was relief crossed over her delicate features, before she asked, "So, how old are you? If you don't mind me asking, of course."

"I'm twenty eight, and I don't mind at all." He gave Emma a genuine smile, and was pleased to receive one in return.

"So, getting back to what we were talking about before, what about you? Do you have any brothers or sisters? From your reaction, I'm guessing you don't come from a big family."

"I have an older brother and sister. They both still live in Hamilton. My sister Lara is married with two little ones, Jacob and Matilda. And my brother Matthew is an engineer. He's not married, but he lives with his partner, Shannon."

"So, you're the baby, huh? I can't picture that." She regarded him thoughtfully, her voice trailing off as she raised the cup to her lips and took another sip of her tea.

"I may have been the youngest, but I held my own, eh? Even when Lara wanted to dress me up for a tea party with her dollies. Or when Matt could still run circles around me. Those days didn't last long, though. He was more interested in books and I couldn't sit still for more than five minutes. Always had to be moving..."

got into a fair bit of trouble, I don't mind saying. My mum took me to the local domain, I think you'd call it a park, to have a run around, to tucker me out. That's where I discovered rugby. Found I was good at it, too. Been playing ever since. Made my mum's life a bit easier after that, yeah? Came home ready for a feed and a nap, instead of chasing around the house driving everyone mad." He smiled at the memory of first discovering his love of rugby. Noah knew how lucky he was to play at the level he did, but he also knew the years of practice and dedication it took to get there.

"I've heard it's every parent's civic duty in New Zealand to have their children play rugby," she stated with a knowing look.

"Suppose it is, but I grew up in a house that was centered on academics, my dad being a professor and all. Don't get me wrong, he loves rugby just as much as every other Kiwi, but it wasn't a priority for my father that we play. It was more important to get a 'proper education' as he put it. But rugby was all I ever really wanted to do, so when the opportunity presented itself, I never looked back."

"Well, you did what was right for you. It's your life, after all. I'm sure your parents just wanted what they felt was best for you, but in the end, it's your choice to make. Isn't it? Good or bad," she offered sincerely, taking another sip of her tea.

"Yeah, I guess so. We don't really talk about it much. But they're proud of me. I know that." Noah knew he'd disappointed his father when he pursued a rugby career instead of something more traditional like a banker or a lawyer. But when he found success, his father seemed to finally accept that he'd made the right decision.

"You followed your dreams. Not many people can say that. Anyway, I can't really see you sitting behind a desk, working nine-to-five." She scoffed at the thought, although he'd probably look damn good in a suit and tie.

Noah huffed out a breath. "No, talk about misery. That would be pure torture. I need to be physical," he winked, and Emma's mind conjured up all kinds of ways they could be physical…together.

Reclining, Noah stretched his arms behind his head, causing his biceps to flex and her heart to flutter. "Yeah, well…it's a good thing for you that you do what you do then." Flustered by his comment and the raw sex appeal that rolled off him in waves, she stopped herself before she started to ramble.

His bare chest and abs were on full display and she wanted to ask him to cover up, so she could concentrate and not be reduced to a blathering idiot. But, on the other hand, it would be a shame to miss out on the show, not knowing when she'd get to see it again.

"Yeah," he agreed simply with a nod of his head. "So, tell me about your family," Noah urged, directing the conversation back to Emma's family.

"Well, let's see…this could take a while."

Noah gave her a sweet smile that had her tummy doing a little flip-flop. "I've got plenty of time." He took another sip of his tea, then relaxed into the cushions of the couch.

"Well, my father's a pediatrician. He has his own practice and my mother stayed home to take care of all of us. And let me tell you, she had her hands full. We weren't the most well-behaved children. But I think she loved every minute of it, or at least that's what she tells us. There were tons of fights and hair pulling, but in the end, we all genuinely like each other, and turned out pretty well-adjusted. And isn't that what's important in the long run?"

Emma was sure they ran their mother ragged, and drove her to drink on more than a few occasions. But she also knew without a doubt that her mother wouldn't change a minute of it. Well, maybe the time her brother Mark jumped off the neighbor's garage and broke his ankle, but other than that, she was a proud momma to her large brood.

"Absolutely," Noah agreed, then quietly waited for her to finish.

"My two oldest brothers are doctors, Luke, is a pediatrician. He works with my dad in Charlotte. And my brother Mark works in an emergency room in New York City."

Taking a deep breath, she continued. "Then there's my sister, Alison. She has a little girl, Abigail." Emma paused and felt a smile spread across her cheeks.

"I miss Abby so much. She's a perfect little angel. She's about six months old now and has started scooting around, so we spend all our time chasing after her. We always joke that she'll never learn to walk because someone's always holding her. But when you pick her up, she'll wrap her little arms around you and snuggle so perfectly." He watched as she mimicked the motion of holding her niece. "She smells like baby shampoo and little girl, and who in their right mind would let go of her long enough to put her down?"

Oh, he was in trouble, he thought, as he lost himself in the blissful smile that struck him like a thunder bolt. "They'd be mad."

Emma's happy glow, as she spoke of her niece, was contagious. One thing he'd figured out pretty quickly, was that you could read her every emotion just by looking at her. Her expressive face didn't hide anything.

"Exactly, there's just something about the feel of a baby in your arms. From the time she was born, I've been completely and totally in love with her, and she isn't even mine. I always wonder, if I feel this way about her, how much more it'll be when I actually have one of my own," she wavered, her brows knitting together in a worrisome pout. "I'm sorry. I'm babbling."

"No worries, I don't mind at all. I know how you feel. When Lara had Jacob and I held him for the first time…God," he exhaled, his mind drifting back to that day. "I would have killed to protect him, and then when Maddie was born, it was even worse. Maybe it was because she was a girl, or that she was so tiny and fragile. But let me just say that I pity the bloke who tries to date her one day," he added, trying to lighten the mood.

Emma sat up straight, like she held the answers to the great mysteries of the universe. "I can just see it. You opening the door to some pimply-faced kid who almost wets himself before you can even open your mouth to ask him what his intentions are. Maybe they're the perfect ones for her to date, though? They'd be too scared to even hold her hand."

He raised his cup, giving her a satisfied smirk. "You have an excellent point, Emma. I'll keep that in mind. Thankfully, I don't have to worry about weeding out the randy buggers just yet, as she's only four."

Emma hated to rain on his parade, but couldn't help herself. "Well, I hate to burst your bubble, but I had my first crush when I was only six, so you'd better get ready. He was either pushing me down on the playground or hugging me," she chuckled. "So typical. Little boys to men, they still can't decide if they want to push the girl away or keep her close."

"Is it that simple, though? Maybe, at such a young age, he just doesn't know how to process his emotions when he sees a pretty girl, so he reacts by pushing her down. Which, now that I think about it, makes perfect sense, because it's where we want her anyway. Underneath us, or on top of us. Either way works for me." He feigned innocence at Emma's shocked expression. "What?"

"Are you kidding me? How'd you go from talking about your precious little niece to talking about sex? That's so wrong, Noah. What's wrong with you?" she protested sarcastically, trying to stifle a laugh.

"There's absolutely nothing wrong with me, Emma." And she had to agree, in fact the thought of being under him or on top of him appealed to her on every level. "But go on, you still have two siblings left, if my count is correct."

"Alright...where was I?" Her head was spinning at the sudden change in topic. Taking a slow, steadying breath, she continued, "Oh yeah, my brother Steven lives in Boone, and is getting his MBA from Appalachian State. And then there's the baby, Katie. She's a sophomore at App, and it's a full time job just watching out for her. She's crazy-beautiful and all the boys follow her around like lost puppies; it drives Steven insane." She suddenly realized she was rambling once again. "Listen to me. I'm talking too much. Aren't I?"

"No, please go on. I like hearing about your family. Must be hard for you to be away from them," Noah stated sympathetically.

She reached up and rubbed at the worry lines that'd formed between her brows. "It is, but I always wanted to study abroad, and with Lily here, it really wasn't a hard decision. My sister Ali came here too." She frowned, remembering how that ended. "Let's just say that Abby was the result of her time here. That, a broken heart, and a ton of disappointment."

"Huh?" He paused as the puzzle pieces fell into place. "Wait a minute, I remember her. Didn't know her very well, but I think she was seeing one of my teammates…Evan Thompson. Met them at the pub a few times, with Lily and Josh. Is he Abby's father?" Noah remembered talk of a child and seemed to recall Evan taking a few weeks leave around the time Abby would've been born.

"Yes, he's Abby's father, and I use that term loosely, very loosely…if you count sending a check every month as a qualification for being a parent." Emma's mossy green eyes, usually so full of light and laugher, were full of sadness. "I really thought, well everyone thought, that he'd want to be an active participant in his daughter's life, but boy were we wrong."

She paused, inhaling a deep breath. "My heart aches for Abby, though, that he's never come back to see her. I'm sorry, but I think I might cry. Shouldn't he be showing off her picture to everyone? Whether they want to see it or not? Isn't that what parents do? Brag about their baby's first smile, first tooth?" she demanded, frustratingly swiping at her cheeks. Noah hated to see her so upset, and couldn't for the life of him understand why Evan would do such a thing.

"Aw, hell, it's supposed to be that way. Please don't cry, Emma." The stricken look on her face tore at his heart and he had to resist the urge to go to her, to pull her onto his lap, to comfort her. Seeing Emma cry brought out an unexpected need to fight her battles for her. "I could talk to him, if you think it would help."

"Thanks, but Ali's going to try to get together with him while she's here with Abby for the wedding. I hope once he sees her again, he'll step up and do the right thing. I don't see how he could look into her eyes and not fall madly in love with her," she sighed shakily, and when her gaze met his, he felt his heart slip a little. Or a lot. He wasn't sure.

"I hope you're right. Maybe that's what he's afraid of, though. If he wants to be in her life, but she lives half way round the world, how would that work, living so far away? Easier to pretend, I reckon, try to forget," he offered, trying to ease her distress, while also trying to defend his teammate. The picture she was painting of Evan didn't make any sense. That wasn't the Evan that he knew.

"Don't you dare defend his actions, Noah." Emma's sudden outburst took him by surprise. Her brow furrowed and her body stiffened as she glared at him. "He doesn't deserve it."

*What the...* "Whoa, whoa, whoa," Noah barked, holding his hands up in protest. "I'm just playing devil's advocate here, you know. I'm not defending him. Personally, I want to punch him in the throat and drag his face through the mud, if he's abandoned his child. But there has to be a reason why he hasn't gone to visit, and he is sending the maintenance."

"Yeah, well there's a hell of a lot more to being a parent than your checkbook."

"I understand. Just trying to help," he answered defensively. He really didn't want to upset her, but didn't appreciate being snapped at either.

"I know, and I'm sorry. I didn't mean to bite your head off, but it just makes me so mad when I think about it. It's not like Ali got pregnant on purpose." Emma took a deep breath and exhaled, her features softening slightly. "But, I guess without him, we wouldn't have Abby, so I try not to get too upset. You want to see a picture of her?" Emma asked, reaching for her phone.

"You're not going to actually bite my head off if I let you sit next to me, are you? Luring me in and then pouncing once I'm close."

"No," she giggled, and he let the sound wash over him, happy to see that her sweet smile was back where it belonged. She was meant to wear a smile. "Now, do you want to see the pictures, or not?"

"Love to." And he meant it, especially if she was going to sit next to him to do it. Of course, he was also curious to see a picture of the wee one that Emma was so fiercely protective of. She was like a momma bear defending her cub.

Emma settled next to him and began scrolling through pictures of Abby and her family. There was no doubt in his mind that Evan was Abby's father; their likeness was uncanny. He was also struck by the pictures of Emma holding and playing with Abby. She was at ease with a baby in her arms, and her devotion to her niece was plain to see.

Sitting so close to her, he had to fight the urge to run his fingers through her hair. And she smelled so good he wanted to nuzzle his nose along the alluringly soft skin of her neck, and just inhale her.

The feel of her bare leg resting against his was sending the blood rushing to his groin every time she brushed against him. He needed to somehow adjust himself quickly, before she noticed the rapidly-growing bulge in his shorts.

Gazing at her long legs, he longed to run his hand up the length of her smooth thigh until he reached the juncture between her legs. To tease her there. He knew he couldn't, that it was out of the question, but it *was* taking every ounce of self-control he possessed not to kiss her. He wanted her. Plain and simple.

Choosing to overlook the fact that she was leaving to go back to America at the end of the year might be a foolish mistake, but all he knew was that Emma was making him feel things he'd never felt before. He could ignore the powerful forces driving them towards each other, but he knew it was just prolonging the inevitable. They would be together. Maybe not forever, but he'd settle for right now and let the rest sort itself out later.

Tomorrow was New Year's Eve, and he wanted to be the one with his lips on hers at the stroke of midnight. He was pretty sure she'd like it too, or at least he hoped she would. He certainly never had any complaints in that department before.

Tracing a finger along her hairline, he gently slid a lock of hair from her face, tucking it behind her ear. The tips of his fingers lingered along the column of her neck for a moment longer than necessary. The gesture was too intimate, he knew, but he needed to touch her, and when she looked into his eyes and gave him a nervous smile, he was stunned into silence.

His need for her was indescribable, and even though he didn't fully understand what was happening, something *was* happening, of that he was sure.

# CHAPTER 6

After spending the day sampling the menu at the country club, tasting cake at the bakery, and securing a membership to the swimming pool, Emma and Lily arrived home in time for dinner. Even though she was tired after the long day, and the lingering effects of jetlag, Emma couldn't deny the rush of finding Noah's too handsome face waiting for her in the lounge.

Leaving her shoes at the front door, she moved swiftly into the kitchen, bags filled with takeout from the Italian restaurant on the corner weighing her down. "Can I get anyone a drink?" she called out, placing the containers in a neat row on the counter.

"A beer would be great, Emma," Noah stated, entering the kitchen behind her.

Startled by his sudden appearance, her hand instinctively clutched her chest as she sucked in a gasp of air. "You need to stop sneaking up on me like that," Emma frowned, then teasingly added. "Don't you have a home that's missing you?"

Letting out a soft chuckle, he looked entirely too pleased with himself and completely at ease. "You need to stop being so jumpy. And, yes, I have a home, but sadly I don't think it cares if I'm there or not." Noah gave her a playful smile as he tugged on a lock of her hair, then let it slowly slip between his fingers.

The gesture momentarily stunned her, and she was left a bit dumbstruck by it. It was so intimate and tender that she instantly felt the dueling need to step away and lean closer. Thrown off balance, she reached for the island to steady herself.

"Yeah, well…here's your beer." She really needed to get a grip and stop acting like a teenaged girl whenever he looked her way.

"Thank you, Emma." Oblivious to her inner turmoil, Noah reached behind her for a plate, his masculine scent invading her senses, then pointed to the takeout containers on the counter. "What would you like?"

You…a generous portion of you, was the first thing that came to mind, but thankfully, she was able to stop herself from saying it out loud.

"I'll have some eggplant parmesan and a little salad, please." Watching as he took their plates to the dining table, she gathered their drinks and took a moment to admire the view.

Worn jeans hugged his incredible backside, and left Emma wanting to reach out and touch it. Based on the looks he'd been giving her, she didn't think he'd mind. In fact, he'd probably welcome it. But other than in her overactive imagination, they hadn't progressed past overtly flirting with one another.

Giving herself a pat on the back for the superhuman act of self-restraint, she kept her hands to herself and followed him into the dining room.

After dinner and one too many beers, they relocated to the lounge and settled comfortably into the same seats as the night before. When Lily asked Emma to play her guitar for them, she initially hesitated, suddenly shy about playing in front of Noah, but then acquiesced and retrieved it from her room.

Perched on the edge of the couch, Emma positioned the guitar on her thighs. The familiar feel of it beneath her fingertips calmed the flutters in her stomach as she took a deep breath, trying to ignore the curious glances from Noah.

"Okay. Let's see," she said slowly, thinking about which songs to play for them, and strumming mindlessly as she pondered her choices. "I think this one's appropriate, it's 'Question' by the Old 97's."

Watching Lily's face light up as she listened to the lyrics, was all the encouragement she needed. Emma couldn't help but smile when Josh pulled her cousin onto his lap. He was incredibly sweet, and she was happy Lily had found such a good man to spend the rest of her life with.

Pausing for just a few beats, she continued with 'January Wedding' by the Avett Brothers.

Too nervous to look at Noah, she focused on her fingers or on Lily and Josh as she played. Their supportive smiles spurred her on and gave her the confidence to continue. "This one I always play for Abby. She loves it…well…she really loves any music, it's 'Banana Pancakes' by Jack Johnson."

Finishing the song, she lifted the guitar off her lap, to set it against the armrest. "Please do a few more, Emma. You're amazing," Lily asked.

"All right. This is one of my favorites, it's 'Rise to Me' by The Decemberists." Finally summoning the courage to look at Noah, Emma began to sing. Would he stand his ground for the one he loved, she wondered?

Wanting to lighten up a little, she continued with 'Sleep Please Come to Me' by Matthew Barber. The fun song about a sleepless night brought back a flood of memories. Of long winter nights spent in her crowded living room in Boone, playing music until the wee hours of the morning.

She couldn't resist adding 'New Slang' by The Shins. Since the first time she'd heard the song, her fingers itched to play it, and it was still one of her all-time favorites.

"And this last song, I dedicate to my lovely home state of North Carolina." She couldn't help but smile at Noah as she started to play the classic, 'Carolina in My Mind' by James Taylor, a song that held such meaning for her. Recognition spread across Noah's face, as he relaxed with his arm stretched out along the back of the couch.

"Emma, you're incredible. Can you write down those songs for me? I'd like to add them to my playlist." Noah's irresistibly charming smile engulfed his entire face and Emma was left a bit dizzy from the impact of it. He really had a beautiful smile.

"Sure. I'm glad you liked them. Trust me, though, the originals are much better. I made a few mistakes, but I haven't played in a while, so I'm a little rusty."

Emma shrugged her shoulders apologetically, embarrassed that she'd flubbed a few of the songs.

Performing in front of family or friends was common for Emma and she usually wasn't insecure at all, but she really wanted Noah to like the songs she'd chosen. For some reason, his opinion meant a lot to her. She wasn't quite sure why, but it did. A lot. And his enthusiastic reaction thrilled her, probably more than it should have.

"Well, we couldn't tell at all, Emma. You're always way too hard on yourself, you know that," Lily pointed out, trying to reassure her.

"You're sweet, Lil. It felt good to play, though. I've been so busy the last few months that I've barely picked it up. It's like an old friend, though. You can pick right up where you left off, as if you just spoke yesterday."

Emma gently ran her fingers along the curves of the guitar, stroking it like she would a lover, and Noah wished she was actually touching him, instead of the polished piece of wood.

"Well, I've never had anyone sit in front of me and play music like that before. Could've listened to you all night. You're very talented, Emma," Noah added cheerfully, in awe of her as she clung to her guitar, like a coat of armor.

She appeared shy and unsure of herself, and he couldn't for the life of him, figure out why. Her gaze was bashfully locked onto her fingers, as they carelessly strummed, filling the air with a soft melody.

"Thanks, Noah. That means a lot to me. It really does," she giggled anxiously, and he wanted to reach out and soothe the worry lines that formed between her brows.

"Well, I've always loved listening to you play, especially with Steven. While he's here for the wedding, we'll definitely find time for the two of you to play together. You'll love it, Noah. They sound so good together." Lily's praise caused an adorable pink tint to spread across Emma's cheeks.

"Give him a couple beers and he'll play all night. He's got an endless playlist in his head. You just sit and listen, totally in awe." Emma turned to Noah and he could see the love she had for her brother written all over her pretty face.

"Well, I'm looking forward to it. Don't know if I'd enjoy listening to him as much as you, though," Noah admitted honestly. As she'd started to play, he was stunned and a bit surprised by her talent, but when she opened her mouth and started to sing, he was utterly blown away.

When she'd gone into her bedroom to fetch her guitar, he'd been worried about how to react if her impromptu concert was dreadful. Thankfully, within a few seconds any worries went right out the window. She was bloody amazing.

"You're too kind, dear sir," Emma joked, lifting herself off the couch. "I need a drink. Can I get anything for anyone while I'm up?"

"I'd love a beer, Emma. If you don't mind," Josh requested.

Calling out over her shoulder, Lily added. "Me too, Emma."

"I'll give you a hand," Noah said, following her into the kitchen, wanting to speak to her in private. "Hey, I was wondering if you'd like to go to the party with me tomorrow night, as my date. Save me from showing up alone." Suddenly insecure, he waited for her reply. To hide his discomfort, he busied himself opening the beers and throwing the caps in the rubbish bin. "Please?"

Emma looked at him sideways for a moment, as if trying to figure out if he was serious. "Really? You sure you want to disappoint all the single ladies by showing up with someone?"

"You're not just *someone,* Emma. And, as far as I know, you're a single lady." Not for long if he had his way. "Anyway, I could say the same to you, eh? I'll be the envy of all the single blokes, especially if I get you to dance with me. So what's it to be, Emma? Will you go with me?"

A wide smile spread across her face, and his heart was beating so loudly he could hear the rapid thumping of his pulse in his ears. She had the best smile, genuine with a touch of whimsy, and he wanted to see more of it. "Well, I'm definitely a single lady, and sure, I'd love to."

Emma took her time getting ready for the New Year's Eve party. Since it was going to be a late night, she left her hair down, letting it fall in natural waves down her back. She spent extra time on her makeup, trying to look her best, not wanting to disappoint Noah. The man was way out of her league, and she knew it. He was an international rugby player and she was just a small town girl from North Carolina.

Studying her reflection in the mirror, Emma suddenly felt extremely self-conscious, seeing all of her imperfections in great detail, and wondered why he wanted to go to the party with her at all. She knew she was attractive, but Noah probably dated celebrities and models, people who made a living from being pretty.

Shaking off the negative thoughts, Emma finished getting ready, and gave herself a much needed pep talk. If Noah didn't appreciate her for who she was and what she looked like, faults and all, then he didn't deserve her time. She was just as worthy as anyone else of his attention, and wasn't beauty in the eye of the beholder anyway?

Lily had helped select her outfit of a sleeveless silk top in a pretty pale blue and black skinny jeans. Completing the look with a pair of high-heeled black sandals, which added another four inches to her height, her spirits were buoyed a little. She didn't look half bad.

Concluding her inner pep talk, she picked up her phone and overnight bag, and walked down the hall towards the living area.

Lily turned at the sound of Emma's heels on the floor as she entered the kitchen. "Noah is going to swallow his tongue when he gets a squiz at you, Emma. You look stunning."

"Thanks, Lil. So do you. You're a lucky man, Josh," Emma hugged Lily, grateful for the confidence boost.

"Too right, I'm going to walk into that piss up with not one, but two beautiful ladies," he boasted, as he pulled them onto either side of him, put his arms around their shoulders, and led them to the door. "Now, let's go pick up your date. And don't worry, Emma, if he swallows his tongue, I'll give you that kiss at midnight. After Lily, of course."

Emma snickered at Josh's comment. "Of course, and I'll make sure to eat something smothered in garlic and onions at 11:45."

"Yum. My favorite," he countered, as the door clicked shut behind them.

Making one last sweep of his house to ensure that everything was in order for later, Noah anxiously paced back and forth by his front door. New Year's had always been one of his favorite holidays, and with the prospect of Emma's kiss waiting for him at midnight, he was ready to get the evening started. Finally spotting the headlights of Josh's car coming down the drive, he practically sprinted for the door.

Settling into the back seat next to Emma, he gave her a quick peck on the cheek. "Hi, Emma. You look lovely."

The warmth of Emma's smile was genuine, and he could see that she truly appreciated his compliment. "Thank you. And you look very handsome."

Just the sight of her had his body humming to life. And she smelled so good, he wanted to snuggle into the sexy curve of her neck as he kissed her there. He wondered if she'd giggle when he nibbled the sensitive spot beneath her ear; he hoped to find out, soon.

"Hey, Noah. Are we still good to spend the night?" Josh asked, as he maneuvered the car onto Lake Road.

"Sure," he answered, then turned to face Emma, giving her a knowing grin. "I put clean sheets on the beds and everything."

Emma let out a hearty laugh that took him by surprise. "Seriously? You're having sex on every surface in your house, too? What is it with you Kiwis?"

*Huh? What?* "Ah...no. That's not why I did it," he stumbled over his words. "I just wanted you to be comfortable, that's all. My house has been sex-free for a while now. Wait...Hold up." He lifted his hands in protest, ignoring the loud snicker from the front seat. "God...Forget I said that. Every surface is covered in body fluids and filthy. DNA all over the place." He gave an embarrassed chuckle, as he shook his head. He'd never been so flustered by a woman before, but he really just wanted her to feel comfortable in his home.

"It's okay, Noah, I like that you changed the sheets for me. I think it's incredibly sweet of you." She placed her hand on his arm and leaned in close before whispering. "I also like the idea that you haven't had sex in a while."

Damn. This woman was going to kill him, he thought, as she straightened herself and adjusted the seatbelt between her breasts. The outline of her lacy bra was visible through the thin layer of silk pressed tightly against her, and thankful for the darkened car, he let his eyes linger there for a long moment, enjoying the view.

Stepping from the car, when they arrived at the party, he felt as if the wind had been knocked out of him. Her long legs went all the way to heaven, and with the added height from her high heels she could almost look him in the eye. They'd align perfectly, he thought to himself.

Smoky makeup accentuated a pair of emerald green eyes that glistened in the moonlight, and when she smiled at him, he forgot his name for a minute. Yes, tonight was going to change everything between them.

He liked the idea of actually having to pursue a woman for a change, taking his time, and getting to know what made her tick. Doing it the right way. He wanted the real thing, a loving partner to share his days and nights with, as well as the ups and down of everyday life.

He couldn't remember the last time a woman interested him this much, and he liked it.

He liked her…

Throughout the night, Noah kept Emma close by his side, not only because he wanted everyone to know she was with him, but also because he genuinely enjoyed her company. It was easy being with her. She didn't take herself too seriously and was quick with a laugh or a witty comment. His mates and their partners seemed to enjoy her company too.

Finally, it was time for the countdown to begin, and the anticipation was killing him. He'd waited patiently to kiss her until now, and with two glasses of champagne in hand, he led her to a quiet corner of the patio, where they'd have a choice view of the Auckland skyline.

"Ten... Nine... Eight... Seven... Six... Five... Four... Three... Two... One... Happy New Year!" They both called out, laughing in unison, then took a small sip of champagne. With his eyes locked on hers, he smoothly took the glass from her, placing it on the railing next to them.

He almost groaned as her tongue slid out to dampen her bottom lip, and when his eyes met hers, he slowly leaned in to kiss her. Their bodies aligned perfectly, just as he thought they would.

As his lips covered hers, he felt the warm touch of her hands as they slowly moved from his forearms to his biceps, leaving a trail of goose bumps in their wake, before finally coming to rest around the back of his neck.

Threading her fingers through his hair, her touch was sending little shivers down his spine while his tongue explored her soft lips, encouraging them to open for him. Tightening his arms around her waist as she complied, Noah's heart took a slow roll in his chest. She tasted of champagne and Emma. Sweetness and light, he thought, as he sipped from her.

Noah's heart was pounding so forcefully, he wondered if Emma could feel the effect she was having on him. Even with her body pressed against his from tip to toe, his only thought was that there was too much space between them. Which made no sense at all considering how tightly they were clinging to each other.

When she softly moaned, he tilted his head and deepened the kiss. Drinking from her as if she was an oasis in the middle of the desert, Noah knew without a doubt that his life would never be the same. He didn't want it to be the same. Just the thought should have made him nervous, but it didn't. Emma's kiss lit him on fire and left him aching for more.

She was heartbreakingly beautiful, but she was also smart and sweet and sassy. And when he held her in his arms, everything just felt right with the world.

Coming up for air, he gently pressed his forehead to hers, trying to catch his breath and his wayward thoughts of forever. One look at her kiss swollen lips and he couldn't help but kiss her again. And again. And again. He would never get enough of her.

"Wow!" he declared, when their mouths finally separated; he'd never been left so gobsmacked by a kiss before.

"Yeah, wow!" she whispered, turning to watch the rest of the fireworks display. "I've always heard of seeing fireworks when someone kisses you. But I really did," she delighted breathlessly.

"Reckon so." Keeping his arm around her shoulder, he tucked her into his side, holding her there, loving the way she felt in his arms.

Sweetness and light...and fireworks.

Noah watched as she took a few pictures and then a short video of the fireworks with her phone. "I want to remember this," she said simply.

Holding her tightly, she leaned into him and rested her head on his shoulder, and he couldn't stop the goofy smile from spreading across his face, as she slid her arm around his waist.

He wanted to remember this, too.

Did she have any idea how exquisite she was, he wondered, as they stood quietly together, watching the colorful explosions. Noah felt like his life had always been in black and white and, all of a sudden, there were colors all around him. Bright, beautiful colors. Everywhere.

Once the fireworks display above the Auckland skyline was over, they sat down at one of the tables on the patio. Emma excitedly sent the pictures and video to her family back home, wishing them a Happy New Year, and he smiled along with her as they replied.

Lily and Josh joined them at the table, taking the seats opposite them.

"So, Emma. Do I have to kiss you now? Or did some other lucky bugger beat me to it?" Josh asked, as he winked at Noah.

She gave Noah a sweet smile, then turned to Josh. "No, someone already wished me a Happy New Year. But thanks for being my back up plan. Thankfully, I was able to avoid the garlic and onions."

On the drive back to Noah's house for the night, he reached over and took hold of her hand, squeezing it gently. Emma felt her stomach flutter anxiously as he entwined their fingers, tracing his thumb along her wrist. Noah's laid-back smile eased her apprehension, as he held her gaze, and left her feeling warm all over.

Emma could sense that something significant had happened between them, and it worried her. His kiss had changed things between them. The innocent flirting had shifted into something more. Something real. At least it had for her, and what did that mean for the future?

The harsh reality was that she lived half a world away, and that wasn't going to change. But Noah was special, that she knew without a doubt. But could she risk her heart, knowing it might be broken? Would their time together be worth the crushing blow, when her time in New Zealand came to an end? Was she willing to take that risk?

# CHAPTER 7

"Nice place you got here, Noah," Emma cheerfully proclaimed, as she crossed the threshold, following Noah into his house.

Nice was putting it mildly, his home was gorgeous, Emma thought, as she looked around. It was deceptively small from the driveway, but once you stepped inside the front door, it opened up to a large sweeping floor plan. And even though it definitely lacked a woman's touch, the layout and finishes were perfect.

Glass doors spanned the length of the outside wall, providing what was sure to be a gorgeous view of the cerulean waters of the Hauraki Gulf. Darkness impeded her vision, but she'd been to Takapuna Beach many times over the years, and knew firsthand how beautiful it was.

The large lounge was simply decorated with a black leather sectional, neatly arranged around a distressed coffee table, and matching end tables. She bit back a laugh at the sight of the massive TV mounted on the wall, with an entertainment console sitting beneath it, covered in framed photographs.

The lounge flowed seamlessly into a sleek, well-equipped kitchen with maple cabinets and a large island covered in black granite. It was a cook's dream, laid out perfectly for efficient food prep. The kitchen overlooked a dining area, furnished with a modern looking table and chairs, flanking the sliding glass doors leading outside.

Spanning the entire living area were wide planked hardwood floors, stained a warm dark chocolate color. Soft white walls stood in stark contrast to the vibrant artwork dotting the space, giving the room a light, airy feel to it. Noah's home was classy, yet comfortable, and surprisingly tidy for a bachelor pad. It felt lived in. Homey.

Noah motioned for her to follow him. "Thanks. I'll show you to your room so you can put your things away."

Leading her down a long hallway, he stepped inside the guest room. The bedroom was tastefully decorated with white cottage-style furniture but, as with the rest of the house, the main focal point was the exterior wall of glass.

"This is lovely, Noah," Emma admitted, as she sat on the bed, letting her bag drop to the floor next to her. "Can I ask you a question?"

"Sure. Anything," he answered simply, smiling as he leaned against the doorframe.

"Can you see the sunrise from here?"

"You might not have the best view from this room, due to a tree out there." Noah lifted his hand, pointing his index finger towards the sliding glass door. "But from the deck or the beach you can. Also, from the lounge. The large trees on the property line give me privacy, but they also block some of the view. Why?"

"I wanted to stay up and watch the sunrise," Emma stated. "I'd like to usher in the first day of the New Year. I know it sounds silly because, technically, we already have, since it is past midnight, but this will probably be my only chance to witness the first sunrise of the year."

Noah shifted his weight from one foot to the other, as he crossed his arms across his chest before settling against the doorframe once again. "Doesn't sound silly at all, Emma. Very thoughtful, actually," he assured her. "I've never done it intentionally. I've stayed awake until sunup a few times, but I don't think I ever paid much attention to the sunrise," he added with a frown.

"I don't know if I'll make it, but I'd like to try. Might need a few energy drinks," she chuckled, examining her toes, thankful Lily had talked her into getting a pedicure the day before.

"No worries. I've got some. Would you like company?" he asked bashfully.

Emma was comforted by his apparent shyness, and appreciated the fact that he wasn't arrogant, expecting her to fall at his feet, begging for any morsel of his attention. "That would be really nice. Maybe Lily and Josh will too."

Noah stepped forward, reaching out his hand to her, tangling their fingers together, as she stood to her feet. They walked to the lounge, hand in hand, the sound of her heels against the hardwood floors accompanying them as they entered the large room.

"Do you want to stay up to watch the sunrise with us?" Emma inquired.

Lily was perched on Josh's lap with her arms draped loosely around his neck.

"No thanks. I'm completely knackered," Josh stated, as he gently slid Lily from his lap, then took her hand and pulled her up from the couch.

"Yeah, me too," Lily added, while hugging Emma and then Noah. "But don't let us stop you."

As Josh and Lily headed for the stairs leading to the lower level, and their chosen bedroom, Noah turned to Emma and noticed her fidgeting with the hem of her silk top.

"Why don't you get changed into something more comfortable and I'll get us a couple of those energy drinks, eh?" he suggested, and as if his arms had a mind of their own, they wrapped themselves around her, hugging Emma securely against his chest. The answering beat of his heart, when her arms slid around his waist, wasn't surprising. At all.

"That's probably a good idea. My feet are killing me," Emma confessed, then turned to walk down the hall to her room.

Watching her retreating figure, he wished she'd be spending the night in his bed. Her shoes may have been killing her feet, but they made her legs look bloody amazing, and conjured up all kinds of images of those long legs wrapped around him, or maybe over his shoulders, while he lost himself in her.

Before he got too carried away, he quickly changed into a T-shirt and a pair of jeans.

Returning a few minutes later, Emma was wearing a pink tank top and a pair of black yoga capri pants, which left very little to the imagination, and showcased her flawless figure nicely. She'd washed her face clean of make-up, and Noah realized that that was how he liked her best…his nature girl.

Emma had a quiet beauty, that didn't need to cry out for attention with heavy makeup or skimpy clothing. She was naturally sexy without even realizing it, which was even sexier, and as he watched her approaching him, he made a mental note to send Lily a lovely bouquet of flowers, to thank her for bringing Emma into his life. He owed Lily…big time.

"So, do you want to hang out in here, or outside?" she asked, coming to a stop in front of him. Her gaze caressed him as it traveled over his body, and he realized that he felt alive for the first time in a long while.

Unable to resist, he placed a quick kiss on her soft lips, then handed her two blankets and picked up their drinks. "I can set the hammock up on the beach, if you'd like. We'll have a good view from there."

"Thanks. Relaxing in a hammock under the stars or in the shade on a sunny day, is one of life's greatest pleasures." With a contented sigh, she draped the blankets over her arm and headed towards the door.

He had to agree, especially with Emma snuggled up next to him. Turning on the porch light, he slid the glass door open. Standing back, Noah gestured for her to walk through onto the deck. "Ladies first."

The placid sound of the waves rolling onto shore called out to Emma, as they crossed the lawn to the edge of the property. A concrete staircase led down to the beach, and she reveled in the feel of the powdery sand between her toes.

Walking over to the retaining wall along the edge of his property, she set the blankets and drinks on top of it, then hoisted herself up. Laying back onto the lawn and gazing up at the stars, she had the sudden urge to play her guitar and wished she'd thought to bring it with her.

"There's a swing under the tree if you'd rather sit there," Noah broke the silence, pointing to a large tree adjacent to the staircase, its thick branches extending over the sandy beach.

"Wow. You even have a tree swing. Could this place be any more perfect?" she remarked, and then instantly regretted it, based on his reaction.

"Oi, hardly perfect," he gently corrected her. "You should've seen the place when I bought it. It's an older house and needed a lot of updating. I ended up completely gutting it. But I was able to make it my own, and it actually stays warm in the winter now." Noah's eyes shifted to the house, sitting proudly as a testament to his success and hard work.

"Well, you've done a great job and the swing is just the cherry on top of the sundae," Emma playfully replied, lowering herself from the wall.

"I can't take credit for the swing. That was all Maddie; she had to have it. It's where you'll find her when she's here."

"Um...hello...What girl can resist a tree swing? None, I'll tell you," Emma declared in a sassy tone, as she settled into the seat, and gently pushed off with her feet.

Noah was left speechless as he watched her lean back, bathed in a pool of speckled moonlight. Delicate fingers clung to the rope as her arms slowly straightened, until she was fully reclined and staring up into the branches above her. Her long hair lightly brushed the sand as it fluttered in the breeze beneath her, and her bare toes left tiny trenches in their wake.

He couldn't see her face, but he was sure she was smiling. She was always smiling.

She was a dream. A very, very pretty dream.

"Hammock's ready," he stated with pride, as he set the drinks in the sand, holding the blanket for her.

Reaching out a hand for the blanket, Emma gave him the easy smile that twisted his heart into a knot. "Thank you," she said, as they sat carefully, with their legs hanging over the edge.

The slope of the hammock caused them to settle against each other, while Noah planted his foot in the sand to smoothly glide them back and forth. "I'm afraid I'm not going to last very long. It's like rocking a baby. Lights out within minutes," she giggled, and he felt the vibration of it all the way to his soul.

"Your drink is right next to you in the sand." He held the hammock still while she reached for it. "Bottoms up. This was your brainchild, so you have to stay awake. And I went to all the trouble of assembling this lovely and relaxing hammock, just for you," he paused, letting out a soft laugh. "Probably a bad idea, eh?"

"Yeah, but I should be fine once I finish this. How many hours till the sun comes up?" Emma asked, as she opened the energy drink and raised it to her lips.

"I'm guessing around three or four. Think you'll make it that long?"

A small frown spread across her face, and Noah felt her bright light dim slightly. "I better. I'm going to be really upset if I came all the way to the place where the world welcomes the new day, and then miss out on it," she took a deep breath, fortifying her resolve. "You know what? I will *definitely* stay up until the sun comes up. How about you, Noah?" Her voice held the hint of a dare.

"Is that a challenge, Emma?" he joked, as her expression shifted from soft to serious in the blink of an eye.

Holding his gaze, her competitive nature came out in force. "I suppose it is, Noah."

"Care to make it interesting?" he suggested with a sinister grin, while rubbing his hands together.

Tilting her head to look at him, he saw the flicker of doubt creasing her brow. "Nothing crazy, right?"

"How about, when I win, you have to...wash my car?" There was no way he was going to lose this bet.

"Okay. That's not so bad. And when I win..."

"Oh, *you are not going to win*, Emma," he interrupted her.

"Oh, really," she protested. "What makes you so sure?"

"Well...you were the one who was just about to nod off; all I have to do is rock you. It's like, how you say...taking candy from a baby," he laughed mischievously.

She poked a finger in his chest and all he could do was smile. Emma was absolutely adorable when she was irritated. "That would not be playing fair."

"All's fair in love and war, sweetheart," he stated resolutely, tapping the tip of her nose.

"Well, we'll see about that. Okay, so *when I win*, you'll have to...give me a back massage. Deal?" She held out her hand to shake on it.

He snickered. "Deal. And, as I see it, it's a win for me either way." He shook her hand, but then didn't let go and laid their joined hands across his chest, twining their fingers together.

As the night wore on, they spoke endlessly about their families, and anything else that came to mind. He'd given in to the urge to kiss her again, a few times, and was relieved she'd kissed him back with equal verve. They weren't the mind blowing, rock your world kind of kisses, but the ones where, midsentence, you leaned in and placed a soft kiss on someone's lips...just because you needed to.

After he'd tried in vain to explain the game of rugby to her, she confessed that it wasn't personal, but it was like going to a football game at home; she always had fun, but had no interest in learning the rules. She just liked to watch and soak up the atmosphere. He appreciated her honesty and it was actually refreshing that she didn't care about rugby, unlike many of his previous dates, who went on endlessly, fishing for gossip to share with their girlfriends.

Not wanting to lose the bet, when it looked like she might make it to sunrise, he thought about rocking the hammock, but in the end, he didn't need to because Emma was sound asleep. Her cheek rested against his shoulder, and with her arm draped loosely around his waist, he had the overwhelming sensation that this was meant to be. That they were meant to be.

Covering her legs with the blanket, he carefully snaked his arm around her, so as not to wake her up, and twirled a lock of her long hair around his finger mindlessly. Holding her in his arms, he watched her sleep. She looked so peaceful and content, like an angel. His angel.

As the dawn was starting to break, he gently nudged Emma. "Wake up, sleepyhead."

Tired eyes blinked open, and he detected the moment she realized she'd fallen asleep. "Oh, no. I lost the bet," she frowned, and he wanted to kiss the pretty pout from her lips. "I can't believe I fell asleep."

"And I can't wait to collect on that bet," he snickered as she rolled onto her back, then silently mourned the loss of her warmth. Maybe she'd let him pick out the outfit she wore while soaping up his car. A sexy swimming costume would suit him just fine, although it might give his elderly neighbor a heart attack.

"Gloating is not an attractive quality, you know," she complained, folding her hands across her abdomen and directing her attention to the rising sun.

They sat together, gently swaying back and forth, reverently welcoming the dawn of a new day, as the sun slowly rose over the horizon, bathing them in golden sunlight.

"God, it's so pretty. It's like a sea of diamonds, glittering on top of the water. I could sit here all day. Right here with my toes in the sand, looking out at that." She gestured beyond the beach to the crystal blue waters of the Hauraki Gulf and Rangitoto Island.

"I don't get to enjoy it as much as I'd like, especially with such a pretty girl in my arms," he confessed, holding her gaze, then placed a chaste kiss on her lips. "But this view is obviously why I bought the house. Didn't care what the house looked like. That could be changed, but you can't change the view. Fell in love as soon as I saw it."

She nodded, as he slid his arm around her shoulders once again, holding her to his side. "Well, I can see why. It's so beautiful."

"I have a stressful job with a lot of pressure. Don't get me wrong, I love it, but it's nice to come home to this." He motioned to the water. "To sit and relax, or maybe go for a walk or jog along the shoreline at the end of the day. Some people love the city life, but I prefer it here, at the beach."

Noah watched as Emma stood and stretched her arms above her head, exposing a small strip of skin along her trim midsection. Cocooning the blanket around her shoulders, she turned to take another look at the gulf, and yawned, staying like that for a long moment, not saying a word.

Emma turned towards Noah and took a minute to appreciate the sight of him. With his eyes closed he looked so at ease, as his large hands cradled his head, forming a pillow. Dark stubble highlighted a strong jawline and his hair stood on end, as if he'd spent the night running his hands through it. From his long legs to the adorable fauxhawk crowning the top of his head, she couldn't imagine a more beautiful sight.

The evening had turned out so unexpectedly. Emma hadn't planned to watch the sunrise with Noah, but now that she had, she wouldn't change a single minute. Sharing the experience with him made it so much more than she ever could've dreamed of.

Emma wasn't sure if he was awake or not, so she whispered his name, careful not to disturb him if he'd fallen asleep. He opened one eye, shifting his hand to shield it from the sun, which was now shining brightly.

"You must be exhausted," she finally spoke. "Did you sleep at all?"

"I don't think so. I think you fell asleep about an hour or so ago. Although, I might've nodded off for a few minutes here or there and not realized it," he thoughtfully replied.

"Thanks for staying up with me, and for not letting me miss the sunrise. I really appreciate it." Noah was such a considerate man. A gentle man, she was quickly learning.

He had every reason to be big-headed. Model good looks, the successful career, women throwing themselves at him, and an amazing beach house. But he wasn't arrogant at all. The opposite really. Noah was a humble man who appreciated everything he had. Took pride in it. Worked hard for it.

"You're welcome. It was nice to watch the sunrise with you." It really was, he thought, as he watched her. She was smart and funny and he was enjoying her company immensely. His first impression of her was based on her physical appearance, but as he got to know her better, he found that there was much more to her than just a pretty face. So much more.

Noah hadn't always made the best decisions when choosing his relationships in the past. He wasn't proud of it, but at times he'd been willing to overlook the personality flaws of the person he was dating if they looked good enough.

And when he wasn't in a relationship, it was always a boost for the ego to be able to go out to a club and go home with whomever he chose. But, he was also old enough to realize that it was an empty existence. He was tired of being lonely, and meaningless sex was no longer as satisfying as it once was. He wanted more.

He wanted Emma.

"I had a lot of fun last night, and this morning. Is it possible that the sunrise looks prettier in the Southern Hemisphere? Because that was the most beautiful thing I think I've ever seen." Emma turned to face him once again with a dazzling smile that felt like a kick to the gut.

Trying to maintain his composure at the sudden flood of emotions stirring in his belly, he looked away from her, his gaze drifting to the swell of the surf as it lazily rolled ashore. "I'm not an expert, but any good Kiwi will tell you that everything is better here. Including the sunrise. Maybe it's because we're the first to see it. By the time it makes its way to other places, it's lost some of its sparkle," he answered, pushing off with his foot, causing the hammock to gently sway back and forth beneath him.

"That must be it. It leaves a little of its beauty along the way." Emma's sleepy smile faded with disappointment as she shrugged her shoulder.

"Well, for what it's worth. It was spectacularly beautiful this morning. I can't honestly say when I last saw one though, so I might not be the best judge. I'm usually in bed, snoring."

"Oh really? You're a snorer?" she laughed, that intoxicating laugh that left him wanting to hear more of it.

"I've had my nose broken a fair few times by now. So, yes, I've been told on a few occasions that I snore," he stated sheepishly.

Ignoring the sudden burn of jealousy ripping through her at the thought of him in bed with another woman, Emma used the opening he gave to observe his handsome face up close.

Faint laugh lines fanned out from the corners of the bluest eyes she'd ever seen, which were lined with a thick fringe of dark lashes. And with an ease that came naturally to him, Noah smiled the smile that made her insides stand at attention.

He really should come with a warning sign, she thought. A smile like that was a threat to even the most jaded of females.

Taking a step closer, she noticed that his nose hooked slightly to the left. He also had a jagged scar on his chin and one on his forehead, above his right eyebrow. A hazard of the job, she supposed. Instead of detracting from his looks, the imperfections made him even more attractive. He wasn't a pretty boy. He was rugged. Real men had scars.

How the players were able to walk away at the end of the game was a mystery to her. She'd be curled up in the fetal position, crying for her mommy after one hit, but they took the constant punishment with glee.

She shook her head. "Did it hurt? Getting your nose broken?" After she uttered the words she instantly wanted to take them back. Of course it hurt, why would she ask such a thing?

He let out a loud laugh. "Like a bitch."

"I'm sure." Still a little embarrassed, she gave him a shaky smile.

Noah stood and reached for her as they strolled back into the house, the feel of her hand warm against his. He needed some sleep. He was too old for an all-nighter and his body ached from the long hours in the hammock. Wishing she'd join him in his bed, as he'd happily forgo the rest, was just that...wishful thinking.

Emma wasn't the type of girl to jump into bed with someone she'd just met, and he was happy for that. But the thought of her cuddled up against his side while they slept, just about brought him to his knees.

He was determined to do it right, though, to take his time with her.

# CHAPTER 8

After a few hours' sleep and a brief stop at Lily's to pack, they embarked on the three-hour drive to Papamoa Beach, on the Bay of Plenty. As they turned into the driveway, Emma's mouth gaped open at the sight of the stately beach house.

Noah pulled his Jeep to a stop in front of a covered walkway that led to the front door. Stacked stone pillars stood sentinel on each side of the slate footpath, with colorful flower beds surrounding them and extending down the length of the walkway, filling the air with a soft fragrance.

Standing in the large foyer, Emma hoped she didn't look as anxious as she felt. With a slight nod of his head, Noah motioned for her to follow him, and as he lifted her suitcase, she dutifully obeyed.

"This is my room, but you can have it. It has a better view than the guest room, and I'll take my parents' room."

"Are you sure? I don't want to put you out. I can take another room. I really don't mind," she insisted.

Noah exhaled an impatient breath, clearly irritable from the lack of sleep. "I know you don't, Emma, but the other guest room doesn't have much of a view and I didn't think you'd be comfortable sleeping in my parents' room."

"I guess you're right. And the view *is* lovely from here." Having three older brothers who were cranky beasts when they didn't get enough sleep, Emma knew to just let it go and move on.

"The bathroom is right down the hall, and since Lily and Josh are staying downstairs, you'll have it to yourself." A lock of hair fell across his forehead, when he tilted his head in the direction of the bathroom, and as she brushed it aside with a gentle stroke of her fingertip, he visibly relaxed.

"Okay, thanks. What's the plan for the day? Do you know?" she asked in a hushed, soothing tone.

"Not sure. Why don't you put your things away and we'll find Josh and Lily and get it sorted."

Shifting through her suitcase, Emma smiled when her fingers landed on her string bikini decorated with the American flag. Feeling slightly homesick, it provided a semblance of comfort. It was also one of her most flattering swimsuits, and if Noah liked the way she looked in it, all the better.

Lily let out a low wolf whistle as Emma entered the lounge. "Damn, girl. You look dead sexy in that. You have to let me borrow it for my honeymoon. It'll honor my mum's heritage."

"Thanks, Lil. Of course you can borrow it," Emma replied, walking out onto the deck overlooking a small grassy area and the beach. Inhaling a deep breath of salty air, she lowered her sunglasses from the top of her head onto the bridge of her nose.

Following the well-worn path leading to the beach, she watched as Noah made his way towards the house, wearing only a pair of aqua board shorts that hung teasingly low on his hips, the color highlighting his deep tan. His easy swagger oozed confidence, Emma mused, as she took in the view.

Noah stopped and eyed Emma appreciatively, his lips curling into a sexy smile, and if she wasn't mistaken, a blush bloomed across his cheeks. "Would you mind helping me for a minute, Emma?" he requested.

"Sure. I'll meet you down on the beach, Lil."

Emma wiped her bare feet on the mat and followed Noah into the kitchen. Leaning against the counter, she watched as he filled a cooler with bottled water and beer, then covered the drinks with a bag of ice. Bending over, his muscular back and arms flexed deliciously as he spread the ice with his large hands. The motion tightened his shorts against his perfect backside, and Emma held back a sigh. He was absolutely yummy.

Bloody hell, trying to stay focused on filling the chilly bin was becoming harder and harder by the minute. He was only human after all, and just knowing that Emma was standing right behind him, practically naked, was wreaking havoc on his nervous system…and his libido.

He'd almost fallen on his knees to thank the heavens for creating such a perfect creature, when he first got a squiz at Emma in her bikini, and had to turn away before she noticed how aroused he'd become. One look at her, in little more than scraps of nothing, held precariously together by a hope and a prayer, and his brain short-circuited.

"Do you think you could take your eyes off my bum long enough to help me carry this?" Noah teased, eyeing her over his shoulder.

Reminding himself to breathe, Noah twisted to face her. He was barely holding it together, and when she started chewing on her lush bottom lip, visions of her pretty mouth kissing its way down to where he ached for her flashed through his mind.

Standing before him was the most beautiful woman he'd ever seen, and the urge to lay her down on the bench and devour her from tip to toe, was completely overwhelming. As a man, he loved and appreciated the soft curves of a woman's body, and Emma's softness was gloriously on full display…other than the three tiny triangles scantily covering her naughty bits.

"Um…I…I wasn't doing that. I was just looking at the cooler," Emma stuttered, her face flushing a bright red. "You wish," she added with a halfhearted chuckle.

"If you say so, Emma. Here, let me get that for you," he smirked, brushing his thumb along the corner of her bottom lip.

"What are you doing? Do I have something on my face?" she startled, snapping her head back and swatting at his hand.

"Just a wee bit of drool," he laughed, trying to keep his eyes on her face, and not on the swell of her round breasts, looking way too tempting for any red blooded man to ignore.

"Liar. I was not drooling. Are you always so incorrigible?" she demanded, reaching for the handle and lifting her side of the chilly bin. He didn't miss the slight giggle as she turned her back towards him and began walking.

Not wanting to push her too far, he silently followed her down the path to the waiting umbrella. Watching the muscles in her shoulders and back flex under the heavy burden was dead sexy, and her bum looked choice in her tiny togs, he thought, enjoying the sway of her hips as they twitched back and forth.

Within minutes of settling on the beach, Emma stretched out on a towel in the sand and closed her eyes and, much to his dismay, was fast asleep.

Wanting to take a walk, but wanting her company even more, Noah waited patiently for Emma to wake up. Sipping his water, while quietly listening to music on his iPhone, he tilted his head back and closed his eyes, letting the sun warm his face.

Turning onto her back when she finally woke from her slumber, her suit slipped sideways. Watching intently as she adjusted the little triangles, she lifted her hips into the air, and lifted his heart rate to an unhealthy level in the process. When she settled her cute little bum against the towel once again, her stomach sunk inward, leaving a mouthwateringly sexy gap between her tanned skin and the barely-there bottoms of her suit.

Mesmerized by the tantalizing view, he was powerless to look away. He knew it was wrong of him, felt a bit pervy even, but he wanted to see what was hidden under there. He wanted to run his fingers along the edge of her suit, then slip them inside, touching her there, in her most private place.

"Where'd Lily and Josh go?" Emma asked, turning her face towards his. Dark sunglasses shaded her eyes as she waited for his reply. "Hello. Earth to Noah," she laughed.

Slowly shifting his focus from her bikini bottom up to her face, he was thankful for his own darkly-tinted sunglasses. She would probably slap him and storm away if she knew the wicked desires her body inspired, if she could see the way he was looking at her.

"Um...they went inside a while ago," he answered shakily, and couldn't stop his eyes from sliding down the length of her toned body, returning to the apex of her thighs once again. It would only take one tug of the thin string to reveal her secret, he thought.

"Now who's drooling?" She shook her head and laughed as she stood to her feet and grabbed a bottle of water, taking a long drink. "Should I get you a bib, Noah?"

"Hey, a sexy woman, in a teeny little bikini...what can I say? I have a new appreciation for the stars and stripes," he smiled, before adding, "I was going to go for a walk. Care to join me?"

"Awe...You think I'm sexy?" she asked demurely, as if shocked by the notion, then quickly continued before he could answer. "Sure, I could use the exercise. I feel like I've either been sitting down or sleeping all day," she grimaced, raising her arms and stretching her long torso.

"I'd have to be blind and stupid to not find you sexy, Emma. And I can assure you that I'm neither of those things," he paused, letting his words sink in. "And I think you may have actually slept the entire day," he chuckled, as they walked, hand in hand, towards the shoreline.

"Thanks, then. And, well, that's what I do when I stay up all night. I sleep all day." She angled her head to look at him. "I'm curious about something. Why do you have this house when you already live on the beach? Why not have one in the mountains or on a lake somewhere?" she hesitated, trying to gauge his reaction, then quickly added, in case he took offense, "Don't get me wrong, it's beautiful. It's just that you leave one beautiful beach to vacation at another."

"Oh, I don't own this house. It's my parents'. They let us use it whenever we want, though. Some of my happiest childhood memories were made right here.

We spent most of our holidays in this house." He exhaled deeply, taking in his surroundings, then continued. "I love visiting other places in En Zed, but I'm happiest at the beach. I bought my home in Takapuna for the same reason. I get to wake up every morning and look out on the water. It's a great way to start... and end the day. Honestly, though, if I were to purchase my own bach, it would probably be on a beach. Maybe up northland, where it's warmer during the winter," he concluded, after some reflection.

They strolled side by side along the shoreline, the gentle waves lapping around their ankles, and Emma couldn't remember a more perfect day.

"Tell me about your childhood," Emma asked sincerely.

"Not much to tell, really. I grew up in Hamilton, about an hour south of Auckland. My dad's a professor of engineering at the university there, and my mum stayed home and kept us in line." A mischievous smile crossed his lips. "I was a perfect child. Never gave her any trouble," he grinned, drumming his fingers on his lips.

"Yeah right. I'm sure you didn't," she laughed, shoving his shoulder with her hand.

He stumbled, but quickly regained his footing at the unexpected push from Emma. "Hey, now. That wasn't nice."

"Who said I was nice? Certainly not me. Nope, never said I was nice," she joked, giving him a light shove once again.

He was prepared for it the second time and didn't budge. "You aren't fooling me, Emma. You have nice girl written all over you, although...your togs don't leave much to the imagination, so maybe you're not so nice after all. Maybe a little naughty," he grinned hopefully. He wasn't necessarily into bad girls, but wasn't opposed to a little mischief in the bedroom now and again, and he had a few naughty fantasies he'd like to fulfill with Emma.

"Hey...This is a very patriotic bathing suit, Noah, I'll have you know. And I was trying to get some sun today while the weather was nice. It wouldn't make sense to wear a matronly cover up," Emma objected, tilting her head to the side, and taking in his playful smile.

"You'll get no complaints from me. I like you in your togs," he admitted, holding his hands up in protest.

"Well, thanks...I guess. Now, tell me something about yourself. I know you were the perfect child and never gave your mother any headaches," she mocked him sassily. "But I want to know something significant." When she smiled, that perfect smile, he would've given her the world if she asked for it.

"I really wasn't a bad kid, but what would you like to know?" he dared to ask.

"I don't know, how about your...best day ever. Stuff like that," she suggested.

He gave her the sweet smile that Emma was starting to fall in love with. "My best day ever isn't really a childhood memory, but it would have to be when I was selected to represent my country, on the All Blacks. I actually shed a few tears when I put the jersey on for the first time. Dreamed about it my whole life, and to have it finally happen was an honor. Something I'll never forget." He looked out onto the water for a long minute and Emma could tell his mind had taken him back to that moment in time. "Now, it's your turn." He nudged her shoulder with his.

"I'm sure it's quite an honor to be chosen. Even I know the All Blacks are the best rugby team in the world. You should be very proud," she smiled, squeezing his hand gently. "Now, let's see... My best day ever would have to be when a few of us went hiking on a trail we hadn't been on before, and after about a mile or so we found this enormous clearing, filled with wildflowers and a massive oak tree in the middle of it. There was a bench under the tree and the view was amazing. You could see forever and the sky was that special shade of Carolina Blue with just a few wispy clouds. It was like we'd stumbled upon Narnia, or someplace magical. I don't know how else to describe it; it was almost too pretty to be real, like your eyes were playing tricks on you."

"Sounds lovely."

"It was." As Emma thought back to that day, she was coming to realize that her time with Noah was just as wonderful.

Making their way back to the house, they found Lily and Josh playing Frisbee on the beach.

"Hey, you guys getting hungry?" Noah asked, as they got closer.

"Starved," Josh replied simply.

While dining alfresco on the deck, Emma remembered how concerned she was that Noah would get on her nerves, and almost laughed at the thought. She was thoroughly enjoying herself. Noah was as charming as always, and certainly wasn't hard to look at in a pair of board shorts.

Too many hours and drinks later, Lily was tipsy and reminding Emma of 'the history of rap', a video they'd found online when Lily had visited her over the summer. With nothing else to do one day, they'd spent hours practicing the dance moves, but Emma had quickly forgotten about it.

Until now.

"Let's do it," Lily demanded.

Emma's stomach sank, as she watched Lily get more and more excited by the horrific idea. "No way. You're crazy," Emma laughed, her anxiety ratcheting up at an alarming pace.

"Oh, come on, Emma," Lily pouted. "It'll be fun. Now get up and let's do it."

Ignoring Emma's protests, Lily reached for her tablet and began searching for the video. With a level of concentration that was actually impressive, based on the amount of alcohol she'd consumed, Lily scrolled through the options until she happily announced that she'd found it.

Emma wanted to crawl under a rock.

This level of humiliation required more alcohol, she thought, and knowing Lily wouldn't let it go, she grabbed her beer and quickly downed it, then grabbed another and started to down that one too.

"Fine. You're such a pain in the ass, Lily. You know that?" she complained, but her own level of intoxication was now easing the burden of her mortification somewhat.

Lily let out a quick burst of laughter. "Of course I know it. Now it's time to shake yours." Lily gave her a conspiratorial smile, playfully smacking Emma's backside.

Josh sat up and took a long pull of his beer. "Oh, you are going to love this, Noah. It's bloody fantastic."

Lily propped the tablet on the coffee table so they could follow along, as they took their places in front of the large fireplace facing Noah and Josh.

"I feel like I should apologize in advance for this. Oh my God, this is going to be so embarrassing. I hate you, Lily," Emma snickered, shaking her head.

Lily hit play and it all quickly came back to Emma, as they started mimicking the video, with Lily acting out the part of Jimmy Fallon and Emma as Justin Timberlake. They messed up in a few spots, but other than that, they were pretty good. Reality was probably closer to marginal, at best, but beer goggles were a wonderful thing when complete humiliation was on tap.

Daring to glance at Noah, Emma found him watching her intently, with what could only be described as a ravenous look in his eyes. His pretty blue eyes actually looked black as he followed her movements. Shifting in his seat, Noah leaned forward, resting his chin in his hands, his lips turning up in a hungry grin that released a swarm of butterflies in her stomach.

When they were done, Josh pulled Lily onto his lap. "Well done, babe."

Emma felt awkward, as she collapsed on the couch, after slipping into the kitchen to get another beer. She'd hoped taking a few moments would calm her sudden bout of nerves, but it wasn't working.

"Well, that was um...entertaining," Noah finally spoke after a prolonged silence.

She giggled nervously, watching him lean back into the couch cushions. "More like utterly humiliating. We were bored that day, and had nothing better to do than surf the web and make fools of ourselves."

"For the record, you didn't make fools of yourselves. It was a lot of fun to watch. Really enjoyed it, actually." A wicked smile spread across his face, as he placed his arm along the couch behind Emma and twirled a lock of her hair around his finger. Emma always loved the feel of a man running his fingers through her hair, and goose bumps rose across her skin as he continued to toy with it.

"Thanks. Like I said, we were bored."

He shifted to move a little closer to her. "You had me at 'push it' and then my brain stopped working at 'I wanna take my clothes off', that little shimmy you did…fucking sexy." His voice trailed off and she watched his eyes linger on her lips before slowly crawling up to meet hers. As he paused to let his words sink in, knowing his brashness would excite and shock her at the same time, Emma never wanted to be kissed more than she did in that moment.

Admitting that he was completely turned on by her was probably a bad idea, but experience had taught him that honesty was the best policy. He felt the attraction growing between them, and loved catching her stolen glances when she thought he wasn't looking. And seeing her cheeks turn an adorable shade of pink when he walked around without a shirt on was totally worth it.

"Oh," she said slowly, as her eyes darted to his lips and then back to his eyes. "Well, it was never intended to be resurrected again. Lily has a big mouth when she's been drinking." Emma started to laugh as she spoke the last sentence loudly for Lily's benefit.

"Do not. I just wanted to have some fun. Admit it. You had fun, Emma. Didn't you?" Lily demanded in between kisses from Josh.

"Yes, Lily, I had fun," Emma begrudgingly admitted, but Noah didn't miss the happy glint in her eye. The copious amount of alcohol she'd consumed may have loosened her up a bit, but Emma wasn't that starchy. She was just a little shy. Which he actually liked.

Lily and Josh made their excuses and went to bed, leaving Emma alone with Noah. Her heart was ready to explode out of her chest at the realization that Noah might actually want to be more than just friends with benefits. She definitely had reservations about beginning a relationship with him, but the memory of their kisses still made her cheeks flush and her heart soar to unbelievable heights. She couldn't stop thinking about the feel of his soft lips against hers and the taste of him. If just his kisses left her breathless, how much more would his touch affect her?

Emma let out a shaky breath, leaning her head against the hand that was still playing with her hair, and as he cradled the back of her neck, she slowly turned her face towards him. Feeling overwhelmed by the flood of emotions, she suddenly felt wary. Taking time to explore the features of his face, from his scruff covered jawline to his gorgeous blue eyes, and everything in between, what she found there, the way he was looking at her, told her everything.

He wanted her. Badly.

Noah sat patiently as Emma checked him out, waiting for their eyes to meet once again. When her gaze fixed on his mouth, a sexy smile crossed her lips and he stifled an audible groan. She was so beautiful, and his thoughts were consumed with kissing her again. He needed to kiss her again.

When her eyes finally landed on his, he slowly pulled her towards him.

"I'm going to kiss you now. Alright?" he asked, once their mouths were only a breath apart.

Words escaped her, along with the ability to think, leaving Emma only able to nod in agreement before Noah's lips were pressed deliciously against hers. The hand that had urged her closer, slid into her hair, holding her there.

Time seemed to stand still as he coaxed her lips to open for him, and she willingly obliged. One thing she knew for sure at that moment was that she could see herself becoming addicted to the feel of his lips against hers as he turned her inside out with only the slightest touch.

Emma placed her hand on his arm and felt the muscles quiver beneath her fingers, as they explored the contours of his bicep before continuing up and over the cap of his shoulder. He was so strong, but still gentle as he held her and it emboldened her. As if they had a mind of their own, her fingers combed through his thick head of dark hair, tugging on it as she gripped the soft strands between her fingers.

Noah groaned, as he gently nipped at her kiss-swollen lower lip, then soothed it with a slow kiss. When Emma softly moaned, he shifted closer to her and slid his free hand around her back. Her raised arms lifted her top, exposing a thin strip of bare skin, and his fingers skillfully stroked her there. And she melted.

"Um. That was…" *Amazing, spectacular, fan-freaking-tastic.* She didn't know where this was going with Noah, but the attraction was too strong to deny. He was looking at her with hunger in his eyes and a goofy grin on his face, and she was sure her expression mirrored his.

No kiss had ever affected her like that before. She couldn't think straight. She could only focus on the impossibly charming man sitting in front of her, and the feel of his thumb caressing her side left her wanting to crawl into his lap and cuddle.

"Yeah, I know," he replied, pressing his forehead against hers, still trying to catch his breath. Gazing into her eyes, he felt his heart twist. He'd never believed in love at first sight, but Emma had an inexplicable hold on him from the minute he'd laid eyes on her in the club. He didn't want to fight it any longer. He needed to be with her as badly as he needed his next breath.

Even though he was pretty sure he'd felt the earth shake beneath his boots every time his lips came in contact with hers, it wasn't like him to be thinking about forever after only a few kisses, so he reminded himself that he needed to proceed with caution.

Noah refused to dwell on the fact that she'd be leaving at the end of the year. When he dared to envision his future, Emma was there with him, by his side. He knew the odds were against them, but it didn't matter, he wasn't a quitter and if they were still together, he'd find a way to make it work.

# CHAPTER 9

The following morning, Noah found Emma relaxing on the deck, reclined on the chaise lounge, with her face tilted towards the sun. A pair of fantasy-inducing legs were stretched out in front of her, and crossed at the ankles, which left Noah unable to swallow past the lump in his throat.

Her eyes were closed and she had a blissful smile on her face. He found himself standing in the doorway quietly observing her, taking in the gentle curve of her long neck and the classic lines of her face. She was exquisite.

Trying to pinpoint the one thing that made her different from all the others was impossible; she was a collection of the senses. Not only was she achingly beautiful, but the sound of her voice was like the finest of wines, smooth and satisfying. Even the slightest touch from her delicate fingers left a wake of goose bumps in their path and his heart flipping over in his chest, and she smelled so damn good he wanted to bathe in her, just to soak up some of her sweetness.

He'd only had the tiniest taste of her, but it left him ravenous and ready to devour her, inch by delicious inch.

Shaking his head and wondering where he'd left his man card, Noah finally cleared his throat and smiled when she turned towards him.

"Good morning, sunshine," Noah said, feeling the full impact of her gaze upon him. Closing the distance between them, he joined her on the chaise lounge, needing to be near her.

Her sweet smile had his heart ready to tumble. "Good morning, Noah. I was just thinking about you."

"Oh yeah? What were you thinking about?" he requested eagerly, then bristled. When did he become so desperate for any morsel of validation?

A pretty pink tint bloomed across her cheeks, and he secretly delighted in the sight of it. "Oh, I don't know. Just how happy I am to be here." Her emerald eyes sparkled in the sunlight, and he was happy she was here, too.

Noah placed his hand on her thigh, his thumb stroking her there, unable to resist the pull she had on him. And as he leaned in to give her a gentle kiss, everything felt...right.

"You look very pretty this morning." Her long hair was pulled back into a ponytail, exposing flawless skin, and she wore a temptingly short pair of denim shorts with a white tank top, which stretched tightly over a mouthwatering pair of breasts.

"Thank you, you're very sweet." The soft touch of her hand as it traced the edge of his jaw distracted him for a minute, as he let her explore, hoping she'd take it a tad further south. "So, what's the plan for today?" she asked.

Feeling a little disappointed when she removed her hand, and ignoring the deep longing in his chest for her missing touch, he filtered through the things he thought she might enjoy. "We could hike The Mount if you'd like. The weather's good and there's a beautiful view from the summit," he added encouragingly.

He needed to burn off some energy, and figured a sweaty bedroom workout with Emma was not an option at this point, so he'd have to settle for a vigorous tramp up the mountain. He also wanted to share one of his favorite places on earth with her.

"That sounds like fun. Are Lily and Josh up yet? Do you think they'd want to go?"

"I'm sure they will, but if not, then we can do it just the two of us," he said, smiling against her lips, just breathing her in, before giving her a proper good morning kiss.

Emma's fingers raked through his hair, and he couldn't hold back the groan as he deepened the kiss. He could not get enough of this woman, he thought to himself. She tasted of mint and something uniquely Emma, and her skin felt like the finest of silks.

Sliding his hand from her thigh, over the soft swell of her hips, he hesitated when he reached her waist. Clutching her tightly as she pressed her luscious curves into him, the feel of her breasts against his chest made his fingers itch with the need to touch them.

She let out a low whimper as Noah inched his fingers beneath the hem of her top, slowly exploring her ribcage, giving her the opportunity to turn him away. But praying she wouldn't. He felt her tense for a brief second, then relax as he finally reached his desired destination, teasing her as his thumb caressed the underside of her breast.

When she sucked on his tongue and released a pleading moan, he completed the journey, gently squeezing and kneading her as she arched her back, encouraging his touch. Her hardened nipple pressed against his palm, through the silky material of her bra, and he longed to taste her there. Just touching her wasn't enough, would never be enough; he was greedy like that.

Emma instantly felt chilled when Noah suddenly slipped his hand from beneath her shirt. The man had magic fingers and she wanted to drag him to her bedroom…more please.

Breaking the kiss, he pressed his cheek to hers and whispered, "We have company," in her ear. Day-old stubble lined his face, awakening her senses as it abraded her cheek.

His touch had the blood pumping through her veins at an alarming rate, and left her feeling dizzy. Taking a deep breath, she smoothed her hands over the length of her shirt to straighten it, as Lily walked outside. Still tingling from his caress, her breasts were heavy with need. As if they knew Noah's skilled hands were only inches from them, her nipples tightened into firm little points, practically reaching out to him.

Damn.

She was thankful Noah had the presence of mind to still be aware of their surroundings, because she certainly didn't. It was as if the rest of the world had vanished, leaving only the two of them. If Lily had witnessed what they were up to, or God forbid, Josh, she'd never have heard the end of it.

"Hey, guys," Lily chirped, practically skipping along the deck.

"Hey. You're way too perky this early in the morning, Lily," Emma pointed out.

"I can't help it, Emma. Life is beautiful." Her attitude was infectious as Lily settled into a chair with a satisfied sigh. "And speaking of beautiful…" Lily smiled demurely as Josh walked outside and took the seat next her.

Josh nodded to Emma and Noah. "Morning."

"Emma and I were just talking about hiking The Mount today. You want to come along?" Noah asked.

Lily let out a loud snort. "Is that what you were doing? Didn't look like there was much talking going on to me."

Emma felt her cheeks catch fire as she quickly glanced at Noah, "Oh, dear God, Lily. Pot, meet kettle."

"Hey, I was just stating the obvious. No judgment here. Good on ya, Emma," Lily responded with a dismissive wave of her hand.

"Well…do you want to go with us?" Noah requested again, getting them back on track, as he turned towards Josh and Lily.

"What do you think, babe? You up for a tramp?" Josh asked Lily, placing his arm over her shoulder.

"Sweet as. I haven't been up there in a while and the view from the top is brilliant, Emma. You'll love it."

"Alrighty then. Let's get something to eat and then head out," Emma said, as she slid her legs off the chaise lounge and stood to her feet.

To say that Noah and Josh set a brisk pace, as they hiked to the summit of Mount Maunganui, was a vicious understatement. Emma was sure they made it in record time, as she breathlessly dropped her backpack and hastily downed a bottle of water. Wiping the sweat from her brow with the back of her hand, her legs were on fire and she was pretty sure her face had taken on the color of a ripe tomato.

She would've preferred a leisurely climb, to appreciate the beautiful scenery, but unless she wanted to be left behind, she had to keep up the exacting pace they'd set. The fact that Noah had barely broken a sweat both impressed and annoyed her at the same time.

Reclining on a large outcropping of rocks, lining the edge of the summit, they were rewarded with the awe-inspiring sight of Papamoa Beach and the Bay of Plenty. Emma snapped a few photos with her phone, wanting to remember the picturesque view, as she caught her breath.

Resting her head on her backpack, she closed her eyes, concentrating on the sound of Noah's voice, letting it wash over her, as he began to recite the legend of Mauao. Emma loved the colorful stories of New Zealand's history and listened raptly as Noah spoke.

"Legend has it that in ancient times The Mount was a nameless hill that was a slave to the most prestigious mountain in Tauranga Moana, Otanewainuku. This nameless hill was in love with the beautiful Puwhenua, but she was in love with Otanewainuku. Well, he was so distraught that her heart belonged to another that he called upon the bush fairies, who possessed magical powers, and asked them to drag him to the ocean so he could drown himself. When night fell, they fastened him with ropes, and began the long journey. The Waimapu River, which means 'weeping waters' now flows through the valley that was created as the fairies pulled him towards the water."

Noah paused to take a long drink of water and then continued. "The problem was that the fairies were people of the night, and as they approached the ocean, morning was breaking. So they abandoned him here, where he still stands today, and fled back into the darkness of the forest. Before they left him, though, they gave him the name of Mauao, which means 'caught by the dawn'. The Maori, who settled here, gave him the name Maunganui, which means 'big mountain', and he's now the symbol of all the tribes of Tauranga Moana." Noah gave Emma a satisfied smile, as he took another drink of water and shuffled closer to her on the large rock.

"That's such a beautiful story, Noah. It's so sad, though," Emma whispered wistfully, as she lifted onto her outstretched arms and turned her face upwards, towards the sun, enjoying the cool breeze that swept over the summit.

Noah took a long drink of water, shrugging his shoulder indifferently. "Yeah, I suppose."

"You're such a guy," Emma balked, nudging him with her foot.

Noah's lips twitched into a sexy smile. "Glad of that. At least, I hope you think so."

"Well, since I like boys, I'm glad you are one." And just because he was so sweet, and without thinking, she leaned in for a quick kiss.

"You ready to head back down? I'm starving," Josh stated, standing up as he offered a hand to Lily.

"Sure. Let's go," Noah answered, pushing to his feet, and reaching for Emma's hand to help her up, then continued to hold it as they set off down the trail.

She gave him an appreciative smile as she wiped the dust from the back of her shorts with her free hand. "Thanks, Noah. I'm glad you suggested this. It's been amazing. And the story of the mountain, well...I'll never forget it."

Thankfully, walking down the mountain was a lot easier than walking up it, Emma thought, as they entered the parking lot. Approaching the car, Emma was surprised to find that people recognized Noah and Josh, and asked for pictures with them. It was unsettling to say the least, but she tried to take it in stride.

Lily suggested they wait for them at the car, as Noah and Josh happily obliged the excited fans. Emma watched inquisitively as Noah interacted with them. He seemed relatively at ease with the attention, even stooping to eye level while speaking with the children.

She was relieved to see that the majority of them were families with small children, who fidgeted nervously, their adoring eyes filled with awe as they posed for photos with their heroes.

When a group of women approached, and proceeded to drape themselves around Noah like a set of cheap curtains, she felt her blood start to boil. Emma knew she had no right to stomp over there and physically remove them, but boy did she want to.

Dammit.

Emma was thankful that Noah just smiled graciously, not encouraging them in any way, only stood for the pictures before politely excusing himself. But the sight of another woman's hands on him infuriated her.

Noah made a beeline for her, placing his hands against the side of the Jeep on either side of her head, trapping her between his hard body and the cool steel of the car, as he leaned in to kiss the scowl off of her face. "If I didn't know better, I'd think you were a wee bit jealous, Emma," Noah teased.

"I...I don't know about that. Well...maybe a *little*," she reluctantly admitted. "But, in my defense, they weren't being respectful of your personal space," Emma declared, offended for him.

The handsy women were still standing together, giggling as they viewed the photos, occasionally glancing over their shoulders to get another look at Noah and Josh.

Eat your heart out ladies...he's with me.

"You'll get used to it, Emma," Lily commiserated, with a deep sigh. "It isn't easy, especially when they're pretty, but it comes with the territory, I guess. Just have to deal."

"Aw, babe. You know that no one can hold a candle to you. Right?" Josh assured her, pulling her to him for a sweet kiss.

"I know. It's just hard sometimes, to see you with another girl's arms around you, is all," she confessed.

"Yeah, well I think someone forgot to teach them some manners, and maybe some boundaries, too. That one girl was about to round third base with you, Noah." Emma had to laugh as Noah choked on the water he was drinking. "What? Her hand was right there. Just a few more inches south and she would've gotten a hell of a lot more than a picture with you," Emma added disgustedly, the scowl returning to her face at the image in her head, as she possessively tucked her thumb into his belt loop, secretly hoping the overzealous fangirls noticed.

Noah reached behind her, placing the empty water bottle on the roof of the car, the heady mixture of sweat and Noah invading her senses. "Third base, huh? That. Would. Not. Have. Happened," Noah spoke precisely, adding a peck on her lips between each word. "Now, let's forget about them and get some food, eh? Because I don't know 'bout you, but I've worked up an appetite. Need a good feed."

"I am kind of hungry. I don't think I've ever hiked that fast before. When we go out back home, it's a casual stroll compared to the pace that you set," Emma admitted.

"Well, good on ya for keeping up. I would've slowed down though, if you'd asked me to."

"No. It was fine. I needed the exercise, but I might not be able to walk tomorrow. Maybe I'll take a hot bath tonight. That should take care of it," Emma stated, stretching her tired legs out to the side one by one.

"Can I watch?" Noah tested jokingly.

"Um…yeah…that would be a…No." Emma ducked under his arm and strolled around to the passenger side of the Jeep, an extra swing in her hips as she went, just because she knew he was watching her. Rounding the front of the Jeep, a quick glance over her shoulder confirmed her suspicion, and from the dumbfounded look on his face, as he stared at her ass, he was enjoying it.

After a quick shower to wash the dirt and sweat off, they tucked into a hearty lunch alfresco, that Noah and Josh had prepared. She hadn't realized how hungry she was until she sat down, but pushing away from the table after quickly devouring the cheeseburger and fries, her gluttonous appetite was more than satisfied.

"I think I need a nap now, to sleep off my food baby," Emma chuckled, rubbing her belly dramatically, walking inside with her empty plate and glass.

"Food baby, eh?" Noah snickered, as he joined her in the kitchen.

"Well, look at the size of my belly. I look pregnant. Maybe four or five months along, I'd say." Emma turned her profile to him and lifted her top, exposing her distended abdomen.

"Um…I don't know. Have you felt him kick yet?" Noah asked, playing along with her.

"*She* isn't acting up yet. Maybe if I add a sugary dessert, that'll get her really worked up," she giggled, smoothing her shirt back into place.

"Ah, ah, ah. Not so fast. I think I need to take some measurements. See for myself how far gone you are. Seeing as I'm the one responsible for your delicate condition." Noah's seductive words were ghosted against her skin, as he moved behind her. Snaking his hand around her waist, he let it rest against her belly, drawing her back into his chest.

Emma's heart did a flip-flop in her chest and then a speedy swan dive into her tummy, as Noah settled her against the firmness of his body. She instantly felt tingly all over. He was warm and solid and smelled like sunshine and fresh air.

His other hand slid her hair across her shoulder, exposing the sensitive skin of her neck. Needing more, Emma tilted her head to the side, giving him permission, then moaned as his lips made contact. Nipping her gently there, he quickly pacified the sting with a stroke of his tongue and a lingering kiss, and she forgot how to breathe.

"Mmm. You smell really good," he whispered in her ear. The feel of his warm breath caused a shudder to race down her spine. "What is it?"

Emma tried to think, but her brain refused to cooperate as his mouth continued lightly suckling on her neck. "Honeysuckle. It's…um…honeysuckle," she somehow managed to say, her voice rough with arousal.

"I like it...a lot," Noah simply replied between kisses. When his large hand slid along her midsection, gripping her tighter, her stomach twisted into delightful knots of anticipation.

"Thanks. It reminds me of home. It grows wild in the woods behind my parents' house. And I'm having trouble thinking while you're doing that, Noah. Oh...that feels...um...so good," Emma sighed, then giggled as he nipped her again.

"Well, it smells delicious. You smell delicious." The tickle of his breath against her skin, as his lips trailed down the curve of her neck, left her fighting for air.

"It tastes good too. We'd pick the flowers and then bite the tip off and suck the nectar out." She gasped as he took the lobe of her ear between his teeth and bit down, then sucked it into his mouth to soothe it. The jolt of pain and pleasure rocked her, and she was thankful his strong arms were holding her up.

"Like that?" he asked seductively, as he repeated the process. "I may have to practice some more so I'll know how to do it. I'm sure it's very delicate, and want to make sure I do it right, savor every drop."

Turning around to face him, Emma laced her fingers around his neck and pulled him down for a slow, wet kiss. "Are you sullying an innocent childhood memory?" She smiled against his lips when they finally parted.

"Who me? I wouldn't do such a thing. You're the one with the dirty mind." Laughing at her shocked expression, he dropped a gentle kiss on the tip of her nose. "But, I like where you're going with that. Gives me something to think about."

"Oh, please," Emma hooted sarcastically.

When he kissed her again, Emma's mind drifted to thoughts of his soft lips discovering other, more sensitive, parts of her body. Then her mind went completely blank as he stroked his tongue against hers, making love to her mouth.

Her world was reduced to the feel of his hard body pressed against hers, and the feel of his hands moving over her, gently caressing as they explored. Knowing how much he liked it, she sucked on his tongue and heard his answering growl in response.

Listening to the sound of the ocean waves as they collided with the shoreline, Emma realized that, like the rise and fall of the tide, being with Noah was inevitable.

"Ah, if you keep doing that. I'm not going to be able to stop. Already half way there," he murmured into the crook of her neck, as he sprinkled kisses along her heated skin.

"You're right," she sighed. Placing her hands on his firm chest, Emma felt the rapid beat of his heart through his shirt and gulped in a deep breath, trying to rein in her own runaway libido before she allowed things to progress further than she was comfortable with. "I'm not quite ready for that. Yet."

Noah was so ready he was prepared to beg, which is something he'd never done before. But he needed to slow down, to do it right. She'd be worth the wait, he told himself, over and over again, while pressing his lips to the smooth skin on her neck.

"I am. Couldn't be more ready." He pressed the hard length of his growing erection against her, wanting to toss her over his shoulder and take her to his bedroom, straight away. "But, no worries. No rush. Just need a minute," he confessed, as he folded his arms around her shoulders, then tucked her head under his chin.

He didn't want to let her go yet, still needed the contact. When she wrapped her arms around his waist and let out a happy little moan, he wondered if he'd ever grow tired of the way she felt in his arms.

After long minutes holding each other quietly, Noah was finally able to speak. "Why don't you get your togs on, and we'll take a walk on the beach. I'll hold your hand, maybe put my arm around you. And even if you want to, I won't let you get to third base with me," he broke off, with a soft chuckle. "Wait, who am I kidding? If you want to, I won't be saying no." He tried to remain serious, he really did, but the sound of Emma's laughter drew a matching response from him.

"I know my manners. Don't you worry, I'll be on my best behavior, Mr. Parker," Emma drawled in an exaggerated southern accent.

Noah let out a hearty laugh. "My own little southern belle. Who knew? You barely sound like you're from the south, though."

"Hey. I'm American by birth, but Southern by the grace of God. Born and raised, baby. But my parents are Yankees, so that's probably why. They met at Duke University, and stayed in North Carolina while my dad was in medical school, then never left. Thank God for that, because I can't imagine growing up anyplace else."

"Yeah, well clearly they raised you right, anyone can see that. Now rattle your dags and let's go on that walk." He reluctantly released her, nudging her towards the hall. Instantly missing her warmth, he almost reached out and pulled her back. Watching her go, he wondered how in such a short period of time she'd become so important to him.

Walking along the beach twenty minutes later, they spotted a pod of dolphins a few meters from the shoreline. Emma quickly pulled the phone from her shorts' pocket, recording the animated creatures as they frolicked in the surf.

"They're amazing. Aren't they? I got to swim with a dolphin once, on vacation in Florida. It was the most incredible experience," she reminisced excitedly, as she slipped the phone back into her pocket, then took his hand and started walking again.

"Never done that, but I'd like to one day," he confessed, squeezing her hand gently, looking out at the expanse of water and then back to her. A wild mass of blonde hair floated around her face as the wind kicked up, and turning her face towards it, the cool breeze provided a semblance of order to the unruly locks.

"You should definitely do it. You won't regret it. It was so much fun." Her voice was full of enthusiasm, practically vibrating with excitement. She had the cutest smile he'd ever seen, the infectious kind that you couldn't help but return.

Noah was surprised when they reached the inlet where the Kaituna River emptied into the Bay of Plenty. He hadn't realized they'd walked that far along the beach. Their easy companionship had the time slipping away from him.

Sinking into the sand to rest for a minute, Noah slid his arm over her shoulder, pulling her close to him, and felt her relax against his side. The ebb and flow of the waves, as they gently crested along the shoreline, was as comforting as the conversation.

"It's so pretty here. Quiet," she observed, resting her head on his shoulder.

"Yeah, not many people venture this far down. Reckon it's too far of a walk." He placed a kiss on top of her head, breathing in the scent of salty air and Emma. "We should be heading back now, though, don't you think?"

"I guess so. We've been gone a while," she frowned, assessing how far down the beach they'd traveled, as she stood to her feet. "Probably shouldn't have walked this far; my legs are tired after the hike this morning. Not used to this much exertion," she chuckled, brushing the sand from the back of her shorts.

Noah stopped and crouched down in front of her. "Get on. I'll carry you for a while."

"What? No. I couldn't. Your legs must be tired too, Noah."

"You forget that I'm a professional, Emma. A highly trained, fine-tuned machine. Now saddle up baby, before this horse trots off without you. It's a long way back from here. I'll carry you for a bit, then you can carry me if you want," he teased, trying to reassure her that he was more than capable of carrying her.

Just the thought of having her nearly naked body pressed against his was worth any additional burden. Looking at her lean figure, he guessed she didn't weigh more than the weights he normally trained with anyway.

"Are you sure?" She hesitated, then jumped onto his back at his nod of approval. Noah held her legs against his side as she draped her arms loosely around his neck. Resting her chin on his shoulder, she tilted her head and kissed him there; the whisper of her warm breath sent delicious shivers across his skin. "Thanks, Noah. The air is much fresher up here at your altitude," she joked.

He reveled in the feel of her long legs wrapped around his waist, her breasts pressed against his naked back, only the thin triangles of her top separating them. The touch of her skin against his made it hard to concentrate, especially when she gently caressed his chest with her fingertips.

Carrying her on his back along the deserted beach, Noah was struck by her gentle nature. She enjoyed the simple things in life, a slow walk along the beach holding hands, laughing as she swayed on a swing, or watching the sunrise. Or riding piggy back, with her chin propped on his shoulder, he added to the list.

Finally putting her down after she insisted he'd carried her long enough, he slipped his arm around her shoulder and mindlessly caressed her skin there. When Emma hooked her thumb into the waistband of his shorts, her soft hand settling on his hip as they strolled back to the house, he let out a contented sigh. This is what he'd been waiting his entire life for.

Once again, he was overcome with a feeling of rightness.

He hadn't felt this happy in a long, long time, and he realized that she was a big part of it.

# CHAPTER 10

Driving to Lily's parents' for dinner after their week at the beach was bitter-sweet. Emma was looking forward to Lily's wedding and seeing her family again, but she was also going to miss spending so much time with Noah.

Having his undivided attention was flattering and had allowed them to grow closer, and she wasn't quite ready for it to be over. She suspected that Lily and Josh had thrown them together on purpose, but as she looked over at Noah from the passenger seat, she was eternally grateful.

Resting her head against the seat, she studied him as he maneuvered the car onto the highway that would take them back to Auckland. His tanned, muscular arms flexed as he gripped the steering wheel, and her fingers ached to touch him. He glanced at her and smiled, while reaching for her hand, lacing their fingers together. It was a sweet and tender gesture…and totally Noah.

Emma would never forget the past week. Even though the house was surrounded by other homes, it felt isolated. She wondered how different things would be when they returned to the real world, once Noah started practicing with the team and she started school.

Life had a way of getting in the way, and vacations sometimes created a false reality of how things would be in real life. An alternate reality of sorts…an illusion. The carefree existence they'd enjoyed the last few weeks would be over.

She'd gotten used to Noah being around all the time; surely that would change, she thought. She knew from Lily's experience that life with a sportsman wasn't always easy. Between the constant travel and the groping fangirls, it could put a strain on any relationship, especially a new one, if that was even what they had. She knew something was happening, but what it was exactly, she wasn't sure.

After dinner, Noah dropped them off at home, explaining that he had team obligations in the morning and needed a good night's sleep, and Emma immediately felt the loss of his company as she sank into the couch cushions.

Emma felt guilty that he'd lost his bed in the city when she'd moved in, but she wasn't prepared to share it with him. At least not yet anyway. He'd made no secret of his desire to take things to the next level, but she wasn't positive they were on the same page, and didn't want to have any regrets when they finally did have sex.

Whenever he was near, her body longed for his touch...physically ached for even the slightest of touches, but she was having trouble reconciling the fact that she'd be leaving at the end of the year.

It would be so much easier if she was the type of girl who could have a casual fling and then walk away after it ran its course, but she wasn't and she knew it. Unable to separate the physical and the emotional aspects of a sexual relationship, she only did relationships one way...all or nothing.

When she dated, it was always someone she could see herself spending the rest of her life with. Admittedly, she'd made poor choices in the past, but she'd tried to learn from each of them. She wasn't going to settle for just so-so, she wanted her happily ever after. She wanted forever.

Noah definitely had her heart wanting forever, and more. But to what end?

After falling asleep with the phone pressed to her ear, Emma woke in the morning and couldn't stop the little giggle that bubbled up from her throat. Noah had called to say goodnight as she was getting into bed, and the last time she'd checked the clock it was two in the morning. So much for him getting a good night's sleep, she thought, reaching for her charger. Plugging in her phone, she called Ali, wanting to talk to her big sister about her trip to the beach and her growing feelings for Noah.

When she finally disconnected the call, Emma was discouraged and more confused than ever. Exhaling as she rolled over onto her back, she stared up at the ceiling. She knew Ali was worried that she'd get hurt, but the extent of her negativity was surprising. To have Ali dismiss her feelings so effortlessly was frustrating. "Why put yourself through that?" she'd asked. Even knowing she had a valid argument, it still felt wrong to deny her feelings for Noah.

Emma decided to go for a swim to clear her mind, and getting a good workout always helped, so she packed her swim bag, put her hair in a topknot, and headed to the kitchen. Finding it empty, she quickly ate a light breakfast, left a note for Lily, grabbed her bag, and set off for the walk to the swim club.

The familiar smell of chlorine immediately calmed her as she slipped into the water. After warming-up with a 200 meter freestyle, she switched to butterfly. Her mind went back to the conversation with her sister. Was Ali right? Was she making a mistake with Noah? She didn't think so, but she also knew the heady rush of a new relationship could be distracting, and being with Noah was the definition of distraction.

She thought back to the night they'd met in the club. From the minute she laid eyes on him, she was sucked into his orbit. He'd turned out to be so much more than a handsome face and a smoking hot body. She truly enjoyed spending time with him; they'd spent countless hours just talking or sitting quietly in a companionable silence, and it never felt awkward or uncomfortable.

Noah was funny and sweet, and when he looked at her with his crooked smile and impossibly blue eyes, he set her on fire. Her body reacted almost instinctively whenever he was near. She was drawn to him like a magnet to steel, but it wasn't just her body that craved him, her mind did too. How do you fight an attraction so strong? She had no idea, but knew she wouldn't try anyway.

Changing to backstroke, she thought about distancing herself from him, but the answering contraction in her chest made it obvious how involved she was already. Her brain could tell her that being with him was a mistake, and it was probably right, but her heart was in total rebellion. Just thinking about their first kiss, and how magical it was, left her feeling all warm and fuzzy. It was the kind of kiss you told your grandchildren about. She could still feel the strength of his arms holding her, as his tongue stoked a fire deep down in her soul.

Reaching the edge of the pool, she pushed off into the breaststroke. Her mind instantly took her back to the morning at the beach house, to the feel of his hands as they slowly inched their way under her shirt until they found their target. She'd wanted to hurry him along, but he'd taken his time, savoring every inch of her. Even now, the memory of his expert fingers, gently caressing her, left her aching with need.

Kicking off the side of the pool, she transitioned to freestyle to finish her workout. Trying to slow her heart rate, she deliberately forced her thoughts from Noah's touch, and his mind-numbing kisses, which had the power to make her forget time and space, and made a mental list of the pros and cons of being with him. The only con she could come up with, unfortunately, was potentially big enough to outweigh all of the pros, and the pros were considerable. The cold reality was that her home was in America and his was here, in New Zealand. Even the most committed relationships would have a hard time surviving that kind of distance for long.

In the end, Emma decided to wait and see where things went with Noah, to take it one day at a time. If the fascination was still there after the wedding, she'd talk to him, to get a feel for what he was looking for. For all she knew, she was stressing herself out over a non-issue. Maybe Noah was only interested in a casual fling, nothing exclusive.

If that was the case, she'd have a good cry and then bow out gracefully. She didn't do casual, and she certainly didn't share, but she was fairly certain Noah felt the same way, and it gave her confidence a needed boost.

With a reassuring nod to herself, she got out of the pool and headed for the locker room. Surely Lily wouldn't encourage her to be with Noah if he was only interested in a casual hook up. It hadn't gone unnoticed that Lily and Josh disappeared for hours on end while they were at the beach. Leaving plenty of alone time for the two of them to get to know each other better.

After a warm shower, which felt like heaven, she quickly dried her hair and got dressed. Sliding her feet into her flip-flops, her heart did a little pitter-patter when she checked her phone and saw a missed call from Noah. Placing her bag over her shoulder, she pushed the door open and stepped out onto the busy sidewalk, pressing the send button to return his call.

"Hi, Emma," Noah happily greeted her.

"Hey. Sorry I missed your call. I was in the pool. What's up?"

"I was wondering if you'd be interested in going to Hobbiton tomorrow. I know you're a big fan of The Lord of the Rings, and you can tour the movie set of The Shire. It's not far from here, and then I thought we'd get a bite to eat." He tried not to think of Emma in her sexy togs, the water sluicing off her smooth skin, her soft curves covered only by a thin layer of material, wet and skin tight.

Without even trying, Emma haunted his dreams and fantasies, and he couldn't wait to fulfill a few of them…the sooner the better. He shifted uncomfortably in his chair at the images his mind conjured up, and after a week at the beach with her, his tired brain didn't have to work too hard. The barely-there bikinis she preferred showcased her athletic body nicely, and left little to the imagination.

On a few mornings, he'd sat on the deck as she did yoga on the beach. When she spread her legs and folded herself in half as she grabbed her ankles, giving him a choice view of her goodies, he actually groaned out loud, and then went as hard as granite, wanting to bury himself there. She was tall, tanned, toned…and limber. And he ached to discover every inch of the luscious body that kept him up at night, and in a constant state of arousal.

"Oh my God, really? I'd love to. I read that they'd left the set up when they finished filming the movies."

"It's about a two hour drive from here, in Matamata, so I'll pick you up 'round nine. We'll have lunch when we get there."

The more time he spent with her, the more time he wanted to spend with her. She was quickly becoming necessary for him. Feeling giddy and uncomfortable at the same time at the realization, he reminded himself that he still had his work cut out for him.

If things progressed the way he'd hoped, he'd have to convince her to leave her family and move to En Zed. And based on the way she lit up when she spoke of them, it was a long shot. Not impossible, but definitely the odds were not in his favor.

"You mean second breakfast, right? I'm so excited, I can't wait!" He could hear the excitement in her voice and reveled in the sound of it. "But how was your meeting this morning?"

"Fine. Fine. I don't much care for having my photo taken, being fussed over and all that. But it's part of the job description I suppose, eh?"

"I guess. What was it for? If you don't mind me asking." He sensed the hesitation in her voice and wished she was standing in front of him, so he could kiss it away. He never wanted her to shy away from asking him anything.

"Promotional stuff with some of the boys, showing off our new jerseys," Noah explained.

He was always embarrassed to see himself on billboards or in magazines. It wasn't why he played, but doing a bit of side work added nicely to his salary. It was always in the back of his mind that his playing days could be over tomorrow, so he banked what he could now, preparing for the future.

Noah didn't have to look far for a reminder of that reality. Josh was one of the best in the world and would probably still be playing if not for the bit of bad luck that ended it all in an instant. Luckily for Josh, he'd taken care of his money, and didn't live extravagantly, other than his flash condo in the CBD. But he'd saved his money and invested wisely, and now he had a comfortable life, with Lily by his side. He was still popular with sponsors, due to the level of success he'd achieved in his career, so that helped to pay the bills too.

Noah hoped to be so lucky. Other than the career-ending injury, of course.

"Well, speaking on behalf of the female population, a hot guy in a tight jersey will always work. Although, when you buy one for your boyfriend and they don't look like the guy in the ad…" she sighed dramatically. "Probably a bit of a disappointment."

"Thanks. I guess. Are you suggesting that I'm hot, Emma?" Noah teased, and he could see her blushing through the phone line. He loved that about her; her shy innocence turned him on and made him want her even more.

A soft giggle greeted him through the phone line. "Oh, please, you know you are. And I like the way you look. *A lot.*" She paused and he wondered if the pretty pink tint of her blush had spread to her chest yet. "And might I remind you that you're a highly trained athlete? A fine-tuned machine, I think you mentioned. It's hard for mere mortals to fill it out as well as you guys."

"Oh, I think you don't give yourself enough credit, sweetheart. You'd fill it out just fine. Might have to get you one to wear. It's time you started pimping more than your university. You are in En Zed after all." He wanted to see her in his jersey. His number 15 proudly displayed across her back.

"Well, you know what they say, 'if you can't beat 'em, join 'em'. I guess I'll need one if I go to a game while I'm here." At the ding of the arriving lift, she quickly added. "I'm probably going to lose you once I'm in the elevator. So I'd better go."

"Yeah. I'll see you in the morning, Emma."

"I can hardly wait. I'm so excited. Don't think I'm going to get much sleep tonight." He could help her with that, he thought to himself.

"Well, I could always come over and keep you company. I can think of a fair few things one can do when sleep evades you," Noah responded hopefully.

"Oh, I'm sure," she snickered. "But, sadly, I must decline your kind invitation. You haven't even taken me on a proper date yet." She had a point, but their outing to Matamata and then the romantic dinner he had planned would qualify as a proper date, and, hopefully, remove that obstacle.

"Um, well…can't say that I'm not disappointed, but I think I'm up for the challenge, Emma," Noah finally stuttered out, momentarily distracted by the thought of their tangled lips and limbs discovering one another.

Emma chuckled. "Well, I hope you are. And on that note, I'll leave it at that, and say goodbye."

"Bye, Emma." Noah leaned back, resting his head on the back of the couch, exhaling a deep breath, and closing his eyes. Visions of Emma, naked and splayed out on his bed, ran through his head. She was the highlight reel that was on a constant loop…tormenting him. Needing to relieve the growing erection that sprung to life every time he thought of her, he lowered his hand and stroked it gently, wishing it was her hand on him.

Hoping a long run on the beach, and then a very cold shower would take care of it, he headed for the door. He knew it wouldn't, though. He doubted the actual deed would satisfy his infinite need for her. Well, he never gave up when he wanted something badly enough, and if she wanted to be properly courted, that's exactly what he'd do. He'd never needed to work this hard to get into a woman's knickers before, but it was good for him, he supposed. She was good for him.


Lily was waiting on the couch when Emma entered the lounge, and by the sly smirk on her face, she wanted to talk. Emma set her bag down by her bedroom door and joined her cousin, knowing she was in for a grilling and Lily wouldn't quit until she got what she wanted out of her.

"Spill it," Lily simply stated, turning to face Emma, folding one leg under the other. "I have to know what's going on with you and Noah."

"I'm not really sure," Emma honestly replied. She'd been thinking about it constantly and still hadn't figured it out. "Wish I knew," Emma added, as her eyes darted around the room, looking for Josh.

"Don't worry, he's not home. It's just the two of us. Now, tell me everything. You two have been joined at the lips since New Year's. How do you not know? Come on, this is me you're talking to." Lily nudged her with her foot as she took a drink, then set the glass back down on the coffee table.

"I'm going to ignore that lovely visual," she grimaced. "But damned if I know. It's really great. He's really great. I'm just not sure if we're dating or just hanging out. Has he said anything to Josh?"

"They're guys, they probably just grunted to each other, but I can tell by the way he looks at you that he likes you, though. I've never seen him so smitten before."

Emma's heart lifted, eager for any sign that he felt the same way she did. "He asked me to go to Matamata tomorrow, to see The Shire, and then to dinner. But I don't want to read too much into it." A slow smile spread across her face as she relaxed into the cushions, and her heart started to race at Lily's reaction.

"Interesting," Lily paused, as she pulled a pillow onto her lap. Looking at Emma's anxious expression, she continued. "He's definitely in serious like with you. He's dated a few women in the past few years, but I can't remember him ever taking them away."

"I don't know if you'd call a day trip going away, exactly. It's not like he asked me to go for the weekend or anything. I find it hard to believe that he hasn't had a serious relationship in a while, though. He's so amazing. I can't understand how he's still single, actually." Emma shook her head in disbelief, wondering why she'd be any different than the others.

"Not for lack of trying. Trust me, there've been plenty who've tried to tie him down. With most of them, we couldn't understand what he was doing, other than the obvious. He is a man, after all, had his head turned by a pretty face." At Emma's frown, she quickly added. "Sorry, Emma. I'm making him sound terribly shallow, and he's not. Quite the opposite, actually. He always wants to see the best in people, even those who don't deserve it. And that's the reason he's still single. He's not willing to settle. He's waiting for the real deal."

"Well, I guess that's a good thing…right? I hate to sound selfish, but I'm glad he's never found Mrs. Right. I really like him, Lily. He's so sweet and charming. Sometimes I can't even form a coherent thought when he's around. I've never been kissed stupid before. He just melts my brain." Emma sighed and felt the resulting flutter in her chest when she realized the extent of her admission.

"Oh yes…it's definitely a good thing, Emma. A very good thing. I, for one, think you're perfect for each other."

"I can't help but worry, though. Half my brain is telling me to run away as fast as I can, and the other half is wanting to wrap myself around him and never let go. But I shouldn't try to convince myself that we have a future together, when we don't. I'm leaving, and he's staying. It's pretty simple. If I let myself get too attached, which as you know, I'm prone to do, then I'm setting myself up for one hell of a heartbreak. Right?"

"Right. But…" Lily raised a finger and pressed it to Emma's lips to prevent her protest. "Isn't every relationship a risk in some way?"

Unable to speak, Emma simply nodded her head.

"And you never know how long it will last."

With Lily's finger still pressed against her lips, she could only nod once again.

"So, how is this one any different? You may not even want to date him by November."

Highly unlikely. Lily finally removed her finger from Emma's lips so she could speak. "I keep telling myself to just go with it and see what happens, but it's hard when you know there's an expiration date on it. I've never been with a guy that I've known up front that on *this* date in time, we're breaking up."

"I know, it's not ideal. But better to have loved and lost than to never have loved at all. Isn't that the old saying?" she stated, almost apologetically. "I still think you should go for it. I don't think you really want to walk away anyway. As much as he can't keep his eyes off of you…you're just as bad."

"Is it that obvious?" She already knew the answer, and Lily's unladylike snort confirmed it.

"Uh…yeah. You'd have to be blind not to see you two ogling each other. It's quite cute, actually. I don't want to see you hurt, though, or him either, for that matter. Just whatever you do, use protection. Your parents will never let any of you come here again unsupervised if you come home pregnant too." Lily's expression reflected the mixed emotions that Ali's unexpected pregnancy always caused. Abby's entry into this world may not have been how Ali envisioned starting her family, but the little angel brought so much joy to everyone's lives that she could never be looked at as a mistake.

"You're right about that. No little Parkers for me," Emma winced, her heart painfully twisting as she felt the full impact of the statement…uttered so carelessly, but surprisingly powerful nonetheless.

# CHAPTER 11

Emma woke bright and early after a fidgety night's sleep, practically pulsating with the anticipation of seeing a little slice of Middle Earth...and Noah. She didn't feel tired, but she didn't feel refreshed either, as her restless brain replayed the conversation with Noah from the previous night, over and over again.

Deciding on a long bath to calm her growing anxiousness, she slid her legs over the edge of the bed and headed for the bathroom.

Sinking into the hot water, the fragrant bubbles filled the air with the scent of honeysuckle. The sweet perfume tickled her senses, as her mind drifted back to a simpler time, of carefree afternoons spent traipsing through the wooded common area behind her childhood home, following the overgrown path along the small creek, and listening to the whispered sounds of the water as it washed over the river stones.

Visions of endless days spent exploring with her siblings and a few neighborhood friends, searching for tadpoles, or sitting beside the small pond deep in the forest, flittered through her mind as if watching a home movie. It was an ideal childhood, and one she hoped to provide for her own children one day.

Once she'd entered her teenage years, the sanctuary in the woods became a secluded place to go with friends, with its tree-stump seats encircling the stone-ringed fire pit; it was the perfect hiding spot to escape the ever-watchful eyes of their parents.

Lily softly knocked on the door, then poked her head into the bathroom, bringing Emma back to the present, to let her know they were leaving for their final meeting with the photographer.

Goosebumps spread across Emma's skin as she lifted out of the bathtub and into the cooler air. Reaching into the shower, she turned on the water, and stepped inside the roomy enclosure. The steady drumbeat from the showerhead relaxed her further, as she dipped her head under the spray to wash her hair.

With the constant threat of rain and the ever-present breeze, Emma decided a fishtail braid was the safest bet, as it would carry her through Middle Earth and onto dinner.

Like clockwork, Noah arrived at nine, looking handsome as ever in a pair of comfortably worn jeans and a navy blue T-shirt that stretched tightly across his broad shoulders. His fingers combed through his dark hair as it fell in soft waves, framing his face. It was her favorite look for him, other than shirtless Noah, or maybe naked Noah. She'd bet her life savings, which granted, wasn't very much, that naked Noah was something to behold.

"You look lovely, Emma," Noah stated appreciatively, as she walked into the lounge. She'd dressed in a purple V-neck T-shirt, and a pair of jeans tucked into black riding boots.

"Thanks, Noah. And you don't look so bad yourself." She tried to appear unaffected as she checked him out, but couldn't stop the goofy smile from spreading across her face as she crossed the room, coming to a stop in front of him.

"Glad to see you're wearing boots, as it might be a bit muddy there," he said, with an approving nod towards her choice of footwear.

"That's what I figured. You ready to go? Lily and Josh had an early appointment with the photographer, so they left about thirty minutes ago."

Noah slid his arms around her waist, and she was acutely aware of the feel of his fingers pinching her side as he lowered his mouth to hers. His lips were soft and tasted like mint with a hint of sexy man. "There. Now that's a proper hello. So we're alone, eh? Sure you want to go after all?"

He could see the internal debate playing out on her expressive face as she considered his proposal. She was adorable when she was deep in thought. "I don't know. As tempting as that is…really tempting actually," she smiled. "But, I really, really want to do this. I've been looking forward to it since you mentioned it yesterday. So…yeah, we better go."

Gripping her waist, he pressed his lips to hers for another slow kiss, then pulled away with a knowing smile. "Now I'm ready to go…on our first official date," he chuckled, patting her bottom and then giving it a little squeeze, letting his hand linger there. It fit perfectly beneath his palm, as if it was made just for him.

"Oh, I see what you're doing, Noah," she laughed, walking past him and out the door. "Just to let you know, it's going to take more than one date."

"How many are we talking about, exactly?" he asked, suddenly sounding breathless as he jogged after her.

"I'm not sure, but you'll be the first to know," she teased, pressing the button for the lift.

Placing his joined hands over his heart, a pleading frown spread across his face. "Ballpark, and please be kind to me, Emma."

"My guess would be anywhere from two to ten." He loved the cheeky grin and playful glint in her eyes, a soft giggle escaping from the lips he desperately wanted to lose himself in. It really didn't matter in the grand scheme of things; he was just teasing her, and he'd wait as long as she needed.

"Oi. Ten," he groaned incredulously. "I might spontaneously combust if I have to wait that long," he pronounced, pulling her against him.

She felt so good in his arms and her sassy smile had his heart doing flips and about to burst from his chest, as he leaned in for another kiss.

"Yeah, me too," she chuckled, as they stepped into the lift for the ride down to Noah's waiting car. "So, I guess it's safe to say that ten is definitely out of the question."

"Taking a *Lord of the Rings* fan to the hallowed ground of The Shire has to rank up there, as far as a first date is concerned. Although, technically, we had our first date on New Year's, but I might be persuaded to let that slide, even though I did ask you to go with me, and we shared a pretty spectacular kiss that night, yeah? I think it should qualify as a date. Don't you think?" Noah nudged her shoulder, amused by the thoughtful look on her face. He could see the gears turning in that gorgeous head of hers.

"I don't know, Noah. At the time, I didn't think it was a *date*, date. I thought it was just two friends going to a party together because they didn't have anyone else to go with."

He huffed out a breath. "I promise you, Emma. If I wanted a different date for the party, I could've gotten one." The moment the words spilled from his lips, he wished he could take them back. A tidal wave of panic engulfed him and he held his hands up in surrender at the livid look marring her pretty face. "Hold up, Emma. That didn't come out quite right."

"I should hope not. I never took you for being so…arrogant," she scoffed, and Noah was thankful they were trapped in the lift, because if the offended look on her face was anything to go by, she probably would have bolted. He needed to do some damage control…quickly.

"Oi. What I'm trying to say is that *if* I wanted to go with someone else, I *probably* could've found a date. But honestly, Emma, the only person I wanted to go with was you," he admitted, as he put his arm around her shoulder and tugged her into his side, then gave her his best smile as they stepped into the lobby, thankful that she didn't push him away.

"Oh, I'm sure you could have." Her sarcastic tone let him know she was still annoyed, as he opened the car door for her, but her features had softened a bit, so all wasn't lost.

Noah jogged around the front of his Jeep nervously, grateful she hadn't gone back upstairs. That was a good sign, he told himself, trying not to worry.

Settling into the driver's seat, Noah turned to Emma and took a deep breath, calming himself. "Okay…let's get one thing straight, Emma. I wanted to spend New Year's with you, and *only you*. I wanted to take you out from the minute I laid eyes on you in the pub that night. I can't stop thinking about you, if I'm being completely honest." He didn't want to push her, but needed her to know how he felt, all the same. He reached for her hand, and when he laced their fingers together, squeezing them tenderly, he was relieved when she held on just as tightly.

She twisted in her seat so that she was facing him; her expression was unreadable and he tried to quell his growing anxiety. "Um…"

"You don't need to say anything," Noah interrupted, not wanting to hear the words if she didn't return his affections.

"No. Let me finish, please." The worrisome crease between her brows softened and Noah was able to breathe again. "Since we're being honest, and baring our souls, so to speak. You should know that I feel the same way, and it scares the crap out of me, that it's all happening so quickly." She shook her head and released a nervous laugh, but then turned and confidently fixed her eyes on him.

It was reassuring to know that Emma felt the same way…that he wasn't in this alone. When he gazed into her emerald green eyes, and saw the same need reflected in their bottomless depths, she gave him a glimpse into her very soul. And he wanted to make himself at home there, cuddled under a blanket by the fire that burned inside of her.

At that moment, he didn't wonder if they'd still be together in November, he wondered how he'd survive the rest of his life without her. No matter how many times he told himself that it was crazy to feel this way already, it really didn't matter, because as she sat next to him, he realized he was falling for Emma. Hard.

Noah brought their joined hands to his lips and brushed a gentle kiss across her knuckles.

"Well, it looks like we're on the same page then, and for the record, it scares me too, but it also feels…right," he paused, with a sigh of relief. "So let's enjoy our *second* date, which will include a walk about the countryside, a nice tea for two, and if all goes well…*a lot* of kissing of that pretty mouth of yours." He leaned over the console and pressed his lips to hers for a quick kiss before starting the car and pulling out onto the busy street.

Emma couldn't believe she was actually having lunch at *The* Green Dragon. It was a dream come true, and as she gazed at the gorgeous man sitting across from her, she was glad to be experiencing it with him. Trying to concentrate, she absorbed every detail, not wanting to forget anything.

She took in the cozy dining area, with its oversized stone fireplace and thick wooden beams, which framed the walls as well as the ceiling. The elaborate wood-work was impressive and reminded her of a pub she'd gone to in Buckinghamshire, while on vacation in England.

The likeness to the movie set was remarkable. She could see Sam and Frodo celebrating with Merry and Pippen…a pint of ale in hand, while Rosie Cotton served drinks from behind the bar as happy Hobbits danced about.

Rounded windows overlooked a small lake and a quaint stone foot bridge, leading to a thatched roof cottage, which had a colorful blue door and working water mill. Impossibly green fields of gently rolling countryside melted into a bright blue sky, and completed the picturesque image that looked more like it belonged in a storybook or was painted by one of the masters, than real life.

Emma couldn't contain her glee as the pint of Girdley Ale settled nicely in her empty stomach. Even the waitress openly flirting with Noah couldn't dampen her spirits, as he ordered two servings of the Stockbrook, without giving the waitress a second look, and she ordered the Green Hill.

"Mmm…This is so good," Emma moaned, as she tucked into her meal, then almost fumbled her utensils at the naughty grin engulfing Noah's face. His pale blue eyes had turned a dark sapphire, revealing a very different type of hunger.

Leaning over the table, he stealthily glanced over both shoulders, making sure no one was eavesdropping. "Please don't do that in public, and maybe not even in private, unless it's me giving you that much pleasure."

Emma felt the sudden spike in her blood pressure as she evaluated the gist of his words, letting them settle over her. She bet he knew how to do it too, or at least she hoped so. What a pity that would be, she thought, if he was all show and no go. "Promises, promises," she seductively replied, taking another bite.

"Oh, trust me. You'll do more than moan when I finally get my hands...and other parts...on you."

Emma went to laugh, but choked on her roast beef instead; she quickly took a drink of ale to rinse down the offending piece of meat, and to catch her breath. Knowing her face was an unnatural shade of red, she hoped he thought it was from her food going down the wrong way, and not his comment, which wasn't necessarily unwelcome, just unexpected.

Of course, the waitress chose that moment to come by, as Noah reclined in his chair, a smug grin spreading across his too-handsome face.

"That was not nice. Are you trying to kill me?" Emma complained, once the waitress had left their table.

"Oh, trust me, sweetheart, killing you is the last thing I'd want to do. There are far too many things I'd like to do to you...and with you, and they require you to be amongst the living."

Two could play this game, she told herself, as she looked around the small dining room. "Someone is very confident in his abilities." Ignoring the heat rising in her cheeks and the cocky smirk on Noah's face, she straightened her back and looked him in the eye. "And I'll have you know that you may feel like you've died and gone to heaven when I get my hands...and um...other parts...on you, too." The stunned look on his face was priceless, and she let out an amused chuckle as she watched him squirming in his chair.

"Touché, sweetheart. Now, we need to change the subject before I either embarrass myself, or take you in one of those little Hobbit Holes you're so fond of."

Her eyes opened wide as she released a startled laugh. "You're funny. A Hobbit Hole? But fine. There's enough wood in this room already, no need to add any more." She smiled mischievously, closing her eyes and taking another bite, teasing him with a breathy moan, wanting to push him just a little.

"You're playing with fire, baby. I'm warning you…unless you want to skip the tour, you need to stop that. We can grab a room back in town, but I don't suspect you want to do that…unfortunately, so you need to behave yourself." He shrugged his shoulder disappointedly, and took another bite, trying for nonchalance, but failing miserably. What he really wanted to do was spread her out on the table and feast on her. The food was delicious and he was hungry, he just wasn't sure if he'd ever be able to satisfy his hunger for the beautiful woman sitting in front of him.

"You're right, I'm sorry. I'll behave, but it wasn't just me, you know. You're just as guilty as I am, so you need to behave, too," Emma stated, pointing her fork at him, a playful sparkle lighting up her face.

"Good as gold. And I will. I know how chuffed you were about coming here today, and I wouldn't want to disappoint you."

"Trust me, Noah. You could take me to lunch in your garage and I wouldn't be disappointed," she stated honestly. "But I'm not going to lie, being here is a dream come true."

"You should set your standards a wee bit higher than a garage, but it's good to know that anything above that will impress you."

"It should be noted that your garage is attached to a very impressive beach house, so they aren't that low," she clarified, lifting her right shoulder to her ear.

"Duly noted." He'd worked hard to be able to afford that house, staying focused on his goals, and taking care of his money. He planned to share it with a wife and children one day, and looking across the table at Emma, he wanted to share it with her, to build a life with her.

As they toured the rolling hills and dales of Hobbiton, strolling hand in hand, Noah reveled in the joy radiating in excited waves off of Emma. He knew she'd like it, but her reaction was exceeding his wildest expectations.

Bouncing from Hobbit Hole to Hobbit Hole, she spiritedly explained to him who each one belonged to, and he couldn't hold back his laughter when she started skipping down the path in front of Bag End animatedly singing, "I'm going on an adventure. I'm going on an adventure." She really was a geek. An adorable geek, but a geek nonetheless.

She took picture after picture of them in front of the various underground homes, built into the hillside, overlooking the bucolic New Zealand countryside. Colorful round doors greeted visitors and endless flower beds exploded with blooms in every shade of the rainbow. You'd have to be dead not to be cheerful in such a happy place, Noah thought to himself. He'd heard it said that Disneyland was the happiest place on earth, and maybe that was true, but as far as Middle Earth was concerned, that honor clearly belonged to The Shire.

The transformation of the typical New Zealand farm into one of literature's most beloved and iconic locations was astounding. From the overflowing vegetable gardens, to the neatly stacked firewood in front of the little houses, and the tiny Hobbit trousers hanging from clotheslines, it really was remarkable how real the little village felt.

Their tour guide happily indulged all of Emma's questions, but was a little too enamored with her for his liking. Noah hadn't missed the glances that held for a beat too long, or the way he sidled up next to her, pointing out something of interest. He couldn't really blame the bloke, she was alluring on her worst of days, but as she danced her way through the green grass, unable to contain her excitement, she was simply irresistible.

Leaning her head against the passenger seat of Noah's car, Emma let out a deep breath and looked over her shoulder, he really was beautiful, she thought to herself. He'd promised her a day she'd never forget, and so far he'd delivered on every count.

Thick dark hair fell in windblown waves, and a stray curl flopped against his forehead. She resisted the urge to brush it back into place, and instead leaned over the center console and ghosted her lips over his in a chaste kiss, which quickly heated into a fire that rivaled the molten lava of Mt. Doom as he pulled her onto his lap, settling her against him with her legs straddling his hips.

Ignoring the fact that they were in a public parking lot and that her knee was painfully wedged between the seat and the door, Noah's hand cradled her head, holding her there as their tongues mated in a seductive dance, guaranteed to shatter any doubts of how badly he wanted her.

Out of breath, she finally pulled away, placing her shaking hands against his chest, fisting his shirt between her fingers. "Thank you, Noah. At the risk of sounding like a total nerd, today's been one of the highlights of my entire life. I first saw *The Lord of the Rings* movies in middle school and dreamed of walking in the footsteps of Hobbits ever since. I will honestly never forget today, so thank you." She was desperate for him to know, to somehow convey, how much it meant to her.

"And I'm not through with you yet. Still have to wine and dine you. But I'm glad you got to check something off your bucket list...with me." He smiled that perfect smile that left nothing to the imagination, as his eyes gleamed with a desire that at once frightened and delighted her.

"I did, and I'm glad you were with me, too. It was even more special sharing it with you, even if you weren't as excited to see a little corner of Middle Earth as I was." She poked him playfully in the chest and then left her hand there, enjoying the feel of his wildly beating heart, rubbing circles with her thumb as his gaze lowered to watch the hypnotic motion.

"I'm finding that if you're happy then so am I, sweetheart. I had a lot of fun today, too. It's funny how, growing up here you forget how beautiful it is, until seeing it through someone else's eyes. You tend to go about your business, not looking around to enjoy the view," he admitted.

"And what a spectacular view it is." Stroking his soft cheek, Emma tenderly gazed into his eyes, hoping he understood the true meaning of her statement.

"You're going to make me blush, Emma," Noah laughed, leaning in for another kiss, this one slow and sweet.

Closing her eyes, Emma focused on the feel of his tongue gently stroking hers as he made love to her mouth. And the steadiness of his hands ghosting up and down her ribcage, his thumbs brushing against the outer swell of her breasts, lingering there before dropping to her waist, and dipping inside the edge of her jeans, before slowly returning to her breasts, left her aching for more.

Emma was left in stunned silence when Noah finally ended the kiss. There were no words that needed to be spoken. Even though it lacked the explosive passion of their earlier kiss, this one conveyed a deeper connection, one not lost on Emma.

The sting of tears burned the backs of her eyes as the full impact hit her, and an inexplicable calm settled over her. She was safe with Noah. Her heart was safe with Noah.

Inhaling a shaky breath, Noah appeared to be as affected as she was, as he searched her eyes for reassurance. Drawing her snugly against his chest, his fingers burrowed into her skin, as if needing something to hold on to. Knowing exactly how he felt, she clung to him for dear life, wishing they weren't sitting in the middle of a parking lot.

They stayed like that for a long while, quietly enjoying the feel of each other's touch.

Finally settling her into the passenger seat, he reached for her hand once he put the car in drive. "We have reservations to keep, and as much as I'd love to sit here devouring that luscious mouth of yours, we need to get a move on."

# CHAPTER 12

The drive back to Auckland was filled with comfortable conversation and, at times, a comfortable silence, as the music from Emma's phone played in the background. She was relieved when Noah didn't retreat like most men would at the first sign of things getting serious, but she didn't want to read too much into the significance of one kiss either, no matter how magnificent it was.

She'd seen the dumbfounded expression on Noah's face in the aftermath, so she was pretty sure it wasn't one-sided, but only time would tell if it was lust or something special on his part.

The restaurant lobby was crowded with patrons waiting to be seated and Emma was glad he'd thought ahead to make a reservation. Knowing she had the tendency to turn into an ogre when she got too hungry, she hoped they were served quickly, because after the long day she was so famished her stomach was cannibalizing itself.

They followed the hostess to a secluded table in the back and Emma would've had to be blind to miss the predatory glances from some of the female diners as they watched Noah stroll by. She also didn't miss the ugly sneers directed her way when they noticed he had company.

Live piano music subtly filled the room, allowing for quiet conversation without the threat of being overheard by the neighboring tables, and candlelight provided a flatteringly warm glow. Even though the dimly-lit room hummed with quiet conversations, Emma felt as if it was just the two of them.

When their food was delivered, her delighted tummy let out a rumble, and she raised her glass in a toast. "Here's to good company, good food, and good beer."

Noah lifted his glass to Emma's. "To a lovely day, spent with an even lovelier woman. Cheers."

"Thanks again, for everything. Today's been one that I'll never forget."

"So, I was wondering when your family was arriving for the wedding." Noah was looking forward to meeting her family. For years he'd heard Lily and Josh rave about them. He also knew how much Emma missed them, since she'd arrived in Auckland.

"They'll be here Monday and I can't wait for everyone to get here. We weren't sure if Mark was going to make it, since he came home for Christmas, but when I spoke to my mother yesterday, she told me he's coming." The smile on her face reminded Noah of a child on Christmas morning. "He can't stay as long as everyone else. Has to leave right after the wedding, but at least he'll be here. I know how much it means to Lily."

"I'm sure...I'm sure you're glad he'll be here, too, and I'm looking forward to meeting all of them."

"I can't wait for you to meet them either. I know I'm not objective or anything, but I think my family's pretty terrific." She spoke with such certainty, that it left Noah utterly conflicted. He loved that Emma was close to her family, but if this thing with her was what he thought it might be, she'd have to choose between them one day, and he was terrified that he'd be on the losing end of that tug of war.

Emma continued with such exuberance that her long braid danced across her shoulder, and he longed to run his fingers through it as he released the tie, watching as it fell in silken waves over her bare chest. The length of it would cover the tips of her naked breasts, her budded nipples teasing him through the veil of long blonde hair, begging his fingers to slowly pull back the curtain...exposing her.

"Hello…hello. Noah." Emma's laugh roused him from his fantasy. "I asked you a question. I thought I'd lost you for a minute there," she giggled, looking at him with perceptive eyes. His stomach stirred and he felt the swell of his arousal pressing uncomfortably against his zipper.

"I'm sorry, Emma. I was distracted for a minute." He felt the temperature in his face heating at his embarrassment. "What did you ask me?"

Her brows knitted together as she eyed him shrewdly. "Well, first off, if you were thinking of someone other than me just now, I'm going to be very upset. And second, I asked you what day you were free next week so I can introduce you to my family. But if that look on your face was for someone else…forget number two." Her blunt reply shocked him, but her apparent jealousy pleased him immensely.

Reaching for her hand, he laced their fingers together across the table, then caressed her wrist with his thumb. Her eyes followed the movement, then slowly climbed back to his, and he took comfort in her response as he continued to hold onto her hand. "To answer your first statement. That was all you, baby. And I've pretty much cleared my schedule until the wedding. Other than a few workouts, I'm free. I wouldn't miss this for anything."

"Okay. Good…and good," Emma sighed, releasing a breath she didn't realize she was holding.

Not normally the jealous type, she felt the sting of it.

If she was being honest with herself, Noah's attention still rattled her a bit. And as if being judged and found wanting by the other women in the restaurant wasn't bad enough, the thought of him fantasizing about another woman made her sick to her stomach.

"Hey," Noah stated softly, tugging on her hand to get her attention. Once she dragged her gaze back to his, he continued. "I meant what I said. I was thinking about you. Only. You. Trust me, Emma."

His tender smile eased the tension building in her shoulders. "I do. I trust you. I'm not normally prone to bouts of jealousy, and I'm not really sure why I feel that way now." Honesty seemed to be her best option when it came to Noah. They didn't have much time together, so playing games would be a waste of his time and hers. "Will you tell me what you were thinking about?"

"Not here. But maybe later I'll show you, if you're a good girl and invite me in when I take you home. Well maybe not a *good* girl." He had to smile at the naughty look on her face, but when her eyes locked onto his, their color changing from emerald green to nearly black, he became painfully hard.

"Well, I'm full. How 'bout you?" Emma stated abruptly, tucking her napkin under the edge of her plate.

"Um…I'm not in a position to get up right now." Discerning eyes skimmed down the length of his torso until reaching the top of the table, lingering there as a sassy smile spread across her beautiful face. "I need a few minutes."

After picturing his granddad in his budgie smuggler…and involuntarily shuddering at the image, he grabbed his wallet and tossed more than enough money on the table, then took her hand and quickly exited the building. He couldn't wait to get her into the privacy of his car so he could get his hands and mouth on her again.

Noah pinned her between the cool steel of his car and the hot steel of his body. Leaving a trail of wet kisses along her jaw, he slowly made his way down her neck. Her breathy sounds and soft whimpers of encouragement sent a jolt of electricity through him, as she tunneled her fingers through his hair. Nipping and licking his way back up to the sensitive spot behind her ear, and without thinking, he lifted his hand to cup her breast and felt her shiver beneath his touch.

Realizing they were still standing in the car park, he reluctantly stepped away and opened her door. "We need to take this somewhere a little more private," he stammered, trying to get himself under control.

"Oh, yeah. Probably a good idea." Her chest was heaving as she caught her breath and he had to fight the urge to put his mouth over the tight peaks protruding through her shirt. Forcing his eyes off the little buds, he watched as she settled herself in the car.

Slamming the door with more force than necessary, he quickly jogged around the front of his car to join her, claiming her mouth again as soon as he shut his door. "Damn, woman, you're killing me. Are Lily and Josh home?"

"They're meeting Josh's parents for dinner, but I'm not sure when they'll be home."

Dammit. "Okay. Then we'll go to my place." It was further away but at least they wouldn't be interrupted.

"I can't. I'm having breakfast with my Aunt and Lily, and then we have our final fittings and a meeting with the florist."

Noah mumbled a string of expletives under his breath, shaking his head, trying to come up with a solution to the problem, when he heard Emma speaking on the phone.

"They're still at dinner. I got the impression that they'll be a while," she stated with obvious relief after ending the call.

It only took a few minutes to get to Emma's, but it felt like an eternity. Surprisingly, he'd held it together long enough to get them home, barely resisting the need to take her against the wall in the lift. Waiting for Emma to open the door was torture, as she clumsily fumbled with the key. His heart pounded violently within his chest as he finally took the key from her trembling fingers and unlocked the door.

Kicking the door shut as he lifted Emma into his arms, his greedy mouth found hers as he carried her to the couch, and he almost lost it when she wrapped her long legs around his waist.

Looking into her eyes, he settled her on his lap, with her long legs straddling his thighs. It was quickly becoming his favorite position to have her in. He couldn't contain the growl as she slowly ran her fingers along the contours of his chest, captivated by her touch.

How he summoned the strength to hold still as she explored every inch of him, he wasn't sure, but when she wound her hand around the back of his neck, holding him to her as she plundered his mouth, his hands started to do some exploring of their own.

Tracing the length of her spine, he settled his hands on her bum, pulling her tightly against him. In the back of his mind, he heard what sounded like a begging groan, not entirely sure who it came from. And not really caring either.

Pressing open-mouthed kisses along the long column of her neck, he slowly ran his thumb under the hem of her shirt. Emma arched her back and rocked her hips along his erection, and whatever control he had left snapped.

He bit down, then sucked hard on her neck, wanting to leave his mark on her, and the feel of her racing pulse beneath his mouth ratcheted up his own need. Running both hands under her shirt, he slid a finger along the waistband of her pants, secretly loving her sexy little whimpers, as he circled her bellybutton with his thumb. Finding her lips again, he slowly lifted her top, exposing her tanned abdomen.

"Oh, Noah. Please don't make me wait. Please. I can't…wait…please," Emma breathlessly pleaded.

"Oh, babe. You're so beautiful."

Finally answering her plea, he lifted her shirt the rest of the way. She may have been the one pleading, but as he stared at the flawless pair of breasts in front of him, covered only by a thin layer of lace, the breath escaped from his lungs and he couldn't think straight.

God, she was exquisite. Hardened nipples teased him through the lace of her bra as he reverently ghosted the tips of his fingers along the edge of the light blue material covering her. She watched as he skillfully explored the swell of her breasts, and he wondered if she realized how sexy it was when the tip of her tongue seductively peeked out from her kiss-swollen lips.

Emma's bronzed skin was like satin, just as he'd imagined it would be. Her chest heaved as she panted with excitement, the motion lifting her breasts mere inches from his lips with each inhalation. His mouth went dry as he ran his thumbs across her nipples, pinching them, and the little breathy sounds she made in response to his touch made him even harder. Needing to taste her, he lowered the lace cups and licked one hardened peak before sucking it into his mouth.

Not forgetting about her other nipple, he lovingly kissed, nibbled, and licked his way from one soft mound to the other, as she held his head to her, driving them both to the brink.

Lifting his gaze to find her eyes on his mouth, watching as he teased the sharp little point with his tongue, her flushed cheeks and hooded lids made him want to beat his chest with the satisfaction of knowing that he'd put that look on her face.

And when she bit down on her plump lip and the corners of her mouth lifted into a saucy grin, his only thought was how amazing it was going to feel when he was finally buried deep inside of her. She cried out as he grazed his teeth over the taut peak, holding it between his teeth, before soothing it with his tongue as he sucked it into his mouth.

He felt the pressure building at the base of his spine as he grew close to release, and if she kept grinding against him, making him feel like he was the king of the world, it wouldn't take long. Incapable of forming a coherent thought at the moment, he was pretty sure he'd lost a few brain cells from lack of oxygen, but he'd never felt so alive.

Suddenly stiffening in his arms, she quickly pulled away and yanked her shirt back into place. She was mumbling something, but he couldn't hear anything over the pounding in his ears.

"What the...?" Noah blurted out at the stricken look on her face, as she hastily slid off his lap and shoved her hand up her shirt to adjust her bra.

Wait a minute...he wasn't done yet, he wanted to be the one with his hand up her shirt, plus all of his blood had pooled in his throbbing erection, which was mourning the loss of her softness rubbing against it.

Still trying to catch his breath, he watched as she removed her hand and then ran it down the length of her top. The rise and fall of her chest mesmerized him as she settled her hand over her rapidly beating heart, trying to calm herself.

Noah was so distracted by her sudden withdrawal that he hadn't realized Lily and Josh had returned home and were now standing in front of them, looking quite amused at what they'd discovered.

Emma's flushed cheeks and plump lips were a dead giveaway as to what they'd been up to, not to mention her aroused nipples, which were clearly evident through the thin material of her shirt. He quickly pulled a pillow onto his lap to cover himself, knowing he wasn't fooling anyone, but he had his pride and didn't want them to see his erection straining against his zipper.

"God, Lily. You scared the life out of me. I thought you were still at dinner," Emma protested, still visibly stunned from their unexpected arrival.

"I spoke to you over an hour ago." Lily was trying not to laugh as she flicked a manicured finger at the obvious red bruise on Emma's neck. "That…better be gone before my wedding."

"What?" Emma's hands went to her neck, found the sensitive spot, and started poking at it, trying to figure out what could have caused it.

Lily turned and pointed that same manicured finger at Noah. "You…keep your mouth off her neck. And any other body part that'll be exposed on my wedding day. I will not…I repeat…I will not, have Emma covered in hickeys in my wedding pictures. Am I making myself clear, Noah?"

"Crystal, Lily. Don't worry. It'll be gone in a few days." He looked at Emma, still dazed from their explosive encounter, and made a mental note to leave another one on the side of her breast, maybe her hip too, if she'd let him get that far. He felt fairly confident that, if they'd been left on their own, she would have.

Josh took particular pleasure in teasing Emma good-naturedly, but she took it in stride, as Noah placed a protective arm around her and curled her into his side, settling into a comfortable conversation about the wedding and the newlyweds' upcoming honeymoon in Bora Bora.

Long hours later, Emma tried to stifle a yawn, but Noah could see the exhaustion in her eyes. Reaching for her hand, he lifted her off the couch. "Time for bed." He didn't miss Emma's startled eyes darting quickly to him and then to Lily.

"I'm tired too," Lily added as she got up. "Good night, and don't forget we're meeting my mum for brekkie. Hopefully, that will've faded by morning."

Emma's hand automatically went back to her neck, worrying the spot once again. "Yeah, I know. Good night."

Noah sensed her unease and pulled her into his arms. "Hey...We don't have to do anything you're not comfortable with. You know that, right?"

"I know, and thanks. I think I may've gotten caught up in the moment before. Got a little carried away." She smiled shyly at Noah through her dark lashes, and he felt the breath get caught in his windpipe. Did she have any idea that with just one look she could bring him to his knees?

"Don't worry, Emma. It's fine. Can't say that I'm not ready, because I'm totally ready to take you to bed straight away...especially, since I've gotten a wee peek at your goodies now, but I don't want to push you."

Emma lifted onto her toes to give him a gentle kiss. "I'm not saying that you can't touch me, because I want that, but do you think we could slow down a little? At least try to?"

"Sure. Don't worry about it, sweetheart." Powerless to resist, he lifted his hands to cup her breasts. "Besides, I could get lost for a while...right here."

Emma arched her back, filling his hands as he caressed her. "Mmm...That feels really nice, but I still can't believe we were here for an hour. It only felt like a few minutes."

"Time flies when you're having fun, baby. I could have feasted on your luscious melons for hours." His thumbs teased her budded nipples, and he hardened too.

"My melons? That's so cheesy," she laughed, then gasped when he smoothly lowered his mouth to hers for a hungry kiss. Her hands scrambled to his hair and held him there, as he seductively sucked her tongue into his mouth. Not too rough, but not too sweet either, just right.

"If we keep this up tonight, I'm going to push. Maybe even beg, Emma. I'm trying to be the man you need me to be, but it's damn hard, especially when I'm sporting this." He rubbed the length of him against her stomach, partially to prove his point, but also to gain some relief. Bloody hell, it was going to be a long night.

The thought of spending the night with Noah was tempting…way too tempting actually. He was so cute and just the thought of his mouth devouring her again had her stomach doing flip-flops and her breasts aching for more of his attention.

She'd been embarrassed when Lily and Josh came home, though, finding them in such a compromising position. She wasn't a prude, but wasn't an exhibitionist either; they needed to be more careful in the future.

"I'm sorry, Noah. I don't want you to think I'm a tease, but it's just that everything is moving so fast and it scares me. I'm not sure about you, but I'm really not a casual kind of girl. I know a lot of women are these days, but I'm not made that way. I know it's not very contemporary of me, but I can't change how I feel. It's not just sex for me," she paused, looking over his shoulder at the wall, anywhere but him, feeling completely exposed by her confession, and afraid she might cry. "God, this is so embarrassing."

Noah placed two fingers under her chin, gently lifting it so that she had no choice but to look at him. "Emma, you never need to apologize to me for being who you are. In case you haven't noticed, I think you're pretty terrific. And for the record, I'm not looking for a casual relationship with you either. Sit down with me and let's have a talk."

Leading her to the couch, he settled her next to him. Emma rested her head on his broad shoulder, drawing strength from him, and braced herself for the potentially uncomfortable conversation.

After a prolonged silence, Noah finally spoke. "Look, I think you should know that I'm not looking for a fling or a hook up, or whatever it's called these days. I'm not going to lie and say that I've never done that, because I have, more than I care to admit. I'm not sure where this thing between us will end up, but I'd like to find out. I really like you, Emma, and I think you feel the same way, or at least I hope you do."

When Emma looked into his eyes, she didn't see arrogance or his usual confidence. She saw insecurity and a vulnerability that melted some of her own insecurities.

"I really like you too, Noah. It's just that…" She took a deep breath to steady herself before continuing. "It's just that I get really attached. Not in a creepy, stalker kind of way," she added with a wobbly laugh.

"That's good to know," he smiled reassuringly.

"But I don't know how to do it any other way, and usually end up getting hurt. The pathetic thing is that I always think the other person feels the same way and never see it coming until they're walking out the door."

"We've all been hurt at some point…thought something was more than it was. You're not alone there. I think that's how you can recognize when the right one comes along."

"I know. That wasn't what I meant to say. I got sidetracked a little. My point was that I tend to become attached…too attached. I'm just afraid of getting hurt again when I have to leave. See, this is what I mean. I'm thinking about ten months from now and we've only had two dates. I'm completely dysfunctional. I probably don't have to worry about it though, because right about now you're wondering how fast you can get to the door." She let out an anxious chuckle, feeling way too exposed.

"It would take a lot more than that to scare me away from you. And we may have only had two official dates…glad to see you're on board with me on that one, by the way, but we've probably spent more time together than most new couples do in months. I think Josh and Lily deliberately set it up that way, but I'm not complaining. You're special, Emma. Anyone who didn't recognize that and walked away from you voluntarily was a bloody fool."

Needing to lighten the mood, Emma cupped his face in her hands and placed a gentle kiss on his lips. "You are the sweetest man. How are you still single? I can't figure it out."

Noah laughed, a carefree grin spreading across his face that let her know everything was going to be alright. "I know, really. I have to beat them off with a stick. I'm a total catch. Why have you not dragged me to bed yet?"

Emma let out a relieved giggle. "I have no idea. See. I must be crazy. Totally dysfunctional."

"But I'd like to point out that I'm not single." At her distressed look, he quickly continued. "I'm with you. I'm not seeing anyone else and I don't want to. And I don't share, so I don't want you to either."

Noah reached for a stray strand of hair that had escaped from her braid and twirled it around his finger, visions of his earlier fantasy flashing through his mind.

"I don't want to see anyone else, either," she admitted earnestly, placing a hand on his chest.

"Good. Got that sorted. Now can we go to bed?" Noah asked hopefully with a cheeky grin.

"Nice try, Noah."

He let out a hearty laugh. "Can't blame a guy for trying."

A few days later, Emma asked Noah to go to the pool with her. Swimming was an important part of her life and she wanted to share that piece of herself with him.

Slipping into the cold water always took her breath away, but when she added Noah's chiseled body in a pair of wet board shorts, it left her heart pounding as if she'd already had her workout.

Kicking off the side of the pool, the familiar rush of the water and the rhythm of her steady breathing relaxed her. After finishing her warm-up laps, Emma waited with her arms stretched along the edge of the pool, her legs lazily dangling in front of her, and watched as Noah approached.

A satisfied grin spread across her face at the realization that she was better than he was. This was probably the only sport that she'd win if they competed and she basked in the glory of that small victory.

With years spent as a summer swim instructor and even more participating in various stroke clinics, she evaluated his form as Noah finished the last few feet, gliding easily under the water to surface next to her, his long muscular physique leaving a small wake in the lap lane.

"Why're you so angry at the water? What did it ever do to you?" Emma couldn't help but laugh at his confused expression, his mouth curving into a sexy pout.

He shook his head quickly from side to side, shaking the water droplets loose, and scraped a hand over the planes of his face. "Huh? What're you talking about?"

Emma pushed off the edge of the pool and turned to stand in front of him as she mimicked his movement. "You slap the water with each stroke, like this."

"Okay," he said slowly. "So, I'm guessing that that isn't the right way."

"Well, it'll get you from one side of the pool to the other, just not very efficiently. If you use the proper technique, you conserve energy and can swim longer and faster. This is how you do it the right way." Emma showed him how to hold his hand to slice into the water and then pull back, rolling from side to side as she reached forward with each stroke. She then turned away from him and swam to about mid pool and swam back to him. "See the difference? Now show me your stroke."

Noah's loud outburst of laughter settled into a mischievous grin as he reached out and snaked his arm around her waist, their bodies slipping against each other in the water, her legs instinctively wrapping around his hips. "I'll show you my stroke if you show me yours." One of his hands slid down to hold her bottom and she stifled a moan as his fingers settled dangerously close to her sweet spot.

"Hardy har har, Noah. Get your mind out of the gutter, and anyway, I've already shown you mine. Now, come on, I'm serious, I want to see you do it. Please, Noah, it means a lot to me." Placing a quick kiss on his still-grinning lips, she tried to stay focused. She wasn't sure if he was doing it on purpose or not, but his fingers were inching lower, and with her legs still wrapped around him, she was spread wide open, making it next to impossible to think about anything other than the aching need to have him slip his fingers beneath her swimsuit.

"Fine. You'll have to show me again, though, because I was a little distracted by your tight togs. Your body's bloody amazing and I never would've thought a swim cap and goggles could be such a turn on." He gave her a devilish grin as he squeezed her bottom and then released her, positioning himself to push off the edge of the pool.

Feeling chilled by the loss of his touch, Emma shook her head. "You're such a guy."

"Guilty as." He simply shrugged his shoulder, not ashamed by the accusation.

"Well, it has to be tight so you have less resistance in the pool."

"I'm not complaining. Although I do prefer your teeny bikinis better."

She sliced her hand through the water, sending a wave of water in his direction. "You would."

Emma spent the next hour giving him a private swimming lesson and was pleased to see him pay attention, once he stopped goofing around and concentrated on what she was trying to teach him. She reveled in the fact that no matter how hard he tried, she would always be faster in the pool, and gave a silent thanks to her parents for providing all the years of swimming lessons.

And with the heated looks Noah was giving her, she was also grateful for the body that went along with the hundreds of hours spent doing laps. When they climbed out of the pool, she could feel his eyes on her as they walked to the locker rooms, and there was no need to glance over her shoulder to see if he appreciated the view, because the agonized growl emanating from his chest spoke for itself.

# CHAPTER 13

Waiting for her family to get through security, Emma could hardly contain her excitement as she stood with her Aunt Mary at the airport. Noah had suggested she use his Jeep to help chauffeur everyone, and also to earn him a few brownie points with her family she suspected, so she'd left him with Lily and Josh at her Aunt's house.

Emma's mother, Dianne, walked in front of the group like a mother duck with a long string of ducklings following obediently behind her, everyone looking tired and rumpled after the long flight.

Abby was the first one to spot Emma and immediately squealed and started to squirm in her mother's arms to get down. Reaching for the irritable baby, Emma fought back tears as she settled her on her hip. Breathing in her little girl scent was like coming home after a long absence.

After the gauntlet of hugs and kisses, and more than a few happy tears, they piled everyone, along with a mountain of luggage, into the waiting cars.

Pulling into the driveway, Emma watched as Noah stepped aside, looking uncharacteristically anxious and fidgety. He patiently waited until everyone had finished with their greetings before inserting himself into the family reunion. Emma stood by his side, putting a comforting arm around his waist, and smiled when he placed a gentle kiss on the top of her head as his hand came to rest along the small of her back, his thumb tracing nervous circles there.

One by one, curious eyes fell on Emma as she stood with Noah, and ignoring the weight of their questioning glares and raised eyebrows, she stepped forward to introduce him to her father.

Moving his arm to lace his fingers through hers, he held her hand tightly as if to ground himself, as he reached out his right hand to her father. She watched as her father's confident gaze analyzed their joined hands, and was relieved to see her father's familiar smile as he shook Noah's hand.

Her father was eyeing Noah suspiciously, but thankfully didn't inquire about their relationship status or Noah's intentions with his daughter, which would've been completely mortifying. If her father disapproved of Noah, he gave no indication, his face remaining neutral as they exchanged pleasantries.

Meeting someone's family usually took place in small increments, over time, not in one fell swoop, but Noah seemed to locate his wavering confidence and didn't shy away from her father's questions. Looking at him, she wondered if she'd ever find another man who'd measure up, or if that was even possible.

Her heart twisted painfully when she thought about Noah's future, which unfortunately didn't include her. At least she wouldn't have to see him with someone else, unless she looked him up on the internet or broke down and asked Lily, which she had no doubt she would at some point.

Just the thought of him with another woman on his muscular arm made Emma's stomach ache. Reality told her that he would eventually find someone else, get married, and go on to have adorable little Noahs running around, but it hurt more than it should to know that those children wouldn't be hers being pushed in his heavenly tree swing.

Pushing aside her aching heart and confusing thoughts, she went about the task of introducing him to the rest of her family. As expected, her brothers gave him the third degree, Ali was polite but noticeably wary, and Katie looked him over and then winked her approval.

She quickly came to realize that her aunt had either been talking to her mother about Noah or she'd filled them in on the car ride. Most likely both. The sisters didn't go long without speaking to one another and her mother would undoubtedly want to know everything that Emma wasn't willingly offering up during their weekly telephone conversations.

With six children, Dianne Anderson had gotten creative over the years when her offspring didn't volunteer information on what was happening in their lives, so pumping her loyal sister for information was expected.

Finally free from the confines of her car seat, Abby rolled around on the floor in the lounge, exploring her new environment, but never letting her mother out of her sight, her pudgy hands clinging tightly to her blanket. Abby giggled in the unrestrained way only babies did when Emma snatched her up off the floor and blew raspberries on her little tummy. God, she'd missed this, she thought to herself.

In all the commotion, Emma lost track of Noah, but relief washed over her when she saw him laughing with her brothers. She was tempted to join them, but resisted, figuring it was best to let them forge a friendship on their own, so she went to find her mother. Might as well get the interrogation over with.

Emerging from the guest room after successfully dodging most of her mother's questions, Emma ran into Ali. Bracing herself for a new round of nosy Anderson women, she held her breath and was shocked when Ali walked right past her. Not wanting to draw attention to herself if Ali was momentarily distracted, she stood frozen in place, holding her breath.

Emma went to move quickly in the opposite direction, but when she heard a muffled sniffle she couldn't walk away. So, like the good sister she was, she turned around and followed Ali into Lily's childhood bedroom.

"Hey. You alright?" Emma sat on the bed next to Ali and gently nudged her shoulder with hers.

"Yeah. I'm fine." Ali didn't sound fine, as she wiped away the tears that were now falling freely down her cheeks.

"What's wrong?"

"It's just being back here with Abby. It's a lot harder than I thought it would be. Everywhere I look, I'm reminded of Evan. And as much as I hate him, I still love him. But, I'll be fine. I just need a few minutes."

Emma's heart broke for her sister. Ali looked defeated as she sat hunched over with her elbows poking her knees, her face buried in her hands. "Are you still going to call him?"

"Yeah. It's scary though. What if he doesn't want to see her? Or me?"

"Then it's his loss on both counts. But you need to be the bigger person and at least offer to let him see her."

"I know. But I'm also afraid of him falling in love with her, too. Does that make me a bad mother? Because that's how I feel."

"No one could ever accuse you of being a bad mother, Ali. One look at that happy and healthy baby out there and there's no doubt about that. But why would you be worried about him falling in love with his own daughter? I don't get it." Emma placed a comforting hand on Ali's back, slowly rubbing up and down the length of her spine.

"What if he wants to share custody of her? I can't be away from her, Emma. It'll kill me. And it's not like he lives nearby." Ali's anguished expression broke Emma's heart in two. She couldn't imagine Ali spending even one night apart from her little girl.

"If that happens, then you'll have to figure something out that works for both of you. But you'll regret it if you keep Abby away from her father, if he wants to see her. And she will too in the long run. You can always come and stay here while she's with him, if it comes to that. You know Aunt Mary would love to have you… or you could stay with Lily and Josh, for that matter."

"I know but…what if he's with someone else?"

"That's a whole nother issue," Emma answered seriously. "And I suspect that it's more about you than Abby. And he could say the same thing about you if you marry someone else. It's inevitable though, isn't it? At some point, both of you will probably get married. I don't see you growing old alone. But I think we're getting ahead of ourselves. Let's see what he says when you talk to him."

"I left him a message before we left, but I haven't heard back from him yet."

"Well then, the ball's in his court. If you don't hear back from him by tomorrow, call him again, and then you've done your part. But hey...I've missed you." Emma wrapped her arms around Ali and hugged her tightly.

"I've missed you, too. So, tell me about Noah. What's going on with you two?"

"I knew that was coming." Emma pulled away from Ali and laughed, releasing some of the tension. "I really like him and we've been seeing a lot of each other since I got here. He's a great guy. Really sweet."

"Just be careful, Emma. I don't want to see you get hurt again."

"Honestly, I think it's inevitable either way, if he left me tomorrow or when I leave. I'm just going to try to enjoy what little time I have with him and then go home and somehow find a way to move on. That makes me every kind of fool, I know, but I can't help myself. He's amazing, and if he lived in North Carolina, I'd be picking out names for our future children." Emma couldn't stop the nervous giggle as she spoke the sobering words.

"Oh, God, you've got it bad, sis. I guess I can't talk you out of it, so I'll give you some sisterly advice. Please take care of yourself and remember that it's not forever. Try to keep that in mind when you're with him. And whatever you do... *Do. Not. Get. Pregnant.*" Ali gently shook Emma's shoulders, emphasizing each word, and released a small chuckle, and Emma was relieved to see the smile return to her sister's tear-streaked face.

"I won't get pregnant and I'm trying to keep things in perspective. Although, I don't think I'm wired that way. But I'm working on it."

"I'll start stocking up on tissues. But seriously, Emma. Be careful." Ali affectionately tugged on a lock of Emma's hair. "I wish I could convince you to walk away now. It'd be a lot easier to do it now. Trust me. But you know I love you and I'll be there for you when you come home."

"I know, and I love you too. I've missed you so much." Emma pulled Ali into a tight embrace. It felt so good to see her again, to talk to her, face to face. She wasn't just a sister, she was her best friend. "Are you alright now? Ready to go back out there?"

"Sure, let's go."

The next few days flew by in a swirl of activities and final wedding preparations. After the rehearsal dinner, they all gathered at Lily's parents' house to continue the celebration. The loud and energetic group were summoned to the lounge by Emma's father with a loud whistle.

Noah entered the room to find Emma, with her guitar slung over her shoulder, standing next to her brother Steven, with their heads together in quiet conversation. Emma's Aunt Mary quickly set two bar stools next to them, before addressing the crowd.

"My sister and I have asked her two very talented children to entertain us with a few songs tonight. The first few are personal requests that they've graciously agreed to play for us, but I think they've got their own ideas for what follows." She let out a shaky breath as she turned to address Lily and Josh. "Lily…you know how much we love you and we're so thankful that you've found a lovely man to spend the rest of your life with. We couldn't be happier to welcome Josh into our family. And Josh…you've brought so much happiness and joy to our Lily's life and we're blessed to call you one of our own. Now, before I start to cry like a baby… Cheers." Her voice trailed off, as she raised her glass and nodded for Emma and Steven to begin.

A hush fell over the room as Emma's beautiful voice quieted everyone. He knew the song was meant for Lily and Josh, but as the words fell from her lips, he felt like he was the only person in the room.

Her eyes met his as she sang of finding true love along the broken road, and he stopped breathing. Emma was the most beautiful woman he'd ever seen, and he wondered if it was possible to be in love with her already. He wasn't sure if what he was feeling was true love or not, but that broken road had led her strait to him and he wasn't going to muck it up.

Looking around the room, his gaze fell upon her mother, who was beaming with pride, her husband's arms folded around her, wiping tears from her face as she quietly sang along with her children.

Noah stood in the back of the room sharing a beer with Josh, resisting the urge to take Emma into his arms and kiss her senseless. To show his love for her like that in front of her family probably wouldn't be well received, and the way he wanted to kiss her would surely get him thrown out on his bum.

Steven smiled at Emma as they began to play another song. More upbeat than the last one, but once again Noah's breath was stolen from his lungs when his eyes met hers. Those expressive green eyes that were a window to her soul were staring back at him. Those eyes held him captive. Those eyes reflected the same love that he felt.

Bottomless pools of green locked onto him. Mesmerized, he couldn't take his gaze off of her, and when she sang the words to the song, everything seemed to fall into place. "Thursday, Friday, short or long. When you got a love so strong. How can it be wrong now? Mercy me. Be mine, be mine."

Whatever piece of his heart that hadn't belong to her already, she now owned. She owned him. Lock, stock, and barrel. Standing with his feet cemented to the ground, as a vision of her as his bride flashed before his eyes, and feeling completely overwhelmed and sobered by the image, he was relieved when the song was over and Steven started speaking.

"Enough of the sappy shit." At his mother's reprimand, Steven lowered his head and added bashfully. "Sorry, Mommy. But now let's change gears and kick this up a bit, shall we?"

Steven sat on the stool and began to play, and all Noah could think was… wow. His gaze moved to Emma, who was watching her brother in awe, with a huge smile on her face as she provided the rhythm for him. Steven's fingers moved along the strings with purpose and skill, showcasing his expertise, and when he added his vocals to the song, Noah wondered why he didn't play professionally, he was certainly talented enough.

When the song was over, Emma raised herself off her stool and bowed in mock worship of him, as her brother Luke called him a show off. Steven flipped him the bird and then quickly apologized to his parents, once again. Their easy camaraderie was evident as the family joked and teased one another.

Steven then turned to Emma and she nodded to him as they started playing an upbeat country song about cold beer on a Friday night and a pair of jeans that fit just right. The song suited Emma and her loving family, and as he looked around the room, his heart sank with dread. Ali was dancing with a giggling Abby in her arms, Emma's parents were clapping and singing along, and her other brothers were laughing and teasing Katie and Lily.

As they played the song that painted a picture of southern living, love, and family, he wondered how he could remove Emma from them. The lyrics weren't just symbolic, they were a reflection of how they lived. She was a part of them and they were a part of her. Would she even consider leaving that behind for him? Could he even ask her to?

It was easy to imagine Emma sitting at a scenic overlook on a mountaintop with close friends surrounding her, laughing, drinking, and playing music together. It was an ideal picture of a life that suited Emma. That was Emma at her core. It was her home.

As they happily performed, unaware of his distress, Noah felt his heart seize painfully inside his chest as his despondency grew deeper and deeper. She had a good life, filled with a loving family and friends. At the moment of realization, he felt defeated, having lost the battle before it had even begun.

Emma set her guitar down when they were done and observed him with concerned scrutiny, as if she could read his troubled thoughts. Making her way to him, she circled her arms around his waist, rocking him into her. Her thumbs threaded through the belt loops of his jeans in an intimate embrace, and her face lit up with that perfect smile he'd miss when she was gone.

Swallowing his heartbreak, he brushed her lips with a gentle kiss. She felt so right in his arms. How could they not be together? Was this karma paying him back for previous wrongs? He'd fallen in love with a woman that he couldn't have.

Tilting her head, she looked at him through squinted eyes. "Are you alright?"

"Yeah, yeah I'm fine," he lied. He was anything but fine…confused, heartbroken, and completely gutted, those were more appropriate words to describe how he was feeling. Definitely not fine. "You were amazing, Emma. Reckon I now have some more songs to add to my playlist, eh?" He let out an unsteady laugh, trying to quell his rising panic.

Emma eyed him inquisitively. "Are you sure? You don't look so good. Let's go outside and get some fresh air. You look like you could use it."

As if he had any choice in the matter, Noah dutifully followed her outside. She sat on the porch swing and patted the seat next to her. "Come over here and sit with me."

For a long while, they sat together in silence, hand in hand, gently swaying. The only noise was the din of laughter and conversation from inside the house.

Noah finally gathered his wits and broke the silence. "You miss home, don't you?"

Emma replied quickly, too quickly for his well-being. "Like crazy." Two little words. That's all she said, but it spoke volumes. Two simple words that left him feeling helpless and alone.

"I've missed you this week." He was pathetic, he thought to himself. If he couldn't go a few days without her presence, he was in trouble. Since her family had arrived in En Zed, her time had been consumed with family outings and maid of honor duties, leaving little time for him, other than a few late night phone calls before falling asleep.

Feeling homesick himself, he'd made a trip to Hamilton to spend the day with his family. The whole time he was there, he'd wished Emma was by his side. He wanted to show her his hometown, to introduce her to his family. He hadn't brought a woman home to meet his mum and dad in years, but he wanted Emma to meet them.

His mum had always been the most important woman in his life, but Emma was quickly gaining equal footing. He'd no doubt his mum would approve of her, and love her as much as he did.

Emma turned to face him and propped her chin on his shoulder, letting out a deep breath that tickled his neck. "I've missed you, too. I've gotten so used to you being there all the time. I love my family to death…don't get me wrong, but at the same time, I missed you. I've been lonely without you. I know that's crazy," she chuckled, her delicate voice trailing off, as her fingers skimmed along the buttons of his shirt, causing a shudder to race up his spine.

Needing to feel her, he reached for her legs and draped them across his lap. Resting his hand on her leg, he rubbed circles with his thumb on her inner thigh. With her like this, he was able to forget his worries. Nothing else mattered but having her tucked securely in his arms. "That's not crazy at all."

Lifting her chin with two fingers, he brought his lips to hers. Needing it to be more than just a kiss, he kept it gentle and sweet, trying to somehow convey the depth of his feelings for her, as his heart swelled with love for the amazing woman who had come into his life and turned his world upside down and inside out.

With her family on the other side of the wall, he couldn't take it any further; it would have to wait until they were alone. Unfortunately, that wouldn't happen for another week when her family returned to the States.

Stealing these few moments would have to hold him over, and he was filled with a renewed sense of hope and purpose. He would love her while he had the chance, cherishing every precious moment, then it would be up to her to decide if they had a future together. When the time was right, he'd present his case for her to stay with him. She'd be his judge and jury, and he would have to live with whatever sentence she handed out.

The night before the wedding, Noah finally found himself sleeping in his bed at Josh's place again, but it wasn't the same. The fragrant aroma of honeysuckle lingered in the room and on Emma's pillow. A scent that would forever be branded onto his consciousness as a reminder of her.

She'd filled the room with framed photos of family and friends, and right next to her pillow, on the night table, was a picture of them from New Year's. His chest tightened with the realization that it was the last thing she saw before she closed her eyes each night. Without thinking, he stretched for his phone.

"Hey, babe."

"Hi, handsome."

"Guess where I am," he teased.

"I don't know, Noah. Where are you?" She answered in a tired voice that sounded breathless and sinfully sexy.

"I'm in your bed, looking at a lovely picture of us." He reached out and picked up the picture to get a closer look.

"Oh, really. I hope you don't mind that I did that." She sounded insecure as she replied and he heard the sheets ruffling through the phone line as she shifted, confirming his suspicion.

"Don't mind at all. In fact, I want one too. Would you make one for me?"

"Sure. I'd love to. So…what did you guys do tonight?" He could hear the trepidation in her voice and wanted to ease it.

"We went out for a few drinks and then came back here and played cards. Your brothers left a little bit ago, with heaps of my money, I might add."

She exhaled loudly into the phone. "Oh, sorry about that. So…no strippers before Josh gets tethered to the old ball and chain, huh?"

"No. No strippers," he laughed.

Her brothers would've probably kicked his ass if he ogled another woman in their presence. Not that he wanted to anyway. The only woman he wanted dancing naked in front of him was Emma. And he'd bet the deed to his beach house that she'd be quite brilliant at it too, he mused.

"Good. I don't think Lily would be too happy if you did. No woman wants her man to have another woman's tatas in his face." And neither would she, he suspected. He quite liked her possessive side.

"Probably not."

"And, I don't think Josh would like it if some oiled-up guy was wiggling his package in Lily's face either." *Oh, hell no*, he wanted to yell. The only wedding tackle that would be wiggled, dangled, or otherwise in Emma's face would belong to him.

"Yeah, I don't think that would go over too well," he snickered.

After a prolonged silence, thinking about getting naked and wiggling with a certain leggy blonde, he asked. "Are you alone?"

"Right now I am. Katie's helping Ali with the baby. Her sleep schedule's all off and Ali's having a hard time getting her to go to bed."

"Oh. Is she going to be a while?"

"I don't know, why?" she questioned with a sexy giggle.

"I was just wondering how long we had to talk."

"To talk? Is that what you call it?" Her soft laugh left his body humming.

He let out a hearty laugh. "Are you propositioning me, Emma?"

"No," she chuckled. "I just thought you wanted to have phone sex or something. I was waiting for you to ask me what I'm wearing."

God, he loved her laugh.

"Would you? If I asked?" His blood pressure spiked and he was instantly as hard as a rock at the thought of Emma pleasuring herself while he listened, giving her instructions.

"I don't know. Definitely not right now, but I've never done that before. Have you?" she whispered into the phone, and he could hear the subtle shifting of the sheets as she moved.

"No, me neither. But there's always a first time for everything." He rolled over and stared at the ceiling, wishing she was there with him, wrapped around him, whispering in his ear.

"I suppose," she paused, sighing deeply. "Noah?" The breathless way she said his name sent a thrill straight to his heart and left his arms aching to hold her.

"Yes," he choked out, feeling the tickle of her breath against his skin through the phone.

"I miss you. Is it horrible of me to wish my family didn't take up all my time?" He could hear the guilt-ridden tone of her voice as she made her confession.

"Maybe. Is it selfish of me to wish they didn't either?" He missed her touch. He missed her laugh. He missed her smile. He missed her everything.

"Maybe," she laughed. "I guess we're horrible and selfish people then. We make quite a pair. Don't we?"

"Yes. We do."

"Well, I better go. Katie just came back in the room. Good night, Noah."

"Good night, Emma."

Ending the call, he rolled over and placed the photo back on the night table and fell asleep with his arms wrapped around her pillow, surrounded by the sweet scent of honeysuckle and Emma.

# CHAPTER 14

Lily and Josh's wedding was taking place on a bluff overlooking the cerulean waters of the Hauraki Gulf, and eighty guests were waiting patiently in their seats for the ceremony to begin. A harpist sat off to the side, providing soft background music, and a welcomed breeze offered relief from the summer sun.

With a quick hug and a dubious promise to try not to cry, Emma left Lily and followed precisely five seconds after her sister Ali, towards the arbor decorated with pink and white roses and the man who would always make her think of colorful fireworks, breathtaking sunrises, and slow sensual kisses under a moonlit sky.

Seeing Noah dressed in a black tuxedo standing at the end of the aisle, it was easy to imagine him excitedly waiting just for her on their wedding day. She knew it was silly, to let her mind wander in that direction, but he looked so handsome standing next to Josh and the other groomsmen that she couldn't help herself. They were all good looking men, but none of them made her heart go pitter-patter... except for Noah.

Emma took a moment to fully appreciate the sight of him; he really was the most beautiful man she'd ever known. His dark hair fell in loose waves, making her want to run her fingers through it, and his piercing blue eyes were like a beacon in the night, calling her home.

Noah's intense gaze made her feel beautiful and sexy, as he watched her slowly approaching the arbor at the end of the carpeted aisle. Emma loved the way he made her feel like she was the only girl in the room, or in this case, on the crowded bluff.

She felt so pretty in her sleeveless floor length periwinkle gown, with her hair pulled up into a chic bun, as she carried a small bouquet of wildflowers. The afternoon sun warmed her skin and Noah's crooked smile warmed her in other, more private places.

Giving her a quick wink, Noah mouthed 'you look beautiful', as she reached the arbor, and when the wedding march began to play, everyone turned to watch Lily stroll down the aisle on her father's arm.

The bride carried a colorful bouquet of forget-me-nots, and her dress was romantic and feminine with cap sleeves, an empire waist, and delicate beading. The A-line silhouette was flattering on her lean figure and the lace detail on the dress was timeless...elegant...Lily.

As the happy couple recited their vows to love, honor, and cherish each other, Emma felt a tear slide down her cheek. She was so thrilled for Lily, that she'd found her happily ever after. And true to form, once they were pronounced man and wife, Josh laid a kiss on his blushing bride that was completely inappropriate for mixed company.

Rowdy cheers erupted from the small gathering of loved ones as the newlyweds practically floated down the aisle arm in arm, laughing and grinning from ear to ear.

The photographer led them away from the ceremony so pictures could be taken of the wedding party and immediate family members, and after an hour of smiling so much their cheeks ached, they finally joined the rest of the guests for the reception.

After Lily and Josh were introduced for the first time as Mr. and Mrs. Josh Thornton, they danced to 'Someone Like You' by Van Morrison. Watching Josh sing the sentimental song to his new wife, as Lily buried her face in the crook of his neck, Emma shed another batch of tears.

When the rest of the bridal party were instructed to join the newlyweds, Noah held out his hand and led Emma to the center of the dance floor. Folding his arms around her waist as they slowly swayed to the music, he was struck once more by how right she felt in his arms.

"Have I told you how beautiful you look?" he asked, giving her a little twirl before settling her against his chest once again.

The moment she emerged from the clubhouse would be etched on his memory forever, and as she made her way down the aisle, he forgot to breathe. She literally took his breath away.

"Um...yeah," she chuckled, then hastened to add. "But I'll never get tired of hearing it from you. And I have to say that you look way too good in this tux. I'm going to have to beat the ladies off with a stick."

"Just *stick* with me, babe, and we'll be fine...together." When she looked into his eyes through her smoky lids and long dark lashes, he was reminded of the night they met. He'd wanted to kiss her so badly that night, but resisted, not wanting to scare her off.

Tonight, however, was completely different. Tilting his head slightly, he claimed her lips with his and lost himself in the taste of her. God, he loved her mouth. Her lips were soft and supple and when his tongue found hers, he found a little slice of heaven.

After long hours dancing the night away, Emma dragged Noah from the crowded dance floor, and finding an abandoned table in the corner, she looked at him with an amused smile on her face. "I have a joke for you."

She was more than a little tipsy and her slightly slurred speech was adorable. "Oh, really?"

"Why are brides unlucky?" she asked, trying to stifle a giggle as she placed two fingers over her lips.

"I don't know. Why are brides unlucky?"

"Because they don't get to marry the best man." Unable to hold back any longer, she rewarded him with a loud laugh, and settled her cute little bum on his lap.

Noah couldn't help but join in, laughing at the delightfully satisfied expression on her pretty face…and the joke, of course. "Very cute, baby."

Long strands of blonde hair hung loosely around Emma's face and down the back of her neck, giving her an 'I was just thoroughly shagged' look, and Noah couldn't resist pulling out the remaining pins, which were still valiantly trying to hold up her thick head of hair after the long night. Finally releasing it from its bonds, he combed his fingers though the silky length of golden sunshine as it fell along her shoulders and down her back.

Burying his face in the warmth of her neck, Noah breathed in the floral scent of her shampoo, kissing her there as she shuddered beneath his touch. He reveled in the feel of her fingers digging into his shoulders, grounding him, as she tipped her head back, allowing him better access to her throat.

When he landed on the sensitive spot behind her ear, she whimpered and gripped him tighter. And utterly incapable of resisting her, he shifted to her full lips and kissed her there, before begrudgingly backing away. It physically hurt to stop, and her squirming in his lap wasn't helping the automatic response his body always had to hers, which left his trousers feeling decidedly uncomfortable.

All he wanted to do was unzip her dress…slowly…watching as it fell in a pool at her feet, to get a squiz at what she was hiding under there. He'd already had a peek at the most spectacular pair of breasts he'd ever seen, with dusky pink nipples that pebbled at his touch, but he longed to see the rest of her. He ached to taste every inch of her soft skin and, after satisfying his hunger, to bury himself inside of her.

Knowing that she wasn't coming home with him was killing him. He wanted her so badly he couldn't sleep at night, longing to hold her in his arms and make love to her until they were both spent and satiated, only to wake up in the morning and start all over again.

Just the thought of Emma crying out his name as she came undone for him, had his hand slipping lower, caressing the round globe of her bum as he claimed her mouth once more, his tongue tangling with hers in a slow seductive dance.

As if they could read his mind, he felt the eyes of at least one of her brothers burning a hole in the back of his head. Happy with the progress he'd made with the male members of her family so far, and preferring to keep his man parts in working order, Noah knew not to take it any further. They were extremely protective of their sisters, and seeing someone groping one of them in public probably wasn't going over too well.

Reluctantly, he lifted Emma off his lap and set her on her feet in front of him, letting his hands come to rest on her hips, enjoying the feel of the soft fabric of her dress and the softness of her body underneath it even more.

He groaned as she stepped between his thighs and raked her fingers back and forth through his hair. Each swipe of her nails against his scalp stoked the fire that was burning for her. Only for her. Needing a moment to gather his strength, to resist tossing her over his shoulder and having his way with her in the nearest closet, he rested his forehead against her soft belly, breathing her in.

Knowing only a thin layer of material stood between his lips and the Promised Land, only increased his suffering. Oi, her brothers were going to kick his ass before the night was through, he was sure of it.

At brunch the following morning, Emma was happy to hear that Ali had finally spoken to Evan and they'd made plans to meet at the local domain. So after strapping Abby into her stroller with visibly shaking hands, Ali set off for the short walk to the park.

A tortuous few hours later, Ali finally returned with a combination of relief, sadness, and happiness tinging her face. After getting Abby settled, Ali collapsed onto the couch with a loud grunt.

"Well, come on now. Let's hear it," Emma's mother finally chimed in, breaking the deafening silence.

"I don't know where to start," Ali replied after a few moments.

"How 'bout from the beginning," their mother stated in her most comforting voice.

"Well…Abby loved him. And I'm pretty sure the feeling was mutual. You know how she's becoming shy around strangers? Well, as soon as he reached for her, she went right to him, didn't even hesitate. It was the damnedest thing. I could see that he was reluctant at first, nervous even, but once he held her…I don't know…everything changed. I should be happy, right?" Ali looked to her mother, desperate for advice.

"It's perfectly normal to be hesitant of change, sweetheart. But sometimes, change is a good thing. Especially if the change is that a father wants to be a part of his daughter's life," her mother said, resting a soothing hand on Ali's knee.

"He wants to see us again before we leave, but should he get off so easily?"

"Be careful about seeking to punish Evan, sweet pea. You need to stay focused on what's best for Abby. And I think him wanting to spend time with her is definitely a step in the right direction," her father added. "As much as I want to throttle the man, maybe he's finally realizing what he's been missing out on. I mean, just look at that angel." Her father's gaze fell to Abby playing contentedly with her toys, oblivious to the turmoil surrounding her, as he wrapped his arms around Ali, giving her a gentle squeeze. "Now, how could anyone not fall in love with her, or not want be a part of her life?"

Emma didn't miss the veiled message in her father's words. He wasn't just speaking of Abby. Their mother may have been the one who always gave them a reassuring hug when they needed it, but the security they found in their father's arms was unparalleled. His warm embrace was where they'd weathered the storms of life.

"He gave her that stuffed animal." All nine pairs of eyes looked to Abby, who was currently chewing on Pooh Bear's ear. "And me this." Ali raised her arm to display a stunning ruby and diamond tennis bracelet dangling from her wrist.

After a noticeable gasp from Aunt Mary, everyone spoke at once. Their reactions ran the gamut from a few choice curse words, swiftly followed by a harsh reminder from their mother that there was a baby in the room, to declarations of admiration for his taste in jewelry. The sudden outburst startled Abby, causing her to cry out for her mommy.

Lifting the fussy baby onto her lap, Ali continued, once the noise level returned to normal. "He told me it represents mine and Abby's birthstones. I tried to give it back to him. Told him I didn't want it, but he wouldn't take it, said to keep it for Abby. For when she's older."

"I hope he doesn't think that thing makes up for bailing on the first six months of her life," Luke added angrily, his face looking like he just drank spoilt milk.

"I'm sure there was some guilt involved," Steven observed.

"Is it real?" Katie questioned, twirling the gems around Ali's wrist.

"It definitely doesn't make up for it, and you're probably right, Steven. But he was always generous with me when we were together. So, I don't think it was only guilt. And based on the fact that it came in a pretty blue box with a white ribbon, I'm pretty sure it's real."

Later when they were alone, Emma finally asked the question that was on everyone's mind, but no one dared to ask.

"So…Abby was fine…but how are you?" she inquired, joining Ali on the porch swing.

"I don't know, Em. I'm so confused," she exhaled, propping her head up with the palm of her hands. "I'm sad for what might've been. I'm mad because he let me go. He should've come for me to make us a family. I'm scared because my heart ached when I saw him again. It physically hurt, Emma. I knew seeing him would be hard, but I didn't expect this. Maybe it's being back here that's churning up all these old feelings and reminding me of when we were together…and happy. God, I'm a mess. What am I going to do, Em?" She looked so lost, her eyes brightening with unshed tears.

"I wish I knew. I think the way you feel is perfectly normal, though. You loved him and he let you down. Big time. Did he ask about seeing Abby after you go home?"

"No. He only asked if he could see us again before we leave. Once we leave, I'll probably never hear from him again anyway, so I don't know why I'm wasting my time, getting so worked up over nothing." Emma didn't miss the way Ali's expression morphed from one of bitterness, to sadness, to acceptance, in the blink of an eye, steeling herself for another round of rejection from the man that clearly still owned her heart.

"Well, if that's the case, then you'll pick up the pieces and move on."

"It's so hard to move on, though, when every time I look at her...I see him. In a strange way, it's comforting. Like I still have him with me," she paused, her lips forming a flat line. "I can't believe I just said that out loud. It's so twisted. Not to mention completely delusional and unhealthy." Ali let out an audible sigh as she picked the polish off her fingernails.

Emma slid her arm over Ali's shoulder and gave her a reassuring hug. "I think you've been holding onto the dream of being a family, which is perfectly normal by the way."

"I know." Ali was quiet for a long time, just staring at her shoes, before whispering so quietly Emma almost missed it. "I'm such a fool, Emma. If he really loved me, he would've come for me, or at least asked me to come back. I would have, you know." She shook her head in resignation. "In a heartbeat. Especially when I found out I was pregnant. But he didn't."

"Aw, Ali. It'll be alright. You never know what the future holds, but whatever happens, you're going to be okay. Let's see what happens when you see him again and then once you get home." Emma lovingly dried the tears that were now streaming down Ali's cheeks, then folded her arms around her, as she cried once more over Evan Thompson.

Finally getting herself under control, Ali lifted her eyes to Emma's. "You're right. I know that, but saying it and believing it are two different things."

Not knowing what else to say, Emma stated the one thing she knew for certain. "I love you."

Letting out a deep breath, Ali flashed a shaky smile. "I love you, too."

The day had finally come to take Emma's family to the airport for their flight home to North Carolina. Cringing at his selfishness, for secretly rejoicing that they were leaving so he'd have more time with Emma, Noah grabbed his keys and headed out the door.

After a tearful send off, he stood by Emma's side as the large group headed through security and finally disappeared from view. When Emma turned to him, her lip trembling as she tried to bite back the tears, he reached for her and encircled her in his arms. Once he had her snuggled against him, she broke down, burying her face in his chest as she fell apart.

Noah shook his head in stern rejection as two fans approached. He was thankful at first, when they kept their distance, but when they raised their phones, obviously taking photos or a video, he wanted to put his fist through something. Noah loved his career, he really did, but sometimes, in times like these, he hated everything about it.

As soon as she lifted her watery eyes to his, he released his hold on her and placed a tender kiss on her forehead, turning her towards the door. "Let's get you home."

Emma was quiet on the drive from the airport, staring blindly out the window, watching the scenery go by, and Noah wasn't sure if she actually saw any of it or not. It was killing him to just sit there and not be able to comfort her, to take her in his arms and make it better. He settled instead for holding her hand as he maneuvered his Jeep through the city streets to her flat in the CBD.

Finally back home, he sat on the couch and pulled her onto his lap, then enveloped her in his arms and held her for a long while as she cried. Not knowing what to say, he gently stroked her back, up and down in a soothing rhythm. He remembered his mum doing that when he needed comfort, and how it always made him feel better.

"Thank you," she finally said, releasing the death grip from his now-aching neck.

"You're welcome, but for what?" he asked, leaning back a few inches from her. Just the sight of her red and swollen eyes completely undid him.

"For being here. For driving to the airport. I don't think I'd have been able to drive home," she replied, still shaky from her bout of tears.

"Aw, babe. I'm glad I was able to be there for you. I want to be the one whose shoulder you cry on. Now, you sit here and I'll make us a cuppa." Easing her off of his lap, onto the couch, he lifted himself up and went to the kitchen.

Returning a few minutes later, he found Emma asleep, curled up like a kitten, with her head resting on the armrest. He stood and watched over her for a few moments, her cheeks still damp with tears, her face blotchy.

He must have it bad, he thought to himself, because she was still the most beautiful girl in the world. Setting the cups down on the end table, he carefully lifted her into his arms and carried her to her bedroom.

Pulling back the duvet, he settled her on the bed, and when she let out a sexy whimper and towed him down with her, it took every ounce of self-control he could muster not to curl up next to her. Knowing she needed a good night's sleep, he unclasped her hands from around his neck, gave her a peck on the forehead, whispered good night, and turned out the light.

Standing in the doorway, he took one last look at her before shutting the door.

Resting his head against the wooden barrier between them, he tried to remember his life before Emma smiled at him from across the table, but couldn't. One smile, one brilliantly sweet smile, from a pretty girl from North Carolina had changed everything.

Another night on the couch wouldn't kill him, he thought, as he stretched out his long legs. Staring at the ceiling, he hoped Emma was in better spirits in the morning. Making a plan to take her to the waterfront café in Takapuna for breakfast and then, hopefully, to his house, he pulled the blanket off the back of the couch, covering himself.

Noah fell asleep thinking about his sweet Emma…in his house…in his bed.

# CHAPTER 15

It turned out that a day at the beach was just what the doctor ordered. Emma loved the beach, and the feel of the soft sand between her toes always cured what ailed her. They'd spent the day playing in the surf and lounging in the sand, and after a long walk along the water's edge, enjoying each other's company and the view, it started to rain, resulting in a mad dash for Noah's comfortably dry home.

Trying to hide her disappointment when Noah merely pointed her to his bathroom instead of joining her, she dropped her sodden clothes and stepped into the large shower. Inhaling the familiar scent of his shampoo before washing her hair, Emma delighted herself in the thought of having his scent on her, while letting the warm water wash away the salt and sand.

The roomy shower was large enough for two, maybe even four people. Not that she would ever want to share the space with anyone but Noah. Just the two of them, doing wonderfully naughty things to each other, as their curious hands explored every nook and cranny of their slippery bodies.

After drying off with a plush towel, she dug through her overnight bag, looking for the sexy bra and panties she'd packed. Stepping into the lacey thong, Emma was taken aback by her lack of nerves. Practically living in a bathing suit, she was comfortable in her own skin, but having sex with someone for the first time was cause for a few butterflies in the tummy.

And without a doubt, she was having sex with Noah...tonight. Maybe even in the next few minutes. They'd circled each other long enough and even though it was her decision to wait until now, she was more than ready. Giving herself one last look in the mirror, Emma combed her fingers through her hair, then set off down the hall to join Noah in the kitchen.

Dressed in a pair of faded jeans, which hung low on his narrow hips, and a crisp white T-shirt, he was the epitome of casual cool. His feet were bare, which was surprisingly sexy, and she stood in the doorway, watching him for just a minute, taking in the view. He hadn't noticed her yet, and she felt the familiar flush and quickening of her heartbeat, as he busied himself gathering the makings for their dinner.

Noah was everything she'd ever wanted in a man. He knew what he wanted and wasn't afraid to go after it, but was still humble enough not to expect it to come easy. But he was also sweet and tender and not embarrassed to show his emotions. And he was undoubtedly the sexiest man she'd ever laid eyes on.

Joining him in the kitchen, Emma picked up a knife and started slicing the carrots for their salad. Working in tandem, they prepared their meal as if they'd been doing it for years, and their comfortable banter continued as they sat at the table to consume their meal.

When Noah stepped behind her, as she finished wiping down the counter, Emma felt the now-familiar tingle at the back of her neck. A rush of heat spread across her chest as he slid his warm hand along her shoulder, exposing her neck.

Shuddering as his lips gently caressed the sensitive skin below her ear, she sucked in a shaky breath. Needing something to hold onto, she wrapped her fingers around the edge of the counter as his fingers skated slowly down the length of her spine, finding the waistband of her shorts, before dipping slightly inside, and teasing her there.

"Breathe, Emma," he whispered against her ear, sending another wave of tingles over her heated skin.

"I'm trying." It was next to impossible to speak or breathe as his hands moved up the length of her ribcage, his callused fingertips brushing the side of her breasts before slowly sliding back down again, in a deliberate seduction.

Leaning back, Emma rested her head against his chest, soaking up the warmth of his body. Two strong hands circled around to her front, covering her stomach, causing the muscles to quiver beneath his touch as his tongue left a moist trail along the length of her neck, the dual sensations overwhelming her.

Gripping her tightly, he pulled her against him, and there was no mistaking how badly he wanted her. He was hard everywhere.

Without letting up the pressure, he slipped his fingers beneath the hem of her shirt, slowly lifting it. She held her breath as he traced the outline of her ribs, until finally reaching the underside of her breast. Teasing her for an agonizing minute before closing over her soft flesh, his large hand kneaded and squeezed her through the lace cups of her bra, caressing her hardened nipples.

She felt the loss of his touch as he withdrew his hand, turning her to face him. Ghosting her hands along the hard planes of his chest, he pressed his erection against her belly, and the yearning in his eyes as he gazed lovingly into hers was nearly her undoing, leaving her all hot and bothered.

Slipping her hands around his neck, she pulled him down for a kiss that started off gentle and then wasn't. Their tongues danced together as they explored every tantalizing corner. Emma heard herself moan as Noah nipped at her lower lip, then sucked it into his mouth before leaving a scorching trail of kisses along her jaw and down her neck.

It was Emma's turn to tease as she kissed her way from his delicious mouth to the sensitive spot behind his ear. When she bit down on his earlobe, then flicked it with her tongue, she smiled at his answering growl. Turnabout was fair play, and she knew he loved it as much as she did.

Gasping as he suddenly lifted her, she landed on the center island, the granite shockingly cold against her heated skin. Stepping between her legs, his hands gripped the backs of her knees, dragging her to the edge of the counter, where his hard cradled her soft. As if they had a mind of their own, her legs wrapped themselves around his waist, and as he rocked his hips into her, she squeezed him tighter, pulling him even closer.

Noah tilted his head back, separating them, and seductively looked her up and down appreciatively. From anyone else she would've been insulted, but as the wicked grin spread across his face, promising delightful things, she didn't mind at all, and visibly shuddered beneath his heated gaze.

"Are you okay with this, baby?" Before they went any further, Noah needed to make sure she wanted this as much as he did. "Because if we go much further, I'm not going to want to stop."

"More than okay. Please, Noah, don't make me beg." Her flustered plea had him grinning from ear to ear.

"Oh, you'll be begging, sweetheart. I promise you that." Finally, there was nothing to stop them now.

His mouth claimed hers again as he picked her up. Holding onto him, with her legs still enfolded around his hips and her arms securely draped around his neck, he carried her down the hall toward his bedroom. Unable to resist the need to kiss her again, he pressed her against the wall and spent a long minute devouring her mouth before continuing the rest of the way.

Leaning over, he placed her on his big bed before following her down, propping himself up on his forearms, hovering above her pretty face. Her expressive green eyes, which had turned dark with arousal, were the window to her soul and he wanted to reach in there and brand her. He needed her in every way, and when he outlined her sexy cupid's bow with a swipe of his tongue, she tasted so sweet he couldn't get enough; he wanted to taste every inch of her.

Suddenly feeling nervous, he took a deep breath to calm himself, breathing in the sweet scent of her. Wanting to take his time, to do it right, but desperately needing her more than his next breath, he mentally counted to ten and placed a calming kiss on her lips.

Emma couldn't wait to get her hands on him, but when she reached for his shirt, Noah clasped her hands between his fingers, and lifted them over her head. Holding her there, he kissed her again. "Not yet," he commanded, between teasingly-slow kisses.

With one hand securing her wrists, the other toyed with the hem of her shirt. Lifting it inch by glorious inch, exposing her bare midriff, as he placed his knee between her legs, spreading them slightly.

"Please, Noah. I need to see you," Emma pleaded breathlessly. She wasn't sure how she was going to survive the night with Noah if she was begging already, and they were both still fully clothed.

"Patience, love," he smiled, releasing her hands.

Slipping her shirt up and over her shoulders, he tossed it onto the floor behind him, and with a look that could melt steel, he traced the lacy edge of her bra. The tender touch of his fingertips as they lovingly caressed her skin had her back arching into his palm, needing to feel his hands fully on her.

Emma's eyes fluttered shut as he circled the firm tip of her pebbled nipple, teasing her there, before pinching it. She cried out as his mouth closed over the hardened peak through her bra, gently biting down, before soothing it with hot strokes of his tongue. He was driving her crazy with his mouth, but when his hand closed over her other breast, she nearly levitated off of the bed.

Needing more, she reached for his shirt, tugging at the hem, pulling it over his head. Lifting up onto her elbows she kissed along the column of his neck and continued lower. He hissed in a breath between clenched teeth as she licked his nipple and then sucked it into her mouth.

Her hands desperately traveled the span of his smooth bare skin. Unable to get enough, they greedily traveled the length of his back, then across his broad shoulders, before clutching his biceps, needing to feel the flex of his powerful muscles as he held himself above her.

Pressing her into the bed as he left a blazing trail of hot wet kisses along her collarbone, her body ached for more. Lowering the cups of her bra, exposing her to his ravenous gaze, he teased her there before taking her into his mouth. As he kissed his way from one hardened peak to the other, Emma fisted her hands in his hair, holding him to her. The feel of his teeth nibbling her sensitive flesh left her gasping for air. He proved adept at multitasking, when he unclasped her bra without skipping a beat, and the lacy scrap of fabric quickly followed the same path as her shirt, landing on the floor.

Just when she thought her heart was going to burst forth from her heaving chest, he sat back and reverently dragged his fingers down the length of her belly, to the waistband of her shorts, leaving a trail of quivering muscles in their path. She almost leapt off the bed when he bent down and flicked his tongue in her belly button, but then he surprised her by sweetly resting his cheek against her tummy, closing his eyes for a moment before inhaling deeply.

Fumbling with shaking hands to undo the button, Emma was relieved to see that he was just as affected as she was. Lifting her hips to help him, Noah slowly slid her shorts down her legs, along with her lace panties, leaving her naked and wanting him more with each passing second. He stood back and took a long look at her, lying supine on his bed, exposed to him, and she resisted the urge to cover herself as his eyes devoured her. She'd never felt more beautiful.

"God, you're exquisite, Emma. Even better than I'd imagined. And what I imagined was pretty spectacular."

Lifting onto her knees she slid her fingers into the waistband of his jeans. Pulling him to the edge of the bed, she kissed him again as she unbuttoned his pants. "Thank you, Noah. And you're wearing too many clothes." She felt her heart pounding violently as she slid his pants over his hips, then watched as they fell to the floor.

When he stepped out of his jeans and boxer briefs, she leaned back and finally got a good look at him. Being a swimmer, she'd seen plenty of nearly-naked men with extremely fit bodies, but none of them compared to the Adonis that stood before her in all his glory. And glory, glory, halleluiah. From his broad shoulders to his long powerful legs, and everything in between, he was magnificent.

She swallowed hard as her eyes settled on the full length of him, he was much bigger than anyone she'd been with before, and she wanted to lick every delicious inch of him. "I must say that you're pretty spectacular yourself. Wow... you're perfect."

As her eyes traveled back to his, he stepped forward, invading her senses with his larger than life presence.

"Lay down, baby," Noah said, in a sweetly seductive voice.

Lifting her leg, he slowly kissed, nibbled and licked his way up the length of her thigh, until finally reaching where she ached for him most.

"Please, Noah. I need..."

"Shh, baby...I know what you need," he whispered, his breath tickling her delicate skin.

Without saying another word, he covered her with his mouth. Her pulse was beating loudly in her ears, and needing something to hold onto, her hands found his hair as she bucked against him. She was groaning and uttering unintelligible words as his lips and tongue teased her mercilessly, the sweet torture driving her right up to the edge, as she cried out his name, again and again.

It was too much and not enough and she heard herself begging and pleading for him to stop and then to never stop. When he added his fingers, he drove her to an explosive release that left her soaring amongst the stars. Her body shook as her muscles contracted around him. Struggling to breathe, her chest heaved as she tried to fill her lungs with air. She was going to die, but what a way to go.

Taking care to make sure she returned safely to earth, he then kissed his way from her hips to her breasts, paying extra attention to them, before moving over her. She opened her eyes to find him watching her as he hovered inches from her face, with the crooked smile she'd grown to love.

With a satisfied smirk, he leaned in and kissed her. Wiping the sweat-dampened hair from her brow, he tucked it behind her ear.

"That was beautiful. You're beautiful," he whispered reverently, as he sweetly kissed her once again.

Emma took a long look at his handsome face, his lips turned up at the corners, forming a confident grin that had her body purring in all the right places. His blue eyes, lined with dark lashes, contained a hint of mischief, promising her everything. She couldn't resist the urge to touch him, running her fingers along his chest and then up to cradle his face.

When he tilted his head and placed a tender kiss on the palm of her hand, she actually swooned. He was such a physically powerful man, but at the same time he was the gentlest of lovers, and the contrast was an incredible aphrodisiac.

"You're amazing, Noah. And that was…" She couldn't think of a word to adequately describe what she was feeling. Her brain hadn't cleared yet from the most powerful orgasm she'd ever experienced.

"Bloody fantastic, yeah?" he stated proudly, burying his face in the crook of her neck, exhaling a deep breath that tickled her heated skin, then kissed her there.

"Yeah, bloody fantastic," she agreed. "No one's ever done that to me before, and I think I just had an out-of-body experience," she chuckled shakily, still feeling the aftershocks.

"Good. There's plenty more where that came from; I'm not nearly done with you yet."

He rocked against her and left no doubt about what he planned to do as he reached over her to fetch a condom out of the bedside table.

They both gasped as he entered her, slowly filling her up, giving her time to adjust to the size of him. Following along at the pace he set, Emma lifted her hips to meet his as they came together as one. Propping himself up on his forearms, he bent his head to kiss her, gently at first and then becoming frantic as his pace quickened. Her hands wound around his neck to hold him there, then skated down the expanse of his back, coming to rest on his perfect backside.

Every nerve in her body was on edge as he slowed his pace. Pressing the weight of his body against hers, his breath was warm as he exhaled, sending a wave of shivers coursing throughout her.

Lacing his fingers through hers, he placed their joined hands above her shoulders, next to her head.

"Open your eyes, sweetheart. Look at me," he gently requested, as he struggled for breath, his face flushed with arousal.

Following his instructions, the love she found in the depths of his bright blue eyes, washed away any lingering doubts she may have had. She loved him completely with her mind, body, and soul.

Fisting her hands tighter and holding them firmly to the mattress, she felt Noah losing control, as his eyes locked onto hers. With every breath, she was whimpering, moaning, and calling out his name in a heated rush, begging for more. Wrapping her legs tightly around his waist, she could feel the tremors from within building as she cried out his name.

She felt her skin flush from her chest to her face, as he continued to move within her. Twisting his body to take one nipple and then the other into his mouth, the added stimulation was enough to send her over the edge. Throwing his head back, he groaned loudly as he emptied himself into her.

They were both spent and out of breath as he turned her into him, his hand coming to rest on her hip, gently caressing her there. Exhausted, she settled her cheek against the firm pillow of his chest, listening to his heart pound wildly beneath her ear, unable to speak, but comforted by the steady beat of it.

After long minutes quietly enjoying the afterglow as his fingers lazily combed through her hair, Noah finally broke the silence. "Are you alright? Because I have to tell you, I'm not. I'm completely shattered."

Almost afraid to hear his answer, she hesitated before asking. "Is that good or bad?" She didn't have much experience to go on, but from her perspective, making love with Noah was absolutely perfect. The earth had literally shifted beneath her. If she'd disappointed him, he wouldn't be the only one who was shattered.

"Oh, it's definitely good, baby. Beyond good, actually. I think *I* just had an out-of-body experience," he said with a satisfied smile, mimicking her words from earlier, as he kissed the top of her head.

"Oh, thank God. Because I've never experienced anything even remotely comparable to what you just did to me, and for me. It was amazing. But for a minute, I thought you were disappointed, that I'd let you down," she stated shyly, not meeting his eyes as she spoke, nervously tracing circles with her finger on his chest.

He lifted her chin, leaving her no option but to look at him. "You could never let me down, Emma. In fact, I'm ready for another round," he chuckled, skimming his finger up the length of her side and then back down again, his hand coming to rest on her backside and squeezing her there, then pinning her beneath him as he claimed her mouth with a passionate kiss.

Waking in the morning to find Emma sleeping next to him, gloriously naked, Noah propped his head on his hand and watched her sleep. He waited for the urge to bolt, but wasn't entirely surprised when it never came. His sister always gave him stick about the revolving door of his love life, told him one day he'd meet his match. And as he watched Emma, cuddled up contentedly next to him, he knew he'd finally met her.

With her back pressed against his chest, her long hair was spread out on the pillow between them as it tickled his face, and their bodies aligned perfectly from shoulders to toes. His arm was draped across her waist, and the weight of her breast rested in his hand. He didn't want to move, but as visions from the night before flashed through his mind, he felt the effects of his arousal, a state he was coming to expect any time Emma was within eyesight.

He'd had lovers before, but none that compared to the insatiable little spitfire currently snuggled up against him. They'd made love three more times before finally succumbing to the need for sleep. He'd never forget the image of her straddling his hips, riding him for all she was worth, her breasts swaying as she moved over him. Not being able to resist, he'd taken them in his hands, and watched as his ministrations drove her higher.

He could still hear her crying out as she rode the waves of her climax; her sexy moans and whimpers as she begged for more drove him insane with need. She made love with an unbridled passion and gave as good as she got, and he couldn't get enough of her.

He tried to put words to the emotions swirling around in his head, but wasn't sure it was even possible. How do you express how one night changed everything? He could only pray that she felt the same way. He'd never needed a woman before, but he needed this woman…his Emma. His sweet and sexy, Emma.

As he watched the rise and fall of her chest beneath his hand, he took comfort in the steady rhythm of her heartbeat. She looked so peaceful as she slept, like an angel, her lips slightly parted in an unconscious smile. He could see himself waking every morning to her beautiful face, her body cuddled up next to his, as they welcomed each new day together.

As she started to wake, her eyes fluttering open, he felt her body stiffen for a split second and then relax.

Noah pulled her tightly against his body as he gently kissed her exposed shoulder. Without thinking, the hand covering her breast started to move, gently caressing it. He watched as her eyes glanced around the room, taking in her surroundings, a serene smile spreading across her face as she turned to face him.

"Good morning." Her hand came to rest on his chest, then dipped lower, her fingers mapping out the deep ridges chiseled into his abdomen, and he was suddenly thankful for the long hours he'd spent at the gym.

"Morning, Emma." He couldn't help but smile at her sleepy eyes.

Leaning in for a kiss, she suddenly backed away from him, scurrying to get out of bed.

"I need to brush my teeth." She looked a bit panicked as she nervously brought her hand to her mouth.

"Don't care. Come here," he demanded, pulling her back so they faced each other, holding her there. "I've been waiting patiently for you to wake up. Been dying to kiss you again."

"But I…"

She didn't get a chance to finish her protestation as he brought his lips to hers and gave her the kiss he'd been waiting for. He felt her relax into his body as she opened up for him, their tongues mating and any thought of morning breath was vanquished.

He'd had countless fantasies that included a naked Emma spread out on his bed, ready and waiting for him to do what he wanted, but none of them compared to her in the flesh. She was so beautiful he ached for her, and she'd given herself to him without reservation. He wondered how he got so lucky to have her.

His hand massaged the length of her back, coming to rest on her naked bottom, pulling her against him as she slid her leg up his, letting it come to rest across his hip.

In one quick movement she pushed him onto his back and sat up, straddling his hips. With her hands resting on his shoulders, she bent down to brush a kiss on his very-happy lips. His hands traced the length of her thighs, up and down, before finally circling around to grip her bum, pulling her tightly against the hard length of his erection.

Emma left a trail of wet kisses along his jaw, then down his neck to his collarbone, then continued lower, paying extra attention to his sensitive nipples.

"Have I told you that you have the most amazing body that I've ever had the pleasure to lay eyes on?" she asked between kisses, as she stroked her hands up and down his arms. "So strong and sexy."

"I don't think so, but I'm having a wee bit of an issue thinking about anything at the moment," he chuckled.

"Well, you do. It makes me crazy. From that first morning I looked up to find you shirtless, standing in the kitchen doorway. It drives me to distraction. I dream about it...and you of course," she added, almost apologetically, as she looked down the length of him and licked her lips.

"Of course," he smiled. "I'm glad you like it...and me too," he laughed.

"Oh, I do. I really, really do." She smiled between kisses as she made her way down the length of his torso towards his happy place.

He moaned as understanding crossed his clouded mind. Running his fingers though her hair, he hissed in a breath between clenched teeth as she kissed the length of him and, wasting no time, took him into her mouth. As he watched her, he thought his head would explode...both of them.

Noah lost all ability to concentrate on anything other than what she was doing. His world was reduced to her mouth, and the pleasure she was giving. Holding her head with his hands, he tried not to push, and ground his teeth as her hair fell across his hips, the silkiness of it tickling him as she bobbed up and down.

When he couldn't hold back any longer, he dragged her up the length of his body and kissed her full on, then with shaking hands reached for a condom. Thankfully, she took it from him and quickly rolled it on, since he doubted he'd have been able to. Gripping her hips, he entered her in one swift movement. She cried out and he froze, thinking he'd hurt her.

"Are you alright?" he somehow managed to ask.

"More than alright. But if you stop, I may have to hurt you," she giggled as she swiveled her hips and started to move over him. Bracing her hands on his chest, she locked her eyes on his and licked her lips, and it was the sexiest thing he'd ever seen.

"No worries 'bout that," he answered with a wicked grin and a thrust of his hips, filling her completely. "In fact, don't think I could stop if I wanted to."

Sitting up, he wrapped his arms around her, kissing her again, just because he needed to taste her, and sucked her tongue into his mouth before nipping at her bottom lip, then rolled her onto her back, and proceeded to show her just how badly he needed her.

Noah would never get tired of hearing Emma cry out his name as she came undone in his arms. Knowing that he'd given her all he had to give and then a little extra measure made him feel powerful.

As they collapsed onto his bed, bodies glistening with sweat and out of breath, he pulled her so that she was splayed on top of him, and smiled when she propped her chin on her hands with a satisfied grin. He reached up and slid a wayward strand of hair behind her ear, letting his hand linger on her face, stroking her cheek.

"Stay with me," he said, as he reverently drew his fingers slowly down her neck and over her shoulder.

He wanted her to stay for the day, but if he was being honest with himself, he wanted her to stay forever, even if he wasn't ready to actually speak those words to her…yet.

As Emma looked into his eyes, the endless pools of crystal blue, there was no place she'd rather be. She loved the feel of his arms wrapped tightly around her as she sprawled against his warm body, so strong and solid; she felt safe and protected…treasured.

"I'd love to, Noah." Smiling she lifted up onto her forearms, her lips inches from his face, and unable to deny the pull, she leaned down to kiss him.

"I have to meet some mates for a workout, but after that, I'm all yours."

"Okay. You hungry?"

"Famished," Noah smirked, rolling her over and showing her just how hungry he was…for her.

# CHAPTER 16

Exploring Noah's home after he left for his workout, Emma admired the craftsmanship and attention to detail he'd employed in the renovation. Gazing at the family photos scattered throughout the living area, she hesitated when she noticed one of Noah. Based on his youthful appearance, it was from his early days with the All Blacks. He looked so happy, standing proudly on the field wearing his tight black jersey. Taking a closer look, she noticed the scar above his eye was missing and he'd added bulk to his impressive frame since the photo was taken. As handsome as he was in the picture, she preferred the man he'd grown into, scars and all.

Continuing her self-guided tour, she went downstairs to the lower level, finding an open sitting area with another TV, along with a fully-equipped home gym and two more guest rooms. French doors opened to a stunning view of the beach and a covered concrete patio that ran the length of the house, with a large hot tub tucked into the far corner for privacy.

Emma could see why Noah had fallen in love with this house. With breath-taking views greeting you around every corner, how could you not? The house was far too big for just one person, but would be perfect for a growing family. Pushing the depressing thought of what wouldn't be from her mind, she finished the tour and went for a walk along the beach.

The water always calmed her nerves and helped to sort through the cluttered and confusing thoughts that constantly rattled around her brain. Being with Noah both soothed and frightened her. He was sweet and gentle, but at the same time, he had the power to do permanent damage. Giving your heart to someone gave them the power to do so. Emma knew she could trust him not to abuse it, but like it or not, she worried his love might very well destroy her in the end.

When he got home Noah found Emma, looking as pretty as ever, sitting crossed legged on the chaise lounge playing her guitar. She was wearing her yellow bikini, one of his favorites, and her golden hair was pulled back into a ponytail. He stood in the doorway watching her for a few moments. Just the sight of her had his heart racing and a dopey grin spreading across his face.

"Hey. I got us a takeaway. I hope you're hungry," Noah said, as he stepped onto the deck to join her.

"Oh my God. You startled me," she gasped, turning to him with a stunned look on her face, her hand clutching her chest and her eyes as big as saucers. "I didn't hear you come home."

"Sorry, sweetheart. I didn't mean to frighten you."

"I'm fine, or I will be in a minute," she chuckled, as she shook her head, reclining against the lounger and exhaling a calming breath.

"Do you want to eat inside or out here?"

"Out here's fine with me. It's so nice out today." Noah wondered if the sun was as enamored with her as he was, because he couldn't remember it shining as brightly as it had since she moved to town.

Sitting down on the chaise next to hers, Noah placed the bag of food on the table between them. "What were you playing just now when I came outside?"

"That was 'Into the Mystic' by Van Morrison. It's one of my favorite songs. I guess sitting here, looking out at the water made me think of it," she replied shyly, setting her guitar on the deck next to her seat.

"Would you play it for me?" Noah loved to hear her play the guitar and her soft voice soothed him. His life was stressful, always feeling like he was being pulled in too many directions at once, but with Emma at his side, he felt at peace for the first time; he was finally able to relax.

The first hit out of the rugby season was just around the corner, and for the first time in his life, it wasn't the most important thing to him. Every year since he was a young fella he looked forward to playing footy with the boys. He still did, but the thought of spending so much time away from Emma made his stomach churn uncomfortably. Everything in his life up until this point had revolved around rugby and anyone he was involved with came in a distant second. It was just the way it always was, but his priorities were shifting.

As he looked at Emma, his heart ached with need. He needed her in a way that he'd never needed anyone before. The realization scared him, but also gave him comfort. He was safe with her; she had no hidden agenda. She wasn't looking for fame or the notoriety of being photographed with a sportsman, quite the opposite actually, she shied away from the attention. She just wanted to be with him, Noah Parker, the man.

Emma tilted her head and looked at him curiously. "Now?" she asked, and at his affirmative nod, she reached for the guitar, then settled it on her still-crossed legs and began to play. He hadn't realized how quiet his house had been until she came along and filled it with the sound of music, and he didn't want her to leave, taking it with her.

Noah had created a world that he could retreat to when the madness of his life became overwhelming, but as he watched Emma, he realized that a house did not make a home. There was no doubt that he had a lovely house and counted himself lucky to have it. But without someone special to come home to at the end of the day, that's all it was, just a house. Emma had turned his house into a home.

When she was done playing, she gingerly placed her guitar on the deck, and he reached for her hand. Taking it in his grasp, his thumb caressed her knuckles as he entwined their fingers together, gently squeezing her there, and she surprised him by joining him on his lounger.

Resting her head on his shoulder, she draped her arm across his abdomen, her curves pressing against him. He'd never really enjoyed cuddling before and usually made an excuse to remove himself before it got awkward, but he couldn't think of a time when he felt more content than he did at that moment. Having her wrapped up tightly in his arms just felt right.

"I love it when you play your guitar for me. Almost as much as when you're playing *with* me," he joked, tracing his fingers along the smooth skin of her arm.

"Oh, that's cute, Noah," she replied, shaking her head at his lame attempt at humor.

"Baby, you can play with me any way you want…any time you want." He turned to face her, nipping at her lip before sliding his tongue along the seam of her mouth, and when she opened for him, he took full advantage. Massaging her round bottom as he pulled her against him, he was quickly realizing that he would never get enough of her; her kisses were intoxicating and left him wanting more, needing more.

Breaking away before he untied her swim suit, leaving her exposed to passersby on the beach, Noah stood up and reached out his hand for her. Without letting go, he gathered up the takeaway and led her inside.

After finally eating lunch, they settled on the couch. Noah sat next to her 'studying' the rugby matches he'd recorded, and she had to bite back a laugh; she couldn't remember enjoying a study session quite so much…ever, but she kept her thoughts to herself. Snuggling comfortably against his side with her e-reader, enjoying the closeness as Noah's arm draped lazily over her shoulder, his fingers mindlessly combing through her hair, she couldn't help but smile.

Rugby season was starting soon and school was about to begin, so she wanted to spend as much time with him as possible. She also didn't see the point of going back to Lily's with only her thoughts to keep her company.

After reading the same paragraph over and over again, yet still unable to focus on the book she was reading, Emma decided to broach the subject of her spending the night in a roundabout way. "What time were you thinking of taking me home?" she asked, once it looked like he was at a convenient stopping point. He paused the game and turned to face her, her heart beating quickly as she braced for his answer.

"About that. I was thinking, um hoping actually, that you'd stay with me until Lily and Josh come home." He hesitated before quickly continuing. "No pressure. It's alright if you don't want to, or if you have other things to do, but I'd really like it if you'd stay. I quite like having you here with me."

He wanted her to stay. Emma felt a smile spread across her face as his words sunk in. He wanted her to stay.

"Well? What's it to be, Emma?" He tugged gently on a lock of her hair and she literally melted into a gooey puddle, complete with an obligatory sigh.

"I'd love to. I wanted to, but I was afraid to ask."

"Oi, please don't ever be afraid to ask me for what you want, Emma. I thought I'd made myself and my intentions where you're concerned perfectly clear. I want you. Here with me. Have no doubts about that. Ever." He snaked his arm around her waist, drawing her closer to him as he leaned in for a kiss, his breath warm against her skin. "Never. Ever. Ever. Think that I don't want you by my side. Ever," he continued sweetly, as he left a trail of kisses along her jaw and down her neck.

"Okay, good. Because I want that, too," Emma giggled as he licked the ticklish spot behind her ear.

"You are the sweet to my heart. The honey to my bunny," he laughed, as he slowly lowered her to the couch and pressed his weight into her.

"The honey to your bunny? Seriously?" she snickered, tilting her head to give him better access.

"Hey, don't make fun of me," he smiled against her neck. "It was off the cuff. And I happen to enjoy a honeybun. Almost as tasty as you, actually. Maybe I'll have to drizzle some honey on *your* bunny, eh? Yes, that sounds delicious. Two of my most favorite things." His naughty smile told her he wasn't joking.

"Sounds messy," she frowned, as the blood started rushing through her veins at an alarming rate at the image that flashed in her mind.

"Sounds fantastic. And I think you'll enthusiastically agree once I'm licking it off of you. In fact, I may even get a 'hell yes' out of you." He gave her a quick wink and a mischievous smile and she felt a shudder rock through her body.

"Oh, well, if you must. Who am I to object?" she exhaled in mock indifference, waving her hand through the air like she could take it or leave it.

"Sweet as." Noah kissed the tip of her nose and then lifted off of her. As he stood to his feet, he reached for her, then led her by the hand into the kitchen.

It seemed that every time with Noah was a new experience for her. He was as adventurous and playful as he was insatiable and she loved that about him.

Sitting on the island with Noah standing between her thighs, she held her breath as he began to spread a thick line of honey along her breasts. The cool temperature of the sticky substance followed by the heat of his breath on her skin as his tongue licked her clean, made her desperate for more. He didn't disappoint when he dipped his finger in the jar and drew a line down the length of her.

"Mmmm," Noah smiled, as he licked his fingers clean, then leaning down, he followed the golden trail with his mouth and showed her how fantastically delicious a little honey and one very talented man could be, complete with Emma's euphoric cry of 'hell yes' when he finished.

After fully exploring each other, they ended up in his shower together to wash themselves clean of the sticky residue that consisted of honey and a few other tasty treats. Noah did a painstakingly detailed job of making sure Emma was polished and scrubbed, which only served to tease and torment her to where she physically ached for him.

When he got on his knees in front of her, mentioning something about doing a thorough inspection to make sure she was clean…everywhere, her mind went blank and she thought she'd faint as he drove her wild, leaving her dizzy and clinging to his broad shoulders for support. He continued his relentless assault until she felt her whole body begin to shake and quiver, then he held her against him until the waves of her orgasm faded, placing tender kisses along her belly.

Lifting her onto him as if she was as light as a feather, he used his weight to press her against the wall. He drove into her as he cushioned her head with one hand, and the other cupped her bottom for support. Wrapping her legs around his hips, her hands raked through his wet hair, the frenzied pace stole her breath as his mouth claimed hers in a kiss so hot it branded her as another climax ripped through her. Noah was right behind her as he nuzzled his face against her neck and groaned her name.

Noah appeared tense after they were dressed and sitting once again in front of the television. Emma guessed it was due to the fact that they'd forgotten to use protection during their feverish coupling in the shower.

"Noah, is everything alright?" she asked, not entirely sure how one approached such a delicate and potentially uncomfortable subject.

"Yeah, everything's fine. But I realized we didn't use a condom in the shower just now. I got carried away in the heat of the moment, I guess. I've never done that before…had unprotected sex. I'm really sorry, Emma. I should've taken better care of you," he frowned, his brows knitting together. As he spoke, his eyes darted from her to the wall over her shoulder and back again.

"Aw, baby. You always take good care of me." She touched his cheek, making sure he was looking at her as she spoke. "This is kind of awkward, but I guess it's good to get it out of the way now. You should know that I'm on the pill and I'm clean." He took a deep breath, and she could see relief ease his worried features.

"So am I. STD free, I mean. I'm not on the pill, though, I'm very forgetful at times and skipped a few, so I'm waiting for my next cycle to start taking it again," he joked. She knew he was going for a feminine pitch to his voice, but with his deep masculine voice, it came out sounding more like a sick cat.

"That's good to know, sweetheart," she chuckled. "And I've never had unprotected sex before either, by the way," she assured him.

"It's funny, but at the time, all I could think about was how amazing it felt… being with you. It never occurred to me that it was because there was nothing between us. I think I could get used to that," he added hopefully.

"Well, I don't mind. Either way is fine with me."

Noah looked so cute, his crooked smile on full display, taking her breath away. "Sweet as. I think I've just died and gone to heaven."

"I think you've just discovered one of the benefits of monogamy." She'd never even considered having unprotected sex before, a condom was always non-negotiable, but with Noah it was different, she trusted him to be faithful to her.

"I like the way that sounds, and since I can't get enough of you, think of all the trips to the market we'll save for late night rubber runs."

"How environmentally-conscious of you." She tried to maintain a straight face at his adorable expression, biting down on her lower lip, but couldn't stop the giggle from bubbling to the surface.

"That's me, just doing my part for the planet, one unused condom at a time."

As the week flew by, they settled into a comfortable routine. Now that he'd discovered the additional pleasure he experienced without the barrier of a condom between them, he'd become even more insatiable than before. On more than one morning, Emma woke to find Noah suckling her breast, which led to an early morning round of hot and steamy sex before showering and eating breakfast together.

The Blues had begun practicing for the upcoming season but as an All Black, Noah hadn't been required to attend until now. He came home at the end of the day worn out and a bit bruised and battered, and Emma delighted herself in taking care of him. Who knew that tending to his cuts and scrapes and having dinner ready for him would be so satisfying? It was all very domestic and she couldn't have been happier. Over dinner, they discussed their day and anything else that came to mind, before washing up together.

On several nights, they relaxed in the hot tub, so Noah could soak his aching muscles. Unable to keep their hands to themselves, especially with so little clothing on, they inevitably ended up naked and satiated before climbing from the water. Their nights spent together in Noah's big bed were filled with passionate lovemaking until finally falling asleep, exhausted and tangled in each other's arms.

Being with Noah was easy, almost too easy. Weren't relationships supposed to be filled with angst and drama? Rarely were two people as concerned for the other person's happiness as they were for their own. Emma had never been with a man as unselfish as Noah. He put her first, always. He had a way of making her feel special and cared for, but it also unnerved her at the same time. It was too good to be true. He was too good to be true.

It was hard to keep the demons of past relationships from creeping to the forefront; she'd had the rug ripped out from under her on more than one occasion, and the experience taught her that if something seemed too good to be true, it usually was. She feared that if it happened with Noah, she'd never recover.

He hadn't given her any reason to doubt him, though. In fact, he'd gone out of his way to reassure her that he wanted her to be with him, and it was getting harder and harder to see herself walking away when her time in New Zealand finally came to an end.

On several occasions, they'd talked about the future, about their hopes and dreams. Even though it was in abstract terms, as if they were afraid to put a face or a name to their future spouses, she always felt like they were picturing each other in those roles.

Noah had told her that he'd purchased and renovated his home with the vision of his future wife and children in mind, and it broke her heart to think of another woman filling that role in Noah's life, another woman taking ownership of his heart and his bed, bearing his children. It wouldn't be her chasing their toddlers through the spacious lounge, listening to them squeal with delight as she encouraged their first steps.

Being with Noah, here in his home, brought out the desire to nest like she'd never felt before. She'd never realized that she was such a masochist, that she would allow herself to fall for a man that she could never have. She was drawn to Noah like a moth to a flame, but unlike the moth, she knew she was going to get burned, but even so, she still couldn't bring herself to turn away.

It was too soon to feel so strongly about Noah, she knew that, but her heart refused to be bound by societal norms that dictated the proper amount of time before you could acknowledge that you were in love with someone. Even knowing that she was heading for a heartbreak so shattering she may never be able to put the pieces back together, wouldn't keep her from Noah.

Unless he broke it off, she'd stay with him until she boarded her flight back to Charlotte. Only then would she allow herself to deal with the fallout, safely tucked into her mother's loving embrace. Somehow, she'd find the strength to pick up the pieces of her broken heart and head back to Boone to finish school.

Hopefully, one day she'd find a man who could hold a candle to the memory of Noah. She wondered if that was even possible. She'd never wanted a man or needed a man as much as she wanted and needed Noah. She quivered at the slightest touch of his fingertips and his kisses lit a fire deep down that grew into a raging inferno as soon as his lips met hers, but more importantly, she enjoyed his company.

It was the simple things he did, like the way he gently squeezed her hand like he didn't want to let her go. Or the way he ran his fingers through her hair while they snuggled on the couch. Or that he really listened to what she had to say and valued her opinion on things. No, she doubted that another man existed who could fill the place he occupied in her heart.

Like a fool, she'd made the fatal mistake of giving her heart to a man who was unavailable to her. Why was she such a glutton for punishment? Of course Noah's unavailability was geographical, not emotional. He was refreshingly open and honest with his feelings and if they didn't have ties that bound them to live half a world apart, she could easily see herself as his wife and the mother of his children.

What a cruel twist of fate, to have fallen in love with the man of her dreams, only to be able to have him for a short while, leaving him to find love and comfort in the arms of another. She felt the sting of tears as they slid down her cheek at the thought of Noah looking at another woman the way he looked at her.

Wiping the tears away, she made a vow to not dwell on the inevitable demise of her happily ever after. She'd focus on the time they had together, cherishing each and every moment…memories she'd treasure for a lifetime. Memories that wouldn't keep her warm at night, but she could pull them out when she was lonely, or whenever she needed a reminder not to settle for second best.

Unfortunately, Noah owned the key to her heart, and he'd broken the mold and destroyed the spare. Maybe one day in the far distant future, another man would come along who would have the proper tools to pick the lock, but he would only be a poor substitute for the original, and she sincerely doubted anyone else existed who possessed the proper equipment.

# CHAPTER 17

While Noah spent more and more time practicing with the team and traveling for promotional obligations, Emma spent her days preparing for classes to begin and doing her part to be supportive when he was tired or irritable after a long day.

Being an All Black made him a huge draw for the fans, so in addition to his grueling workouts with the team, he was required to show up for whatever luncheon or photo op the PR department set up for the players. Knowing how uncomfortable he was with the attention, Emma always tried to make it easy for him when he got home, so he could relax.

Emma's phone chimed with a text from Lily as she was putting dinner in the oven, and she couldn't help but smile at the picture Lily had sent. The image of Lily and Josh's legs, tanned by the tropical sun, melting into the powdery white sand and clear blue waters of the lagoon was a vision of paradise.

Quickly sending a picture of herself in front of the open oven, excitedly pointing to the meatloaf, Emma wasn't entirely surprised when her phone started ringing within seconds, knowing Lily would instantly recognize Noah's kitchen.

"Hello! When were you going to tell me?" Lily stated impatiently, without waiting for Emma's greeting.

"Hi Lily. How are you? How's married life treating you?" Emma replied playfully.

"Yeah, yeah. No worries there. Couldn't be any better. Now stop avoiding my question." Emma knew Lily had the patience of a two-year-old, so it was fun to mess with her just a little.

Ignoring Lily, Emma continued. "Are you bored with Josh already? Is that why you're calling me?"

"Don't try to change the subject, Emma. You know exactly what I'm talking about. Now spill it," she demanded.

Emma chuckled as she took a drink of water, prolonging Lily's suffering just a little while longer. "Poor Josh, I see married life has already turned you into a demanding shrew."

Lily let out a loud laugh, before quickly returning to the matter at hand. "Shut up, Emma. Now, I want to know everything."

"Seriously, are you that bored already? Is Josh not entertaining you properly?" she teased.

"Oh. Trust me. If Josh entertained me any better I wouldn't be able to walk. The man's insatiable," Lily giggled, as Josh mumbled something that Emma couldn't make out. "Now, stop dodging."

"Fine. I've been staying at Noah's since you left. He asked me to stay with him while you're gone, so I wouldn't be alone in the apartment."

"Yeah, right. Is that why? Somehow, I don't think that's the only reason."

"Probably not," Emma stated honestly, suddenly feeling shy and thankful Lily couldn't see the blush spreading across her cheeks.

"Of course that's not the reason and you know it. The man's crazy about you. I'm happy for you, Em. So…how was it? Is he *entertaining* you properly?"

"Amazing. He's amazing, Lily. I really don't know how else to describe it. And yes, he's entertaining me just fine." Emma couldn't help the silly grin quickly spreading across her face as she tried to come up with adequate words to explain how she felt.

"Well, let's see. Hot. Sweaty. Mind-blowing. Orgasmic. Multi-orgasmic. Shall I go on?"

"All of the above. Plus sweet, and throw in a healthy portion of can't get enough," Emma laughed, relaxing into the comfortable banter she was used to with her cousin.

"Well, then, it's a good thing you're staying with him," Lily snickered.

"Yeah, it's been really great. Now, tell me about your honeymoon."

"It's so pretty here, and we've done a bit of exploring around the island. Honestly, Emma, I can't imagine a more beautiful place to spend your honeymoon. It's perfect." Lily giggled once again as Josh commented on her current state of undress, and Emma took that as her queue to hang up.

"Okay. On that note, I really need to go. Noah's going to be home soon and I want to finish dinner."

"Aren't you the happy homemaker?"

Emma laughed at the truthfulness of Lily's comment. "Yeah, I guess I am. Tell Josh I said hi."

"Will do. You're still picking us up from the airport, right?"

"Yes, of course." Emma was glad Lily was coming home, but also disappointed that her time playing house with Noah would be coming to an end as well.

"Miss you and give my love to Noah."

Hanging up, Emma felt relieved to have spoken to Lily about the change in her relationship with Noah. It was easy to talk to Lily, since she was actually encouraging it, as opposed to Ali, who always tempered her comments with words of warning and unsolicited advice.

Knowing her sister had her best interests at heart eased the sting a little, but it always hurt just the same. She just wanted Ali to share in her excitement, not constantly frown upon it.

Noah made her happy and she was sticking with him for as long as he wanted her. She'd deal with the consequences later. Right now, she wanted to concentrate on how happy he made her.

Noah opened the garage door and dropped his bag by the door. "Honey, I'm home," he joked, as he called out for Emma. When she strolled into the kitchen, he couldn't help but pull her into a long embrace. "Something smells delicious."

"I made meatloaf. I hope you like it," she stated sheepishly, wrapping her arms around his waist.

"Well, if it tastes half as good as it smells, you've got yourself a winner," he assured her, bending down to give her the kiss he'd been thinking about all day.

"It'll be ready by the time you get changed, so go on," she said, smacking his bum playfully.

Sitting down for dinner, Noah stared appreciatively at the plate she set before him. "You're spoiling me, babe. I could get used to coming home to you every night and to a home cooked meal like this." His mouth watered at the sight of it, mounded high with thick slices of meatloaf, along with heaps of mashed potatoes and vegetables.

"I like spoiling you," Emma stated bubbly, with a slight blush tinting her delicate features.

It was their final night together before Lily and Josh returned from their honeymoon, and Noah wasn't thrilled with the prospect of Emma leaving. He enjoyed having her around. Their time together may have been brief, but it felt like he'd known her his whole life. He'd never felt so at ease with another person, even when they were sitting quietly reading the paper or watching TV.

He'd grown used to the warmth of her next to him as he slept, their limbs tangled together after a night of lovemaking. And waking up to her sleepy smile was something he'd never get tired of.

He always prided himself on the fact that he could take care of himself, but he liked being cared for by Emma. She was a nurturer. He'd never had a need for someone to fuss over him, but it was special with her. And he found that he actually enjoyed it. When she wanted to play nursemaid, how could he refuse? He'd be a fool to turn down a good massage or an offer to kiss his aches away, or a delicious home cooked meal.

New relationships usually started out with a flood of emotions and an insatiable desire for the other person, he wasn't blind to that, but Emma was different. Everything with her was different, and he couldn't foresee a time when he wouldn't want her by his side.

Just a smile from her was like a jolt to his system, and when she looked at him with hooded eyes filled with desire, nothing else mattered. Only her. She'd worked her way into his heart, and he ached at the thought of another man taking his place. He wanted to be the one she grew old with.

He loved her. Three little words that changed everything. He'd never said those words to anyone before. They weren't meant to be bandied about frivolously, carelessly.

As they cuddled together in the hammock under a blanket later that evening, with the stars as their canopy, Noah's heart beat wildly with nervous anticipation.

He wanted this night to be perfect and was finally ready to confess his feelings for Emma. Entwining their fingers together to calm himself, he took a deep breath before baring his soul. "I know we haven't been together for long, but I hope you know how much I care for you." He placed his finger against her mouth when she started to say something, tracing his thumb along her bottom lip. "Let me finish, sweetheart. Please. I'm a little nervous, so bear with me."

"Okay." She spoke so softly he almost missed it.

Lifting her chin so she looked him in the eye, he took a deep breath before he spoke. "God, I love you, Emma. I'm so in love with you, it scares me sometimes. I know there are probably rules for this, and I'm surely mucking it up completely," he paused, inhaling a deep breath, thankful to have finally spoken the words.

Suddenly worried he'd said the wrong thing, his heart sank into his stomach. He knew he should've told her over a candlelit dinner with a champagne toast. "You don't have to say it back to me, but I needed to say it. I wanted to tell you, here…in the spot where I was completely captivated by you." Holding his breath, he watched as the full impact of his words registered on her pretty face.

Emma's beautiful emerald green eyes were suddenly rimmed with moisture as she touched his cheek with a trembling hand. He watched a tear spill from her eye, and slid his thumb across her cheek to wipe it away.

"I love you too, Noah. And, for the record, you didn't muck anything up. It was perfect. You're perfect. And I must say that it was also very romantic…very, very romantic. I need you to kiss me now."

"Your wish is my command, my love." He couldn't stop the goofy grin from spreading across his face and didn't want to. She loved him and that was all that mattered.

"I like the sound of that."

The convenience of being under the cover of darkness with a blanket to hide their wandering hands and lips was overridden by his need to get her naked. Now. Trying to maintain his balance so they didn't flip the hammock over was virtually impossible as their movements became more and more erratic.

Pulling away from her, Noah tried to catch his breath, to calm himself long enough to make it indoors. He doubted he'd make it to their bedroom, but the couch, or even the floor would have to do, or maybe against the wall.

Being a recognized figure had many blessings, but privacy wasn't one of them. Sportsmen were held to a high standard in En Zed, a standard Noah strived to always live up to, and public fornication would not be looked upon favorably. He also wanted to protect Emma from the scrutiny of the media's obsession with the private lives of footy players, the All Blacks in particular, for as long as possible.

Not willing to lose the connection, he lifted her from the hammock and into his arms, cupping her bum in his hands as she crossed her long legs behind his back. He couldn't help but smile as she slid her arms around his neck and kissed him there.

Finally in the house, he set her on her feet. "Drop your gear," he commanded a little too sternly, based on her shocked expression. "Please," he amended softly, quickly kissing her before turning to close the blinds.

He felt the thrill of anticipation as he turned to find Emma completely naked, still standing where he'd left her, a pile of clothes discarded at her feet. "Good girl. Now come and sit on the couch for me."

"I shouldn't follow orders like this, but I haven't seen this side of you before, and well…it's kind of a turn-on." Her sassy smile was almost his undoing, but he stood back and let her walk on by.

He was holding on by a thread and his last ounce of control was spent resisting the need to reach out and touch her as she sauntered past him. What he really wanted was to throw her over his shoulder and take her to bed. But he'd fantasized about having her like this for some time now and needed to see it through.

"Now, lean back and spread your legs for me." He watched as she complied and almost lost it right there. She was so damn sexy; he was instantly so hard he could pound nails. "Damn. I want to do so many things to you right now, I don't know where to start."

"How about here?" his little minx smiled seductively, raising her hand to her mouth, skimming her fingers along her full lower lip, and when her tongue peeked out, grazing the tips of her fingers, he groaned. "Or maybe, you'd rather start here?"

Noah watched in amazement as Emma slowly ghosted her fingers down the long column of her neck and cupped her breasts with both hands, caressing them gently before teasing her hardened nipples.

"As much as I adore the lovely options you've put on offer, I'm not sure they're where I want to start, though. Anything else you have in mind? I'm open for suggestions." He quickly lost his clothes and stood before her naked, waiting for her next move, hoping she was going where he thought she might.

His heart was racing riotously and he felt out of breath. Needing some relief, he stroked himself as he watched her bite down on her lower lip, while the corners of her mouth twitched up into a suggestive smile. Her eyes opened widely as she scanned his naked body before coming to rest on his hand sliding up and down the length of his painfully hard erection.

"Mmm. Well, maybe, just maybe, this is more to your liking?" Watching, frozen in place, his heart pounded violently, as she left one hand on her breast and lowered the other over her ribs. As if in slow motion, her fingers splayed across her stomach before dipping between her legs.

Letting out a loud growl, he got on his knees and replaced her hand with his mouth. She'd teased him long enough and now it was his turn. Using his shoulders, he opened her further, and watched as she writhed in ecstasy, her hands flailing about as they searched for something to hold onto, finally landing on his shoulders. Listening to her whimper and moan his name as he drove her up and over the crest of her orgasm, almost had him joining her.

Sitting back on his haunches, he gave himself a moment to take in the sight of her, all flushed and flustered. "Turn around and get on your knees and hold onto the back of the couch," he requested, pleased to see her hurriedly comply without question, and the sight of her waiting for him was better than he'd imagined.

Tracing the length of her spine with his fingers, they finally came to rest on her perfect round bum and he caressed her there, enjoying the silkiness of her soft skin. The feel of her warmth surrounding him was overwhelming as he entered her, and if he didn't get himself under control quickly, it'd be over before it began, so he held still as he took in a deep breath before continuing.

Bending over, he licked a trail up the length of her spine to her neck before kissing her there. Unable to resist, he reached around and filled his palm with her breast. Moaning out a shaky breath, she watched him over her shoulder, crying out as she started to climax and it wasn't long before he joined her, collapsing breathlessly onto the couch.

Encircling her in his arms, he pulled her tightly against his chest, thrilled he'd put the satisfied look on her face.

"Holy shit. That was...um...hot." Still overwhelmed from their explosive encounter, he tried to calm his racing heart with the sweet comfort of her softness.

"I never knew you had such a bossy side," she giggled. "Or that I'd comply so easily."

"I'm thinking I may have to explore that hidden side of my personality more often."

"I'm a little embarrassed. I've never…you know…done that in front of anyone before. Not sure what came over me." He watched as her cheeks turned an adorable shade of pink at her candid confession.

"Don't be embarrassed, Emma. It was dead sexy. I was this close to coming in my trousers." He pinched his fingers together for emphasis. "I wanted to let you finish, but I couldn't. I think every man fantasizes about watching his lover pleasure herself. It's pretty much a given. We may have to try that again sometime and see if I can hold out long enough for you to make my dream come true."

"Oh, my God. You are such a guy," she chuckled, slapping his chest, then to his delight, she left her hand there, gently caressing him.

"Well, since you didn't say no, I'll hold out hope."

"Keep dreaming," she laughed, lifting off the couch and holding out a hand for him. "Now take me to bed, Noah."

"Just where I want you." He laced his fingers through hers and gladly followed her, primed and ready for another round.

Finally succumbing to the need for sleep, Noah held her in his arms and closed his eyes, replaying the evening moment by moment, not wanting to forget a thing.

"I love you." He loved the sound of those three little words and his heart swelled with contentment before he leaned in and sweetly kissed her on the lips.

"I love you, too. I don't think I'll ever get tired of hearing you say that to me," she whispered, reaching up to gently brush his cheek with her soft fingertips.

"Then it's a good thing I'll never get tired of telling you," he admitted happily. "I love you, sweetheart."

Resting her head on his chest, she fell fast asleep in his arms. Holding her tightly, he watched the way her lips curled into a sweet smile as she slept and he knew, without a doubt, that she was the one he'd been waiting for.

He lay awake for a long while, thinking about the future. He had the girl of his dreams in his arms, in his bed, and now he needed to figure out a way to keep her.

Moonlight spilled into the room, casting a silvery glow over her soft skin, giving her the appearance of an ethereal goddess. Waves of golden hair surrounded her like a crown of shimmering silk, and her hand rested against his still-pounding heart.

He felt a sudden burst of panic at the thought of losing her. Mentally corralling his wayward thoughts, he discarded them to the rubbish bin where they belonged. He wasn't a quitter, and he never gave up when he wanted something badly enough.

The only thing he'd ever wanted this badly was to play footy, and from a very young age, he set out to accomplish that goal. He'd worked hard and sacrificed a good chunk of his social life to make it a reality, with no regrets, and never looked back. Over the course of his career, he'd had the privilege of sharing the stage with royalty and international celebrities, but none of that compared to the honor of having the love of his sweet Emma. What they shared was precious.

She was precious.

# CHAPTER 18

Emma was relieved when Noah asked her to stay with him once Lily and Josh returned from their honeymoon, happily making room in his home for her as she shifted some of her belongings to his house. Living with Noah was everything she could've hoped for, but at the same time, it wasn't forever and she needed to keep reminding herself of that pesky little fact as they happily lived in a bubble, blissfully ignoring the elephant in the room.

Emma knew it wasn't in her best interest to move in with Noah, especially since they were behaving like a married couple, but she selfishly wanted to spend as much time with him as possible. Even knowing it would make it that much harder when her time in New Zealand was up, it was impossible to walk away.

Deciding that suspending reality until she boarded the plane for home was the only option at this point, Emma was determined to enjoy every minute she had with him. Waking up to the sound of Noah's beating heart beneath her ear, tucked securely in his arms, made it easy to forget her worries and forge ahead.

The next few weeks flew by as classes were finally beginning and Noah was busy training with the Blues. It made her proud to see how hard he worked, and his dedication to the team and his teammates was unparalleled. Sharing in Noah's excitement for the game, Emma was looking forward to attending her very first rugby match at Eden Park. By now, she'd watched what felt like hundreds of them on TV with Noah, but she knew nothing would compare to being there when he stepped onto the field.

Noah had secured tickets for her, Lily, and Josh to attend the match together, and the anticipation and excitement in Auckland had ratcheted up to a level like nothing she'd ever experienced before. She didn't know how he dealt with the constant pressure. Every time you opened the paper or turned on the news, there was another story speculating on how this or that player was performing, or not performing.

Wanting to help him succeed in her own small way, Emma made sure his home life was as stress-free as possible. Seeing the wives and girlfriends of professional athletes back home blamed for poor performance, she was determined to keep her name out of the conversation. The thought of being publically excoriated made her queasy. Noah was a national hero and, as such, was expected to perform his best at all times...no mistakes and no excuses.

Since Valentine's Day fell midweek, they'd gone to his parents' house on Papamoa Beach the prior weekend, where they'd blissfully played in the sun by day and made love by night. The weather had cooperated for the most part and, when it didn't, it gave them an excuse to stay in bed. Not that staying in bed with Noah was a hardship...far from it.

On Valentine's Day, they'd planned to share a quiet dinner at home, and he'd arrived with a huge bouquet of wildflowers and a takeaway from a local café. She didn't care about a fancy dinner out, for her it was the simple act of spending time together that she cherished the most, plus staying home would guarantee an uninterrupted meal.

Taking in the sight of Noah's little boy grin, as he held out a beautifully wrapped gift for her, Emma couldn't help but rip into it. She'd never been one to slowly unwrap presents anyway and Noah's enthusiasm was contagious.

"Oh, Noah. It's so beautiful," she exclaimed excitedly, touching the heart-shaped pendant hanging from a delicate silver chain with her fingertip.

"I'm glad you like it. Here let me help you put it on," he said, reaching for the necklace he'd given to her.

"Thank you," she delighted, lifting her long hair, then stroking the pendant as it rested against her chest.

"You're very welcome. It looks lovely on you," he smiled, pulling her onto his lap.

"I have something for you, too. Although, it doesn't seem adequate after this," she said shyly, placing a gift wrapped in bright red paper in front of him.

"I'm sure I'll love it," he assured her, taking the gift she offered him.

"But before you open that, I'd like to play a song for you." She lifted off his lap and retrieved her guitar, settling it on her thighs as she sat on the coffee table facing him. She'd been practicing Adele's 'Make You Feel My Love' and hoped she could get through it without crying. Knowing Noah was as sentimental as she was, she knew the heartfelt lyrics would touch him as deeply as they did her, and she wanted it to be perfect for him.

"Cheers, sweetheart. That was brilliant." Noah heard the quiver in his voice and swallowed past the lump forming in the back of his throat, completely overwhelmed. It was truly the nicest thing anyone had ever done for him. He could listen to her sing to him all day long, and the way she held his eyes as she sang the meaningful lyrics made it even more special.

"Thanks. I've wanted to play that song for you, but it took me a while to be able to sing it without breaking down. It's like it was written from my heart to yours." She settled on his lap once again and he held her against his chest, wanting to consume her. He'd never felt so loved and was on the verge of tears. "Now, on a much lighter note, open your gift. I'm dying for you to see it. I hope you like it."

As he unwrapped the pressie, he couldn't help but smile, looking at the framed photo of the two of them taken at the top of The Mount with the gorgeous Bay of Plenty and Papamoa Beach as the backdrop. They looked a little worse for wear in the photo, but were happy as they held hands, laughing at something he couldn't remember.

"It's perfect, love. I was chuffed to show you one of my favorite places that day. When we'd go there on holiday as a boy, I used to hike to the summit and sit there for hours, just looking out at the view, thinking…dreaming. To have a picture of the two of us in that very spot…well it means a lot to me. Thank you, baby." He set the photo on the table and draped his arms around her waist, pulling her against him, as he placed his lips on hers for a gentle kiss.

"You're welcome. I know you said you wanted a copy of the picture of us from New Year's but since I brought it with me from Lily's, I thought a different one might be nice. I'm so glad I picked this one now that you've told me that."

"Well, now that the gift-giving is done and dusted, I think there's one more present I'd like to unwrap." He couldn't stop the mischievous grin from spreading across his face, as he traced his finger along the V of her shirt, sliding it between her breasts, tickling and teasing her there.

"I think you're a mind reader," Emma smiled, letting her hand come to rest on his chest before easing herself off his lap and reaching for his hand.

Noah quickly lifted off the chair and took her hand in his, leading her to the bedroom where he planned to unwrap her…layer by delicious layer.

Noah had a light practice, a captain's run, and they'd invited Lily and Josh for dinner. After a few days of constant rain, Emma spent a few blissful minutes soaking up the sun on the deck, while Noah prepared the grill for dinner.

Opening the door to Lily and Josh a short while later, they both stood back and watched curiously as Josh carried in a large package and set it down on the floor, leaning it against the back of the couch in the lounge.

"What's that?" Emma asked, inquiring about the colorfully wrapped package, after giving both Josh and Lily a hug.

"It's a gift for you and Noah," Lily answered brightly.

"Can we open it now, or do we have to wait?" Emma pleaded, giving Lily a hopeful smile.

"I've been dying to give it to you, so please don't make me wait any longer," Lily requested anxiously.

Inside the large parcel were three individually-wrapped boxes, one larger than the other two. "Is this one of those things where each box contains another box?" Emma laughed, reaching for one of the smaller packages.

"No, cheeky bugger. Open the bigger one first," Lily demanded, when she saw Emma's hand settle on one the smaller boxes.

"Alright. Oh, I'm so excited. Can't imagine what it is," she said, gently shaking the gift, lifting it to her ear and listening for a clue as to what it could be.

"Stop that and open it already," Lily chastised her.

As Emma opened the larger box, she heard herself gasp for air and tears immediately stung the backs of her eyes at the sight of the picture of her and Noah. It was printed on a large canvas, and Emma guessed it was about four feet tall by three feet wide.

It was from the New Year's Eve party, taken from behind as they watched the fireworks display. Noah's arm was draped over her shoulder as her head rested against him. Their silhouettes were highlighted by the colorful explosions over the Auckland skyline, and on the bottom of the picture was a quote that read,

*"I've always heard of seeing fireworks when someone kisses you. But I really did."*

"I don't know what to say, Lily. I'm speechless. It's so beautiful. I think I'm going to cry." Emma reached for Lily and hugged her tightly in a long embrace. "How'd you know what I said, though?" She inquired, still reeling from the thoughtful gift.

"Josh was taking a video of the fireworks as we stood behind you. I downloaded everything off my camera when we got home from our honeymoon and I found it. With all the craziness of the wedding, I'd forgotten about it," she sighed dramatically, taking a deep breath. "Now hurry up and open the others. I'm dying for you to see them."

The next photo was slightly smaller than the larger one and was of their first kiss. Noah's arms held her closely around the waist and her arms were clasped around his neck, with the colorful sky behind them serving as a backdrop against their profiles.

She quickly moved to open the last photo, desperate to see the final image of Noah's forehead pressed to hers as they both smiled, gazing adoringly into each other's eyes. It was such an intimate photo and, in light of the fact that they'd only just met, it was even more telling. The love she saw in their smiles brought her back to the night she and Noah shared their first kiss, and how she'd known, even then, that she'd met the man who would own her heart.

Looking at the three pictures laid out before her, she felt Noah's arms slide around her waist as he stood behind her. Leaning into him for comfort, she felt the tears slide down her cheeks.

Swiping at the dampness on her cheeks, she turned to Lily who was looking at her with a satisfied smile on her face. "Oh, Lily. I had no idea. I don't know how to thank you. They're so beautiful, and thoughtful. And thank you too, Josh," Emma said, as she tried to collect herself. She couldn't remember ever receiving such a special gift. She'd cherish them forever.

"Cheers, Lily," Noah finally commented with a voice that quivered slightly. "I think they'll look perfect over our bed. What do you think, Emma?"

"I want to hang them right now, but I think I'd like to look at them while we eat dinner," Emma said, carefully arranging them along the back of the couch as Noah and Josh cleaned up the debris. "I don't know how to thank you. They're amazing," Emma continued, gushing over the photos.

"I'm glad you both like them and you can thank us by enjoying them. I was quite pleased when they were delivered. They transferred nicely to canvas, don't you think? The fireworks in the background along with the Auckland skyline came out just as I'd hoped. And don't even get me started on how adorable the two of you are."

"Well, I love them, and you." Emma placed a kiss on Lily's cheek and held her in a tight embrace before releasing her. "Now, let's eat. I'm starving and I made a strawberry angel food cake for desert."

"Yum," Noah and Josh said in unison, as they stepped onto the deck.

After cleaning up from dinner, they debated where to hang the photos. Deciding they looked best on the wall over their large king-sized bed, Noah removed the generic landscape that currently occupied the spot and replaced it with the personal photos. The larger canvas was flanked on either side by the smaller images and took up most of the wall over their bed. Standing back to admire his handiwork, he wanted to kiss Lily for such an amazing gift.

Making love that night took on an added lightness when he whispered in Emma's ear as they lazily cuddled together. "I've always heard of seeing fireworks when you come. But I really did."

Emma laughed out loud before smacking him on his arm. "Oh, my God. I can't believe you just said that to me." She laughed again until he kissed her.

"Next time, you can be on top so you can see fireworks, too," he chuckled. "It's the least I can do. Only fair, yeah?"

"Of course." She wrapped her long legs around his hips and flipped him onto his back, and he swore he'd never seen a more beautiful sight. "I'm ready for the show, big boy. How about you? You going to show me some fireworks, baby?"

"No worries there, sweetheart. Got you covered. Get ready for a few explosions."

"Promises, promises," Emma said seductively, circling her hips along his growing erection.

"I never make promises I can't deliver, sweet cheeks," he grinned, sliding his hands along her hips, then slowly inching his way up until finally reaching her breasts, caressing them, loving the little moans she uttered as she arched her back and rocked against him.

"Um…hmmm." She braced her hands on his chest and her sexy smile stole his breath. "Well, I think it's time to settle up. I'm ready for the show. Are you?" He answered with a single thrust of his hips, filling her completely, as she cried out.

Taking her seat in the large stadium the following evening, Emma was filled with nervous excitement. She'd been to plenty of football games back home with friends and family, but this was unlike anything she'd ever experienced before, and hearing the large crowd cheer for the man she loved was surreal. When Noah was getting ready to take his position in the backfield, she saw him glance her way before turning his focus to the match. Emma was sure she blended in with the rest of the crowd, but it was comforting to know he was thinking of her.

According to Josh, Noah was considered one of the best full-backs in the world, and he had a keen sense of being able to anticipate the opposition's next move. Having an expert sitting with her was proving helpful as the match progressed and, thankfully, Josh only shook his head and snickered at a few of her questions.

Emma held her breath quite a few times as Noah was taken down by the opposing team. It was hard to watch him be repeatedly knocked to the ground, but he seemed to be able to shake it off and continue. She wished he wore the pads and helmet that American football players used to protect themselves. His position wasn't as physical as the forwards, but he was still taking a beating.

She had to laugh at herself at the realization that she mistakenly thought rugby was like football, just without the protective gear. This was nothing like football. This was badass, she thought, as she watched them run into each other at full speed without regard for the pain inflicted.

Emma still didn't understand the rules of the game, but as a spectator, she enjoyed watching rugby much more than football. Having a vested interest in one of the players probably had a lot to do with it, but it wasn't the only reason. It was fun to watch them expertly toss the ball to one another as they moved the ball down the field towards their try line.

At the beginning of the match, she refused to cheer when Evan Thompson made a good play, out of principle and solidarity with her sister, but as she watched the camaraderie he shared with Noah on the field, she had a hard time keeping herself in check. When Evan scored a try, she stood and cheered for the team, not Evan, she told herself.

Emma wondered if Noah had told him he was dating Ali's sister, and wondered what Evan would think about it, then wondered why she wondered what he would think.

She thought back to when she'd first met Evan on her family's annual vacation to Auckland to visit Lily and her family. Ali had been studying abroad that year and had met Evan at his parents' horse farm. Emma's first impression of him, at the time, was that he seemed like a nice enough guy, and Ali was over the moon. She'd never seen her sister so smitten before.

Evan missed Abby's birth, but arrived the next day with flowers and Abby's now-favorite teddy bear in hand. He'd stayed at the hospital and then at her parents' house in the guestroom and had been good about helping with diaper changes and bath time, but with Ali breastfeeding, there really wasn't much else he could do.

Emma would never forget how fragile Abby looked as her daddy cradled her in his massive arms. It was still impossible for Emma to reconcile how, after spending a week and a half with Abby, he'd left and hadn't come back. She understood he had obligations to the team, but shouldn't his daughter take precedence?

The loud roar of the crowd mentally shook her from her wandering thoughts and brought her back to the game unfolding before her.

She cheered as Noah assisted in scoring a try, but cringed when he took a hard hit as he unloaded the ball to the player who scored, and was slammed to the ground. Shaking it off, he jumped back up immediately, even though it was enough to bring most men to their knees, and charged towards his teammates to celebrate.

As the game progressed, the score went back and forth in a nerve-wracking roller coaster of emotions. It was just a game, she knew that, and losing was a part of it, but she really wanted the Blues to win.

Jumping to her feet, along with the majority of the capacity crowd, Emma's heart swelled with pride when, after a long march down the field, Noah scored a try. Watching him dive over the line after sprinting the last few yards, she felt the welling of tears in her eyes, and reached out for Lily and hugged her tightly. She really wanted to hug Noah, but that would have to wait until he got home later.

After an agonizing back and forth, the Blues finally took the lead and held onto it as the clock ran out. Emma watched as they lined up and shook the hands of the players from the opposing team, and Noah's easygoing nature showed as he lingered on the field, laughing with the other players after he made it through the line.

The crowd had thinned by the time he headed for the changing room and, this time, when Noah looked up, he smiled and gave her a slight wave. He looked battle-weary in his grass-stained and sweaty kit.

With his game face still on, he smiled for the crowd gathered along the railing calling out his name, but she saw the exhaustion hidden behind the smile. She didn't expect anything less from him, knowing how dedicated he was. Noah would give everything he had, and then find a little more, and give that too. It was the way he lived every aspect of his life, and she counted herself lucky to be a part of it.

Not sure what time Noah would be home, she got ready for bed and waited for him in the lounge. Settling into the cushions with her e-reader and a cup of tea, Emma felt the heaviness settle behind her eyelids. It'd been a long day full of excitement and a surprising amount of stress.

Ignoring her book, she let her mind drift back to the sound of the crowd cheering for Noah and the team, and how proud she was of him. Recognizing he was a role model for young boys still dreaming of reaching the pinnacle of the rugby world, he never took it for granted, and appreciated everything he had. Noah never forgot that he was once one of those young boys, looking up to his heroes, and he didn't want to let them, or his teammates, down, or disappoint them by slacking and not giving his all.

Noah dropped his bag by the kitchen door and went looking for Emma, anxious to see her, wanting to celebrate the win with her. His aches and pains were forgotten when he found her sleeping on the couch, her hands in the praying position under her cheek, and he wanted to bow his head and give thanks to the heavens for her.

It seemed a sin to wake her, but he really needed to relax and she'd become his preferred method, and since she was on the couch and not in bed, he guessed she'd intended to stay up for him. Gently stirring her, his heart did a little flip-flop in his chest when her eyes fluttered open.

"Hey, baby," Noah whispered, while he stroked her hair, leaning over her.

"Hey," she sleepily responded, and he couldn't help but smile as she sat up and stretched. "I tried to stay up, but must've fallen asleep."

"Your tea has gone cold," he mentioned, nodding towards the full mug abandoned on the table next to her. "Can I get you something to drink?"

"No. I just want some water, but sit down, and I'll get it." Emma stood and put her hands on his shoulders, guiding him onto the couch. "What would you like?"

"I'll just have some water too. You up for some conversation? I'm still a bit amped. Not quite ready for bed yet."

"Well, I had a great time tonight," Emma proudly exclaimed, as she sat next to him, handing him a bottle of cold water. "It was exciting to watch you play. And when you scored that try, let me tell you...that was absolutely amazing. I wanted to run down there and kiss you, I was so happy."

Noah reached over and pulled her onto his lap, hugging her tightly. "How about you give me that kiss now, eh," he stated without question.

"Gladly," she smiled against his lips, leaning in and giving him a slow wet kiss. "Congratulations on the win. And, can I just state for the record that you were the sexiest man on the field tonight and I'm glad you're all mine?"

"Thanks. Cheers for that, and I'm glad I'm all yours, too. And I had the pleasure of coming home after a hard day at the office to find sleeping beauty in my lounge." She snickered and Noah couldn't help but kiss her full lips again at the happy smile on his beautiful Emma's face.

"Yeah, well, I felt more like Maleficent when I was watching you get tackled. A couple of times I wanted to take off my earrings and throw down. You must be sore, though." Emma ran her hands along his shoulders and down his arms, gently massaging along the way, her touch soothing his aches and pains.

Noah chuckled at the image of her all hot and bothered, coming to his defense. "I would've loved to see that. But it's nothing serious. I'll be right in a few days. Just a few bangs and bruises. But feel free to keep that up. It feels good." Unable to resist, he ran his fingers through her hair, reveling in the silkiness of it.

"It was helpful to have Josh with me so he could explain what was happening. I was worried about you, though. Josh said when that guy grabbed you by the back of the collar, that he should've gotten a penalty for that. That it's not allowed." He reached up to soothe the worry lines between her eyes, touched by her concern.

"Yeah, but sometimes we get by on something too, so it usually all works out. Not to worry, it looked worse than it was." He tried to ease her worries, even though it had hurt like hell when he came down hard on Colin's knee in his back, and was sure he'd have a pretty nasty bruise there tomorrow.

"I don't know how you do it. If someone dragged me down to the ground like that, I'd cry like a baby."

Tamping down his rage and the overwhelming need to protect her, he shook his head as he thought about what she said. "If someone *ever* laid a hand on you like that, it would be the last thing they ever did."

It was so natural to kiss her, he realized, as she placed her hands around his neck and he brought his lips to hers. She adjusted herself and slid one leg over his, straddling his hips. "This is better," she whispered against his lips before kissing him again.

"I have a better idea. Wrap your legs around me," he said, lifting off of the couch and heading for the bedroom, his hands cupping her backside, holding her against him. As her soft cradled his hard, he didn't even try to hold back the groan at the contact.

"I thought you wanted to talk," she giggled, as he squeezed her bum.

"Talking's overrated. I can think of a better way to relax and enjoy a hard-fought victory."

"To the victor goes the spoils," Emma laughed, as he dropped her on the bed.

"Uh huh. Now, since I entertained you all night…I think it's my turn." He gave her a naughty grin as he sat down on the bed.

"What'd you have in mind?"

He maneuvered her between his legs, his hands coming to rest on her hips. "How about a little dance for me?"

Taking a few steps back, he watched as her eyes grew dark with desire and she seductively circled her hips. Tilting her head back, she ghosted her hands down the column of her neck, lowering them slowly over her collarbone. Filling her hands with her breasts, he felt the muscles in his jaw twitch as he adjusted the now-painful bulge behind his zipper. Her pebbled nipples begged for his touch, and as she reached for the hem of her top, slowly raising it over her head, he licked his lips.

Needing to feel her, he crooked his finger and smiled as she closed the gap between them. His hands came to rest on her hips, gripping her tightly as he licked her budded nipple and then sucked it into his mouth. Throwing her head back, she let out a loud moan as she raked her hands through his hair, holding him to her as his hungry mouth feasted on one firm peak and then its twin.

Finally pulling away from him, she hooked her thumbs in the waistband of her sleep-shorts and slowly lowered them, inch by inch. Resisting the almost-uncontrollable urge to touch her was painful, but he was mesmerized by the skin she was revealing, and he didn't want to distract her.

The pounding in his ears was deafening, and he couldn't stop himself from reaching for her, crushing his lips to hers in an explosive kiss.

"Cheers for that, sweetheart. I wasn't expecting all that. That was the sexiest thing I've ever seen. Ranks up there with that night on the couch."

"I'm not done yet, and you're wearing too many clothes, baby." He was speechless as she undid his belt and slid his trousers and boxer briefs from his hips.

Kneeling in front of him, she stroked his erection before taking it into her mouth, and not wanting to miss a thing, he pulled her hair back and held it in his hand. Needing to touch her, he reached between them to caress her breast and her sexy moan vibrated in the back of her throat, almost finishing him off right then and there. Holding back, he tugged gently on her hair.

"I wasn't done yet," she frowned. "Didn't you like it?" she asked demurely, as she traced her finger along the length of him, teasing him, as she slid her thumb over the top.

"If I liked it any more, it would've been over already and I didn't want to finish like that. I want to be deep inside you when I do. Now, come here," he commanded, as he lifted her to her feet.

Noah groaned as she shoved him onto his back and lowered herself onto him with her hands resting on his chest as she moved over him. He was awed by how beautiful she was as she lost herself to her own pleasure. Her sexy moans became increasingly unsteady as she started to climax, turning into sighs and exclamations of his name. Her perfect breasts swayed as she moved and he cupped them in his hands, teasing her nipples, and the added sensation was enough to put her over the precipice as she cried out.

He was barely hanging on as he gripped her hips and plunged into her. It only took a few thrusts before he followed her in his release. Still joined, she collapsed onto his chest, their hearts beating in unison, as Noah mindlessly traced the length of her spine, trying to gather his thoughts.

"How can it be that every time I make love to you I think it's the best ever... until the next time and I think the same thing?" Noah wondered out loud, hugging her tightly to him.

"I know. That was amazingly good," she beamed, as she circled his nipple with her fingertip, then softly kissed him there.

"That was all you, baby," Noah observed, lifting her chin to give her a kiss.

"You make me feel sexy and safe when I'm with you," she admitted.

"I love you, Emma, and I always want you to feel that way when you're with me."

"I love you, too, and congratulations on your win tonight," she said, before leaning in for another kiss.

# CHAPTER 19

Having grown accustomed to falling asleep with the whisper of her breath tickling his chest as he held her, Noah couldn't help but wonder how he'd survive without her once she moved back to America. He hadn't realized how lonely he was until she came along and filled his life with the joys of companionship. Life with Emma was fun and exciting, and it was the little things she did that made him the happiest.

When he returned home after a long day, he was now greeted with flower gardens bursting with pretty flowers of every variety, instead of the once barren landscape. He'd offered to hire someone, but she wouldn't hear of it, insisting they do it themselves, so his free time had been spent getting his hands dirty digging in the dirt, along with the satisfaction of a job well done.

She surrounded herself with beautiful things, and his once-quiet house was now filled with the sounds of music and his sweet, sweet Emma. Just knowing she was waiting for him, he found himself rushing home to be with her.

He may have spent countless hours agonizing over every detail of the renovation, but he hadn't a clue when it came to decorating, and watching her face light up when she'd found a treasure at the market, knowing just the spot for it, was surprisingly satisfying. Emma had filled the empty spaces with love and a few strategically-placed bits and pieces, turning his house into a home one knick-knack and scented candle at a time.

A few pictures from Josh and Lily's wedding and her family's visit were added to the growing mixture of photographs scattered about the different rooms. He knew it was her way of surrounding herself with family and friends, even though they were far away, but his stomach twisted every time he caught her longingly gazing at a photograph of her family, seeing the sadness in her pretty green eyes, knowing how much she missed them. At times, he resented having the constant reminder of her family, their smiling faces silently mocking him, knowing they'd be the victors in the battle for Emma's loyalty.

Noah's heart ached as he thought about living in his house without her. She'd left her mark in every corner of every room and on every surface. He wondered if he'd have to tear down the house and start over, but even then it would still be a painful reminder of what they'd shared, when every time he walked in the door he'd remember that it was different because she'd left.

He wanted her to stay, and had spent hours trying to figure out if she felt the same way. He'd been reluctant to bring it up, not wanting to pressure her, but he didn't know how much longer he could stand the uncertainty. Noah knew, without a doubt, that she loved him, but she was also a member of a fiercely-loyal and close-knit family, and family meant everything to her.

Noah knew it was a big ask for Emma to give up everything and everyone to stay with him, and he'd seen how distressed she was when her family went back home, but as he looked at her pretty face, so peaceful as she slept, he could only pray that when the time came, she'd pick him. He'd do everything in his power to make sure she had a happy life, and it wasn't like she'd never see them again, he told himself, trying to convince his doubting mind that he had a chance to keep her.

Noah was traveling to Hamilton for his upcoming match against the Chiefs and he'd wanted Emma to join him so he could introduce her to his family. Knowing he was leaving for South Africa a few days later, he wanted to spend as much time with her as possible before leaving town for two weeks. When she'd told him she had an exam that she couldn't miss, he'd been disappointed, and even though he understood, he still groveled a little, trying to convince her to skip it and follow him to the bustling metropolis of Hamilton, New Zealand.

Feeling a bit homesick, Noah was happy to be home, but spending time with his family was always a mixed blessing. He was able to recharge his batteries in his childhood home, but he'd always be considered the baby of the family, no matter how old he was or what he accomplished in life. His mum would fuss over him and his dad would lecture him, wanting to make sure he was being responsible with his finances.

Walking in the back door, he kicked off his shoes and dropped his bag on the floor.

"Oh Noah. I'm so glad you're home," his mum gushed, hauling him into a tight embrace before setting him aside as she lovingly gazed at him. "I've missed you, my boy." Her smile always had a way of brightening even his gloomiest of days.

"Missed you too, Mum. Something smells good," he smiled, looking around the familiar kitchen. It was small and outdated, but it would always be home.

"I made a roast for tea tonight. Pity Emma couldn't come. I was so looking forward to meeting her," she frowned, patting his hand in the way she always did.

"She really wanted to come, but had a class she couldn't miss." He wanted to smile, but couldn't bring himself to force one. His mum would've known it wasn't genuine anyway. He missed Emma terribly, and had hoped to be introducing his family to the woman who'd stolen his heart, instead of pining away for her in his mum's kitchen.

"Well, I can see that she's quite special to you, sweetheart. I can't wait to meet the girl who finally has you so enamored you want to bring her home." He knew his mum worried about him and wanted him to settle down and start reproducing, so the fact that he'd found someone had her overjoyed. "Your father's in the lounge. Why don't you go say hello while I finish up in here? I'll call you when your tea's ready. We'll talk later."

"Okay, Mum." Noah reached for his mum and hugged her tightly. "I've really missed you. It's good to be home."

His dad was sitting in his favorite chair reading a book, and setting it on the table next to him when he heard Noah enter the room, he stood to his feet. "Hello, Noah. Good to see you, son."

"Hi, Dad. It's good to see you too," Noah smiled, as his father gave him a quick hug before returning to his chair, and he settled himself on the couch.

"How long you in town for?"

"I'm leaving Saturday morning, so I have a few days to get ready before I leave for South Africa."

"You've got your work cut out for you tomorrow against the Chiefs, I'd say. They're looking good."

"We'll give it a go," he replied, trying not to be defensive. He'd learned long ago that, as much as he'd wished he was, his dad really wasn't all that interested in rugby.

"I've been doing some reading and they're predicting good things for the Blues. Last year was rubbish, but after the win this last week, things seem to have turned around nicely."

"Yeah. It was a squeaker, but in the end we came out on top. Did you watch it?" Why he still yearned for his father's approval like a little boy, he wasn't sure, but he anxiously scrutinized the features of his father's face for signs of acknowledgment.

His dad's smile gave him his answer, and he wanted to jump for joy. "Of course we watched it. You make us proud, son. I hope you know that, and we're looking forward to seeing you play tomorrow."

"Thanks, Dad. It means a lot to me to hear you say that."

"Well, I don't say it enough. But I'm getting old and don't want to leave things unsaid. Had a colleague fall dead with a heart attack last month. He was only a few years older than me. Gets you thinking about your own mortality, I reckon," he frowned, looking at his clasped hands in his lap and then back to Noah.

"I'm sorry to hear that, Dad. Must've been a shock."

"It was, but it got me thinking. Want to make sure my affairs are in order and all that."

"You're making me nervous, Dad. Is there something wrong?" Noah asked, feeling his stomach lurch.

"No. No. No. It just rattled me a bit. Got me thinking, that's all," he tried to reassure his son.

"That's a good thing then, I suppose. Never know when you're time's up, eh?" Noah agreed.

Looking at his father, Noah couldn't imagine a world without him in it. He was a good and decent man, who always put his children first and took good care of his family.

Thankfully, when Noah was first picked up by the Blues, his father sat him down and went over his budget. He'd followed his advice and never lived beyond his means, and made sure to put away money for the future. When some of his mates were going on holidays and purchasing flash cars, he was saving his money, setting himself up for the day when his rugby career ended. And after almost ten years, he now had a comfortable cushion to fall back on. He planned to continue playing for another four or five years, then transition into coaching or broadcasting, but even if it all ended today, he'd be fine financially.

"Come sit down for tea," his mum called out from the kitchen, and Noah was relieved to be done with the depressing conversation. He knew it would happen one day, that it was inevitable, but he needed to focus on the match tomorrow night, not something as distressing as losing his mum or dad.

Tucking into his mother's cooking always made him feel better. For some reason, everything tasted better when she made it. The small kitchen table, which once seemed so large but now barely held his large frame, still bore the scars from where he'd done his homework as a little boy, the little indentations spelling out the story of his life, one letter at a time. It was a witness to his childhood, and was something he wanted with his own children one day.

He'd been thinking more and more about starting a family with Emma. He could picture her swollen belly growing larger as she carried his child, and how beautiful she'd look. Up until this point in his life, he never saw himself living anywhere but New Zealand, but when all was said and done, home was where Emma was.

"So, Noah," his mum hesitated, looking at his dad before continuing hopefully as they made their way into the lounge after they'd finished eating. "It sounds like things are getting serious between you and Emma."

"Yes, she's moved in with me, actually," Noah stated, sitting down on the couch.

"Oh, my." His mum took a deep breath and he didn't miss the excitement that flashed across her face. "That's quite a step."

"I love her, Mum. I want her with me," he replied honestly, and felt the smile on his face as he thought of Emma waiting for him at home.

"She's American, right?" At Noah's nod, his father continued. "Have you spoken about the future? You've worked hard to get where you are in your career, and it's not something you can do in America, at least not at your level."

"I know, and I'm planning to talk to her about it, soon. I want her to stay with me, here…marry me one day. Maybe in the future, when my playing days are over, we can move to America to be close to her family, but I have obligations and am under contract, so I can't move right now. Barring any injuries, I probably have another six years, tops. I always thought I'd stay involved in some way, but if she really wanted to go back to America, then I'd have to, eh? It would only be fair."

"Yes, I see," his mum said, as her hand came to rest against her chest, unable to hide her distress at the prospect of her future grandchildren leaving before they'd even been born. If she were wearing her pearls, she'd surely be twisting them between her fingers.

"Well, girls are different than boys. They tend to stay close to their family," his father commented seriously.

"She has family here, though. She's close with her cousin, Lily. Her Aunt and Uncle are here, too. And I'm here. I'm hoping that's enough to convince her to stay," he stated with more confidence than he felt.

"Well, it sounds like you've got your work cut out for you, son. You'll know when the time is right to ask her. Don't put too much pressure on yourself. Or her. From what you've told us, she sounds like a nice girl. And you obviously care deeply for her."

"I do, Dad. She's the one for me. Never thought it would be so difficult, though," Noah confessed, rubbing his hands along the length of his thighs nervously.

"Anything worth having is worth working for. You've proven over the years that, once you put your mind to something, you're willing to go full stop until you accomplish it. If she's the one, then it'll all work out in the end. She'd be lucky to have you, I'd say."

"Thanks, but I'd be lucky to have her. She's an amazing woman." He took a deep breath to calm himself. "But I need to get some rest. Have a big day tomorrow." Standing to his feet, he bent down to give his mum a long hug.

"Good night, Noah," his mum said, before kissing his cheek.

"Night, Mum, Dad." He turned to grab his bag from where he'd left it in the kitchen, then headed up to his childhood bedroom.

Noah's arms felt empty, as he settled himself in his small bed. He missed Emma's warm body and the sweet smell of her hair as it fell in gentle waves over the pillow. Needing to hear her voice before he let sleep come, he reached for his phone.

"Hey, babe."

"Hi, handsome. Are you at your parents' house?" He felt himself relax at the sound of her voice, and her sleepy whisper brought an instant smile to his face.

"Yeah. Just going to bed now, but I wanted to say goodnight. Did you stay at Lily's?"

"I met them for dinner and was going to, but I really just wanted to stay here. Do you mind?" The uncertainty in her voice broke him. How could she think he wanted her anywhere but there? In their home.

"Oi. Of course I don't mind. I just thought you might want to stay with Lily while I was gone, that's all." His words sounded harsh as he exhaled in frustration.

"I know it sounds pathetic, but I'm lonely without you and I can smell you on your pillow and it makes me feel better." Her voice trailed off and he could hear the longing that matched his own.

"About as pathetic as I am. I wish you were here with me. Although this bed could barely fit us both," he chuckled. "But I'd make it work."

"God, I miss you, Noah," she sighed into the phone, sending chills down his spine. "But I wouldn't feel comfortable sleeping with you at your parents' house. Call me old-fashioned, but it wouldn't feel right if we weren't married."

"I know, and my mum wouldn't like it either. They were sorry you couldn't make it, though. They really wanted to meet you."

"Maybe we could plan to have them come up for a visit soon. I'd love to meet them, too."

"I'll talk to them about it in the morning before I leave. But I'm telling you right now, if they come to visit, you're sleeping in our bed. With me." He was a grown man, damn it, and she belonged with him, in his bed, whether his parents frowned upon it or not.

"I think it's different when it's your house and not your parents'. I know my parents wouldn't allow it. They'd think it was disrespectful, and I wouldn't even ask. Their house, their rules." She mimicked her mother, and he was sure she'd heard those words spoken on more than one occasion.

"I can understand that, but it's my house, my rules. And you sleep in my bed, where you belong. Wrapped around me and preferably naked," he chuckled, reflexively reaching out for her, but finding the space empty.

"There's nowhere else I'd rather be, baby. You know that, right?" she paused, exhaling a deep breath. "I love you, Noah." At the sound of her declaration, his heart ached to touch her.

"I love you too, babe. But just the thought of you naked in my bed is making me hard."

"I'm not naked, Noah," she giggled into the phone, reminding him of the sound she made when he tickled her. "But why don't you tell me about your day. Change the subject to something a little less um…stimulating."

"Probably a good idea." He rolled over and took a long breath to clear his mind. "We had an easy day, then knocked off early. I went to Lara's before dinner, since she couldn't make it tonight because Maddie's sick. I didn't stay long, though. She sends her love and Maddie drew a picture for me to give to you."

"Aw. That's so sweet. I can't wait to see it."

"It's no masterpiece, so don't get too excited," he laughed.

"Now, Noah, don't you know that children's artwork is more precious than any masterpiece because they made it just for you?" And that is why he loved her so fiercely. He knew she'd treasure the mess of scribbles that somehow made up a rainbow, stars, and a unicorn, if you looked very, very closely, that is.

"Well, I have it tucked away in my bag, safe and sound for you. So what did you do today?" he asked.

"After class, I went for a swim, and then met Lily and Josh at that café down the street from them for an early dinner. I was planning to stay with them, but when the time came, I just wanted to come home. Lily was disappointed, but I think Josh was relieved," she snickered. "I think he likes having the place all to themselves."

"I'm sure. Just like I like having you all to myself. We're selfish like that, eh?"

"Yeah," she giggled softly before continuing. "I came home and took a walk on the beach. It was a little chilly, but it felt good, then I sat on the swing for a while and just looked at the view. It never gets old, does it?"

"No. I don't think it does. I wish I was there to enjoy it with you, though."

"Me too. Do you think it'll get easier, being away from each other?" she asked in a quiet whisper.

"I don't know, but this sucks. A lot of my teammates have partners, and it's easier for some than others."

"Maybe it's because it's still so new for us, that's why I miss you so much." She sighed into the phone and he longed to comfort her, to hold her in his arms.

"Somehow, I don't think time will make it any easier, baby. The more I have you, the more I need you. I don't think that's going to change."

"I think you're right. It's only been one night and I want to cry. It doesn't feel right without you here." The sadness in her voice ripped a hole in his heart, and he desperately wanted to jump out of bed and drive home to her.

"I'll be home day after next, and you better get your rest, because I'm going to keep you up all night."

"Promises, promises," she chuckled. "And I could say the same thing to you, Noah."

"Great minds think alike." A slow grin spread across his face and he was sure she could see it through the phone line.

"Well, this girl just misses her man's arms around her, and as much as I try to fool myself, your pillow isn't doing the trick. It may smell like you, but it's much too soft."

"There're so many things I could say to that, but cheers to your liking my hard body."

"Among other things." Her suggestive tone made a certain part of his anatomy stand up and take notice.

"Emma...please don't go there. I haven't had to take care of myself in this room since I was a randy teenager." Reaching down, he stroked the front of his shorts, as he adjusted himself.

"I'm sorry, baby. But is it bad of me to find that kind of hot?"

"Very bad. And you're not helping, Emma." If he didn't change the subject soon, he'd have no choice but to take care of business himself, and the thought of that wasn't exciting at all.

"I'm sorry, sweetheart. I'll stop. But it wasn't just me."

"Duly noted. Now let's talk about something else to take my mind off of the growing problem I seem to have...please."

"Umm...let me think." She paused for a long moment. "Okay, my nanny called today to tell me that she finally decided to have her varicose veins taken care of."

"Well...that did the trick. Problem solved." He frowned, and then couldn't help but laugh. "Did she really call you, or are you just telling me that?"

"No. I mean, yes. She called me and we spoke about that, among other things. But she just wanted to say hello and see how I was doing."

"That was nice of her. I'm sure it was good to hear from her."

"Yeah, it was. I miss her so much, and it was good to hear her voice," she paused, and he could hear the sadness in her silence, and the ruffling of the sheets as she shifted in bed.

"I know, sweetheart. Why don't you get some sleep? Will you be watching tomorrow night?" he asked hopefully, rolling onto his back as the bed creaked beneath him.

"Of course. I wouldn't miss it. I'll be cheering you on, baby. I'll even wear one of your jerseys, too."

"I'd like that. Goodnight, sweetheart. I love you." The tone of his voice surprised him; he sounded soft as he professed is feelings.

"I love you more. Goodnight, my love," she whispered before disconnecting.

Staring up at the ceiling, the conversation with his parents replayed over and over in his mind. He kept coming back to the point where he mentioned that he wanted to marry her one day. The admission should terrify him, but it didn't. He wanted more from her than just living under the same roof. He wanted it all.

He wasn't ready to make any grand proposals yet, and he suspected that she wasn't ready to hear one. But one day, he could see himself making her his wife. The thought of her pregnant with their children brought a sudden warmth to his chest. She'd be a great mum. And he had no doubt that she was the one for him, and didn't see that changing…Ever.

Thinking back to the night they'd met, he'd been so taken with her. Without a doubt, she was gorgeous, but there was so much more to her than met the eye. She gave herself freely and honestly, and her thoughts were written all over her pretty face. She was an open book, and it was one of the things he loved most about her. As he closed his eyes, it was Emma's pretty face he was thinking of as he drifted off to sleep with a contented smile on his face.

# CHAPTER 20

The first day of mid-semester break, Emma found herself at Auckland International Airport, waiting for Noah's flight to arrive from Melbourne. She had the next two weeks off from school, and thankfully, other than an away game in Dunedin, Noah would be home for most of it.

They were leaving the following day to spend Easter weekend in Hamilton with Noah's family, and surprisingly, the thought of meeting them was making Emma anxious. She wasn't usually nervous about meeting her boyfriends' parents, but knowing how important it was to Noah, she desperately wanted them to like her and wanted to like them in return.

"Excuse me. Are you Emma?" Interrupted from her thoughts, she turned to find a pretty brunette looking expectantly at her.

"Yes," she answered.

"I'm sorry. I'm Suzanne O'Neill. I'm married to Noah's teammate, Tucker." Suzanne's warm brown eyes and easy smile instantly set Emma at ease as she held out her hand. "Tucker told me you'd be here to pick up Noah, so I thought I'd introduce myself."

"Oh, hi. It's nice to meet you. I haven't met Tucker yet," Emma stated, shaking her hand, and quickly glancing at Suzanne's swollen belly, but knowing better than to inquire if she was pregnant.

"Yes. I'm expecting," Suzanne knowingly laughed, her hand coming to rest on her small baby bump.

"I thought so, but there was no way I was going to ask you. That's one of the fastest ways to gain an enemy," Emma chuckled. "So, how far along are you?"

"Five months now and this is Isabella Grace. She's two." Suzanne smiled adoringly at the little girl taking a nap in the stroller next to her.

"You're going to have your hands full in a few months," Emma stated, remembering the years she'd spent babysitting children that age. It was a lot of fun, but also a lot of work.

"I know, but I can't wait for this little one to get here." Emma watched as Suzanne's hand instinctively returned to her stomach. "You're going to school here, right? At the university?"

"Yes. I'll be here until the end of the year," Emma replied, and felt a sudden pain in her chest at the thought of leaving. New Zealand was feeling more and more like home to her, and the thought of leaving it…and Noah just hurt.

"We don't live that far from there. In Mt. Eden. Maybe we could meet for lunch sometime."

"I'd love that. And, hopefully, Isabella will be awake next time." Emma couldn't help the silly grin that quickly spread across her face as she gazed longingly at the toddler sleeping with her thumb firmly planted in her mouth. She could stare at a sleeping baby for hours, and always marveled at how their peaceful innocence belied the holy terror they could unleash during their wakeful hours.

Emma had found herself thinking more and more about having children of her own lately. Her life plan had always included being married by her mid-twenties and a mother soon thereafter. That plan was currently out the window, since it was going to take years, maybe even decades to get over Noah. Her eggs might've dried up by the time she was ready to date someone else, let alone marry someone whose name didn't start with Noah and end with Parker.

"Give me your number, and I'll give you a call. I'll be staying here when they travel to Dunedin for the match against the Highlanders. Are you going?"

"No. I'll be here. Would you like to meet then?"

"Sure. That sounds lovely," Suzanne smiled, scanning the length of the terminal as the first of the players made their way out.

Emma followed her line of vision and stood straighter at the sight of Noah walking towards her. She felt the hair rise on the back of her neck as their eyes met and he gave her a sweet smile. Noah stopped as a few fans approached for a picture, and then finally made his way to her side.

"Hey, baby." His strong arms enveloped her in a tight embrace, lifting her off the ground as he placed a quick kiss on her lips. Setting her down, he turned to face Suzanne, who was still waiting for her husband to arrive. "I see you've met Suzanne."

"We were just making plans to get together for lunch while you're in Dunedin," Emma answered excitedly at the prospect of making a new friend.

Emma was used to being surrounded by family and friends back home, and missed the constant buzz of energy around her. With Noah traveling as much as he did, she'd been feeling a bit forlorn, and it would be nice to have someone who could relate to the loneliness brought on by the frequent separations.

She'd made a few casual friends since school started, but none she felt comfortable confiding in about her relationship with Noah. She wanted people to befriend her for her, not as a means to get an introduction to Noah, or to score tickets to a match. Noah was a private man and didn't seek the spotlight; she also enjoyed his company way too much to share his attention when he was home.

It was selfish, she knew, but their time together was precious and, much to her dismay, quickly slipping away. New Zealand was going to have him forever, but she'd only have him for a few more months, so she planned to greedily steal him away while she could, keeping him all to herself, and not feel the least bit guilty about it.

"Here's Tucker now." Suzanne's affection for her husband was obvious in her delicate features as her face beamed brighter the closer he got to them.

Tucker's eyes were fixed on his wife as he strode with purpose towards them. His dirty blonde hair framed a face that was classically handsome, and his smile revealed a slight gap between his front teeth. Brown eyes smiled down at his beautiful wife as he hugged her gently, careful not to squeeze her distended belly too tightly, then turned to look lovingly at his sleeping daughter.

"Tucker, this is Emma," Noah introduced them, once he'd properly greeted his wife.

"Nice to finally meet you. I've heard a lot about you," he smiled, and Emma found herself engulfed in his arms. "Emma this and Emma that, is bugger all I've heard lately from this one."

"Oh. Good things, I hope," she giggled as he released her. "And it's nice to meet you, too."

"Of course," he smiled and gave Emma a subtle wink, then turned back to his family.

Noah picked up his bag and led them to the exit, and by the look on his face, he was as anxious to get home as she was. The feel of his fingers as they traced light circles on her palm was distracting as they said their goodbyes to Suzanne and Tucker, then made their way to the car.

Emma didn't miss the grimace that marred his handsome features as he settled his large frame into the driver's seat. He always assured her that he was fine and would be 'right as rain' in a few days, so she usually let it go, but he appeared to be in genuine agony.

The match against the Rebels was particularly brutal, and she'd felt his pain as he was taken down hard on more than one occasion. He was obviously paying the price for it now, even though he was trying his best to hide it.

"Sorry about the loss."

"Thanks. It was a quiet flight back, and you can't help but wonder what you could've done differently. But in the end, you can't win them all, so you just have to learn your lessons and prepare for the next match. But I'm not going to lie, I was gutted."

"I'm sure. Hey..." She lifted her hand to his cheek and smiled when he leaned into her palm. "I didn't miss that face you made when you were getting in the car. Are you alright?"

"Other than a wicked bruise on my ribs, I'm fine. Nothing a few days of rest and some tender loving care from a certain leggy blonde won't fix." He gave her a cheeky grin, but winced as he reached for her hand.

"Oh, baby," Emma drawled. "Why don't I drive so you can relax?"

"Might be a good idea," he confessed, as he moved very gingerly, getting out of the car slowly.

As Emma started the car and headed for home, she took a deep breath. She was glad to have Noah home again. She'd missed him terribly while he was away, and was growing more and more anxious about meeting his family. Having him home relaxed her, and his presence gave her peace of mind.

"Suzanne seemed nice," she stated, as Noah took her hand in his.

"Yeah. She's a saint and been good for Tucker. She keeps him focused and out of trouble."

"Is that a nice way of saying that he was a bit of a bad boy?" Emma chuckled.

"I guess you could say that. He was a mess before he met her. Always going out on the piss and getting into trouble. Not taking care of himself. She keeps him in line."

"Well, then she's been good for him."

"Having a good woman waiting for you at home makes all the difference, eh?" The gentle stroke of his thumb against her wrist was both soothing and exciting, and when she turned to look at him, she had to remember she was driving.

Noah's eyes were a dark sapphire and, even though they were having an average conversation, there was nothing average about the way he was looking at her. His eyes were full of pent-up desire, and suddenly, she couldn't get home fast enough.

She felt the caress of his gaze as it slid from her lips to her breasts, as if he was physically touching her, and her nipples puckered in response.

"Yes, it does," she agreed, and when they got home, she'd show him just how good it could be.

After what felt like an eternity, Emma was finally pulling the car into the garage. Noah's large hand had drifted to her thigh and was slowly tracing a blazing trail up and down the length of it, inching higher with each trip. His constant ministrations were driving her mad with need, and if she had to wait another minute to get her hands on him, she may have burst into flames or pulled the car over and had her way with him on the side of the road.

Dropping his bag by the door, Noah crushed his mouth to hers in a hungry kiss that lit her already-aroused body on fire. His strong arms circled her waist, holding her firmly. She couldn't get enough of him as she pulled his shirt from his trousers, needing to feel the touch of his skin. Within seconds he had her top off and her pants quickly followed, falling in a pile on the kitchen floor.

"Not here. I want to take my time with you," he said, as his appreciative gaze caused a shiver of anticipation. It still amazed her that just one look from him could cause her insides to flutter and her body temperature spike to a fever pitch within seconds. "I want to do too many things to you right now. God, I've missed you, Emma."

"I've missed you, too. So much." She gently kissed him and then started towards their bedroom.

Emma giggled as he licked the sensitive spot behind her ear and his arms banded around her waist from behind, as they marched in step down the hall. She had to focus on putting one foot in front of the other, as one hand covered her breast and the other slid into her panties. The dueling sensations were overwhelming, and by the time they reached their bedroom, she was already on the verge of climax.

Laying her on the bed, Noah stood back just to look at her. He'd missed her so much while he was gone, and the sight of her spread out and waiting for him left him aching to sink into her. He'd missed the rosy blush to her cheeks after he'd satisfied her, and her sexy moans and breathy sighs as she came apart for him.

"You're a sight for sore eyes, baby." He quickly lost the rest of his clothes and reveled in the way she watched him, her eyes following his every movement. She was so pretty in her pink bra and panties, the silken material almost as soft as her skin, but he needed to feel the real thing.

When he joined her on the bed, his lips instinctively found hers as their tongues mated and danced. The taste of her was as intoxicating as her sexy whimpers, but it wasn't enough, he needed more.

Propping himself on his forearms, he leaned down and gently kissed her, loving the glazed look on her pretty face. "I love you, Emma. It's good to be home."

"I love you, too. I've missed you so much. I've missed this." Her fingers softly traced his cheek before wrapping around his neck, pulling him down to her lips for another kiss.

Burying himself in her was like coming home…she was home. And as he made love to her, he made a vow to himself that he wouldn't lose her. Ever.

Collapsing against her, he rolled over onto his side, taking her with him. She snuggled in close, ghosting her fingers along his ribs, as her cheek rested against his bicep, using it as a pillow. Her gentle touch was like a healing balm to his aching muscles.

"This is a really bad bruise, sweetheart. Are you sure you're alright?" He could see the concern in her eyes as she watched her fingers gently ministering to the ugly patch of skin on his ribcage.

"Yeah. I'll be fine. The doctor looked at it. It's just a deep bruise."

"Would a bath help?"

He instantly perked up at the thought. "Will you be in there with me?"

"Maybe," she answered coyly. "Only if you think it would help."

"Oh…I do believe it would. And put some of that honeysuckle stuff in there too, please."

"Aw, you want to smell pretty, baby," she teased.

"Well, I do love to suckle your honey, if you haven't noticed." Her eyes opened wide and even after everything they'd done together, her cheeks tinted with the hint of a blush.

Sinking into the jetted tub full of bubbles, he watched as Emma stood naked in front of the mirror, putting her hair up in a knot on the top of her head. He rested his head against the tub and sighed as she gracefully lowered herself into the hot water, but as he watched her luscious body sink beneath the fluffy cloud, he instantly regretted requesting the bubble bath.

She was a vision of loveliness as she closed her eyes, laying her head back, and the feel of her legs sliding against his under the water was making him hard already.

"This is nice," she smiled, as her hand found his leg under the water and gently massaged it. "I can't believe this is the first time we've taken a bath together."

"You know what they say. The family that bathes together, stays together."

With a sassy grin, she pushed herself off the edge of the tub and quickly closed the distance between them. "Umm hmm, I've heard that a time or two."

He winced. "I'm going to pretend that I'm the only man you've ever shared a tub with. Okay?"

"Mmm, Okay. And I'll pretend that I'm the only woman you've had in this tub." By the pained look on her face, she didn't like the idea at all, and he liked that she didn't like it.

"Well…honestly, you are."

Her face instantly brightened as she settled herself against his growing erection. "Well then, let's christen this bad boy properly…right now." When she pressed her lips against his, he couldn't think of anything he'd rather do than bury himself deep in her sweetness. His hands found her breasts and teased her there as she sank onto him and started to move.

"You are a naughty girl, aren't you?"

"Very," she simply stated, as he stroked her bottom and squeezed it before thrusting into her once again.

The erratic motion caused the water to splash over the edge of the tub and onto the floor, but he didn't care, and as Emma cried out her release, he swiftly followed. Pulling her to his chest, he held on tight as he caught his breath, and wondered how he had gotten so lucky to have her.

"That was amazing. But I think we made a mess." Her laugh tickled his neck as she snuggled against him.

"Don't care. That was worth it. The house could have been on fire and I would have let it burn."

Falling into bed after a shower and a quick dinner, Emma had never felt so good. Having Noah home made everything better...made everything right. While he was away, she'd worked herself into a near-panic over meeting his family, playing out all the different scenarios in her head over and over again. Would they approve of her? Would they be upset they were living together out of wedlock?

Would they wonder why he was wasting his time on a girl who was only temporary? That thought, in particular, made her cringe every time. She refused to believe they were wasting their time. What they shared was special, and as she cuddled next to Noah in their big bed, she had no doubt as to just how special he was.

She never understood the urge to have another person complete you, but as she looked at Noah, that's exactly how she felt...complete. Maybe that's what true love was, completely trusting another human being with your heart. Willingly giving them the power to crush you, but at the same time, opening yourself up to fully experience the power of true love. It was a relief to know she could trust Noah with her heart, that it was safe with him, just as his heart was safe with her.

She wanted to make love to him again, to show him how much she truly loved him, but as she gazed into his tired eyes, she just snuggled against him and rested her arm across his chest. She'd missed the simple act of falling asleep tucked securely against his side, drifting off to sleep with a contented smile on her face.

It was dark outside when she woke with a moan from a very erotic dream where Noah's skilled hands and mouth teased and tormented her, but as awareness settled upon her, she quickly realized it wasn't a dream at all. Noah's hands expertly worshipped her backside as he kissed and licked a path down the line of her spine.

After thoroughly ravishing her until she was gasping for air, driving her higher and higher until she was flying amongst the stars, fireworks exploded behind her eyelids, and she was sure her cries of ecstasy were heard all the way down the beach, but she didn't care.

Noah followed her in his release and collapsed his full weight on top of her, pressing her into the mattress. She could feel his heart pounding against her and his breath tickled the back of her neck as he kissed her there.

Finally lifting off of her, he turned her to face him and hungrily kissed her as his arm slid around her waist, pressing her against his chest. He loved to make out after sex and she loved that he just didn't roll over once he was finished, but kissed her like he couldn't get enough...like she was a treasure. And he was such a good kisser. A girl could get lost in his kisses...In him.

"Wow...you sure know how to wake a girl up," she smiled demurely.

"I needed you, and you didn't seem to mind." His sexy smile had her body waking up all over again.

"Not at all. Feel free to wake me up like that any time you want. I thought it was a dream at first, and was about to wake you up to finish me off." She blushed at her candid confession.

"I'll gladly do it again. Anytime. You just say the word and I'm there." He sounded like a little kid, and she couldn't help but giggle at his dramatics.

His happy expression melted her heart, as he dazzled her with his childish grin. "You're too cute for your own good. You know that?"

"Glad you think so. If you give me just a minute to recover, I'll be ready for another round." He buried his face in her neck and nuzzled her with his nose, then started to nibble on the sensitive spot behind her ear. "Then we can start all over again in the morning."

"You're exhausting," she stated sarcastically, wrapping her legs around his waist, pressing herself wantonly against him.

"You love it and you know it." His knowing look as he hovered over her had a swarm of butterflies fluttering in her stomach and her body instinctively responding to him.

"Yes, I do. Now kiss me, Noah."

She couldn't hide how much she wanted him and delighted in the fact that she didn't have to. One of the things she loved most about being with Noah was the honesty they shared. She always knew exactly where she stood with him and it gave her the security to be herself.

It was such a heady feeling, and she now realized that this was how it was supposed to be. The drama and anxiety that took up too much of her time in previous relationships was draining, and eventually sucked the life out of her, but time spent with Noah was refreshingly drama-free.

If possible, she'd go back in time and save herself for him. If she only knew then what she knew now, she would have. Nothing compared to being with him, and experiencing his love and the act of wholly becoming one with him was more than she'd ever dreamed of.

This was what a healthy relationship was supposed to feel like. It was what her mother tried to describe to her over the years, while trying in vain to talk some sense into her when she mistakenly confused lust and infatuation for true love. This was what her parents shared. Wincing at the thought of her parents having sex, especially the crazy hot variety she'd just shared with Noah, she scrubbed her memory of the disturbing thought.

But this was what her mother wanted her to wait for. For her to not settle for anything less than complete and total surrender, and a love that was equally shared by the other person. Loving someone with all of your heart left you wide open for heartache if the other person didn't feel the same way, but she knew beyond a shadow of a doubt that Noah was just as vulnerable as she was, that he loved her as deeply as she loved him.

# CHAPTER 21

Noah watched as Emma's anxiety level slowly ratcheted up the closer they got to Hamilton. Her fingers had been wrung to within an inch of their lives, and now she was chipping away at her fingernail polish. He'd never seen her so nervous and it was starting to make him edgy too.

He really wasn't sure what to say to ease her anxious mind. "Relax, sweetheart. They won't bite. They're going to love you, almost as much as I do." He tried to give her a reassuring smile, but based on her reaction, she wasn't buying it.

"I'm not usually this nervous and my nervousness is making me nervous. Does that make sense?" She cocked her head and gave him a sweet smile that left him no choice but to smile back at her.

Even though she was clearly worried about meeting his family, she was still the prettiest thing he'd ever seen. Looking at her distressed face, all he wanted to do was pull the car over and hold her in his arms. The need to comfort her was overwhelming.

"Perfect sense. But you really do need to calm down. You're getting yourself worked up for nothing." He spoke in soothing tones, not liking the strained look on her face. This was supposed to be a fun get-together with his family, and he didn't like causing her such discomfort. His family may not have been the life of the party like hers was, but they were genuinely nice people and would welcome her with open arms.

Her beautiful face grew serious as she turned to look at him. The vulnerability he saw in the depths of her green eyes just about undid him. "But, what if they don't like me, Noah? God, I sound so needy, I'm making myself sick." Her quiet chuckle and subtle headshake relaxed him slightly, as he saw her take a deep breath and settle against the seat. She briefly gazed out the window before locking eyes with him once again, looking for reassurance.

"I don't know what else to tell you, baby. They can't wait to meet you. My mum even called to make sure you'd like lamb for Easter. And trust me, if I didn't like it, we'd still be having it. But she was going to make whatever you liked." He gave her an uplifting smile as he tried to lighten the mood.

His mum strictly adhered to the mindset of 'you'll eat what I make or go without', so for her to even offer to modify the dinner menu was monumental, but Emma had no way of knowing that. Other than his birthday, his mum had never consulted with him on the menu offerings, ever. Emma was so worried about making a good impression, but so was his mum. She made no secret of wanting him to settle down with a good woman, and start churning out the grandchildren, so she was willing to pull out all the stops.

"That was so sweet of her." Emma gave him a genuine smile and some of the tension eased from her eyes. "We always have lamb for Easter too, though, so not having it would seem wrong to me. You know, Jesus is the Lamb and all." Her serious tone caught him off-guard as he turned to look at her.

Dressed in a casual outfit of jeans and a lightweight navy sweater, she looked so pretty. She wore her hair down and had fussed over it so much that he'd wondered if they'd ever leave home. It didn't look all that different than it usually did when she let it dry naturally, but he didn't dare ask what had taken her so long. He just gave her a supportive smile and told her how beautiful she was. And she was beautiful, achingly beautiful.

"You're seriously putting too much pressure on yourself." He reached for her hand and gave it a gentle tug, bringing it to his lips and was relieved when the simple gesture appeared to calm her nerves a bit more. "Trust me. They're going to love you. Now, take a few deep breaths and stop worrying yourself. Let's turn that frown upside down, shall we?"

At her sudden outburst of laughter, he turned to see that her pretty smile had returned. "That's my girl."

A soft smile turned up the corners of her lips and his heart skipped a beat. "I know I'm being unreasonable, but this is really important to me, that they like me."

"I know, sweetheart. Just be yourself, and everything will be fine."

Turning onto the tree-lined street that led to his childhood home, he felt at ease for the first time since they'd left home after lunch. He watched as Emma checked her makeup in the mirror, swiped some gloss across her lips, then flipped up the visor and took a deep breath to fortify herself.

Parking in front of the Tudor-style home he'd grown up in, Noah leaned over the console for one last kiss. When he pulled away, she tugged on the nape of his neck and brought her lips to his once more, then wiped the gloss off his lips with her thumb. The tender gesture left him unable to move and a bit breathless as their eyes locked onto one another's for a long moment.

Walking in the front door, he carried their bags, while Emma clutched the cake that she'd made that morning. It felt strange using the front door, as that was reserved for guests, but Emma had marched up the front walkway so quickly once they'd gotten out of the car that he didn't have the heart to tell her otherwise.

"You must be Emma." She was instantly enveloped in his mum's arms as soon as they crossed the threshold, before he'd even had the chance to introduce them. "Well, aren't you lovely?" his mum smiled as she pulled away, taking a good look at her.

Once his mum released her, his dad took her into his arms for a warm embrace. "Hello, Emma. It's very nice to finally meet you."

"Hello Mr. and Mrs. Parker. It's nice to meet you too, and thank you for having me." Noah could tell she was still struggling with her nerves by the slightly elevated tone of her voice, so he placed their bags on the floor and rested a reassuring hand on her lower back. Feeling her lean slightly into his touch, he gently caressed her with his thumb and felt her relax further.

"We're happy you're here, Emma. Noah's told us so much about you. But, please, call us Carol and Jim; we try not to be too formal around here." His mum's smile was warm and genuine as her eyes drifted to the cake tucked against Emma's side. "What have we here?"

"It's a mandarin cream cake. I hope you like it. It's one of my favorites. I made it this morning. It's an Easter tradition in my family."

"Well, thank you for making it for us then. I can't wait to try it. It looks fantastic." She eyed Emma appreciatively as she reached for the cake. "Noah, why don't you take Emma upstairs and get her sorted. I've set up the guest room for her."

He knew it was his mum's way of being subtle, letting him know they wouldn't be sharing a room. His bed was only a single, but he'd have found a way to make it work, or he could join her in the guest room. Either one would work for him, as long as his sweet Emma was wrapped around him. Where she belonged.

Sleep without Emma snuggled against him was restless, at best, and he wasn't looking forward to the long nights alone in his cramped bed. He traveled so often that, when he was home, he didn't want to miss even one single night with her, sinking into her. Melting into her.

"Thanks, Mum. We'll be down in a few minutes." Noah moved to embrace her before heading upstairs with Emma. "It's good to be home. I've missed you."

"I've missed you too, my boy. Now run along." He chose to ignore the childish way his mum addressed him and the blush he felt rising in his cheeks, and reached for their bags. With his free hand, he laced his fingers through Emma's and led her up the stairs.

"So, this is where it all began?" Emma teased, as she stepped though the doorway and into his childhood bedroom. It was a small room with a single bed along the outside wall. A wooden dresser occupied the opposite wall, and there was a small desk in the corner. She struggled to visualize Noah sleeping in the tiny bed, knowing he couldn't roll over on the narrow mattress without falling onto the floor.

She took a seat on the rolling chair that sat in front of the desk and watched as Noah sat down on the bed, seeing it sink beneath his weight. She'd been so nervous on the drive to his parents' house, but now that the introductions were done, she finally felt at ease. Noah calmed her, relaxed her, and his parents were very welcoming. She knew that Noah rarely brought women home to meet his family, so she'd really wanted to make a good impression, to make Noah proud.

"I guess you could say that," Noah answered her. "Is it different than what you'd imagined?" She knew he was probing, looking for her approval.

"Your parents' home is beautiful, but honestly, I hadn't really thought about it, other than when we spoke that night you stayed here. I can't picture you sleeping in that small of a bed, though." She swiveled back and forth in the chair, watching his eyes on her.

Noah looked the bed up and down and then turned back to Emma. "Yeah, it is small. A big bed was the first thing I bought when I got a place of my own. I got tired of my feet getting cold from hanging off the edge, eh?" He let out a slight chuckle as he reached for her knee, gliding the chair from the desk, along the hardwood floors, and situating it between his legs. "And as much as I enjoy a good sleep, I also enjoy sharing my bed with a warm woman wrapped around me, and that would be a wee bit of a problem in a single."

Emma braced her feet on the edge of the bed and straightened her legs, backing away from him. "A warm woman?" She tried not to be jealous, but his words stung.

"You know what I meant, Emma. You know that you're the only warm woman I want in my bed." He gave her the sweet sexy smile that never ceased to unleash the butterflies in her stomach and snaked his fingers around the backs of her knees, bringing her back between his legs. She planted her feet on either side of his hips, her legs bent at the knees and enjoyed the feel of his hands as they stroked up and down her thighs.

"I know." She couldn't help the smile that spread across her face. Trusting Noah was easy, and he'd never given her any reason to question his loyalty. "I just don't like to think about you with other women, that's all."

"I know it sounds cliché, but you've ruined me, Emma. Anyone who came before you has literally faded away. Can't remember them, and I don't want to."

His honest words melted her heart. "You always say the sweetest things, Noah." She paused and exhaled a deep breath as she gazed into his gorgeous eyes, getting lost in them. "I love you...so much."

"I love you too, babe." His grip tightened and curled around the backs of her knees as he slid her off the chair and onto his lap.

Adjusting herself so that she was sitting on his thighs, Emma draped her arms around his neck. Nothing felt better than being held by him. His strong arms enveloped her, holding her against his broad chest. Bringing her lips to his, she smiled against them. "You know, this is kind of naughty, Noah."

"Yeah, I know. But I see you and I want you. Period. And...this is one of my favorite positions to have you in." He gave her an unapologetically wicked grin as he closed the gap and kissed her. It wasn't enough. It would never be enough.

Emma felt herself shudder at his words, as his tongue slid along the seam of her lips, requesting entrance. She complied instinctively and their tongues mated and danced in the comfortable rhythm that they'd perfected over time. It was familiar, but new at the same time. His lips were warm and soft against hers, as he maintained the gentle pressure of his kiss.

The memory of their lovemaking from the night before and that morning were still fresh in her mind as he continued the slow seduction. His hands were roaming up and down her back, softly massaging her as they traveled, then finally landed on her backside, pulling her tightly against the hard bulge pressing against her belly.

Breathlessly, she backed away slightly and placed a chaste kiss against his lips. "We really need to stop. I don't want your parents to think poorly of me if they find us like this."

Noah rested his forehead against hers, releasing a shaky breath. "Remind me again why we came here, because I'm ready to leave and take you home. Straight away." His breath tickled her lips and unable to resist, she kissed him again.

Regaining her thoughts and her last ounce of self-control, Emma cupped his face in her hands while she stroked his cheeks and lifted her eyes to meet his. "You wanted me to meet your family...I wanted to meet your family. Remember?"

The low growl emanating from his chest expressed his displeasure, but he reluctantly pulled away, after pressing his lips against hers for one more taste. "Yeah, you're right. How about a walk? We're only a block from the lake and the domain. Let you see where I ran amuck as a wee fella. I'm going to need a few minutes before I'm ready for mixed company, though. Go sit over there." He pointed to the desk that sat in the corner of the room. At her questioning look and raised eyebrow, he added with a pleading smile. "Please." Emma complied as she slid the chair across the small room, settling at his desk.

They leisurely strolled hand in hand, their fingers entwined, along the path that encircled the lake at the end of his street. A cool breeze chilled Emma and she leaned against Noah's side, wanting to absorb some of the heat that radiated off of him. The man was hot, literally and figuratively.

The path led them to a picturesque park that sat along the edge of the lake. It was the place where Noah first discovered his love and talent for the game of rugby and held so many of his childhood memories. There were several young boys gathered in the center of the field, running and tossing the ball to each other.

Leading her to a bench, they sat and watched the boys for a long while as Noah regaled her with story after story of his early days as a promising, but unskilled boy, daring to dream of the life he would one day achieve. After a while, one of the boys realized that it was Noah Parker sitting on the bench and the group rushed over to them with nervous smiles on their eager faces.

Emma watched as Noah patiently posed for pictures and then joined them on the field to give them a pointer or two. He was reluctant to leave her, but seeing the hopeful look on the boys' faces at the possibility of having a private coaching session, there was no way she could let them down. After the initial excitement and nervousness wore off, they got down to business.

An hour quickly passed as Noah worked with them, helping to perfect their technique. Emma kept busy by getting caught up on her various social media sites and texting back and forth with family and friends. It was starting to get dark when Noah said his goodbyes to the now-fatigued boys and made his way back to where Emma waited on the bench.

"Sorry about that. Didn't mean to be gone so long," he frowned, his eyebrows knitting together, but she could tell he didn't really feel that sorry about it at all. He may have felt guilty for leaving her sitting alone for so long, but he'd definitely enjoyed himself as much as the boys did, and she loved him all the more for it.

"Don't be sorry. You just made their day. Maybe even their year," she chuckled, lifting off the bench to join him.

Noah lazily draped his arm over her shoulders and placed a kiss on her temple. "Yeah, maybe, but you must have been bored, just sitting here watching us."

"I wasn't bored at all. I don't need you to entertain me, Noah. Anyway, I liked watching you run around and that one boy was almost as fast as you are. He certainly gave you a run for your money." She bumped her hip against his and slid her arm around his waist as they set off for the lakeside path back to his house.

"If he stays focused and puts in the hard yards, he may just have a future as a footy player. Not many young fellas get stuck in, though. There're plenty of boys who have the physical ability, but lack the mental focus and vice versa. You have to possess both to make it in super rugby, especially to be selected for the All Blacks. It takes a lot of hard work and a lifetime of sacrifices to get there. But there's nothing that compares to the feeling of putting on that black jersey." He gave her a thoughtful smile and clutched her shoulder, pulling her tightly against his side. "Well, maybe one thing."

She tilted her head and looked up to find him smiling at her. "Oh yeah... what's that?"

"At the risk of turning in my man card…the feeling I get when you smile at me when you first wake up in the morning with your sleepy eyes. It does something to me. In here." He rubbed his chest over his heart, then finished his thought. "Nothing compares to that."

Emma felt her heart swell and she stopped walking, turning to face him. "You are the sweetest man, you know that? And you make me so happy, it almost hurts sometimes." She hugged him tightly around his waist, then gave an extra squeeze as she lifted onto her toes and pressed her lips against his, reveling in the feel of his warm lips against hers. "And you don't have to worry about losing your man card. Real men can admit their feelings and make a girl dizzy by saying what you just said. That, my love, is a real man. At least in my book."

"You mean you don't want your man to come with a ton of baggage and mummy issues?" he laughed sarcastically.

"God, no!" The sound of her laughter echoed over the expansive lake. "Been there done that and it left me dizzy for all the wrong reasons." They started back down the meandering path beside the lake, strolling quietly along the trail. Noah watched as she was deep in thought.

He could tell she was gathering her thoughts, so he remained silent and waited for her to continue. "I've watched my mom virtually swoon when my dad walks into the room or whispers in her ear. She actually blushes. It used to embarrass me, seeing her giggle like a schoolgirl. Especially when I had friends over. But I've come to realize that I want that too. I want to spend my life with a man who loves me so much that, even after thirty years of marriage, he can still make me feel that way. Most people think that's unrealistic, and maybe they're right. But I grew up in a house that was filled with love and laughter, so I know it's possible. I don't want to settle for anything less than that…and I won't."

Noah listened intently as she spoke. He could give her that life, wanted to give her that life, the one she longed for. He'd spend the rest of his days making her happy, just so he could hear the sound of her laughter and see her pretty smile, knowing he played a role in it. "You deserve that, Emma. Any man would count himself lucky to have you. Should want to spend his life making you feel loved and cherished for the gift that you are."

"Thank you, Noah. And I could say the same things about you, you know. I think you're pretty amazing. I watched you with those boys. You were so patient with them. I could almost picture you with our…" She stopped so suddenly that he almost tripped. Her hand went to her lips, as if it would prevent the rest of her thoughts from tumbling out.

After a brief moment, realization settled over him as her words registered. Was she picturing him with their children? Was she actually thinking of staying with him? He didn't dare bring it up, didn't want to make the rest of their stay awkward if she said no.

He'd been thinking more and more about broaching the subject with her, but he wasn't going to do it at his parents' house. He wanted to be able to celebrate with her if she was agreeable or even just agreed to think about it. Or, if things didn't go as he hoped, he needed the ability to lick his wounds in private if she turned him down. So, he bit his tongue and pretended he missed her slip of the tongue.

"Well, I love kids. I've thought about coaching once my playing days are over. And, if I'm lucky enough, I hope to have a house full of my own one day." They'd spoken about their mutual desire for a big family before, and he was more convinced than ever that Emma would be the mother of his children. He just needed to gather up enough courage to ask her to stay with him.

Where Emma was used to laughter and good-natured teasing at family gatherings, Noah's family quietly tucked into their meal. Between bites, the banter consisted of local gossip, workplace happenings, and Jacob and Maddie's various milestones. It was very formal and polite and not at all what she was used to; no one spoke over each other or needed to raise their voices to be heard.

She couldn't help but miss the chaos that accompanied family get-togethers at home. This was the first time she'd ever spent a holiday away from her family and, even though Noah's family had gone out of their way to make her feel at home, it just wasn't the same. She missed her rambunctious family.

She'd spoken to her mother the day before when she couldn't remember the recipe for the mandarin cream cake she'd wanted to bring with her to Noah's parents' house. It just wouldn't have been Easter without it, and she needed to bring a little slice of home with her. As winter approached, it was getting colder in New Zealand, but back home, spring had sprung, and her mother had gushed over her blossoming flower gardens, and Emma ached for the familiar sounds and fragrances of springtime in North Carolina.

"So, Emma, Noah tells us you're a student. What're you studying at university?" Noah's father's words snapped Emma out of her ruminations and back to the cozy dining room where she looked up to find seven sets of eyes watching her expectantly.

Swallowing her food, she gave herself a moment to gather her thoughts. "Yes. I'm a business major. I'll have one semester to go once I get back home, and then I'll finally be done. It's taken me longer to get my degree because I started off as a pharmacy major, but changed my mind after a few years, so I basically had to start over again." She knew she was babbling, but she always felt the need to explain why she was still working on her undergraduate degree.

"I see that quite often, actually, but it's better to realize it while you're still in school than after you graduate. Too many people are afraid to change course, or feel they're too far gone to start over, then are unhappy in their careers." His warm reassuring smile reminded her of Noah's and set her at ease.

"Well, I'll just be glad to be done. I'm tired of school and ready to start the next chapter of my life."

"What do you see yourself doing, once you graduate?" Noah's sister Lara chimed in.

Her future was once clearly-defined in her mind's eye, but now was murky and uncertain. Emma wished things were different, that Noah worked in a field that he could transfer to America so they could have a future together, but the harsh reality was that he couldn't play rugby at his level in America, and she couldn't see herself living half a world away from her family.

Or could she? The thought didn't induce the aching homesickness it once did, and as she looked at Noah, she was sure he was the main reason why. New Zealand was a beautiful and magical country, filled with awe-inspiring vistas and friendly people, and she'd always loved visiting throughout the years, but she had no doubt that the man sitting across from her in the cozy dining room was the reason why New Zealand was feeling more and more like home to her every day.

Realizing she'd still not answered Lara's question, she quickly filtered through her cluttered mind to remember the question. "I served an internship last semester at the firm my mentor owns, and he's mentioned that he might have a position for me if I want to stay in Boone. But I'm not really sure what I want to do yet. The job market isn't good right now and, as much as I love Boone, I'm not sure if I want to live there permanently." She purposefully remained vague, not quite sure how to answer the question.

It was easier to ignore the reality of their situation than to acknowledge the fact that they both knew going into the relationship that it was only temporary. They could pretend it was forever until the clock stroke midnight, but instead of Cinderella's coach turning into a pumpkin, it was turning into a jumbo jet, whisking her away from her prince charming.

Emma looked to Noah, wanting to gauge his reaction to her answer, and found his brows knitted together and his handsome features twisted into a grimace. He was visibly upset. Knowing how they felt about each other, she wondered why they hadn't discussed their futures, except in vague platitudes. She knew long distance relationships rarely worked for the long term, but Noah hadn't even asked her to stay.

Would she stay if he asked? Was he going to let her board the plane and leave like Evan let Ali? Just the thought left her feeling a bit nauseous. She wouldn't force herself on any man, but if he loved her as much as he said he did, how could he let her walk away? The barrage of questions racing through her mind left her confused and a bit heartbroken at the thought of Noah letting her leave without even asking her to stay.

After dinner, which consisted of a delicious leg of lamb and enough side dishes to feed a hungry side of footballers, Emma and Noah took Maddie and Jacob for a walk to the local park. Maddie insisted on holding Emma's hand while they strolled along the winding lakeside path. Her little fingers clasped Emma's, holding tightly as she skipped along next to her new best friend. The little girl had attached herself to Emma's hip from the moment she'd arrived with her parents and her older brother Jacob.

Noah walked a few paces ahead of them, encouraging Jacob on his new bicycle. Emma couldn't help but imagine what life would be like with their own children. She'd no doubt that Noah would be a loving and attentive father. He was also patient and kind, taking care of the people and things he cared about, and he gave selflessly of himself and asked for nothing in return. All were excellent qualities for a husband and father to possess, and what she'd hoped and prayed for in a man.

He also looked damn fine in a pair of faded blue jeans. His long legs ate up the ground as Jacob picked up speed. The worn denim hugged his perfectly rounded bottom and if she wasn't holding the hand of an impressionable four year old, she would've reached out and pinched it. Her mind easily drifted to the soft skin of his naked backside cradled in her hands as he did wonderfully wicked things to her. She felt the flush of heat in her face, and feeling guilty for her naughty thoughts, she forced herself to avert her eyes back to the innocent child prancing next to her.

When they arrived at the park, Maddie dragged Emma to the swing set, which sat on the edge of the picturesque lake. Crawling onto Emma's lap as soon as she'd settled on the wooden seat, Maddie made herself comfortable, then pushing off with her feet, they started to gently sway back and forth.

"Do you like my Uncle Noah?" Maddie asked with complete sincerity, tilting her head to look up at Emma, her precious smile melting her heart.

"Yes. I do like your Uncle Noah. Very much." Emma felt the corners of her mouth curl into a smile as she looked into Maddie's pretty blue eyes, which were identical to her uncle's.

"My mummy said that you're leaving soon."

"Yes. I have to go home to my family in America. I'm only here for a little while longer." Like always, Emma's chest twisted painfully when she thought about leaving New Zealand, and Noah.

"But don't you like it here?" Her questioning look had Emma sitting up straighter on the suddenly too-hard wooden seat beneath her.

"Yes. Of course I like it here."

"But if you like it here and you like my Uncle Noah, then why would you leave?" Out of the mouths of babes, she thought to herself.

Emma made sure to speak in a soft tone when she answered Maddie's question. "Well…first of all, I miss my family, and just because I like it here, doesn't mean I can stay. And second of all…your Uncle Noah hasn't asked me to stay." It was probably too much information for such a little girl to process, but Emma couldn't help the words from spilling out of her mouth, barely disguising her inner turmoil.

She'd begun to wonder more and more why Noah hadn't raised the subject of her staying with him. Did he not want her to stay? Was he going to let her go back home and that would be the end of it?

"Oh." Maddie scrunched her little mouth into a frown before thoughtfully finishing. "Well, I'd like you to stay. I don't want you to leave."

If Emma hadn't already fallen in love with the little girl, she'd have fallen right then and there. "You are such a love bug. I could just eat you up." Emma squeezed her tightly around the waist and placed a kiss on the top of her head, inhaling a deep breath of fresh air and strawberry shampoo.

Emma knew Maddie was getting tired when the little girl leaned back against her chest and let out a deep sigh. It had been a long day and even Emma was feeling a bit knackered, so she wasn't surprised at all that she was ready for a nap. Picking Maddie up, Emma turned her around and settled the sleepy child against her chest as her little legs dangled freely behind her. Maddie slid her arms around Emma's waist and closed her eyes, her soft cheek using her chest as a pillow. The placid glide of the swing was enough to lull Maddie to sleep and, after a few minutes, Emma felt her little arms go slack along her sides.

When Noah and Jacob were ready to head back, they made their way across the field to the swing set. Noah couldn't help but smile as he watched Emma rocking his sleeping niece, holding her gently as she swayed to and fro on the swing. He'd watched all day as she patiently tolerated Maddie's incessant questions and demands for her attention, never once getting frustrated. Jacob had been a bit standoffish with Emma, but he suspected it was more about Emma being a girl than about her personally. Jacob was at the age where boys started to notice the difference between the sexes, especially a beautiful woman like Emma.

The urge to make babies with Emma had surprised him at first, but the more he thought about her swollen belly, pregnant with his child, the more he wanted it to be reality. He knew asking her to come back to En Zed once she graduated was easy for him, but a massive sacrifice for her. She'd have to leave her family, friends, and everything she was familiar with. He'd gain the world, but give up nothing in exchange. But they'd have a good life together; he'd see to it. He'd take care of her and they'd fill their home with children, along with the happy sounds of love and laughter that she'd grown up with, and was accustomed to.

And if she said no, well, for the first time in his career, he'd considered an early retirement. He was set financially, so they wouldn't have to worry about putting food on their table, but they'd have to be cautious with their money and he'd probably have to sell his home. He'd planned to play for a few more years to cushion his bank account some more, but he could start a new career in America. Doing what, he didn't know, but as long as he had Emma by his side, everything would be fine.

Approaching Emma, Noah held out his hands to relieve her of her charge. "We're ready to head back. I can take her if you want."

Emma carefully stood to her feet to join them, lifting up easily and adjusting Maddie so her head came to rest on her shoulder. "No, I can take her for now. But if my arms get too tired, you can take over."

"She looks good on you." Noah said, as he watched Emma lovingly stroke Maddie's hair, brushing it off her face, as she soothed her back to sleep.

Comfortable. That was the word that best described the scene as they lazily strolled back to his parents' house with Maddie tucked securely into Emma's embrace and Jacob racing up and down the path under the watchful eyes of his Uncle Noah and Emma.

It felt good…It felt right.

# CHAPTER 22

Noah strode through the car park towards his car with purpose, quickly eating up the pavement, when he heard his name being called out from behind him. Turning to see Evan Thompson jogging in his direction, he reluctantly paused to wait for him. He'd been wanting to speak to Evan about Ali and Abby, but was uncomfortable butting into the situation without invite, and for a brief moment, he considered broaching the subject before changing his mind once again.

As Evan reached his side, Noah slowly started in the direction of his car once again. He was anxious to get home to Emma after a long day, knowing she'd prepared a special evening for their six-month anniversary. He'd always considered it overkill to celebrate monthly milestones, but it was important to Emma, so it was important to him. He even offered to take her to a flash restaurant in the CBD, but she'd insisted on a quiet dinner, just the two of them at home.

Waking that morning to the sight of her in the sexiest negligée he'd ever seen, the thin straps holding up a scrap of transparent black satin and lace with a matching thong, he was sure he was dreaming. No living creature could be that perfect, but as she wiggled her hips, he shook off the last vestiges of sleep and worshipped every inch of her. Just the memory of it had his blood heating and his heart beating faster and left him wondering why they weren't celebrating monthly anniversaries. He was game if she was.

"Hey, Noah. Do you have a minute?" Turning to look at his teammate, Noah couldn't miss the uneasiness in his tone and his stiff posture. Evan was normally a pretty laid-back guy, but as Noah observed him closely, the only word that came to mind was…pinched.

"I'm in a bit of a hurry, but I can spare a few. What's up?"

"Well, I've been wanting to talk to you about your girlfriend. Give you some friendly advice."

"Oh yeah? What about her? I didn't think you knew each other well enough for you to be giving me advice about Emma." Noah felt his back straighten and the hair rise on the back of his neck. He slowed his pace and looked Evan in the eyes as he spoke, knowing his clipped tone and aggressive stance revealed his irritation with where the conversation was headed.

"I don't know her, other than the few weeks I spent at her family's home with Ali, when Abby was born. But I do know that you're wasting your time with her. No matter how much you want her to stay, she won't. She'll get on that plane when her time here is up and that will be that." Noah didn't miss Evan's bitter tone as he gave voice to Noah's worst nightmare, and he felt like he'd been sucker-punched in the gut.

*What the…?* Where did that come from? For the first time ever, Noah felt the urge to pummel one of his teammates. He'd always liked Evan, and had even defended him to Emma on more than one occasion, but as he looked at the man standing next to him, he felt his hand curl into a fist and had to hold himself back from letting said fist connect with his jaw. "*Oh*…that's rich coming from the man who, for all intents and purposes, has abandoned his only child. You've got nerve, I'll give you that, but you don't know the first thing about my relationship with Emma. And maybe you should worry more about your daughter and less about me, eh? Now, if you don't mind, I need to get home."

As Noah turned away, he felt the press of Evan's hand on his arm. "Look, Noah. I'm speaking from experience. She's not going to stay, mate." Noah's hard gaze went from Evan's hand to his face and Evan received the stern unspoken warning, wisely removing his hand and quickly taking a step back.

Noah needed to get out of there; he needed the sanctuary of Emma's warm body. "How would you know? You never even asked Ali to stay, or to come back when she fell pregnant for that matter. Now you're going to stand here and tell me that, when you never even bothered to ask? Perhaps she was waiting for you to step up and be a man. Did you ever think of that? And ask her to stay with you. But you never gave her the chance to turn you down, did you? So forgive me if I don't heed your warning."

"Call me a coward if you like, and I'll accept that, but I knew all along that she wouldn't stay. Her bloody horse meant more to her than I did. A man's ego can only take so much rejection. So yeah, I may not have asked her the question that I already knew the answer to, but I never deceived myself otherwise. And, as far as Abby is concerned, I'm trying to make amends there. I let my pride and bruised ego bugger everything up, but I'm going to fix that. I'm going to make sure that I'm a part of her life." Noah saw the softening of Evan's features and his tone as he spoke of his daughter. The deep regret was evident on Evan's face. Seeing that eased some of his own anger a bit.

He knew Evan was projecting his broken relationship with Ali onto his relationship with Emma, but nevertheless, his words stung. Evan was voicing Noah's greatest fear. He'd known all along that it was a possibility that Emma might not stay, but refused to believe it, he needed to believe that, when the time came, she'd stay. That she'd pick him.

"Well, good luck with that, Evan. I truly mean it. Your daughter needs you. But don't pretend to know bugger all about what Emma will or won't do."

"Fair enough. But when she boards that plane and leaves you gutted, don't say I didn't warn you. Hey, how 'bout I buy you a drink and we can try to drown our sorrows when it happens? And it will happen, mate." It was obvious that Evan was trying to lighten the increasingly tense mood, but his words punched a hole through Noah's gut and left him feeling sick to his stomach at the thought of Emma leaving him.

Noah tried not to cringe at the certainty of Evan's words, but failed. "I'll tell you what…if she gets on that plane, without the intention of returning to me, I might take you up on your offer. After I bloody your nose, that is." Noah bit back the chuckle at Evan's loud outburst of laughter. The man may have thoroughly infuriated him, but his heart was in the right place. He'd clearly been hurt by Ali's leaving and was still bitter about it. Knowing he'd be feeling the same way if Emma left him, and not one to hold onto a grudge, he couldn't stay mad at his friend and teammate.

"And I'll probably let you do it too. Can't promise I won't hit you back though. Fair warning, bro." At that, Evan turned and stalked to his own car, leaving Noah standing alone in the car park, stewing over their conversation.

Evan had no one to blame but himself for the way things had turned out, but Noah couldn't help but feel sorry for the man. He'd never get back the time he'd missed with his daughter, that was lost to him forever, but hopefully, he could make amends with Ali and become the father he needed to be.

Driving home, no matter how hard he'd tried to squelch them, Evan's words ricocheted around in Noah's head.

'She's not going to stay. She's not going to stay.'

The taste of bile was bitter in his mouth as he held his emotions in check. He'd always been satisfied with his life and career; it was what he'd worked so hard for. But pulling into the garage, he hated everything about it.

As he stepped through the kitchen door, the delicious aroma from the dinner Emma was preparing for them filled the room and made his mouth water. He dropped his bag on the kitchen floor at the sight of Emma, dressed in a flirty dress and a pair of high heels that were so sexy they should be illegal, and all the air escaped from his lungs. He quickly crossed the room and swallowed her in a tight embrace. He didn't know what he'd done to deserve her, but the goddess that stood before him was created for him and him alone.

His heart was insatiable with its need for her, but his mind was telling him to face reality, to protect himself from the inevitability of her leaving. From the moment he'd laid eyes on her, he never wavered in his pursuit, but as he held her in his arms, he found himself letting her go.

Taking a step back to gather his thoughts, he took a deep breath and surveyed his surroundings. The table was covered with the cloth his mum had given him, but he'd yet to use, and lit by candlelight. A bottle of wine waited on the kitchen bench next to two wine glasses, and a platter was artfully arranged with an assortment of cheese, crackers, and grapes. It was clear to see that she'd gone the extra mile to make tonight special for them, and he didn't want to disappoint her.

Deciding it was best to deal with his insecurities at a later time, when he could sort through his emotions without mucking everything up, he forced the earlier conversation with Evan to the deepest recesses of his mind. He knew Evan's opinion was clouding his judgment and influencing his emotions, but it was hard to deny the truth of his sentiments.

He'd accused Evan of being a coward, but in reality, he was just as much of one himself. He knew he needed to have the conversation with Emma, about her staying with him. It was long overdue, but he always found an excuse to keep putting it off. The thought of losing her terrified him, and he knew if she turned him down, everything would be different between them. He would have to begin the process of emotionally detaching himself from her, and that was actually the opposite of what he wanted to do. He wanted to permanently *attach* himself to her.

Turning his gaze back to Emma, he couldn't help but smile. She was so lovely; his heart ached just looking at her.

She wore a little black dress that hugged every delicious curve of the athletic body he worshipped on a daily basis and her sky-high heels were made for sin. But it was her smile that stole his breath and his heart. One look from her and he was lost. How would he survive without her in his life, in his home, in his heart? Every fiber of his being cried out for her, ached for her.

He hissed in a breath as she closed the gap between them and swathed him in her embrace. Holding him tightly to her, she nestled her cheek against his neck and he felt the warmth of her breath against his skin. When she shifted her head and pressed her soft lips to his neck, he forgot his name. His world was reduced to the softness of her lips.

Instinctively, he slid his arms around her, and before his mind could remind him to stop, he kissed her. His lips whispered over hers reverently, before tilting his head and sliding his tongue along her plump bottom lip. She tasted of mint and Emma. The added height from her heels brought her almost to eye-level with him, as he crushed his mouth to hers in a possessive kiss. She opened to him immediately and met the thrust of his tongue stroke for stroke.

Breaking away, he allowed his eyes to rake over her from head to toe. "Hey, sweetheart. Dinner smells amazing, and you look good enough to eat."

Emma's arms rested lazily around his waist, her hip cocked to one side. "Thanks." Her knowing chuckle at his suggestive comment left him weak in the knees. "I wanted tonight to be special. And I found these shoes while I was out with Lily the other day and thought…why not get dressed up? Celebrate." His tongue suddenly felt too big for his mouth as he watched her shift her leg out to the side, twisting her foot back and forth so he could get a squiz at her new shoes. The sexy high heels had a black leather strap that extended up the back of her heel before wrapping around her delicate ankle. The motion hiked the hem of her dress up several inches, exposing a pair of lean legs that went all the way to heaven, as she rested her hip against the counter.

"Well, you won't find me complaining about them. I may have you leave them on when I take you to bed tonight." Forget dinner, he wanted to strip her down to her bra and panties…and those shoes, right now.

Emma angled her head and gave him a seductive grin. "I was hoping you'd like them. I bought them with you in mind."

Noah ghosted the tips of his fingers from her bare shoulder, down the length of her arm, to her hand. The tender gesture left a trail of goose bumps on her soft skin. He loved how responsive she was to even the most innocent of touches. "Sweetheart, you could be standing here in a burlap sack and I'd still want you more than my next breath. But the way you look tonight…" He paused, as he let his eyes slowly take in the sight of her. "Well, I don't even know how to express how I feel. It wouldn't do you justice, you're so beautiful."

He laced his fingers through hers and brought their joined hands to his lips.

Emma's soft giggle left him unable to breathe. "Mission accomplished."

"Do you have any idea what you do to me?"

"Uh…yeah," she said playfully and he had to bite back a laugh at her sassy retort. "Because you do the same thing to me, just by walking into the room."

He was startled as she poked him in the stomach, but recovered quickly enough to get ahold of her wrist before she pulled it away. Snickering at her surprised gasp, he circled his arm around her back, her wrist still bound in his hand. The stretch of fabric across her breasts distracted him for a moment as his eyes lingered on the swell of her cleavage. A hint of black lace was visible as she took a shaky breath, the motion lifting her breasts and making his mouth water.

Reaching behind her with his free hand, he picked up a grape and placed it to her lips. Without taking her eyes from his, she opened her mouth and sucked it in along with the tip of his finger. Her lips closed around it and he felt the sting of her teeth biting playfully, mixed with the flood of juices from the grape.

The platter was slowly emptied of its contents as they fed each other in a game of seductive one-upmanship that only served to leave him hard as a rock and so turned-on that he almost bent her over the bench and had his way with her right there in the kitchen. It wouldn't have been the first time they'd made love in the kitchen, but it would have been one of the most memorable. They'd already licked and sucked each other to near climax without shedding a single piece of their clothing or touching any of their naughty bits.

The ding of the timer had Emma turning her attention to their dinner. She looked at the oven with a hint of regret in her eyes before turning back to him. "Dinner's ready," she uttered unenthusiastically.

He bit back his disappointment at the end of their seductive game. He was hungry for more than the food she'd prepared for them, but he knew the effort she'd put in, so his raging libido would have to wait. Releasing her, he took the few steps to the oven and removed the tray of homemade lasagna. It had quickly become one of his favorite meals and was pleased she'd made it for him.

Emma opened the refrigerator door and removed a large bowl of salad, placing it next to the lasagna on the counter. He smiled as she waved her hand through the air as if she'd just conjured the dinner up from nothing. "Dig in."

Noah raked his fingers through her silken hair as she slept in his arms, unable to find sleep himself. His restless mind focused on visions of Emma in nothing but black lace and the sexiest pair of high heels he'd ever seen, as he'd brought her to an explosive climax. He'd taken her seven different ways to Sunday before stripping off the shoes, and he still wanted more. He was sure he had heel marks along his back and would probably catch stick for it in the sheds, but it was worth it. Her breathy moans and exclamations echoed in his head and the feel of her naked body pressed against his left him ready to go again.

He wondered if he'd ever tire of having her, because he couldn't imagine a day when he wouldn't look at her in awe. And that thought inevitably brought his mind back to his conversation with Evan.

He hated that he let Evan have such a negative influence on him and his relationship with Emma, but he just couldn't shake the uneasy feeling his words had left behind. He would survive if she left, Noah knew that, but he didn't want her to leave. It was that simple. In his heart, he'd already found his mate, his lifelong companion, and couldn't envision ever wanting to be with anyone else.

He'd once heard that God created Eve from Adam's rib, so that when he found his Eve, she completed him. He was whole again. Noah now understood that without his Emma, he would be forever missing the part of him that only she possessed...that only she could satisfy.

Wanting to shout out to the heavens at the unfairness of it all and giving up on sleep, he gently slid from her arms, trying his level-best not to wake her. Quietly donning his running shorts and trainers, he slipped out the back door for a moonlit run on the beach.

An hour later, he was no closer to resolving his problems, but he was bone tired, so he gave thanks for that and quietly slipped into the shower. The feel of the warm water relaxed him as he rinsed the sand and sweat from his tired limbs.

Noah wasn't surprised to find Emma sitting on the counter when he stepped out of the shower, dressed in the shirt he'd worn that day. Her confused expression mingled with sleepy eyes as she stifled a yawn. "Where'd you go?"

"Couldn't sleep, so I went for a run. I didn't mean to wake you." He really didn't and felt the sting of guilt that he'd worried her as he wrapped a towel around his hips.

"Oh…Is everything alright?" Her confused expression turned to concern as she scrutinized him, a frown marring her pretty face.

"Everything's fine. I'm fine. Just couldn't sleep, is all. Worried about the match tomorrow, I guess," he lied, but hoped she didn't catch the nervous twitch in his voice.

She gave him a sad look and slid from the counter. "Well, go lie down and I'll make you some warm milk. It always helps me sleep when I have trouble."

He was helpless to resist the pull of her and enveloped her in his arms. "Thanks, baby. You're too good to me." It was true, he thought, as he patted her bottom before giving it a gentle squeeze.

Between the warm milk, the moonlit run, and Emma's warm breath against his chest, he finally found the sleep his weary mind craved.

Sitting cross-legged in Albert Park with Isabella in her lap, Emma finished off the remnants of her turkey sandwich. She'd met Suzanne for a picnic lunch in the park so Bella could run around without drawing the ire of the other patrons that frequented the busy cafes that encircled the university campus. Bella was a whirling dervish while she was awake, and Suzanne had to practically tie her to the chair to keep her out of trouble. With her pregnant belly getting larger by the minute, it wasn't an easy task to chase an energetic two-year-old through a crowded restaurant.

Emma and Suzanne had struck up an easy friendship and had managed to fit in a few lunches since they'd met in the airport while waiting for their significant others to deplane. As she gazed at the puffy woman, whose pregnant belly had grown significantly since they'd first met, reclining on the quilt next to her, she envied her. Suzanne was living the life that Emma had always dreamed of, a husband who adored her and about to give birth to her second little girl. They'd already picked out a name and excitedly decorated the nursery. Little Sarah Elizabeth O'Neill was coming into this world surrounded by a loving family that could hardly wait for her arrival.

Emma was enjoying the few minutes of rest between classes and soaking up the sun as it peeked through the clouds. The spirited two-year-old was just the distraction she needed to take her mind off her troubles and the stress of her exams. The rare sighting of the sun as it broke through the clouds had lifted her dragging spirits, slightly. The weather that had descended upon Auckland for the last few weeks was a perfect reflection of her mood…gloomy.

Things had been strained between her and Noah and it was wearing on her last nerve. For the first time, she was questioning their relationship. When they were together, everything was…fine…at least on the surface. They'd gone about their normal routine, but there was a growing distance between them, and their comfortable connection felt tense and awkward at times.

On more than one occasion, she'd woken up in the middle of the night to find Noah sitting alone in the lounge, watching TV in the dark, or missing altogether. She'd panicked the first few times she'd woken to an empty house, searching every room for him, only to hear him sneak in the back door some time later and head straight for the shower.

Noah had been traveling for most of the last week, first with The Blues to Australia, for their final game of the season, and then with the All Blacks to Christchurch, so she'd had plenty of time to obsess over what could be upsetting him.

Had she done something to cause him to pull away from her? Had he met someone else? Just the thought of Noah with another woman, or even wanting another woman, left her seeing red…and wanting to throw up. Every time the crushing image of Noah with someone else came to the forefront, she tried her best to mentally shake it off. It was always in the back of her mind, eating away bit by bit, but when she looked into her heart of hearts, she knew Noah would never be unfaithful.

Deciding that infidelity was unlikely, she still knew something was terribly wrong and she'd resolved herself to take the bull by the horns and insist he talk to her. She wasn't all that comfortable with confrontation, but things couldn't go on the way they were. One of the things that formed the foundation of a healthy relationship was trust. And if he didn't trust her enough to confide in her, to tell her whatever was bothering him, then they had a problem. A fixable problem, but a problem nonetheless, and she was determined to figure it out. She wasn't ready to cut her losses yet, but she wouldn't force him to stay with her either, if it wasn't what he wanted any longer.

Every time he didn't quite look at her, but through her, her heart broke a little more. The faraway look in his eyes betrayed him, and as much as he insisted that everything was alright…it wasn't. Nothing was alright, and if he wanted out, then she'd let him go, even though it would kill her to walk away from him.

She couldn't help but wonder if he stayed with her out of some misguided sense of obligation because of his friendship with Josh and Lily. She was no one's pity date, so if that was the case then she'd set him straight and move out, with a shattered heart that would probably never be right again. Trying to prepare for the inevitable, she'd even thought about bringing a few of her things back to Lily's to make it less awkward if she had to leave. She hadn't let her growing insecurities drive her to such drastic actions yet, but she didn't want to be caught off-guard and left scrambling to pack everything she'd accumulated at Noah's either.

He'd gone quiet on her and that was never a good sign. She'd been there before in relationships past and it never ended well...it just ended. Just the thought of losing Noah left her with a herd of stampeding elephants wreaking havoc on her insides, and, alternately, on the verge of hysterics or an ulcer.

As much as she tried to prepare herself, she wasn't ready to let him go, so she hung on with every ounce of grit she could muster and pasted a smile on her face that didn't feel quite as genuine as it once did. Her mother always told her she was as stubborn as a mule, and she was relying on that tenacity. Like a good southern girl, she'd get through it with her chin held high and a smile plastered on her face.

After chasing Bella around the fountain until the little tornado was exhausted, Emma carried her back to the waiting arms of her mum.

Emma bit back a laugh as Suzanne struggled to raise herself to a standing position. She was in the final stages of pregnancy, making even the most routine tasks difficult. "Is everything alright, Emma? You seem quiet today. Not your normally-cheerful self." Emma wanted to confess her deepest worries to her friend, but she needed to get to class and didn't want to burden her with her troubles.

"I'm fine." She was really beginning to hate that word. "Just stressed with exams and everything." It wasn't a complete lie, she told herself. Her exams were causing her stress and her issues with Noah could fall under 'everything'.

Suzanne paused and looked closely at Emma, causing her to fidget under the scrutiny. "Well, if you need anything, just let me know. I remember living off of junk food and coffee during exams, so if you want to pop in for tea, just give me a call. I'd love the company."

"Thanks. I may just take you up on that."

"Well, try to get some rest. You look...tired."

Ouch. "I didn't think I looked that bad," Emma laughed, but it rang hollow in her ears.

"You're still gorgeous and you know it, but you just look...weary. Maybe that's a better word." Her concern was sincere, so Emma knew not to take offense.

Emma let out a small chuckle. "I think weary or tired would both work. Just look around campus, everyone looks like a bunch of zombies. And I'm both weary and tired of school. I'm so ready to graduate I can't stand it anymore. I just want to be done."

Suzanne's firm grip encircled Emma's biceps, holding her tightly at arm's length. "Well, give me a call and I'll have a nice meal and some tea waiting for you. And in case of the zombie apocalypse, remember to 'Keep calm and head to the Winchester'."

Emma's sudden burst of genuine laughter caught her by surprise. "Thanks, I needed that. Best zombie movie *ever*." She suspected Suzanne knew there was more to her weariness, but thankfully, she didn't push the issue. "I just need to get though another week, and then I'm off for the next three weeks. It's what's keeping me going at this point, I'm so exhausted. But I really do need to get to class. Thanks for lunch and for letting me chase the little munchkin around for a little while." Emma leaned back on her haunches, lowering herself to eye level with Bella, and gave her a hug. Her heart swelled when the little girl hugged her tightly before smacking a wet kiss on her cheek.

With the impending conversation she needed to have with Noah still weighing heavily on her mind, she crossed the street and made her way across campus to her next class. Lingering outside the building, she pulled her phone from her back pocket and called Lily. Her cousin knew Noah better than most, and maybe Noah had talked to Josh. If that was the case, then Lily knew what was upsetting him, because they shared everything.

"Hey, Emma," Lily's cheery voice greeted her. "What's up?"

"Oh, well let's see, where should I start?" Emma chuckled into the phone. Just the sound of Lily's voice lightened her heavy load. "I'm exhausted, hungry for a good meal, and lonely. I need my Lily."

Lily's laughter rang through the phone. "Well...I don't know...it's a pretty big ask, Emma," she teased. "Of course I can help. Come over after class and I'll take care of you. I know just the thing."

Lily's enthusiastic giggle left Emma slightly afraid of what her cousin had in mind, but she was happy for the distraction and the company. "I get out of class at three, and I'll come over then. I'm so tired, Lily, I just want to pull the blankets over my head and forget about the real world for a while."

"Well, come on over when you're done. Why don't you spend the night here tonight, since Noah's out of town? That way you can just collapse in your bed instead of driving home after dinner."

"I think I might just do that. But I have to go. I'll see you later. Love you." Emma ended the call and rolled her shoulders, feeling better already.

Lily opened the door and immediately handed Emma a cold beer. "I've booked us for massages at the spa at four. You're getting the Aromatherapy massage, and I'm going to try the hot stones. The Aromatherapy massage is supposed to help reduce stress and promote relaxation. It sounds delightful. And then we're going to have dinner, just the two of us. Make it a ladies night." Lily was so excited, she forgot to breathe, finally sucking in a deep breath when she finished speaking.

Emma wanted to cry at Lily's thoughtful surprise. It was just what she needed. "Oh, my God...that sounds perfect. Thanks Lily."

"Well, I think we deserve a little treat, don't you?"

"Abso-freaking-lutely!"

Settling in the lounge after their massages and dinner, Emma was finally ready to speak to Lily about Noah. She'd gone over the conversation repeatedly in her mind over the last few hours, but she found that actually expressing her emotions was a lot harder than she thought it would be. It gave a sense of finality to her situation, but at the same time she felt foolish for questioning Noah's commitment.

She took a long pull from the beer Lily had given her, the cold liquid sliding past the lump in her throat, as she tried to organize her jumbled thoughts.

Lily gave her a concerned look, her normally upturned lips forming a straight line. "Alright. I can't take it anymore. Talk to me Emma. What's wrong?"

Emma filled her lungs and exhaled the deep breath, gathering the courage to voice her concerns. "Well, I wanted to talk to you about Noah. Something's wrong, but he won't talk to me."

"What makes you think something's wrong?" she asked, setting her drink on the table and shifting so she was facing her cousin, giving Emma her undivided attention.

"It's not just one thing, but everything's just…off. Like he keeps waking up in the middle of the night and going for a run, or I find him watching TV. And the way he looks at me…" She couldn't stop the flood of sudden tears from spilling onto her cheeks. Wiping them away abruptly, she continued. "It's different. I can't explain it really. It's almost like he doesn't see me. He's miles away. But I was wondering if Josh has said anything?" Trying to quiet the desperation in her voice was futile as more tears fell against her cheeks.

"Oh, Emma." Lily's kind eyes were wet with tears as she reached out and banded her arms around Emma, holding her tightly. "Josh hasn't said anything to me. But I didn't know to ask him. I'll talk to him tonight and see if Noah's said anything to him. I wish I knew what went through the minds of men. Why they push away the best thing that's ever happened to them. And trust me, Emma, you are the best thing that's ever happened to that man. He'd be a bloody fool to let you go." Her heartfelt words did little to ease the weight of her affliction.

Emma sat up, trying to be strong and bite back the tears that refused to stop. "Do you think he's met someone else?"

"No way! I've seen the way he looks at you, cuz. He truly only has eyes for you. Are you sure it's you and not something going on with the team? I know when Josh was still playing, he got testy when they didn't do well. That's probably what's got his knickers in a twist."

"See, that's the problem, though. I'm left to guess what's bothering him. And something's definitely bothering him, but he doesn't trust me enough to talk to me about it." Emma was fairly certain that if he would just talk to her, they could work it out, but without knowing what the problem was made that impossible.

"You know, he's been on his own for a long while now. Maybe he's just used to figuring things out on his own."

"But he's not alone anymore, and when you're a couple, you figure things out together. At least that's how I think it should be. How I want it to be. I don't want to be left guessing if I've done something to upset him or whatever." Emma's voice ticked up a few notches as her sadness mixed with anger.

"No, you're right. And I'm not trying to say that he's right, because he's definitely wrong for shutting you out. But I just want you to keep that in mind."

"I know. I'm going to talk to him when he gets home tomorrow, and if he doesn't open up, then I need to think about what I'm going to do. I can't go on like this any longer. It's killing me." Emma's weak chuckle rang empty in her ears. The strain of the unknown had taken its toll on her and she was mentally exhausted.

"Well, you know you always have a home here with us." Lily gave her a soft smile, and Emma could see the worry in her eyes as she continued. "But let's hope it doesn't come to that."

"Yeah. I hope not. I love him, Lily."

Emma knew deep-down that Noah loved her, and that was why his behavior hurt so badly. He was pushing her away for no reason, and it left her unsure of her footing and grasping for any explanation that would justify his behavior.

"I know you do, Emma. And he loves you too, I know he does."

# Chapter 23

Emma was waiting in the lounge when the flicker of the sun's reflection off Noah's windshield lit the room, and the sound of the garage door opening announced his arrival. Bracing herself for the conversation she both needed to have, but dreaded at the same time, she held her breath at the sound of his footsteps.

Standing to her feet as he entered the lounge, Emma steeled her resolve, but almost faltered as she took in the sight of him. He looked just as exhausted as she did, and it was evident that whatever was troubling him was taking its toll.

Unable to resist, she moved to take him into her arms, reveling in the feel of his warm embrace and the scent of him. She was at home in his arms. There was nowhere else she'd rather be. The steady beat of his heart beneath her ear was like manna from heaven.

Her resolve began to dissolve as she worried the confrontation would be the end of Emma and Noah. She was so afraid she'd lose him if her fears were confirmed. Could she continue with their relationship the way things were going? Should she just hold her tongue and wait to see if it blew over? Maybe his worries *were* over something that was happening with the team and had nothing to do with her. Even so, he should trust her with his burdens and not shut her out, she reminded herself.

Emma's thoughts were a jumbled mess, but when Noah lifted her chin to look into her eyes, she had her answer. Unless he forcibly removed her, she wasn't going anywhere. She might be every kind of fool, but she loved him, and just the thought of walking out the door was unbearable.

Noah's crooked smile melted her heart and what was left of her resolve. "Hey, sweetheart. I've missed you. I'm so glad to be home." His arms tightened around her and she was a goner.

"I missed you, too. Sorry about the yellow card." She'd watched the test match between the All Blacks and Ireland with Josh and Lily the night before and saw the devastation in Noah's eyes when he was interviewed by the media. Knowing how he hated to let the team down, she knew he'd beaten himself up over it.

"It happens. I try not to dwell on it, but I was compete rubbish out there." A genuine smile crossed his lips as he gazed longingly into her eyes. "Coming home to you makes it better, though."

His soft lips met hers and all other thoughts were banished; his tongue begged for entrance and she instinctively complied. Strong arms gripped her tightly as she lifted onto her toes to meet him. This is where she belonged, securely enveloped in his loving arms.

She heard herself moan as his hands slipped down, coming to rest on her backside as he lifted her off her feet like she weighed nothing at all. As if they had a mind of their own, her legs wrapped around his waist as he moved to the couch. He settled her against his chest as her legs straddled his hips, never breaking the kiss.

Pressing his forehead to hers, they both struggled for breath after the long heated kiss. "God, I love you, Emma. I've missed you so much. Missed this. Just holding you, babe, you have no idea."

His sweet profession of love melted her heart and emboldened her to make her own declaration. "I love you too…so much. I ache for you when you're gone, you know. Sometimes at night when I wake up and you're not there, I just feel… lost." She couldn't stop the flow of tears at the overwhelming sensation of being completely in love with the beautiful man who sat before her.

"Stay with me, Emma. When you finish university, that is. Come back to me," he whispered reverently against her lips.

His words startled her, causing her to suck in a deep breath of air. Within the span of a few weeks he'd gone from the man of her dreams, to pushing her away, to asking her to give up everything and move to New Zealand permanently.

She was dizzy as his words tumbled over and over in her exhausted brain. Unable to organize her thoughts, she took a moment to really think about the words he'd just spoken, letting the implications of his request settle over her as a thousand questions raced through her mind, each one leaving another in its wake.

Apparently, she took a moment too long, because when she looked into his eyes for reassurance, expecting to see the same softness from a moment ago, she found...anger? What was that about? "Noah, I don't know what to say."

"You know what...forget it. The look on your face just said everything. Forget I asked." Her heart sank as he abruptly slid her off his lap and stood to his feet. He'd never snapped at her that way before, and it took a few seconds for it to register. Anger radiated off of him in waves as he looked at her as if she was a stranger.

Emma took in the sight of him standing rigid in front of her, his jaw clenched and his eyes hard slits. She had no idea what she'd said or done to elicit this reaction, but she didn't deserve it. He started to pace back and forth across the lounge in obvious frustration, raking his hands through his hair.

"Noah, what's the matter? What did I say?" The desperation in her tone shocked her, but she straightened her spine and continued. "I don't understand. You didn't even give me a minute to think. Why are you being this way? And, to be honest, Noah...I don't appreciate it."

"It's not you, Emma. It's me, I..."

"Oh, no you don't, Noah! Don't you dare!" she interrupted him. She was yelling now, but didn't care; his anger was infectious, and as far as she was concerned, hers was justified, but his was not. "Do not give me that. That's a total cop-out and I deserve better than that." She felt her anger rise to the surface and didn't hold back. "You've been giving me the push for the last few weeks, and whenever I asked you to talk to me about it, you brushed it off. And now you expect me to jump up and down when you ask me to stay. Don't you get it? I was actually worried you'd found someone else, but didn't have the guts to break up with me." She felt the flush of her anger from the tip of her head to her toes, but it was of little relief to release the pent-up frustration from his behavior the last few weeks.

She watched as he cringed from the sting of her words; his expression went from pained to heated in the blink of an eye, and she wasn't sure if she'd imagined it. "How could you possibly think that I would want anyone other than you? That's complete and total rubbish. You have to know that."

Emma softened her tone and tried to rein in her temper. "You know what? Two weeks ago I'd never have thought that, but lately, I wake up in the middle of the night and you've up and left. Like you don't want to be with me. Something changed, and every time I asked you about it, you gave me the *oh so enlightening*, *'I'm fine'*…when I knew something was wrong. I could feel it in here." Emma rubbed her aching heart, as she felt the sting of tears once again. She'd tried to stay calm, knowing if she didn't her emotions would get the best of her, but it was of no use. For the first time, she really believed it was over. Her heart was breaking into a million pieces as she stood in front of the man she loved, watching him slip away.

"You know what? It wasn't fine. I wasn't fine. But did you ever think that it was something I was trying to deal with? My own insecurities? That it had nothing to do with you?" She desperately searched his eyes for some sign of hope, but came away empty.

Emma felt like he'd just reached into her chest and crushed what was left of her heart. "What the fuck, Noah?" Her harsh words hit their mark as she watched his handsome face twist into a painful grimace. "How can you stand there and say that to me? Of course it had everything to do with me. I can't believe you just said that. If there was something upsetting me and you asked me about it, I would talk to you. So we could work it out…*together*. But you know what the pathetic thing is? I really thought you trusted me to share your worries, your troubles. Because that's what couples do, or at least, that's what they're supposed to do. Be there for each other." She took a deep breath, her head was pounding in unison with her racing pulse, and she was so mad and sad she couldn't think straight. "Boy, was I a fool. But thanks for opening my eyes before I made an even bigger mistake."

"Wow, that's priceless coming from the girl who's going to be leaving in a few months! You know what? Oh, never mind…I need to get out of here." He turned to leave, and Emma wanted to throw the nearest object at his retreating backside. It was either that or jump on his back and beg him to stay.

"What! You're leaving…now?" He paused and looked back at her over his shoulder, his face a mixture of sorrow and anger.

"Yeah. I need to clear my head, and I can't do it here. I'm really sorry, Emma. I never meant to hurt you, you have to know that." Emma watched in amazement as he stalked out the door he'd just entered a few minutes earlier.

Collapsing onto the couch, clutching her throbbing head in her hands, she wondered how things had gone so wrong, so quickly. She'd let her temper get the best of her, and now she was left alone to suffer the consequences. She'd never seen him so angry before, his face hardened as he stared at her, the tick in his jaw as he clenched his teeth. She looked around the room in which she'd felt at home just a short while ago and felt sick to her stomach.

She thought back over her time with Noah. From the first night they'd met, she felt connected to him in a way that she'd never felt with anyone else. His request hadn't come as a complete surprise. They'd carried on their relationship as if it was forever, so asking her to come back shouldn't have shocked her. But he'd been so distant the last few weeks that it *had* shocked her. And she'd needed a minute to process it and then maybe to sleep on it, too. They at least needed to sit down and talk about it rationally.

If he expected her to stay with him permanently, was he going to want to get married? Would she move without some sort of commitment from him? Should she? She could definitely see herself as Noah's wife, had fantasized about it even. Would she be able to work? Her student visa prohibited her from getting a job, but surely he'd want her to contribute, at least until they started their family. Oh,

God, just the idea of being so far away from her family when she had children twisted her already-sickened stomach into a painful knot.

He was asking her to give up everyone and everything she loved in America. Well, maybe not give it up entirely, she could always visit, but it wouldn't be the same. In Boone, if she was feeling homesick, she could always just hop in her car and be home within a few hours.

Just thinking about living the rest of her life half a world away from her family left the wretched taste of bile in the back of her throat. And sweet little Abby would grow up so quickly, without her. And her own children would grow up without the influence of her parents and brothers and sisters.

That might be a good thing, she lied to herself, after watching Ali deal with their mother being constantly underfoot. She'd always pictured her children baking cookies and learning to swim on their Sunday visits to Nanny and Pop-pops for dinner. Could she leave it all behind and start a life in New Zealand with Noah?

As she looked around the lounge, a wave of despair washed over her as she realized it was probably too late to worry about it anyway. He'd walked away, he'd left her.

She waited on the couch for him to return, hoping they could talk, for what felt like hours. Wondering if he was staying away because she was still there, and suddenly feeling an overwhelming need to escape, she picked up her phone with trembling hands and called the one person who would always be there for her.

At the sound of Lily's greeting, she broke down, sobbing uncontrollably into the phone. "Lily, will you come and get me?" she finally muttered, and wondered if Lily understood the unintelligible words she'd just barely mumbled.

"Emma, what happened?" Lily's compassionate tone took some of the sting away, but she needed to get out of there, away from the memories that mocked her from every corner.

"We had a fight and he left. I just want to get out of here before he comes back. Can you come and get me, please?" she begged, and hoped Lily didn't probe any deeper. She didn't have the strength left and didn't think she could explain what had happened when she didn't understand it herself.

"Of course. I'm leaving now. I'm going to kill that man when I get my hands on him. Do you want me to stay on the phone until I get there?" Lily's steadfast support bolstered her as she stood to her feet and headed down the hall.

"No. I'm going to pack a few things and I'll wait outside for you. But, please hurry, Lily."

Ending the call, Emma braced herself before entering their bedroom. She sucked in a deep breath and exhaled slowly, stepping through the door as if entering a minefield. They'd shared so many amazing moments within the four walls that, just crossing over the threshold, took a herculean effort and the sight of their photos hanging over the bed was more than she could bear. Swallowing another round of tears, she quickly threw a few items into her suitcase, and finally releasing a breath, rushed from the room.

She'd had a few messy breakups in her lifetime, but this one put them all to shame. Her heart had been shattered into a million pieces, and she wasn't sure how she'd make it through another minute, let alone the rest of her life without Noah. Replaying the evening over and over again did little to help her comprehend how it all had gone so wrong so suddenly. Noah went from asking her to stay to walking out the door in a matter of minutes. He'd walked away from her and hadn't looked back.

Noah wasn't surprised when his cell phone rang and Josh's face lit up the screen. He was sure that Emma had talked to Lily by now and his best friend was either calling to rip him a new one or to lend his support. He swiped the screen and answered the call. "What the hell have you done, mate?" Josh's angry voice bellowed through the phone, and Noah had his answer.

"I've blown it all to hell, that's what I've done," Noah growled in frustration, knowing he'd ruined the very thing he was so desperate to hold on to. The sting of the cold sand beneath his bare feet felt like a thousand tiny daggers, and he deserved each and every one of them, welcomed them even, as a reminder of the pain he'd caused the one woman who meant the world to him.

"Too right, you wanker. You want to tell me what you did and why Emma called Lily crying? Don't you know that you should never, and I repeat, *never* make your girl cry? Only happy tears, mate."

Noah was ashamed of his actions, and looking back, he knew he'd overreacted. When she hesitated for just a moment, he took it as a no, and things spiraled out of control so quickly, his head was left spinning and his heart was broken beyond repair.

He couldn't get the vision of Emma's tear-stained face out of his mind, the image a painful reminder of how wrong the evening had gone. He'd just thrown away the one thing that meant the most to him in this world, and it was all his fault. "Yeah, I know, but I've ruined everything man. I asked her to stay and when she didn't throw herself at me with gratitude, I got mad and walked away."

Josh's snicker sent a wave of irritation through him. "You know, I never took you for a bloody fool before, mate, but you, my friend, are an idiot. Now, what are you going to about it?"

"I don't know what to do. I can't lose her, Josh. I just can't. But I don't know how to fix it, either. I let my temper get the best of me, and now I don't know how to make it right again. I'm such a bloody fool. I can't believe I walked out and left her standing there. Oh my God, Josh, what have I just done?" His grieving heart ached and his voice cracked as he felt the burn of tears against his cheeks. The crushing realization brought him to his knees in the hard sand.

He couldn't remember ever shedding tears over a woman before, but he welcomed them. He took it as a sign that he still had a heart, that he wasn't a merciless bastard. If he was to convince her to take a chance on him, he was going to have to expose his deepest desires and fears. She'd accused him of pushing her away, and as he looked back over the last few weeks, he knew she was right. He'd foolishly allowed his insecurities to convince him that she wouldn't stay, and by pushing her away, he'd made it happen.

"You haven't lost her yet." Josh's softened voice was reassuring as Noah looked out over the water in anguish. "Now, first off, why are you not groveling on your hands and knees begging her to forgive you? And, second of all, why would you walk out on her, bro? That was a really stupid thing to do, you know that, right? Where are you anyway?"

"I thought we needed a time out, so I went for a walk on the beach to clear my head and try to figure out where it all went wrong and how I can fix it. Things were getting out of control." As he spoke the words, he realized that what seemed like a good idea at the time was actually the worst thing he could've done and may have cost him everything. "I can't lose her, Josh."

"I know, man. Look, I know you love her, but I've got to make sure you're in this wholeheartedly, because if I help you and Emma gets hurt again, Lily will kill me. I'd take a bullet for you, you know that, but Lily comes first...always. And Emma's a sweet girl who's like a sister to me, so if this isn't a forever thing for you, then let her go now." Josh's sympathetic tone eased his panic level from complete despair to utter misery. Noah wanted to be upset with Josh for questioning his commitment to Emma, but his concern for her touched him.

"Josh, I appreciate you looking out for Emma." Just saying her name sent a dagger of guilt through his heart. "I really do, but I think you know me well enough to know that I wouldn't have asked her to stay if I wasn't stuck in. She's everything to me. If she leaves me, I'm following her. I just have to find a way to get her to listen to me, to let me explain." His heart ached with need for her. He'd fall to his knees and beg her to forgive him if necessary. How he'd let things get so out of control, he still didn't know, but he'd do whatever it took to put it right again.

"Take it from me, just be honest with her. They have this sixth sense and know when you're holding back anyway, so it's not worth it. And you've buggered everything up, so you better do it right the first time. You may not get another chance."

Noah lifted himself off the sand and quickly headed home; his bare feet were numb from the cold as they churned up the sand. He never should've left in the first place and prayed it wasn't too late to make it right.

The sun had set, and as he approached his house, his stomach sank. For a brief moment he was frozen in place; his normally-welcoming home looked like an empty shell, dark and abandoned. It had lost its heart. Regaining his momentum, he hurried up the path and entered the door, looking around the darkened space. Quelling his rising panic, he called out Emma's name as he darted from room to room, only to be met with the deafening sound of silence.

Oh, God, she's left me, he muttered to himself, as he lowered his soulless body to the couch in the lounge. Looking around the room, seeing Emma in every square inch of it, he put his face in his hands, and for the first time ever, broke down and cried. He'd lost her. He was too late.

Movement outside the front door caught his attention, and by the light of the porch, he saw the silhouette of the body that he'd recognize anywhere. Thinking he must be hallucinating, but needing to check just to make sure, he lifted his shattered body from the couch.

As he opened the door, he prayed his eyes weren't playing tricks on him. "Emma?" he softly whispered, afraid that if he spoke too loudly, she'd disappear.

"What do you want, Noah?" She sounded defeated as she hunched over, refusing to look at him, her arms wrapped around her knees. As if it was possible, her quiet whimpers made him feel even more wretched.

"What're you doing out here?" He was so relieved to see her, he didn't even realize he'd ignored her question. All he wanted was take her in his arms and never let go. He knew he hadn't earned the privilege, so he shoved his empty hands in his pockets.

"I'm waiting for Lily to come and get me," she sniffled, rubbing her cheek against her knee. Her back had flattened against her thighs and he watched as she slowly rocked back and forth. The movement was almost undetectable, but he knew she was trying to soothe herself. He'd done this to her, to them.

Hoping he still had a chance to change her mind, he reached for his phone. "Go home, Lily," he spoke only those three words before ending the call, and carefully moved the last few steps until he was standing next to Emma. He wasn't sure how she'd respond to his sending away her means of escape, but he couldn't let Lily take her.

Without turning her head to look in his direction, Emma spoke so softly he almost didn't hear her. "Why'd you do that?"

"Please, come inside, Emma. Let me explain everything. Please." He'd never begged for anything in his life, but as he stood next to his reason for living, he'd beg, plead, or supplicate himself just to have her hear him out.

He wished she'd look at him, but at least she was listening, and he gave a silent thanks for that. "Why, Noah? I think we've both said enough, and I'm too exhausted for round two. And you had no right to send Lily away."

"I know, but I can't let you leave before we talk. If you still want to go, then I'll take you to Lily's myself, alright?" He was sure his heart had split in two and was bleeding out inside his chest, it hurt so badly. Her soft whimpers squeezed what was left of his heart painfully as he moved to stand in front of her.

"I'm not sure what you want from me." She finally lifted her face and the devastation he saw there wrecked him. He hated himself at that moment.

Everything. "I just want to talk. Let me explain why I reacted so poorly. Maybe you can find it in your heart to forgive me? I'm so sorry, sweetheart. The last thing I ever want to do is hurt you."

Her features softened as she held his gaze. He didn't deserve to breathe the same air as the exquisite woman sitting before him. "I'm sorry, too. I got so angry, and I said some things I didn't mean. No matter what, you could never be a mistake, Noah. I've loved every minute with you. Excluding the last few, of course." Lifting his hand to her cheek, he gently wiped away the tears that still flowed from her sad, bloodshot eyes. She gifted him with a wobbly smile and some of the crushing weight lifted from his shoulders.

"I said things, too. Definitely not my proudest moment, sweetheart. Please, come inside and I'll make us a cuppa and we can talk." He tugged on her hands, lifting them from where they clutched her knees, and pressed them to his chest. The empty hole that his heart used to inhabit, filled slightly as she stood to her feet and turned for the door.

Wanting to fall to his knees to give thanks, he reached for her suitcase and guitar and followed her inside.

Lifting his face towards the heavens, he mouthed, "Thank you. Thank you. Thank you."

Noah sat patiently as Emma spoke to Lily on the phone, assuring her that she was alright and that she'd call her later. He knew Lily would give him hell the next time she saw him, but he'd gladly pay the price if it meant he still had Emma in his life.

After countless promises to call if she needed anything, Emma finally disconnected the call and turned her beautiful face towards Noah. She was still the most gorgeous woman he'd ever seen, even with puffy red eyes and a runny nose.

Sitting next to Emma on the couch, Noah took a deep breath and decided to start at the beginning. Emma deserved the full explanation for his petulant behavior, and if he wanted any chance at a future that included her, he had to be honest. He was embarrassed that he'd let Evan's comments influence him, that he was so weak. But he'd been worried about asking her to stay and Evan's remarks had sent him over the edge, clouding his judgment.

He desperately wanted to take her in his arms and pull her onto his lap, as it would make it so much easier for him; he was free when she was in his arms, but he didn't dare touch her, afraid she might run away.

He felt worthless for causing her such pain, and as she looked at him with swollen eyes, his confidence wavered. He didn't deserve her. If she'd give him another chance, he'd spend the rest of his life trying to be the man she needed him to be.

Steeling himself, he inhaled deeply, slowly reaching for her hand, and was relieved when she thread her fingers through his, giving him a gentle squeeze. The tender gesture gave him the courage to begin. "From the first moment I saw you, dancing with Lily, you owned me. I didn't understand it; I wanted to know everything about you. And the more I found out, the more I wanted to know. You were so beautiful, but it was more than that. There's so much more to you than the way you look." Giving her a genuine smile, he thought back to the beginning of their courtship. "I'd never met anyone like you, so sweet and kind, and even though you could've had anyone, you chose me. You've filled this house with the sounds of laughter and music...and love. You've made it a home."

"You made it easy, Noah." He released the breath he didn't realize he was holding when she gave him the sweet smile that he'd fallen in love with. For the first time since he foolishly walked out the door, he had hope.

"When we first kissed..." Pausing, he felt a dopey grin spread across his face at the memory. "I knew from just that one kiss that you were the one I'd been waiting for. And when we finally made love, well...that was it for me. I'd found my forever."

He wanted to cut out what was left of his heart when he saw a tear slide down her cheek. "I'm sorry, Emma. Please don't cry, sweetheart."

She placed her fingers against his lips to quiet him. "Shhh, Noah. They're happy tears. Everything you just said, I've felt the same way." She looked at him with her soulful green eyes and he felt his heart come back to life as it beat wildly. "You've made me so happy. But at the same time, I've been so conflicted. I want to be with you, but I can't imagine living so far away from my family. It's so unfair. Why should I have to choose between my heart and my home?"

He couldn't resist any longer and pulled her onto his lap, breathing a sigh of relief when she circled her arms around his neck and rested her head on his shoulder. The feel of her weight in his lap and her warm breath against the sensitive skin of his neck comforted him, giving him the strength to continue.

"I know, baby. But I'm not going to pressure you to stay, and I'll give you the time you need to make up your mind. If we have to, we'll do the long distance thing until my contract is up and then I'll come to you." He'd thought about following her to America a time or two, but never seriously thought it was an option. But as he held her in his arms, he knew without a doubt that he'd follow her anywhere, without regret.

"You'd do that for me?" She lifted her head from his shoulder, her red rimmed eyes meeting his, and he knew he'd do anything for her.

"Don't you know, Emma? I'd follow you to the moon and back again. Nothing means anything without you here to share it with me. When I think of this house, without you filling it with love, it's just a house…you make it home. I designed it with my future family in mind and don't get me wrong, I'd like to raise my children here. But their mother has to want that too." He felt the vise that had gripped his heart loosen at her beautiful smile.

"Their mother wants that, too. I want that too, Noah. I can't tell you how many times I've dreamed about our children running around this house. Our home." She reached her hand up and gently touched his cheek before running her fingers through his hair and he wanted to fall prostrate at her feet. "But at the same time, I want my children to have a close relationship with my parents, and their aunts and uncles and cousins. I don't see how that's possible if we live so far away from them." She was being torn in two, and he didn't have an answer that would satisfy both halves.

"I know, sweetheart, we'll figure it out…together." He took the tips of her hair between his fingers, reveling in the softness of it. "I need to tell you something else, though, and I hope it doesn't change the way you feel about me." He could hear the nervousness in his voice and tried to subdue it.

"Nothing could change the way I feel about you."

Fortifying himself, he continued. "Well, I'd been wanting to talk to you about staying here with me, but it was never the right time. No…I take that back…I didn't have the balls to ask you. I was so afraid you'd say no that I kept putting it off. Then, a few weeks ago, I had a conversation with Evan. He wanted to warn me that you'd never stay and that I was kidding myself to think otherwise."

She pulled away, looking in his eyes, her skin flushing a deep red, and he wanted to cheer at her righteous indignation. "He what? Well, if he'd bothered to ask Ali, she would've stayed. She told me so herself. So, he's a fool. He lost everything for nothing. He just let her walk away, without a fight."

"I'm so ashamed to admit it, but I was scared, and when you didn't answer me right away…well, I assumed you were about to crush my future with one little word…no. And I couldn't bear to hear it. So…I did the cowardly thing…and ran." He forced himself to hold her gaze when all he wanted to do was hide himself away.

"Oh, Noah, you know what happens when you assume?" She gripped his face gently with both hands as she gave him a smile that was tinged with sadness.

"I make an ass out of you and me?"

"No, you break my heart." Her voice soothed his soul as her soft hand caressed his cheek. She brought her lips to his in a feather-light kiss that was over much too quickly.

"I'll remember that." He'd learned his lesson the hard way, and thankfully it hadn't cost him the one thing he couldn't live without.

"Please do, and promise me that, in the future, you'll talk to me when something's bothering you. And if you want to ask me something, however big or small, ask me instead of stewing over it. And no matter how hard things get, never ever run away from me again. I thought I'd die when you walked away from me."

"I promise." He was so relieved to hear her speak of the future, their future, his eyes welled with tears as he squeezed her tightly to his chest and kissed her.

"I love you, Noah. Now and forever."

"I love you too, baby," he confessed, smiling against her soft lips before claiming her with a kiss that healed his soul and left him needing all of her.

"Hey…we just had our first fight." She gave him a saucy grin while tracing her fingers along the planes of his chest.

"Does that mean we can have hot and sweaty make up sex?" he asked hopefully.

"Yeah. And I think the hotness of it should correlate to the magnitude of the fight, which in this case was off the charts. You up for that, big boy? Because I think I need you to take me to bed now."

"I think I'm the luckiest guy on the planet."

"I don't know about that, but you are about to get lucky." With that, she rose to her feet and reached out her hand to him, and he gladly followed her down the hall to their bedroom, watching the sassy sway of her hips.

Emma woke with the sun following a restless night, thinking about her life with and without Noah. It had been a week since their argument, and he'd kept his word and hadn't pressured her to make up her mind. She was relieved that he'd given her the time to work through her feelings.

After their argument, things had returned to normal as she'd carefully weighed her options, not wanting to regret the decision she made. Uprooting her life wouldn't be easy, but she could see herself living in New Zealand permanently, and being happy here. The country and the people had always held a special place in her heart, and she felt equally at home here and in North Carolina.

She'd traveled to Hamilton to attend the All Blacks test match against Ireland and cheered for Noah, alongside his family. It quickly became obvious to her that Noah had told them he'd asked her to stay and about their subsequent fight, but thankfully they were very discreet about it.

Lara had pulled her aside to let her know she hoped she stayed and would be thrilled to have her in the family. Emma was stunned when Lara confided in her that when Noah had visited her back in January, he'd gushed about the girl he'd only just met, but could see himself marrying one day. Emma remembered the trip he'd made to Hamilton when she was busy with her family during their stay, but had no idea at the time that he'd felt so strongly about her and their future together.

Now that they were back home, she was finally done with exams and on break from school and Noah didn't have another test match with the All Blacks for two months. Having made up her mind, she couldn't wait for him to wake up so she could give him the news. Emma still had some questions and felt she needed some guidance from him as to what he saw as her role, what he expected of her. But as she watched him sleep, his features soft and relaxed, she knew she'd never leave him. He was her other half, the part of her that had been missing all along.

Her mother had read her a quote after one of her nastier breakups that said, 'Once you meet the right one, you'll realize why it never worked out with anyone else' and as she looked back now, she knew it was true. There would never be anyone else for her, and she couldn't stop the sappy grin from spreading across her face at the thought of waking up in his arms every morning for the rest of her life.

Giving Noah a gentle nudge to coax him out of his deep slumber, she almost trembled with excitement as he started to stir. Pressing her lips to his chest, she watched as the corners of his mouth twitched up into a smile. Noah's eyes fluttered opened as he rested his hand on her arm; the smooth motion of his thumb as it caressed her was intoxicating as he turned to face her. She lifted her head and rested it on her hand and he did the same as they faced each other.

Unable to resist touching him, she reached out and ghosted her fingers along the arm that was now draped lazily around her waist. "Ask me again," she stated with certainty, looking him in the eyes.

"Excuse me?" His confused expression left her feeling a bit frustrated, but she held his steady gaze before asking him once more.

"Ask me again." She gave him a cheeky grin as she watched him, knowingly.

As realization dawned on him, he shook off the last remnants of sleep and gave her a satisfied smile as he leaned over and caged her beneath him. "Stay with me, Emma. Will you come back and stay with me?" He brushed a chaste kiss against her lips and it wasn't enough. She needed more, but first he deserved an answer.

"Yes, Noah. I'll come..."

She didn't get the chance to finish as his mouth came against hers in a kiss so possessive, it curled her toes.

"Oh, trust me, you'll come…repeatedly. And you'll like it." She shuddered at his promise as he traced his lips along the length of her neck and kept going.

She arched her back as Noah lifted the hem of her tank top, slowly uncovering her breasts, before slipping it over her head. His eyes darkened to a deep sapphire as he licked his lips at the sight of her hardened nipples.

Emma cried out as his teeth grazed the sensitive peaks before suckling one and then the other. His teasing nibbles were driving her mad with need as she writhed beneath him. Each press of his lips was a bolt of lightning straight to her core.

"Noah, I need you now," she begged wantonly. Unable to resist the need to touch him, she reached between his legs and stroked the length of him.

"Don't worry, sweetness, I know what you need." He hissed in a breath at her touch and his mouth came against hers, their tongues mating in rhythm with the stroke of her hand.

She needed more, as she left a trail of kisses along the curve of his neck. His groan of approval left her feeling powerful as she kissed her way down the length of his chest to her intended destination. She felt his strong hands tangle within the strands of her hair, holding her head as she took him into her mouth.

Glancing up at him, she loved giving him so much pleasure as he watched her move up and down over him. The blissful look on his handsome face turned serious as his fingers twisted around her hair, tugging her gently, then pushing her back down. She knew he was getting close and the strained look on his face indicated he was doing his level best to hold back.

Finally bringing him to the brink, he gave her hair a tug and lifted her up and over his body before crushing his mouth to hers and entering her in one swift thrust. Her muffled moan was replaced with the cries of frenzied lovemaking, every touch branding her as he made her his in every way. At once gentle and rough, he worshipped every inch of her body before finally taking his own release with a loud growl against her neck as he bit her there.

After the most thorough shower she'd ever taken, Emma cuddled against his chest, loving the feel of his arms holding her snugly. Noah had reverently washed every inch of her, before making love to her until the water ran cold. She could still feel his lips against her sensitive skin as she screamed out her climax, and without letting her come back down, he drove her to another before taking her against the wall. All the while, he whispered professions of love and forever that left her heart spilling over with pure unadulterated pleasure.

# CHAPTER 24

Emma's family was coming to Auckland to celebrate Emma's and Abby's birthdays in two weeks' time, and Noah wanted to take her away to celebrate her birthday privately, just the two of them.

Looking for any excuse to get Emma back into her swimming costume again, he'd booked a private villa in Bora Bora for the week, and couldn't wait to give her the surprise. Remembering that it was on her bucket list, he wanted to tick the box with her. The villa was perched over a pristine lagoon with a private plunge pool on the terrace and an unobstructed view of the mountainside. And he'd arranged for a couples massage and a romantic candlelit dinner for two on the terrace of their bungalow, knowing she'd love them both.

The resort offered an assortment of excursions and water sports, but he hadn't wanted to over-plan their time. If she wanted to spend the day in bed or relaxing in the villa, that would suit him just fine. He did want to do some paddle boarding and snorkeling in the lagoon while they were there, but other than that, he was game for just about anything she wanted to do, or not do.

Handing her the birthday card with the brochure tucked inside, he was bursting with anticipation. "Happy Birthday, baby. I wanted to give you your pressie early."

Watching as she sat up, the sheet slipped from her breasts, leaving her bare as she sat cross- legged facing him. Her breasts, perfectly rounded with tight nipples, drew his attention, and knowing she was naked under the sheet that draped lazily over her legs distracted him for a moment before he dragged his gaze up her long torso, finally reaching her eyes.

The look on Emma's gorgeous face was worth the price of the trip as her eyes opened wide and her mouth hung open. He was beaming with pride as she turned the brochure over and over, as if she couldn't believe her eyes. "I booked us for five days in that villa…right there," he said, pointing to the location at the end of the row on the cover of the brochure. "And we leave tomorrow. So get your bags packed, baby, because we're headed for some fun in the sun."

"Oh, Noah, I want to say you shouldn't have because it's too much, which it is, but I love it, so I won't. Thank you, baby. It's the best birthday present *ever*. I love you. I love you. I love you."

Throwing herself at him, she banded her arms around his neck and pressed her lips to his. The motion left the sheet that was covering her in a puddle at her knees, and his mind in the gutter.

Unconsciously lifting his hand to the back of her thigh, he enjoyed the feel of her soft skin. Tilting his head, he deepened the kiss as his hand traced up and down the length of her leg, before settling on the round globe of her perfect backside.

Her soft chuckle against his lips as he squeezed her bum left him hungry for more. Sitting up and rolling her onto her back, he proceeded to get the birthday celebration off on the right foot.

Standing in the arrivals area of Auckland International Airport, Noah could feel the excitement radiating off Emma so strongly he could almost reach out and touch it. She was literally trembling in his arms. Her parents were staying with her Aunt Mary and Uncle Bob, while Steven, Katie, Ali, and Abby were staying with them.

They'd stocked the fridge with food and beer, and Emma had baby-proofed the entire house, including baby gates to block the staircase. Looking at the purchases as investments in the future children they'd have, he even went with her to pick them out and they'd spent the day installing them. Abby was walking now, and they wanted her to be free to explore, safely.

Emma's excited squeal signaled their arrival, and once the hugs and kisses were taken care of, they loaded the luggage into the waiting vehicles and headed to Noah's home in Takapuna.

Noah was apprehensive, knowing they'd be informing her family of Emma's decision to come back to live with him permanently after she finished school. Emma had assured him they wouldn't throw him to the sharks, and that her happiness was of utmost importance to them, but a little niggle of doubt still lingered. Knowing how close they were worried him. He wanted to be welcomed into the family fold, not looked upon as the man who stole away a beloved piece of the family puzzle.

Once everyone was settled in the lounge, Noah followed Emma into the kitchen to help set out the food she'd prepared for brunch. Standing in the doorway, he surveyed the room. He had no idea the kitchen was capable of producing so much food at one time.

She was pulling food from every nook and cranny, arranging each dish precisely, so that everything fit and had the proper flow. He wasn't sure what the 'flow' meant exactly, but Emma assured him that she knew what she was doing, so he didn't question it.

As Emma stood back to examine the smorgasbord of platters and casserole dishes she'd laid out buffet style on the kitchen island, Noah stepped up behind her and wound his arms around her waist. Having her securely enveloped in his arms, his shoulders relaxed as she leaned into his chest. He loved the way she felt in his arms. Bending down to bury his face in the curve of her neck, he inhaled the familiar scent of honeysuckle and his sweet, sweet Emma.

"Everything looks great, baby. You've outdone yourself," he said, resting his chin on her shoulder, taking in the display of mouthwatering food.

Twisting in his arms so she was facing him, Emma let her hands come to rest on his hips. "Thanks. And thanks for letting everyone stay here. It means a lot to me."

"Emma...this is your home, too. There's no need to thank me. Of course your family's welcome to stay with us. And it'll give me a chance to get to know them better too." Tucking a strand of hair behind her ear, he pressed his lips to hers for a quick kiss.

She gave him a sweet smile as her eyes found his. "I was thinking that, after brunch, before my parent's leave, we should talk to them about me moving here, to get it out of the way so we can enjoy the rest of their visit." He knew she was nervous about telling her parents, and the slight uptick in her voice confirmed it.

"Sounds good to me. The sooner the better. Don't worry, sweetheart. Everything will be fine." Giving her a gentle squeeze, Noah hoped he sounded more confident than he felt.

"I know. I just don't like upsetting my parents. And I'm warning you now... my mother's a crier. She's very sentimental. The woman gets broken up over television commercials. So when her baby girl tells her she's moving to the other side of the earth...well, it's not going to be pretty." Worry lines formed between her brows, as she frowned.

He couldn't resist the need to kiss away her troubles, and the thought of her mum breaking down in tears worried him too. Like most men, he never handled it well when women cried, and it was usually his cue to exit the building. "I'm sure that, after the initial shock wears off, she'll be fine."

"From your lips to God's ears," she laughed, and gave his bum a sharp pinch.

"Ouch...That hurt," he chuckled.

"Should I kiss it and make it better?" Emma playfully teased, as she soothed the sore spot with the palm of her hand, and he instantly felt the stir of arousal.

Noah pressed his hips against hers to express his discomfort and gain some relief. "You're seriously going to do this to me with your family in the next room?"

"I'm sorry," she giggled. "That wasn't nice of me."

"No, it wasn't," he said, leaning down for a kiss that would have to hold him over until they could be alone.

"Break it up, you two. I'm starving and the food's getting cold," Steven bellowed, as he walked into the kitchen and picked up a cinnamon bun before taking a large bite.

After everyone had been given a tour of the house and were settled in their respective rooms, Emma and Noah asked her parents to join them on the terrace. The weather was chilly, but the sun was shining and it would give them the privacy they needed to have the potentially-uncomfortable conversation.

Noah could feel the watchful eyes of Lily, Josh, and Emma's aunt and uncle upon them as they anxiously waited in the lounge. They'd already heard the news and were thrilled that Emma was staying in New Zealand, but also knew how hard the revelation would hit Emma's parents.

Walking onto the field for the first time with the All Blacks was nothing compared to facing Emma's parents as they sat across the table from them with curious expressions. Having their blessing meant a lot to Emma, and he wanted to get it right. He'd imagined the conversation many times, but the reality of them sitting across from him was nerve-racking. Noah's heart was pounding a mile a minute and his palms were clammy as he tried to organize his thoughts.

Taking a deep fortifying breath, he cobbled together the words to start the conversation that would make her moving to En Zed official. "Mr. and Mrs. Anderson, Emma and I wanted to talk to you about our future together. I've asked her to come back to New Zealand once she graduates, and she's said yes." Pausing to gauge their reaction, he looked to Emma for a needed confidence boost. The gentle squeeze of her hand on his thigh gave him the encouragement he was looking for. "I love your daughter very much and I'm honored she's chosen to stay here with me."

"I really want you to be happy for me," Emma chimed in, looking from one parent to the other. "Mom, you once told me that I'd know it when I met 'the one'. Well, I found him. He's a good man, and he makes me happy." She gave him the sweet smile that always took his breath away, never looking prettier.

Noah watched as her parents shared a meaningful look and then turned to face them once again.

"Well, I can't say that I'm surprised," her father stated, as he smiled at his daughter. "Emma, you know your mother and I just want you to be happy. But I'm not going to lie and tell you that I like the idea of you living so far away from us." Hesitating at the sound of his wife's quiet whimper, they all turned their attention to her. Sure enough, the tears were flowing, and Noah wanted to crawl under the table.

"Please, don't cry," Emma pleaded, lifting off the chair and circling the table, the frown returning to her pretty face as she knelt in front of her mum. "Believe me, if there was any other way, I'd take it. But Noah's job is here, and he can't leave. And I can't be apart from him." She spoke with such confidence and surety, and he'd never loved her more than in that moment.

Noah watched as her mum softly caressed Emma's cheek, her eyes filled to overflowing with love for her daughter. "Oh, sweetheart, I've missed seeing your pretty face and now to think of you living so far away…well, it just hurts. I knew your heart was here with Noah, but hearing it somehow makes it real. You've always followed your heart; it's who you are. It's what makes you…you. And, yes, I told you that when the right one came along, you'd know it, and that he'd cherish you for the priceless jewel you are."

Emma's mum turned to Noah, holding his gaze, and he acknowledged her statement with a nod of agreement. "That you'd be safe with him, and take good care of each other. That you'd be good to each other." Facing Emma once again, she gently swiped at the tears that were falling from her eyes. "That's all I've ever wanted for you, my precious angel."

"I love you, Mommy," Emma said, enveloping her mum in a tight embrace. "I've missed you."

"Noah, why don't you and I go for a walk?" Emma's father stated without question and Noah immediately raised himself from his seat and followed him down the path to the beach.

After walking quietly next to each other along the water's edge, Mr. Anderson stopped, turning to look out on the blue waters of the Hauraki Gulf and Rangitoto Island in the distance.

Without looking at Noah, he began to speak, and Noah stood quietly, listening intently. "Emma's a special girl. Out of my three daughters, she's the most sensitive. She's as stubborn as the day is long; they all are, really," he softly chuckled, but Noah could see the love for his children written all over his face. "But she has a tender heart. It's obvious how much she cares for you, and that's not something to be taken lightly or for granted. It's a blessing for the man who recognizes it for the rare gift that it is; she'll give you everything she has, plus a little more. She has a lovely soul, my Emma...a sweet and gentle soul."

"It's one of the things I love most about her. I'm not sure what to say, but I love everything about Emma. From the moment we met, I knew she was special. I'll take good care of her, and I'd never intentionally hurt her in any way. I can promise you that."

"I understand you're a bit of a celebrity here in New Zealand." He stared blankly at the gently rolling surf as it broke on the shore, and Noah felt his back stiffen, unsure of where her father was going with the comment.

Trying not to take offense, Noah answered honestly. "I suppose so. Although, we live a pretty quiet life. I've never sought attention because of my profession."

Finally turning to look at Noah, his steely regard demanded respect and Noah stood up straight and looked him in the eyes. "I'm sure that with the focus as it is on rugby here, you garner the attention of quite a few of the female fans." Noah felt his shoulders relax as he realized what he was getting at. "Am I right?"

Holding his gaze with confidence, Noah replied. "Yes, sir, but I can assure you that I've never encouraged that and would never be unfaithful to your daughter. My profession puts me in the spotlight and that's part of it, I guess, but Emma is my life and I come home to her...and only her. That will never change."

"I'm glad to hear it. I also hope you'll protect her and keep her safe from the unintended consequences of living your life under the scrutiny of celebrity and what comes with it."

Noah let out a breath, and felt the bands around his stomach ease. "Of course. I enjoy what I do for a living, don't get me wrong, it's what I dreamed of my whole life. And it's afforded me a good life that I'm thankful for. But if it ever threatened my relationship with Emma, or Emma in any way, there's no question as to who'd prevail. She will always be my number one priority. I can assure you of that. I recognize how lucky I am to have her, and I'd never take that, or her, for granted."

"Good. Now…I know it's a cliché, but I need to ask it anyway, because if I don't, I'll never hear the end of it from my wife. But I'd like to know what your intentions are with my daughter." He gave Noah an apologetic chuckle, but the firm set of his eyes let Noah know he was completely serious.

He should have seen the question coming, but it still took him a bit by surprise. "Well…I'll be honest with you…I'd like to marry her one day. I've known from the beginning that she was the one for me. And I want you to know that I'll do everything in my power to make sure she's happy."

Emma's father finally cracked a smile and Noah breathed a sigh of relief. "Did Emma ever tell you how I met her mother?"

"Only that you met in college."

"Yes, that's true. I was at a party on campus when she walked into the room. She looked at me and smiled, and I felt like I'd been hit by a bus. I'll never forget it. It took my breath away…it still does. We spent the rest of the night talking and laughing, and I knew that she'd be my wife and the mother of my children one day." Noah watched as a faraway look was quickly replaced with a goofy grin, and he could only guess he was reliving that moment in time.

"Emma's told me so much about you both, about her childhood. I can only hope that our children will look back as fondly on their childhoods as she does."

"She's going to make a great mother," Emma's father stated proudly, with a huge smile on his face.

"Yes, sir, she will."

"I think it's time we head back. Thanks for talking with me, Noah. When Emma graduates, if she still wants to settle here with you, then you'll have our blessing." Holding out his hand, Noah took it in a firm handshake, as the weight of the conversation lifted from his shoulders.

"Thank you, Mr. Anderson…that means a lot to us. And I told her that if she changes her mind and decides to stay in America, I'll have to consider an early retirement, because I can't live without her."

"Please, call me Jonathan. And as long as Emma's happy, then I'm happy. I don't suspect you'll need to hang up your boots just yet, son. I think she's grown quite fond of living here with you." His firm hand slapped Noah on the back as they headed towards the house. "She's always loved the water, you know. It's funny to think that we've been coming to Takapuna all these years and now she's going to be living here. I've walked past this house countless times…" His steps hesitated as he looked up at the home that was now brimming with life with a pleased look on his face. "You've done a remarkable job with it."

Noah had to swallow back the lump forming in the back of his throat at the compliment. "Thank you. I'd love to show you the photos I have of the reno."

"And I'd love to see them."

With that, they turned and walked up the path to where Emma sat with her mum, laughing with a giggling Abby on her lap.


Sitting around the campfire on their final night in Auckland, Noah was genuinely sad to see them leave. He'd grown quite fond of her family, and after an initial ribbing by Steven, on behalf of her other brothers, they'd all taken the news of Emma's leaving in stride. Her parents had gone home earlier with Emma's aunt and uncle, and had left them with strict instructions to be ready on time and preferably not hung over.

Music played from Emma's phone, which sat cradled in the portable speaker, and as a new song began, all four Anderson siblings instantly froze, and all conversation ceased. Noah watched curiously as they enthusiastically sang each and every word of the song about a guy crashing his car and breaking his parole to have a good time.

Listening to Emma utter the curse words in the song was kind of hot, if he was being honest with himself. She normally never spoke anything harsher then hell or damn, but hearing her drop the f-bomb so casually was surprisingly a bit of a turn on.

Dissolving into a fit of giggles when the song came to an end, he knew she'd had a few too many beers. Emma was adorable when she was drunk, and her slurred words left him wanting to throw her over his shoulder and take her to bed. She also got horny when she was tipsy and her persistent touches and provocative whispers in his ear, her warm breath against his skin as she described in detail what she planned to do to him once they were alone, had been driving him to the brink of insanity all evening.

Finally taking the party inside so they didn't disturb the neighbors, the large group gathered in the lounge.

Listening to Emma recount their holiday in Bora Bora had his chest puffed up a bit with pride as she pulled out her tablet to show everyone the pictures and videos they'd taken. She and Lily had already chosen a few of the photos to develop on canvas, one of the view from their villa and one taken of them paddle boarding, the crystal blue waters of the lagoon on full display in both images. They'd decided on the location to hang them once they arrived, and Noah loved the idea of filling the walls with meaningful images instead of the generic landscapes he'd decorated with.

As she spoke of going for long swims in the crystal blue waters of the lagoon, Noah's mind drifted back to the night they'd jumped off the terrace into the warm water, the taste of salt water on their lips as they made love to each other under the stars. Glancing at Emma, her knowing smile told him she was remembering that night also. He'd never forget how beautiful she looked under the soft moonlight, the way they circled each other before finally coming together. She truly took his breath away, in every way.

It was a week he'd never forget, mornings spent making love to the sounds of the water gently lapping at the terrace, and nights spent skinny-dipping in the warm lagoon. He could still hear Emma's soft giggles as she dared him to join her, stripping off her clothes before diving into the water.

Lazy afternoons were spent playing in the lagoon or lounging on the terrace, enjoying the view and each other's company. The beauty of the island was only surpassed by the beauty of his companion.

Emma's beauty was effortless and he'd never get tired of looking at her. Especially in her teeny bikini doing yoga on the terrace, while he enjoyed his tropical drink, and a spectacular view of her perfect posterior…no that would never get old…Ever.

Standing in front of the fridge later that evening, Noah inhaled the familiar scent of honeysuckle and Emma, as her arms snaked around his waist and she pressed her breasts against his back.

"God, you are so freaking hot, Noah. Have I told you that lately? And I love your ass in these jeans. Just sayin'." Her hand was creeping down the front of his pants, and he grabbed her wrist to stop the movement. He was already getting hard, and he figured a hand job in the kitchen was out of the question, so it was best to stop now.

"I'm glad you like it, but we have a house full of guests, sweetheart. And as much as I like where you're going with this…and trust me, I think you can feel how much I like it," he snickered, taking a calming breath, "but it's going to have to wait."

Reaching around, he pulled her in front of him, caging her against the cabinets, between his arms.

"I know, but I don't want to," she pouted, and he leaned down to kiss her pretty lips. She may've had the worst timing on the planet, but he loved it when she got frisky. "I crave you, you know. The more I have you, the more I want you."

"Trust me...the feeling is mutual, sweet cheeks." God, he loved this woman; she was so sexy it hurt to even look at her sometimes. Pulling her hair back, he exposed her long neck and the heart-shaped ruby earrings he'd given her on her birthday; she softly moaned, and he felt her shudder as he kissed the sensitive spot beneath her ear.

It was going to be a long night, Noah thought, as they headed back into the lounge and he settled her on his lap. The feel of her in his arms would have to satisfy him until he could take her to bed, and let her have her way with him.

# CHAPTER 25

It was the day Emma had been dreading for months. Noah was leaving with the All Blacks for the European tour, and they wouldn't see each other again until the first week of December. He was flying to Charlotte after the final match in London, and he'd already booked them a room at the Ballantyne Resort, so they could make up for lost time and have a private place to escape to when they wanted to be alone.

As much as she'd miss the physical nature of their relationship, she was going to miss his company even more. They'd grown quite attached to one another, and the loss of his presence was what she'd miss the most. It was the simple things like waking up beside him, discussing their day as they strolled hand in hand along the shore, sitting together as they read the paper or watched TV, or seeing him smile that perfect smile that never failed to melt her heart…those were the things she'd miss more than anything.

The pain in her chest grew as she watched him slowly pack his bag as if it might bite him. She could see the matching despair in his eyes, and knew he was hurting just as badly as she was. They'd stayed up the previous night making love with a passion and hunger that, even hours later, just the memory of the things they'd done with each other, sent a shiver down her spine. The same spine he'd run his tongue down the length of, as if he could somehow devour her and take her with him when he left.

A month was a long time to be apart, but trying to look on the bright side, it would ease them into the four-month separation they'd have to endure while she finished school. The plan was for him to stay in Boone with her, after Christmas with her family, until he had to return to Auckland in mid-January, then he'd come back for her graduation and they'd make the return trip to New Zealand together.

They'd spent his birthday at his parents' beach house on Papamoa Beach, making new memories in the location that had initially set them on the path to where they were today.

One afternoon they hiked The Mount once again, taking their time, enjoying the view of the Bay of Plenty as well as the long stretch of powdery white sand laid out before them. She'd packed a picnic lunch, and they ate and drank while soaking up the sun and each other.

The breathtakingly beautiful beach would always hold a special place in her heart, as it was where she'd fallen in love with the wonderful man who now stood before her, ready to go.

Following him to the car, Emma somehow found the strength to smile as he settled into the seat next to her, and reached for her hand. Noah was struggling for composure as he raised their entwined fingers to his lips, his eyes moist with unshed tears. This was never going to be easy, and she tried to remind herself that she needed to get used to it. Separation was one of the sacrifices they'd have to make for him to pursue his career, and she'd support him like a pro, knowing he'd come back to her...always.

Driving in silence, she stared at the road ahead of them, loathing every inch of it.

"I'll call you as soon as I get to Edinburgh." Noah's comment lifted her from the morose stupor she'd found herself in.

Turning to face him, Emma wanted to focus on what little time they had left together. There'd be plenty of time over the next month to wallow in her despondency. "Okay," she quietly said, her voice cracking as a tear spilled onto her cheek.

"Oi, sweetheart. Please, don't cry. I'll be back before you know it." His shaky smile twisted her heart. Noah was trying to be strong for her, and she needed to do the same for him.

"I know. It's just that I'm going to miss you. And I'm a little jealous that you're going to all those romantic cities without me." Attempting levity, she returned his shaky smile, even though she felt neither.

"Tell you what. We'll travel there together after you graduate, on my next break, alright?"

Pulling into the parking spot at the airport, Emma felt sick to her stomach and finally lost the strength to hold back the tears. She'd tried so hard to be strong, but as Noah clung to her with a desperation that equaled hers, she gave up the fight, breaking down in body-shaking sobs against his chest.

Hauling her over the console and onto his lap, as he shed silent tears, his lips came against hers. Emma wound her arms around his neck as she matched the thrusts of his tongue and drank in the taste of him, until they ran out the clock and he had to leave. Reluctantly, she opened the door and stepped onto the hard pavement, watching as he boldly swiped away the remnants of moisture from his cheeks, holding her gaze without even the slightest hint of shame.

Walking hand in hand into the airport, Emma swallowed the lump in her throat and maintained her composure until he disappeared from view into the terminal, after a long wet kiss that would have to hold her over until she saw him again.

Hurrying back to the car before she made a spectacle of herself, Emma finally let loose with the sobs that demanded they have their due. Leaning her head against the steering wheel, she acknowledged the loss of Noah's presence and gave herself a mental reprimand. He wasn't going off to war or doing something that put his life in jeopardy; he would return to her safe and sound. She needed to keep things in perspective and remember how lucky she was.

Emma turned to her phone at the sound of an incoming text. Recognizing Noah's assigned ringtone, she quickly swiped the phone to open it. "Twenty nine days. Why does it feel like an eternity right now?"

Knowing he was surrounded by his teammates and other passengers waiting to board their flight, she sought to lift his spirits. And even though she wanted to send him a sentimental reply that would match her disposition, she wouldn't. "We can do it, baby. One day at a time and I'll be all up in your business doing really naughty things to you before we know it."

"Don't write checks your ass can't cash," came his quick reply.

Emma chuckled at his cheeky comment. "Not only can my ass cash that check, but I've got overdraft protection." She wasn't sure what she meant by that, but it was all she could come up with off the top of her head.

"hahaha…I'll be buried deep in your credit when I get my hands on you again."

"As much as I love your hands…I'm counting on a deposit from another part of your anatomy…please. Pretty please."

"I don't know if this would even count as sexting, but I'm getting a little hard. I may have to excuse myself in a minute."

"Poor baby…I love you and if I can be of service, you've got my number."

"You're killing me, you know that, right?"

Emma sat in the car, the weight of his departure lifting with each exchange, until he boarded his flight. Deciding to spend the night at Lily's instead of facing the deafening silence at home…alone, she headed for Auckland's CBD.

Staring at the canvas photos of them, holding court in the place of honor above their bed, Emma couldn't believe it was time to head back to North Carolina already. Time had flown by so quickly. She was packed and ready to go, and waiting for Lily and Josh to arrive. They were going to have an early dinner at her aunt and uncle's before heading to the airport to catch her flight.

Packing was quick and easy this time, as her suitcases held only the gifts she'd purchased for friends and family, her toiletries, and a few outfits. Smiling, she turned her face towards the sound of the surf wafting in from the open door.

Summer had returned to Auckland, and Emma wasn't looking forward to the cold temperatures and barren landscape awaiting her in Charlotte. She didn't even want to think about the frozen tundra of Boone that she'd be returning to when school started again in January. Thankfully, she'd have Noah to keep her warm through the long nights once they transitioned to the small mountain town that she loved, but now couldn't wait to leave.

Emma smiled as her phone blared 'Say Hey (I Love You)' by Michael Franti, signaling an incoming call from Noah. "But I know…one thing…that I love you," she sang happily into the phone, as she answered his call.

"I love you too, baby. You packed?"

"Yup. Just waiting for Lily to pick me up and in twenty-something hours, we'll only be separated by the Atlantic Ocean."

"Aye…I can't wait to hold you again."

"Eight days and counting. We got this baby."

Emma arrived at Charlotte Douglas International Airport ahead of schedule and anxiously waited for Noah's flight to arrive from London. The December air blew her hair around her face as she made her way through the parking garage and across the marked path to the arrivals area. The hustle and bustle of the crowded airport whirled around her, but she fixed her eyes upon the escalator, ignoring the commotion, waiting for Noah.

Unable to control herself, she ran to him as his imposing figure came into view. Dropping his bag, he welcomed her into his embrace. The feel of his muscular arms enveloping her was overwhelming…she was home. Lifting her off her feet, his lips crushed hers with the intensity of a starving man.

Finally putting her down, Noah casually slid his arms around her waist; his blue eyes shimmered with a suggestive sparkle and his crooked smile matched her own. "If I'm dreaming, please don't wake me up," he said, and Emma felt his fingers grip her hips tightly beneath her winter coat.

Noah's sweet smile left her breathless and unable to think of anything but needing to be with him. "I've missed you so much, baby. It almost feels like a dream, doesn't it? I'm so glad you're here. I can't wait to show you around, but first…" She leaned in to whisper her desires in his ear, reveling in the way he met her halfway, as if he knew what she wanted. "I need to get you naked. I need to feel you." Averting her eyes, Emma felt the blush as it bloomed across her cheeks.

Noah brushed his lips against hers and gave her a quick kiss. "Well…you know I can't deny you anything, so what are we waiting for? Lead the way."

Emma had already checked them into the large suite…that, thankfully, came equipped with a king-sized bed. Excusing herself, she slipped into the bathroom to change into the lingerie she'd left there.

Stepping out of the bathroom, dressed only in a sheer black baby doll top with lace cups and flyaway front, paired with a matching thong, Emma watched as a wide smile spread across his face. Noah crossed the room in one long stride as he came against her with fervor; his large hand gripping her bare bottom as his mouth crushed against hers. He'd stripped to just his boxer briefs and the thin fabric did little to hide the erection that impressively tented the front.

She'd never felt more beautiful as Noah gently set her on the bed, coming to rest alongside her. His fingers slowly traced the edge of the garment, his eyes trailing the movement, taking in the sight of her as he separated the flyaway bodice, exposing her toned midsection.

Emma held her breath as her eyes fluttered closed, focusing on the feel of his fingers as they whispered reverently over her skin. Her every nerve was on high alert as his lips gently touched the swell of her breast. "You're so beautiful, Emma. I need you so badly, but I just want to enjoy this moment a little while longer," his warm breath tickled, as he whispered against her skin.

Opening her eyes, her heart leapt from her chest when she met his gaze and found his crystal blue eyes watching her with ravenous desire. Reaching up to caress his cheek, she was struck with the depth of her love for him.

Noah had the brute strength to take what he wanted, but he was the gentlest of lovers. "I'm in no hurry, sweetheart. But I don't know how long I can wait to feel you inside me."

A loud groan emanated from her chest as Noah's fingers outlined the lace edging of her panties, before slipping between her legs. "I'm going to take my time with you, play with you for a while. I want to see you come for me…so pretty as you cry out my name."

"Yes," she moaned breathlessly, as his fingers moved against her sensitive skin. It had been too long since she'd felt his touch. "Oh, God, Noah. I want that so badly. Please, don't make me wait," she begged, reaching out to stroke the front of his boxers, unable to keep her hands off of him for another second.

"Patience, my love. Oh yeah, that's good," he hissed in a shaky breath, as he nibbled on the firm peak of her nipple through the lace cups that still covered her breasts.

Her hand gripped him tightly through the cotton fabric of his boxers as stars exploded behind her eyelids and she cried out, his expert touch bringing her to a quick orgasm.

Noah quickly stripped off her panties and stood as he lowered his boxers. Emma's eyes took in the exquisite sight of him, magnificently naked before her.

"I'm not going to last long, sweetheart. I really want to, but it's been too long and you are the sexiest thing I've ever seen. I could come just looking at you." His eyes darkened as he sucked in a deep breath, exhaling slowly through his teeth, as if he could will himself the control he was losing.

"That's alright. We've got all night."

Positioning himself on the bed, stretching out, Noah reached for her hand. "Come here, baby. I need you now." His tongue demanded entrance as he pressed his lips against hers for a long sensual kiss that curled her toes and left her desperate for more.

Noah couldn't hold back any longer, he had to be inside her…right now. Quickly rolling her onto her back, he entered her with one swift thrust of his hips, and Emma cried out, still feeling the effects of her climax.

"That's it, baby. I've got you. Open your eyes. I want you to watch as I make love to you," he whispered against her lips, as her back arched and another breathy moan escaped from her pretty mouth.

Emma's eyes drank him in as he moved over her, propped on his forearms, hovering inches above her. Flushed with arousal as she tried to focus, her eyes scanned his face, as if taking a mental picture. He let her take her time, a sexy smile crossing her lips, as her fingernails dragged down the length of his back, coming to rest on his bum and squeezing him there. Unable to hold back any longer, he emptied into her with a loud groan as they climaxed together.

Lazily combing his fingers through Emma's hair as they held each other in the comfortable bed, Noah could finally relax as she sprawled on top of him, her chin resting on her hands, a wide smile on her beautiful face.

"I've missed this...you. I'm so glad you thought to get this room, or I may have had to kick Ali out of her house so I could get my fill of you," Emma giggled, pressing a gentle kiss to his chest.

"Too right," he stated, without removing his eyes from hers. "I missed you too, baby. Thankfully, we won't have to resort to that, and I must confess that it was rather selfish of me, eh? I wanted a place to whisk you away to so I could have my wicked way with your gorgeous body, without disruption. Phone sex may tide me over temporarily, but nothing compares to you...in the flesh."

"I know. I ached for you when you were gone. I would dream of you, touching me, and wake up needing you...so badly."

"I'm here now and I need you too...again. Right now."

"Please." Her wish was his command as he wrapped his arms around her back and kissed her. He would never get enough, even though they had all night.

Christmas at the Andersons' was best described as organized chaos. The smell of cookies and gingerbread, fresh from the oven, filled the comfortable home with the familiar aromas of Christmas. The large house brimmed with laughter as the close-knit family gathered to celebrate the holiday.

Noah helped decorate the outside of the stately brick home with festive lights along the eaves and across the front shrubbery, and fat red ribbons adorned the columns of the front porch, along with a large wreath on the front door.

A large Christmas tree stood tall beside the fireplace in the lounge, its oversized mantle covered in garland and twinkling white lights, and Noah was pleased to see a stocking next to Emma's with his name on it.

Christmas morning, Noah woke to the feel of Emma's warm body, as she settled against him. Instinctively reaching for her, he held her tightly against his side. He'd missed waking up to the feel of her next to him, her warm breath tickling his chest.

"Merry Christmas, baby. I wanted to give you a present while we're alone," she said, handing him a brightly wrapped gift.

"Thanks and Merry Christmas, sweetheart." Noah sat up, resting his back against his pillow as he took the gift from her, shaking it gently, trying to figure out what it was.

Emma reached out, holding his hand steady. "We don't have much time, so you need to open it quickly. Plus, I'm dying for you to see it."

Noah ripped the paper off the small framed photo of Emma naked on their bed, beneath a sheet that strategically covered her private parts. Barely. Her golden hair fell in soft waves on the pillow, and her arms were stretched high above her as if reaching out to him. She was so beautiful; he was left speechless as he lost himself in the image.

"It's probably inappropriate as a Christmas present, but I wanted you to have something to take with you when we're apart. It's small enough to fit discretely in your bag but it's tasteful, so if someone were to find it, it wouldn't be too embarrassing. Although, I wouldn't want anyone seeing it...but you."

There was no way he'd ever let anyone lay eyes on the sexy photo...ever. "It's so beautiful. You're beautiful. I love it. It won't keep me warm on those lonely nights, but it will definitely heat me up." Placing it on the bed next to him, he clasped his hand around the back of her neck to pull her towards him. Lifting onto her knees, she settled herself on his thighs as she leaned in for a kiss that was over much too quickly.

Sitting around the lounge, Noah was blown away by the generous gifts from her family. He'd received tickets to that weekend's Panthers game, a pair of gloves, a watch, a Segway tour of uptown Charlotte, and even a chocolate Santa in his stocking.

But the gift that left him struggling for composure was the photo book from Emma. It was one of the digital ones filled with page after page of pictures from their first year together. There were photos of them from the first night they met in the pub, all the way to their time in Charlotte with her family, with thoughtful quotes sprinkled throughout.

As he turned the pages of the book he said a silent thanks to Lily and her camera for capturing so many images of the two of them. It was the story of them, and he loved it. As she excitedly passed the book around, patiently showing it to each family member, he wondered how he'd gotten so lucky to be a part of her life.

He'd given Emma a Tiffany's bracelet and her sharp intake of breath and the adorable squeak that followed, along with the ooh's and ahh's from her family as she put it on, left him bursting with pride. She was definitely a Tiffany's girl, as were her sisters, he'd come to find out. Knowing she'd be flying back to Auckland, his gifts needed to be small enough to travel, so jewelry was the perfect choice.

He also gave her a round-trip ticket to Auckland for New Year's. It was their first anniversary, and he wanted to watch the sunrise with her, on the hammock, wrapped securely in his arms.

But the gift that meant the most was still tucked away in his bag upstairs… waiting until the right time.

"Ten… Nine… Eight… Seven… Six… Five… Four… Three… Two… One… Happy New Year!" They called out in unison as the clock struck midnight.

"Happy New Year, baby," Noah smiled, as he leaned down for a kiss. This was going to be a good year, he thought to himself, as she welcomed the glide of his tongue for a long sensual kiss that left him weak in the knees.

"Happy New Year, sweetheart. I can't believe it's been a year already. In some ways, it feels like yesterday, but in others it feels like a lifetime ago." Emma's pretty smile reached all the way to her eyes as she turned to watch the fireworks over the Auckland skyline, resting against his side.

Noah slid his arm around her shoulders, hugging her tightly. "I know; it was an awesome year, wasn't it?"

"Yes, it was, and you know what?" she exclaimed, turning towards him, momentarily ignoring the colorful display.

"What?"

Lifting onto her toes, she placed a gentle kiss to his lips. "The best is yet to come."

"You are absolutely right," he said, as she leaned against him, smiling as Lily and Josh joined them.

As they drove home after the party, Noah listened as Emma excitedly chatted about their time in North Carolina. Like the same night one year earlier, Josh and Lily joined them at his home in Takapuna, and knowing what Noah had planned, they excitedly left him alone with Emma to watch the sunrise.

Noah was nervous as he gathered the blankets and took her hand, leading her down to the beach and the waiting hammock. He'd planned everything down to the last detail and prayed it all went according to plan. Patting his pocket one last time, he settled Emma against his side for the last few hours until the sunrise, welcoming the first day of the rest of their lives together.

Just like the year before, they talked and laughed under the stars, enjoying each other's company. Noah couldn't resist pointing out that he never collected on the bet she'd lost, but when Emma offered to give him a bath instead of his car, he wholeheartedly agreed to change the means of settlement.

As the sun started to rise over the horizon, Noah took a calming breath and lifted to his feet, bringing Emma with him. He'd gone over what he'd say to her a thousand times, trying to find a way to impart how much she meant to him, but as he looked at her, so pretty with the blanket wrapped around her shoulders, the glow of the sunrise tinting her features, his mind went blank and he forgot everything.

He'd have to wing it and hope he didn't muck it up, he thought, as he took her by the hand.

"Emma, I've known since the night we met that you were the one for me. My mate. One year ago, we sat in this very spot watching the sunrise together and you stole my heart. I love you so much, baby. And I told you that for the first time here, too." He smiled before continuing. "Before you, I was drifting along, knowing I was missing something, but nothing made sense until you came into my life...completely captivating me...Completing me."

Noah watched as tears spilled from her eyes. "Oh, Noah. I love you, too."

Watching curiously as Noah lowered himself to one knee and reached into his pocket, Emma's eyes opened wide with astonishment, and a tiny gasp fell from her lips.

"Emma Lynn Anderson, will you please do me the honor of becoming my wife?" he asked, clutching her hand in his. She covered her smile with her right hand as he slid the ring on her outstretched ring finger. "Will you marry me, Emma?"

"Yes! Yes! Yes! Noah, of course I'll marry you," she cried, throwing herself into his waiting arms, hugging him tightly as he sealed it with a kiss. "I love you. I love you. I love you."

"You've just made me the happiest man on the planet, baby. I love you so much, and I can't wait to marry you."

"We're going to be happy, aren't we?" she stated, before kissing him again. "And I can't wait to marry you either. *Oh, my God, we're getting married! I'm so happy*," she excitedly declared, kissing him again, and squeezing him tightly around the neck.

Noah still had one surprise left for her. Retrieving her guitar from where he'd hidden it, he nervously lifted the strap over his head, settling it against his chest.

He'd been practicing a song, without Emma's knowledge, to surprise her. He'd heard it on her playlist and had looked it up on the internet, finding a demo video on how to play it on the guitar. He didn't have the best voice, but hoped to impress her by playing one of her favorite songs, even if it was off-key and a bit shaky.

Emma looked on with a confused expression as he started strumming the chords to 'The Greatest Sum' by The Avett Brothers. The look on her face, as she realized what he'd done for her, was worth the endless hours spent preparing, and the aching fingers. He knew it by heart, after filling his down-time while in Europe practicing with a teammate who knew how to play the guitar.

No words could ever express the depth of his love for her, but the song was a small gesture he hoped would give her some idea of how much she meant to him, and hopefully make her happy. Nothing would ever hold him back from her, and as he sang the lyrics, he meant every word. He couldn't believe he was going to spend the rest of his life with her. Her worth was immeasurable.

Watching the sun welcome the new day, Emma stared at the elegant ring on her finger, the stunning cushion-cut diamond solitaire with small stones lining the platinum band, glistened in the sunlight. It was beautiful and everything she'd ever dreamed of.

But most importantly, it went with the promise of, one day soon, becoming Mrs. Noah James Parker. His wife.

Looking at Noah, so handsome as he gazed adoringly at her, she couldn't help but smile back at him. Life with Noah would never be boring or without love and laughter, and as she thought back over the last year she wouldn't change a second of it.

A thousand questions and ideas tumbled over and over in her mind. Like most women, Emma had dreamed of her wedding day since she was a little girl. Picturing her handsome groom dressed in a black tuxedo, waiting breathlessly for her as she strode down the aisle towards him. The adoring way he'd gaze into her eyes as they exchanged their vows. And their first kiss as husband and wife, sealing their commitment, as they embraced the future together as one.

# EPILOGUE

As they strode through Auckland International Airport, Noah's hand securely entangled with hers, Emma couldn't help but reflect on the past few months. So much had happened since the day he'd left her in a puddle of tears, when he'd returned to Auckland and she'd remained in Boone to finish her studies. Noah had waited until the last possible day, not wanting to leave her, but duty called, so he reluctantly departed.

Her family had all swooned over her gorgeous engagement ring and, depending on who was doing the commenting, his proposal was either the most romantic thing they'd ever heard or Noah was completely whipped. The whipped remark came from her brothers, but she knew they were just teasing. They genuinely liked Noah and appreciated how much he loved their little sister.

She'd taken him to all her favorite spots in Charlotte and Boone, and given him a tour of Appalachian State, secretly loving her girlfriends' reaction when she introduced him. He was a catch, and she knew how lucky she was to have him in her life. Of course, everyone loved him; his easygoing nature fit in well with the Boone crowd, and it was nice for him to finally be able to put a face to the names of all of her friends.

It was too cold to go on any long hikes, but she'd taken him to a few of the shorter trails off the Blue Ridge Parkway that led to breathtaking overlooks and stunning waterfalls. It was important to her that he felt a connection to her childhood home and the place she'd spent her college years, and seeing him enjoy them as much as she did pleased her immensely.

Having Steven and Katie in Boone allowed them to grow closer to Noah, as well as comfort her once he left, keeping her company through the long lonely nights. Katie often spent the night with her, so she didn't have to sleep alone, especially in the early days after he'd left.

Emma concentrated on her studies and enjoyed the last few months with her friends and family. Once the weather broke and the warmer temperatures returned, she'd gone on long hikes through the forest on familiar trails and found undiscovered ones too.

Emma loved Boone, and it had been a wonderful place to live, but it was time to move on. Most of her friends graduated along with her and were now leaving Boone for jobs in other cities, or were moving back home to be closer to their families.

Her future was in Auckland with Noah, and even though she wouldn't see her friends on a daily basis, it didn't mean they wouldn't keep in touch, she repeatedly reminded herself. Distance couldn't break the strong bonds of family and friendships, forged over the ups and downs of finding their way into adulthood.

Finally finishing school was such a relief. The added years had drained any excitement she'd once felt about going away to college. And knowing what was waiting for her, left her wanting to chuck it all and run straight to Noah. She knew she'd look back with regret if she didn't get her degree, so she stuck it out, counting the days until graduation, and having him there to celebrate the accomplishment made it even more special.

It hadn't been easy being separated from Noah. She'd flown to Los Angeles for a quick rendezvous, where they'd checked into the airport Hilton and didn't leave the bed the entire time, except to answer the door for room service. But they'd survived the separation and had come out on the other side stronger and more committed than ever to each other.

The Super Rugby season was in full swing once again, and Noah was in demand on and off the field. He'd come for her graduation, and she was grateful for that, knowing what it took for him to get away. She'd offered to just meet him in Auckland so he wouldn't have to make the trip, but he'd insisted on attending her graduation ceremony, and secretly she was thankful for his presence.

Her parents had thrown a going away party for her and Noah and even though she could see the heartache in their eyes at her leaving, she knew they were happy for her. She'd made a point to come home as often as she could over the last few months of school, wanting to spend as much time as possible with her family before she left for her new life in New Zealand.

The promise of a future with Noah was everything she could have hoped for, but leaving her family almost broke her. Noah as usual was her rock and a strong shoulder to cry on as they boarded their flight, assuring her that they'd see them again in a few months.

Emma couldn't help but smile as Noah parked the car in front of their home. Letting out a relieved sigh at the sight of it, Emma opened the door and inhaled the familiar scent of salty air, instantly feeling at ease. Taking in the sight of her home, she was glad to see that Noah had kept the flowers they'd planted alive while she was away.

It had been five long months since she'd last seen the beachfront home in Takapuna, and as she started for the door, anxious to be inside, Noah swept her off her feet. "Noah, what are you doing?" she giggled, as he cradled her tightly against his chest.

"I'm carrying you over the threshold, silly."

"You don't do that until we're married, but feel free, I like the feel of it," she joked, her lips touching the tender skin on his neck, and breathing in the scent of him.

He set her on her feet in the familiar kitchen, and looking around, she was pleased to see that everything was just how she'd left it.

Leaning into him, she slid her arms around his waist, her head coming to rest against his broad chest. "I'm so happy to be home. I've missed everything about this place. But most of all, I've missed you."

"This is the first day of the rest of our lives, sweetheart. You're finally home... with me."

And as she walked around the spacious lounge...she was home. Pausing to take in the view of the blue waters, she couldn't believe how incredibly lucky she was.

They were going to spend the rest of their lives together. His handsome face would be the first thing that greeted her as she welcomed each new day and the last thing she saw as she drifted off to sleep each night.

This was where they'd raise their family, filling their home with children... where they'd grow old together.

North Carolina would always hold a special place in her heart. It's where her family lived, and where she'd grown up. But New Zealand was her home now... her future. Along with the amazing man who made her feel beautiful and sexy and treasured...but also more than anything else...loved.

After taking her to bed and making slow, passionate love to her, Noah held onto her tightly, as if he was afraid to let her go. She was finally home where she belonged, tucked securely by his side.

"I love you, Noah. Now and forever," she whispered against his lips, his arms circling her waist as he leaned into her for a slow wet kiss that took her breath away and left her dizzy.

"I love you too, Emma. Now and forever."

They'd found their forever...together.


THE END

**Please continue reading for a first look at the next book in the series, *Belong With Me*, The Andersons Book 2...**

# EXCERPT FROM
# BELONG WITH ME,
## THE ANDERSONS BOOK 2

Staring up at the Carolina blue sky from the back of her horse, Captain Jack, Alison Anderson found a quiet respite from her hectic life. Her fingers drifted mindlessly along the smooth sheen of Jack's coat as she relaxed against his bare back. The gentle rocking back and forth of Jack's hindquarters, as he lazily grazed in the pasture, would have lulled her to sleep had she not needed to maintain her balance.

The warm caress of the sun shining above her and the warmth of Jack's soft coat beneath her back felt like being cocooned in a fuzzy blanket, only better.

In the distance, two hawks circled in the sky, zeroing in on their prey. Their wings spread wide as they silently stalked their target. She watched as a third bird joined the two, falling in line as they orbited the sky above her. A cool breeze kicked up the aroma of fresh-cut grass and sent a wave of shivers over her heated skin. Snuggling deeper into the warmth of Jack's coat, she welcomed the heat radiating off of him. Protesting as her elbow accidentally poked him, Jack snorted and shook his head, but quickly returned to the buffet laid out before him.

The cloudless sky and unseasonably warm temperatures for November in North Carolina were a welcome reprieve from the bone-chilling rain that had enveloped the Charlotte area for the past few days. Winter weather in the Carolinas was notorious for extremes from week to week, or even from one day to the next, so she'd packed up her rambunctious fifteen-month-old daughter, Abigail, and headed to the barn to take advantage of the warm weather while it lasted, and to enjoy the sunshine.

Ali had boarded Jack at Stoney Brook Stables since she'd adopted him her sophomore year in high school. The owners, Claudia and her husband Reginald Morrison, had been patient and kind to her when, as a teenager, she felt invisible and lost in the crowd at home. And what began as a way to indulge her love of horses with an afterschool job at their farm, quickly became more like a home away from home than a job, and the attentive owners had become like family.

The picturesque stable, nestled amongst rolling green pastures and creeping sprawl from the neighboring city of Charlotte, wasn't unique for her home town, which was dotted with similar farms and estates, but she was at home at the quiet retreat and never considered shifting stables.

Ali's mother had met Claudia Morrison at a local charity event and Claudia had agreed to hire Ali in exchange for free riding lessons. Since the farm was conveniently located adjacent to her school, she'd not only spent her assigned work days there, but just about every other day too.

As soon as the bell rang, she'd happily sling her backpack over her shoulder and make her way through the lush green pastures overlooking the school's tennis courts and baseball field, towards the barn on the far side of the meadow, eager to help out in any way they needed her.

She'd never forget the day Jack arrived, skittish and in desperate need of a bath, but otherwise in good condition. His long mane and tail were clumped with mud, sticks, and leaves, and the combination reminded her of Johnny Depp's character from the Pirates of the Caribbean, Captain Jack Sparrow, and the nickname stuck.

His dark reddish-brown coat and black legs had been caked in mud and the white blaze that ran the length of his face was nearly invisible, but underneath the dirt and grime was a beautiful soul just wanting to be loved and cared for… just like the rest of us.

Jack had spent the first few years of his life as an unsuccessful race horse and then was bounced from home to home until Claudia had seen him listed on a local rescue organization's website and, without hesitation, picked up the phone and made the necessary arrangements to pick him up from his current owners, who were no longer able to care for him.

It only took one look at Jack, and Ali was hopelessly in love with him, and she'd cried when Claudia and Reginald asked her to adopt him a few months later. Her parents had offered to pay for the gorgeous five-year-old bay thoroughbred, but Claudia refused, insisting she only wanted him to have a loving forever home. Since Ali would've no sooner parted with her heart than part with Jack, and practically lived there anyway, his home had remained at Stoney Brook.

Jack wasn't used to a loving hand, so it had taken a few months for him to trust her completely, but once he did, he'd transformed into the sweetest and most tenderhearted horse in the barn. He'd wait for Ali along the pasture fence every day after school, excitedly shaking his head and whinnying to her when she emerged from the building, and Ali happily hitched a ride bareback across the field, where she'd reward him with a hug and a carrot.

It was her favorite time with her horse, just the two of them, with nothing between them but a mutual trust and dedication to one another. Without reins, Jack was in complete control and he'd never failed to transport her safely from one side of the large meadow to the other.

Her current life definitely lacked the uncomplicated ease she'd enjoyed before Abby entered the world, but even though her daughter was unexpected, she was the best thing that ever happened to her. Ali knew she had it much better than most single mothers, but being a single mom wasn't for the faint of heart, no matter how much support you had from friends and family. And she'd spent more nights than she cared to think about lying awake in bed worrying about…just about everything.

Thankfully, Abby's father deposited more than enough money into her bank account each month to cover the bills, so that was one thing she didn't have to worry about. Ali appreciated the money, now that she'd moved out of her parents' house with Abby and was settling into a home of their own a few miles away. But, what she really wanted, was for Abby's father to care enough to spend time with his daughter and not just show he cared with his wallet.

Ali tried to cut Evan Thompson some slack, since he lived half a world away in New Zealand and couldn't relocate, but in Abby's short life, she could count on both hands the number of days he'd spent with his daughter. And now that she was getting older, Ali was afraid she wouldn't be enough for Abby. It was one of her greatest fears that Abby would grow up resenting the fact that she didn't have a father, that she'd feel like she was missing something…because she would be…her father's presence in her life.

She was sure one of her brothers would happily escort Abby to events like the father daughter dance at school, when the time came for things like that, but it wouldn't be the same. When her sweet baby girl looked around at all the other girls laughing and dancing with their doting fathers, her little heart would break. And the thought of Abby standing in the middle of a crowded room, feeling completely alone, had the power to reduce her to tears every time, and left her questioning how she had been so wrong about Evan in the first place.

Just thinking of Evan sent her stomach roiling uncomfortably. He was undeniably the love of her life, and she'd be lying to herself if she denied it, but he'd shattered her heart into a million pieces, and as much as she wanted to hate him for letting her and Abby go so easily, she'd always love him. The heart was funny like that, and just looking at Abby with her silky dark brown waves and whiskey-colored eyes, so much like her daddy's, it hurt to look at her sometimes; she was thankful to have a little piece of him to hold onto…as twisted as that was.

Friends had encouraged Ali to start dating again, but her heart just wasn't into it. What little free time she had was best spent with Abby and Jack, or her family, and she wasn't ready to add another complication to her already overly-complicated life. She'd gone out on a couple of dates since Abby was born, but there hadn't been even the tiniest of sparks with any of them, let alone the intense chemical reaction she'd always felt whenever she was within eyeshot of Evan Thompson.

Just the thought of having another man around Abby made Ali uncomfortable anyway, so it was probably for the best, at least until Abby was older. Maybe one day, in the far distant future, she'd meet someone and fall in love again, but her heart was still healing, and she wasn't ready to go down that road again, at least not yet.

With his six-foot-four frame of solid muscle, dark brown hair that begged to be touched, and eyes the color of malt whiskey, Evan's physical appearance didn't just appeal to her baser instincts, but lit every single inch of her on fire. Evan was undeniably what her friends would call 'eye candy', with rugged good looks, abs you could bounce a quarter off of, and a rakish smile that did funny things to a girl's insides when he bestowed it on her, but Ali's attraction to him went much deeper than what was on the surface.

Evan Thompson was a triple threat...smart and funny and could ride a horse, the three most important qualities in a man, as far as she was concerned. The fact that he knew his way around a woman's body, a knowledge he set out to prove repeatedly...and she'd enjoyed way too much and far too often, was a delightful bonus and made him downright dangerous.

Sinfully dangerous.

But even with their undeniable physical connection, it was their emotional connection that kept her interested.

They'd spent countless hours talking about everything and nothing, while exploring the sprawling horse farm he grew up on, and for someone raised with a silver spoon in his mouth and a trust fund worth more than most third-world nations, he was surprisingly normal.

Evan didn't flaunt his wealth and didn't let it define him, but never denied its existence either. For someone who could've easily rested on his laurels and enjoyed the pampered lifestyle of a stereotypical trust fund baby, his pride wouldn't allow it. He relentlessly pushed himself to succeed and never quit once he put his mind to something.

He had a subtle confidence and determination that was both unexpected and enormously attractive. And Ali had been unquestionably drawn to him from the moment she laid eyes upon him.

Even though she'd boarded the plane that carried her from Auckland, New Zealand back home to Charlotte, North Carolina almost two long years ago, it still felt like yesterday. Ali had never felt so alone as she had on the twenty-hour flight home, and the crushing realization that the man she'd hoped to spend the rest of her life with didn't care enough to ask her to stay, was absolutely devastating.

Shaking off the threat of tears, she reminded herself that she had a full and complete life and didn't need a man to mess with the delicate balance of things. And between her nosy brothers and her father, she already had enough testosterone in her life...thank you very much. She swore they were worse than women sometimes.

Jack was the one male in her life who didn't feel the need to offer an opinion on the state of her love life, her finances, or her baby girl. When she felt overwhelmed by how her life had turned out, he'd simply nuzzle her neck and listen intently as she vented or cried on his shoulder. His broad shoulders had seen Ali through the trials and tribulations of her high school and college years, and then her unplanned pregnancy, with steadfast loyalty and devotion, and just seeing his beautiful face brightened even the gloomiest of days.

Knowing her family loved her, and only wanted what was best for her and Abby, eased the frustration of their butting into her business all the time, but sometimes a girl just needed to be left alone. Being a member of a large close-knit family had many blessings, and she tried to remember to count them each and every day, but solitude wasn't one of them.

Lacing her fingers behind her head, Ali closed her eyes and allowed herself a few more minutes of blessed silence before heading back to the barn. The swishing of Jack's tail as he swatted the occasional fly and the accompanying ruffled exhale of breath as he happily grazed in the field was the only sound she heard, soothing her in a way that nothing else could.

Being a single mother left little alone time, or even a minute to go to the bathroom or shower in peace, so she refused to feel guilty or selfish for carving out some time to spend with her first child, Jack. Her fur baby. But she'd left Abby in the barn with Claudia and didn't want to take advantage of her babysitting services for too long, in case she had other things to do.

Inhaling a deep breath of fresh air, she sat up, then leaned over and rested her chest against Jack's long neck, wrapping her arms around his neck and hugging him tightly. Lingering there for a long minute before lifting up and rubbing the lean stretch of muscles that ran the length of his mane, she gave him a gentle squeeze with her legs and led him back to the barn.

The large eight-stall barn had a long center aisle, flanked on either side by rows of square stalls, tack and feed rooms, and two wash bays. A wide breezeway divided the long aisle in half and a small living quarters occupied the second story above the breezeway. The rustic design of the exterior complemented the appearance of the main house, which sat perched on a hill overlooking the luxurious estate.

The leisurely click-clack of Jack's hooves against the concrete floor announced their arrival and Ali smiled as she took in the sight of Abby perched on Claudia's hip, chatting away, as she helped her brush the newest arrival to Stoney Brook, a chestnut pony named Nutmeg.

Ali slowed Jack to a stop and attached his halter to the set of cross ties in front of his stall so she could give him a good grooming before settling him into his stall for the night. Taking a deep breath, Ali inhaled the familiar scent of wood shavings, hay, and molasses, and wondered if it was odd to be comforted by the smell of a barn.

"Hey there, sweet girl. Are you behaving yourself for Miss Claudia?" Ali questioned Abby, tickling her side as she brushed past her to get Jack's grooming kit from the tack room.

Claudia smiled back at Ali. "She's been a perfect little angel. Haven't you, Abby?"

Ignoring them both, Abby twisted in Claudia's arms and reached out for her mommy as Ali stepped past her to set the wooden box of grooming supplies on the ground next to where she'd left Jack. "Up-up."

"Come here, baby." Ali settled her daughter on her hip as she placed a kiss on the top of her head. "Do you want to help Mommy brush Jack?"

Ali ran her free hand down the length of Jack's neck, his coat silky and smooth beneath her fingers, and leaned in so Abby could do the same. Ali had become an expert at completing most tasks one handed since giving birth to Abby, and Jack remained relatively unfazed when Abby stroked his neck before pinching her little fingers around his mane and yanking it abruptly.

"No, Abby. Gentle hands," Ali spoke in the firm tone that usually got Abby's attention, as she untangled her fingers from his black mane, which she noticed was in need of trimming. She then took Abby's tiny hand in hers and reinforced the proper way to pet an animal. "Nice hands, Abby...Good girl," she stated, as she rewarded Jack's patience with a solid rub along his withers and down the length of his back. "That's the way you like it, don't you, boy?"

"Goo grr," Abby repeated, concentrating adorably, trying to form the words as she puckered her little ribbon lips.

"Yes, good girl," Abby mimicked the way Ali rubbed Jack's neck, then turned her attention to her mommy and softly pet the side of Ali's head as she bent down to pick up a brush and got to work.

After helping Claudia feed the horses and lock up the barn, Ali secured Abby in her car seat and headed home for dinner and a bath. Waiting for the security gate to open, she looked in the rearview mirror and smiled at the sight of Abby wiggling and singing along to the *Frozen* soundtrack playing through the speakers. Well, maybe not singing exactly, but she was mumbling along to the words, and knew when to hit the high notes.

Even though her life hadn't turned out as she'd planned, Ali really was happy and in a good place.

Life was good.

Snuggling with Abby on the couch before bedtime, Ali hugged her little girl close as they watched *Winnie the Pooh and the Blustery Day* on the television, the smell of watermelon shampoo and little girl filling the air and warming her heart.

She reached for her phone as it started to ring. Seeing Evan's handsome face on the screen had her heart quickening and her stomach twisting with a mixture of excitement and trepidation. He was, at once, the bane of her existence and the wishful center of her universe, the dueling emotions always bubbling just beneath the surface and setting her off-kilter.

Ali had visited Auckland in July with her family and spent a fair amount of time with Evan while she was there, and since she'd returned home, he called almost every night to say goodnight to Abby. Before disconnecting, they'd usually talk for a few minutes, and on a handful of occasions their conversations had continued into the wee hours of the morning. He was trying to be a better father and she was grateful for that.

It was a good thing, she reminded herself every time his smiling face appeared on the screen of her phone, but it still left her feeling raw and exposed.

Ali suspected the regular phone calls were one of the reasons she was having such a hard time moving on from her relationship with Evan, but she couldn't tell him not to call when he was trying so hard to maintain a connection with his daughter.

She'd made a vow to herself when Abby was born to never be one of those parents who used their child as a weapon to hurt their ex, no matter how tempting, and she'd remained true to her word and never denied Evan access to his daughter. She'd never admit to it, but she secretly looked forward to his calls each evening and enjoyed hearing about his day, or even the weather.

His voice was deep and smooth like chocolate, with a sexy fusion of a Kiwi and British accent that left her hypnotized, and she'd always loved just listening to him speak.

Once upon a time, he'd enjoyed teasing her by reading steamy romance novels out loud to her, but listening to him read the phone book would've been sexy too. She'd cuddle against his chest and close her eyes, just letting the words wash over her until he'd put the book down, pretending to be horrified by the sex scenes. All the while, he gave her the crooked smile she loved so much, which told her that he wasn't horrified at all…quite the opposite, in fact.

Shaking off the sudden flush of lust at the memory, she braced herself for his nightly phone call. "Look, Abby, Daddy's on the phone," she cheerfully announced, as Abby sat up and pointed to the picture.

"Dada, Dada."

Swiping the screen to answer his call, she took a calming breath. "Hey."

"Hi, Ali. Can you switch to FaceTime?"

"Sure. Hold on a second."

Pressing the circle on the screen, she smiled at the sight of Evan sitting in his hotel room. "Look, sweetheart. It's Daddy."

Abby touched the phone and then wrapped her little hand around it as she pulled it to her face. "Dada."

"You just caught her before bedtime," Ali softly giggled, as she watched Abby fumble with the phone. "Here, sweetie. Hold it like this so you can see Daddy."

"Yeah, that's what I figured. I was just getting ready for bed myself, but thought I'd give you a call first." Ali could see the sadness in his warm brown eyes as he watched Abby intently through the phone, his gaze trying to keep up with her erratic movements. "Hi, sweetheart. How's my girl?"

Abby continued babbling incoherently, oblivious to her father's distress, but Ali could read him like a book, always could, and knew how severely he was hurting. He also looked a bit battered.

Evan had followed in his father's footsteps and was a professional rugby player with the Blues, Auckland's super rugby team, and New Zealand's national team, the All Blacks. He was currently on the European tour with the All Blacks, and if her dates were correct, he was now in Edinburgh, Scotland.

When Abby rubbed her eyes for the third time and let out a dramatic sigh, Ali knew she needed to get her little angel to bed quickly, before she got a second wind. Which soon thereafter would be followed by a complete and total meltdown when she became overtired, and a set of horns would miraculously sprout from the top of her head.

Letting Abby hold onto the phone, she picked her up and climbed the stairs to her bedroom. Tucking her in, Abby continued to babble to Evan as Ali settled on the bed next to her.

Her baby was growing up so quickly, and Ali wanted to cherish every moment. Before she knew it, Abby would be too old to have her mommy tuck her in at night and would be full of sass and vinegar, rolling her eyes and asking to be dropped off around the corner to escape the horror of her friends catching a glimpse of her mother.

The creep of time was inevitable, but Ali just wished there was a way to bottle this moment in time…to hold onto her little girl for just a little while longer.

After they'd moved into their new home, Abby had startled her by climbing out of her crib in the middle of the night. In the process of looking for Ali, Abby had made her way past the open staircase. The full-on panic attack that followed, as Ali clutched her baby tightly to her chest and the reality of what could've happened sunk in, was something she never wanted to relive. Once was more than enough. The frightening images of Abby injuring herself as she dropped to her bedroom floor, or tumbling down the stairs in an effort to find her mommy, had her shopping for a bed the following day.

Even though she wasn't mentally prepared to have her baby in a big girl bed yet, Ali added the bed to Abby's room, bought a guard rail for the new bed, closed the baby gate at the top of the stairs at night, and without further ado, officially transitioned to the next stage of development.

Time waited for no one, not even distraught mommies who were desperate to keep their babies as…babies for just a little while longer. Even if you recited a litany of prayers, begged and pleaded, or when all else failed…stomped your feet in a temper tantrum worthy of a temperamental two-year-old, time marched on.

"Give Daddy a goodnight kiss, sweetheart," Ali instructed, after she'd read her favorite bedtime story of Goodnight Moon, and smiled as Abby brought the phone to her lips, placing a smacking kiss on the screen.

Ali leaned down and placed a kiss on her little girl's forehead. "Goodnight, sweet pea. Mommy loves you." As she took the phone from Abby's hands and turned out the light, she quietly turned for the door, then gently closed it behind her.

"Hey, don't hang up just yet. I wanted to talk to you," Evan stated, as she made her way down the wide staircase to the family room.

"Okay. What's up?"

"I'd like to come for Christmas. Would you mind?" Confusion at his unexpected announcement caused her to stumble, and she reached for the railing to steady herself.

"No. Of course I wouldn't mind, Evan. You're always welcome; you know that." She tried not to sound defensive, but knew it came out that way. "I've never kept you away from Abby."

"I know, and I'm not saying that." He let out a frustrated breath in an exaggerated huff. "I also wanted to let you know that I'm announcing my retirement from the All Blacks after this tour."

"What?" Ali felt her heart rate kick into high gear at his abrupt proclamation, but cautiously reminded herself that his retirement had nothing to do with her. He was never one for beating around the bush, but it would've been nice if he'd eased her into it, instead of just blurting it out. "Really?"

"Yeah, I reckon it's the right time. Go out on top and all that. And I'd like to be able to spend more time with Abby." Ali's heart sank when she was forgotten once again. Of course he wanted to spend time with Abby, but the realization that she wasn't a factor in his decision still stung. "Plus, I don't bounce back as easily as I used to, and I'm tired of the constant travel."

The room shifted off-kilter and her heart rate surged again for an entirely different reason, as her mind raced with endless questions…each one more troublesome than the next. Would Evan want to take Abby back to New Zealand for extended periods of time? He'd never mentioned it before, but now that Abby was getting older and he'd have a longer break between rugby seasons, it was entirely possible.

And, stupidly, she'd never insisted on a custody agreement.

Stupid. Stupid. Stupid.

How could she have been so lax? Securing custody of Abby should've been on the top of her priority list.

He was making an effort to be more involved with Abby, and wanting her to visit him would be a natural progression of their relationship, but the thought of being that far away from her baby left her lightheaded and a bit queasy.

Well, if he insisted on Abby staying with him in the off-season, he'd get two visitors for the price of one. Mother and child were a package deal, take it or leave it.

Feeling like she'd just run a marathon, she collapsed into the overstuffed couch cushions and tried to remember the breathing techniques she employed in the yoga classes she took three times a week at the neighborhood clubhouse.

Breathe in through the nose…hold…and out through the mouth. No need to panic yet, she tried to convince herself.

She could taste the bitter bile in the back of her throat as she swallowed past the lump forming there, and for a moment, thought she might actually throw up.

"Congratulations…I guess," she managed to mumble after a stretch of silence that lasted a beat too long.

"Thanks. This is a good thing, Ali."

Well, that remained to be seen, but she didn't want to give him any ideas, so she quickly changed the subject as she bit back the sting of nervous tears and settled into the corner of the couch, covering herself with a throw blanket to ward off the chills and the growing rush of panic threatening to whisk her away.

**Thank you for reading *Stay With Me*! I hope you enjoyed it. If you did, please help other readers find this book:**

If you enjoyed *Stay With Me*, please consider leaving a review at the retailer of your choice or on Goodreads to help other readers find my book.

Make sure you're on my mailing list to receive notification when Book 2, *Belong With Me*, is available.

Visit Alexa's website at:

www.alexapowers.com

Follow Alexa on twitter at:

www.twitter.com/alexapowers5

Join Alexa on Facebook at:

www.facebook.com/alexapowersauthor

I'd love to hear from you at:

alexa@alexapowers.com

# Emma's Playlist

Question – Old 97's

January Wedding – The Avett Brothers

Banana Pancakes – Jack Johnson

Rise to Me – The Decemberists

Sleep Please Come to Me – Matthew Barber

New Slang – The Shinns

Carolina In My Mind – James Taylor

God Bless the Broken Road – Rascal Flats

Be Mine – David Gray

Zeplike – Slightly Stoopid

Closer to the Sun – Slightly Stoopid

Chicken Fried – Zach Brown Band

My Lady and the Mountain – Avett Brothers

Someone Like You – Van Morrison

Into the Mystic – Van Morrison

Make You Feel My Love – Adele

Bartender Song – Rehab

Redemption Song – Bob Marley

What I Got – Sublime

Drop It Like It's Hot – Snoop Dog

Say Hey (I Love You) – Michael Franti & Spearhead

The Greatest Sum – The Avett Brothers

# ABOUT THE AUTHOR

Alexa Powers lives in North Carolina with her children and the furry friends her children have collected over the years. When not daydreaming about the cast of characters which have taken up residence in her head, Alexa Powers can be found in front of her computer or spending time with her three beautiful daughters. A ferocious reader from a young age, Alexa is a sucker for a happily ever after and considers herself lucky to be able to call herself a writer.

www.ingramcontent.com/pod-product-compliance
Lightning Source LLC
Chambersburg PA
CBHW071041250626
47159CB00002B/325